MAGPIE

GEORGIA HILL

Copyright © 2025 Georgia Hill

The right of Georgia Hill to be identified as the Author of the Work has been asserted by them in accordance with the Copyright, Designs and Patents Act 1988.

First published in 2025 by Bloodhound Books.

Apart from any use permitted under UK copyright law, this publication may only be reproduced, stored, or transmitted, in any form, or by any means, with prior permission in writing of the publisher or, in the case of reprographic production, in accordance with the terms of licences issued by the Copyright Licensing Agency.

All characters in this publication are fictitious and any resemblance to real persons, living or dead, is purely coincidental.

www.bloodhoundbooks.com

Print ISBN: 978-1-917705-30-1

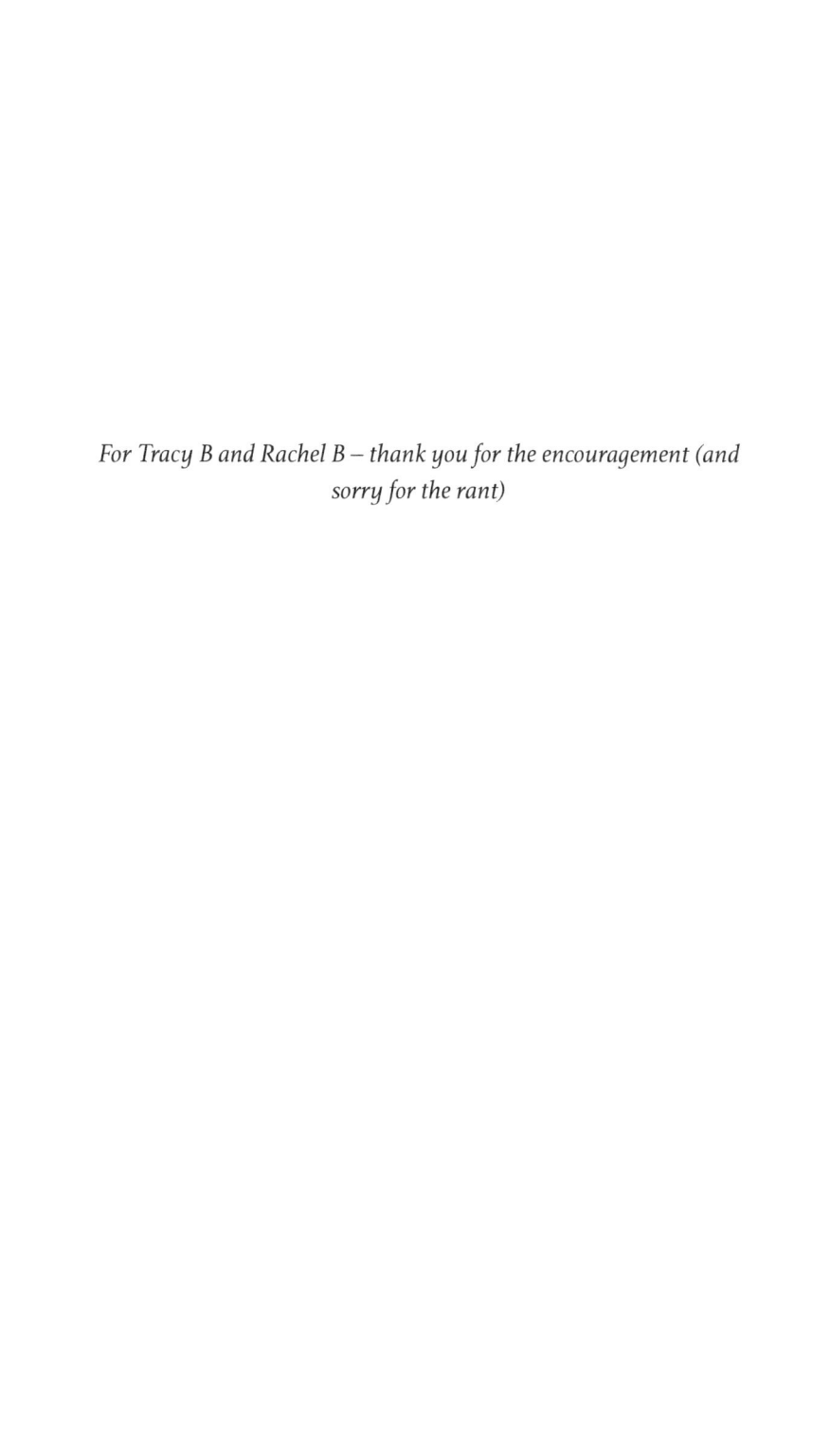

For Tracy B and Rachel B – thank you for the encouragement (and sorry for the rant)

PROLOGUE

FLETE, DEVON, OCTOBER 1660

She had no time. She had to think fast and she had to think clever. There was little she needed but one thing she must take. After she had tightly bound it into layers of oiled cloth, she gave a last look around the house she'd called home. A gulp of emotion caught in her throat, but she couldn't give in to either sentiment or fear. Her fate was decided. Hearing the horse snort and stamp outside, she dragged a stool to the inglenook. Standing on tiptoes and precariously balanced, she shoved the knife handle high onto a ledge above the dead fire. She would not take this with her. It had caused problems from the first and she cursed it. Choking on clouds of displaced soot, she reached into the pocket tied around her waist and added the green glass bottle to the same hiding place. She would take her chance without it.

'May it protect whoever lives here in the future better than it did us,' she hissed. Clambering off the stool she fell still for a moment, pressing her hands against the chimney, nails biting into the brick. The horror at what she had done overwhelmed her. 'What have I become?' she wailed. 'Will God ever forgive me for what I did? Will I ever forgive myself?'

A shout came from the street, urging her to make haste. With one last despairing cry, she swung open the heavy oak door and stepped out. Overhead a magpie flapped its wings and cawed. Black and white, its tail trailing iridescent blue green, it soared into the cruel autumn wind.

CHAPTER 1

FLETE, DEVON, MAY 2018

Beth Loveday inserted the enormous old-fashioned key into a lock corroded by time and salty air and pushed at the door.

'Get on with it,' Lorna said from behind. 'Can't wait to see inside.'

Beth grinned. Lorna was the impatient one. 'Hold your horses, as Gran would say.' Gran was also prone to say the sisters were chalk and cheese. Lorna, a bubbly honey blonde in contrast to Beth's auburn hair, freckles and introvert nature. Forcing the door with her shoulder, it eventually gave, and she led Lorna into what would, eventually and with a lot of hard work, become the main selling space. Beth stood, hands on hips, gazing around. Her uppermost emotion bewilderment.

Lorna elbowed her in the ribs. 'You could at least *look* a bit excited. You never show your feelings, do you?'

'Trust me, my insides are a bundle of nerves.'

Lorna gave her a hug. Although younger by three years she always assumed the mother role. 'Oh, Bethie, I'm so proud of you. Your own shop. Come on, admit it, you must be over the moon.'

Beth returned the hug. 'I am. And nervous. Worried to hell. Not to mention knackered.' She noted her sister's concerned expression. 'I'm okay, just inside I'm a bubbling mess.'

Lorna pulled a face. 'Better not be the curry from last night. I've just caught a glimpse of the downstairs loo. Grim isn't the word. Add bleach to your list of stuff to buy.' She whirled around, kicking up dust. 'Along with an industrial strength hoover. So this will be the main shop space?'

'Yup.' Beth switched on the lights. 'That's better. We can see properly. The sooner I get those window boardings down the better.'

'I like the half-timbered walls.' Lorna ran a finger along one ancient oak beam and scrubbed her hand clean on her jeans. 'It's in a good location too. Seems to be lots of quirky shops along the lane.'

'Yeah, shame I couldn't get anything nearer the seafront, but the house sale money and my redundancy only stretched so far. Plus, I need a cushion of funds when this old place is repaired. Not to mention savings if the whole thing goes tits up.'

'Which it won't, Beth.' Lorna wagged a finger. 'Be positive.'

Beth swooped to pick up a pile of junk mail to hide her anxiety. Everything was riding on this. The offer of redundancy from her office job in a timber firm had been a sign, the push to follow her long-stifled dream. She'd taken it, retrained and, with heart in mouth and wondering just what she was doing, had sold her little house; the one she'd scrimped and saved to buy. Her entire future now rested on making her handmade soaps and lotions business a success. And if it wasn't, she'd end up incomeless and homeless. For a person who craved routine and security it had been a leap of faith. Possibly an insane one. Her two closest friends were moving on with their lives, it was time she did the same. Stifling the fear, she straightened and looked around her. What had possessed her to buy a half-timbered shop in a run-down seaside town? Normally the most practical, least fey sort of person, something about the place had called to her, invaded her brain. And, once she'd viewed it, no other would do. It might have been an equally insane decision. 'It won't go tits up.' She sent the words out into the universe, feeling ridiculous. 'Tenpenny House will do very nicely indeed. Not huge but just big enough for what I want.'

'So, what are you going to do with it?'

'Display shelving along there.' Beth pointed to the wall that ran perpendicular to the shopfront. 'Freestanding as the walls are so uneven. Rustic and scrubbed oak, or maybe pine,' she amended hurriedly, 'as it'll be cheaper. With stacked woven baskets to put the soaps in.' She strode to the middle. 'A central table just here for seasonal stock or special offers.' Her tone became more animated. She turned to her sister; eyes gleaming. 'Or maybe curated collections like lavender-themed products, or skin cleansers for problem skin?'

'That's more like it,' Lorna approved.

'And the counter for the boring stuff like the till and card machines can go over there facing the windows so I can look out.'

'And what about that bad boy?' her sister asked, nodding to the fireplace.

Beth edged closer to the enormous inglenook that dominated the back wall. 'No idea.' She sniffed. Burned wood and soot prickled her nostrils. A gout of ash fell, making her jump back. 'Used recently then. Do you think it'll need sweeping?'

Lorna joined her and slipped an arm through, eyeing the blackened chimney with distrust. 'Almost certainly.'

'And do I need rugs to cover these old stone slabs, or will that be a trip hazard? Rush matting would look cool.' She peered down, ideas beginning to fizz. 'The flooring could be original, you know. The estate agent reckons the place dates back to at least the seventeenth century, possibly even before. I might research life in seventeenth-century Flete when I get the chance.'

'You and your research. You love your books.' Lorna laughed. 'Think you'll be too busy getting the shop up and running to do any learning.'

A thrill electrified Beth. Excitement finally winning through, bypassing the stress and angst of the lead up to Tenpenny House's purchase. This was going to be her dream come true. Her very own shop! On the other side of the chip-boarded windows she heard footsteps tripping along the pavement. In a few short weeks those feet could be wandering in. They could be her first customers. She hugged Lorna's arm and did a little happy dance, stirring up clouds of dust that made them sneeze.

'Aw, that's better, Bethie. It's good to see you getting enthused about it all.'

'Well, you know me, I warm up to things slowly–'

'And are always cautious and overthink things. Now you've finally taken the plunge to do this, you've got to go all-out.'

'Stop nagging.'

'It's my job,' Lorna replied crisply. 'Come on, let's have a decko at the rest of the place.' She disappeared into the hallway.

As Beth dropped the latch on the solid oak door, shutting off the selling space, a noise behind made her freeze. 'What's that?'

Lorna turned to her. 'What?'

'There's someone in the shop.'

'Don't be daft. We've just come out. Only thing in there is dust and cobwebs. And you locked the front door. No one could walk in.'

Beth shushed her sister. 'Listen!' She put her ear to the door.

Lorna joined her. 'I can't hear anything.'

There was a frozen silence as the women listened, their ears pressed to the ancient oak. From within the shop came an eerie slithering sound. Beth felt her pulse leap in her throat. The room had been empty when she'd left, she was sure of it.

The slithering rose and sank. It stopped, began again and turned into a thumping flapping sound. A violent bang against the door had them rearing back in terror.

'Shit!' Beth clutched on to Lorna, her insides liquid with fear. The horrible unearthly sounds continued, becoming frenzied. 'A ghost?' Thankfully the words died on her tongue. Her sister would never let her live that one down.

Lorna put her ear against the door again. 'I think,' she screwed up her face in concentration, 'it might be a bird.'

'A bird? But how?' Beth asked.

'Windows boarded up. Door locked. Chimney? Remember that ash that fell down? Must have been a bird trapped.'

Another thump resounded against the door before whatever it was sounded as though it fell to the ground.

Beth's heart rate hitched. Trapped birds were horrible to deal with. They'd had a starling fly into the office one summer. Panicked, it made a hell of a mess before she'd been able to release it. 'Suppose it could be a bird. We'll have to let the poor thing out.' Feeling calmer now she knew what she was dealing with, she added, 'We go in, you close this door as quickly as you can. Last thing we want is for it to escape into the rest of the building. I'll unlock the front door and we shoo it out. Ready?'

Lorna nodded.

They burst into the shop. A chaos of whirling blackness flew at Beth's head. Protecting her eyes and trying not to scream, she ran to the front door and scrabbled at the lock.

'It's gone.' Lorna's voice went brittle with relief. She'd obviously been putting on a brave front. 'Well done, Bethie.' Joining her at the open front door, she asked, 'Did you see what it was? Blackbird maybe?'

Beth had seen the bird as it soared up over the rooftops. Beneath its blackened feathers gleamed white, shot through with iridescent blue. Its long tail left a trail of choking soot. 'It was a magpie.'

'Oh, Beth.' Lorna stared at her with huge eyes. 'You know what Gran always says.'

Beth nodded. 'One for sorrow.'

Lorna shivered. 'Look, I'm sure it'll all be fine. You'll be fine.'

Beth wasn't sure who her sister was reassuring.

Shaken, they went towards the hallway.

'Hold on, Lor. What's this?' Beth bent and picked up an object off the floor.

Lorna peered at it. 'Who knows? Something the bird dropped?' She shuddered. 'Throw it away, Beth, it's filthy.'

'It's some kind of handle, I think.' Beth rubbed away the soot, revealing carved bone. 'It must have been in the chimney, there was nothing in the room.'

Lorna had already made her way out of the shop. 'I don't like it, whatever it is,' she called over her shoulder. 'Throw it out.'

Ignoring her, Beth wrapped the handle in a tissue and shoved it into the pocket of her jeans.

'Come on, show me the rest of the place,' Lorna said, tension making her voice high-pitched. 'What's upstairs?'

The hallway was heavily beamed, narrow and had the same uneven stone slabs as the shop. The commercial kitchen, left over from the building's days as a tea room, however, was all stainless steel and twenty-first century. Levering open a door, Beth switched on another light to reveal a crooked and worn set of bare wooden stairs. Still shaking, she peered up, half afraid of another trapped bird. 'Follow me, this is the living space.' Hanging on to the thickly coiled rope that acted as the handrail, she hauled herself up them, hoping in time she'd get used to their steep rise and odd camber.

'It's not huge up here, is it?' Lorna observed once they'd conquered the stairs and were standing on the creaking floorboards of the sitting room.

'Bedroom, shower, kitchen and this room. It's all I need. There's only me. Just as well I don't have a tribe of kids like you.' Beth looked around in dismay. 'It's in a right state though.'

Lorna shrugged. 'What can I say? Make the most of me now. You won't see me once the kids break up for the school holidays. Until then, you've got the best scrubber in town.' Her nose wrinkling, she added, 'And I think you'll need me.'

Beth wasn't listening. Drawn to the diamond-paned window, she stared out at the view. 'It's like going back in time,' she murmured. 'Hardly anything's changed since the place was built. Look at the old rooftops and the way they hang over the lower storeys.'

Lorna gave her a surprised look. 'Under that no-nonsense independent exterior lurks a closet romantic, doesn't it? Of course it's changed. I can see at least three Sky dishes from here.' She went nearer and rubbed a clean patch on the window. 'Ooh, now you're talking. I can see the sea. Just... I mean, it's all a bit run-down, but–'

'It was what I could afford,' Beth finished. 'Sidmouth and Lyme were too expensive. And Clappers Lane is marketed as "The Cultural Centre of Flete". Don't scoff, Lor! As well as the scenic cobbles–'

'The ankle-breaking cobbles!'

After the encounter with the magpie Beth was glad of an excuse to laugh. Lorna had tripped up on the walk here. 'Your own fault for not looking where you were going.'

'Couldn't help it. Steve texted with a crisis.' At Beth's questioning look she explained. 'Couldn't find the dishwasher tablets.'

'You haven't trained him very well.' Beth giggled, feeling the tension dissipate. She loved her brother-in-law, but he could never be called domestic.

'What can I say? I'm happy to be the homemaker. He's better at earning money. I know it's not for you, Miss Independence, but it works for us. Tell me more about this cultural quarter then.'

Beth decided it was a genuine question. It looked as though Lorna needed a distraction too. 'Well, there's a Tudor half-timbered pub on the corner, the Moroccan rug shop, one selling fancy lingerie, and an upmarket cookware shop. The town museum's just round the corner too. It's all nicely eclectic. Don't laugh!'

Lorna managed to ruffle her sister's hair before she ducked. 'Soz, Beth. I was only teasing. Looks like the ideal place to attract the sort of customers you're aiming for. The ones wanting fancy artisan soaps.'

'I hope so.' Beth's gaze returned to the fingernail of sea she could see. It was a vivid blue. Positivity was blossoming. She'd sacrificed everything to follow her dream but this bright shiny day as she held the keys to her future made it all worth it. Lorna was right, Flete was a little down at heel in comparison to nearby Sidmouth but, if it was, then there was only one way and that was up. 'I just hope my optimism isn't misplaced.'

'Oi!' Lorna hectored. 'Don't start doubting yourself. What did I say about overthinking stuff? Look how much fun it'll be living here. Only a short walk to the beach, that lovely long prom and harbour.'

Beth sucked in a breath, chasing the misgivings away. 'You're right. There's so much to look forward to. And, whatever happens, it's bye-bye to the boring old nine to five.' She leafed through the pile of circulars and junk mail she'd picked up from the shop floor. Sifting them into a recycling pile, the local newspaper caught her eye. It was dated the week before and was barely thicker than a pamphlet. 'Look at this, Lor.'

'What is it?'

Beth held the newspaper up and read the headline, 'Local GP finds mysterious book.'

'Oh, Beth, give up with the books already.'

'No, it's interesting. Listen. "Local doctor finds old book of recipes in an attic".' She peered at the grainy black-and-white photograph showing a man holding up a small book. It was impossible to see the man or the book clearly in the terrible picture but something about the story reeled her in. '"It's now with an expert in the museum",' she continued. '"Initial analysis suggests it's at least four hundred years old". As old as Tenpenny House, Lorna.' She shivered. It was cold up here, in the way old buildings get when they're unoccupied for a while. She longed to throw open the window and let in some warmth and fresh air but, glancing at the archaic window latches, didn't trust them.

'We haven't time for old books in attics,' her sister chided. 'Stop daydreaming. We need to get started on cleaning this flat. Get it half decent so you can move your bed in at least.'

Beth shook herself. Lorna was right, there was tons to do. Just as she was going to suggest making tea before they embarked on the clean-up, her phone buzzed a text. A little jumbled and in shouty capitals but she could excuse her friend that:

> BABY HAMISH HERE AT LAST! HUGH & ME
> BESOTTED. LONG LABOUR. JUST
> SURFACED. GORY DEETS 2 FOLLOW.

She collapsed onto the window seat.

'What is it?' her sister asked sharply.

'It's Jade. She's had the baby.'

'Oh, love.' Ignoring the filth, Lorna slid alongside and put an arm around her. She rested her head against her sister's in solidarity.

Beth went to text her reply, but her thumb refused to co-operate and hovered uselessly. She was thrilled for Jade but the news was bittersweet.

'I've told you before, you need to ghost those two. Hugh's a complete dick, splitting with you and then marrying that bitch Jade. And don't get me started on why he kept those pics of you in the nuddy. Why the hell are you still in touch?'

'I don't know.' Beth's voice cracked with emotion. 'Habit. History. They're my closest friends. Or were. We go back a long way.'

'Then treat this not only as a new start to your professional life but also your personal. Get rid, Beth. They're toxic.'

'I know.' Even as Beth said the words tears prickled and a solid lump of longing sank into her stomach. She wished she knew why she was still in touch with Jade and Hugh. She couldn't work it out herself, but she was unable to let them go. Staring at the text, the letters jumped and blurred. This could have been her baby, and she could have been Hugh's wife. If only things had worked out differently.

The tissue-wrapped knife handle lodged uncomfortably in her jeans pocket, the image of the terrified magpie fleeing the chimney seared into her brain. One for sorrow, indeed. She just hoped it wasn't an omen.

CHAPTER 2

MAY 1660

'Mistress Lacey fared well.' Susanna reached up for the dried lavender bunch hanging from the oak beam and began shredding it. It was last year's. Soon it would be time to harvest the fragrant flowers and store them again. The year's rhythm rolled around relentlessly; the season's demands predictable. This spring, however, politics had thrown something new into their path. She scattered the lavender so it mingled with the rushes covering the earth floor.

'And delivered of a bonny boy. Mother and son doing well and the child bellowing lustfully. We did a good deed today, Susie.' Prudie Tenpenny collapsed onto her husband's chair nearest the fire and held out her hands to warm them. She shivered and pulled her kerchief more snuggly around her neck. 'Even though summer's on the door frame, there's still a mighty wind out there. Fare chilled my old bones on that walk back. The sea's raging. The men spied a lone mock a pie. A true sign theys won't have any fishing today, I reckon.'

'I'm sure the Lacey's are grateful for the safe deliverance, praise be to God.' Susanna looked at her fondly. 'Now rest a while, we've had a long night. I'll warm us some ale.'

'You're a good child.' Prudie squinted up gratefully. 'The day I took you in was my blessing.'

Susanna came to her and kneaded the knots out of the old woman's shoulders. 'As was mine.' Going to the fireplace, she poured ale into a pan hanging over the fire and stirred in some honey. She cocked an ear to the sounds coming from the distant town church. 'The bells are ringing.'

'Aye. To acknowledge a king is back on the throne. The streets were already wild with revellers, weren't they? Twas a rowdy walk from the Lacey's manor and through crowds of men already up to their cups in ale and rough cider outside The Cock.' Prudie shuddered. 'I'm glad we're home.'

'Flete is welcoming the news then.'

'It would seem so, child.'

It was said conversationally but both women heard their underlying tension. To have a king back in power was not cause for celebration for those who had fought on the opposing side.

Susanna filled two tankards to the brim, handed one to Prudie and perched on the bench opposite. The women lapsed into silence. Star, their aged lurcher, crept nearer Prudie and lay at her feet. 'And what will Mistress Agnes name the babe?'

'Charles, I suspect. In honour of the new king.'

'That would fit,' Susanna replied drily. 'The family always did bend with the prevailing wind. Had he been born in old Mr Lacey's time he would have been an Oliver.'

Prudie gave a scoffing laugh. 'Ain't that the truth? There are some folks hereabouts who turned tailcoat, which way and that and got away with it.' She settled back against the high-backed chair. 'But I cannot bear a grudge against an innocent. Let him grow and thrive.'

'And let us hope he sees a world not rift apart by war.'

Prudie raised her mug. 'Amen to that. Let us hope we all have peace, for God knows we have need of it. Praise God, there'll be an end to family against family, brother against brother.'

Susanna raised her own pot in salute.

'We need to be careful though, young Susie. There are still some folks who likes to make mischief.'

As Susanna was about to agree, the door blew open, and in came her adopted father. 'Get out of my chair, woman!' John Tenpenny roared.

Prudie stood up, easing into her bones slowly. 'Husband, get ye to the fire and heat yerself.'

John wheezed as he slid into the warmed space she'd vacated. Holding a raw knuckled hand to his chest, he coughed painfully, his body convulsing, unable to speak.

The women looked on in concern. The chill had settled on John's chest and once there had refused to budge these past four months. The bitter winter and cold spring showed no sign of easing it.

'The mustard plaister had no effect then?' Prudie hovered anxiously but he batted her away.

'Get thee away, woman. Your fussing makes me feel worse. Yes, I still cough and my chest feels sore tight. The plaister's only saving grace was it stank so high I could not smell the privy. 'Tis cleared now, wife. The night soil men will take their goods and it will be clean again for the summer.'

John had been at work repairing the shelter and emptying the privy's foul contents, the privy shelter wall having collapsed in the night making it unusable.

'You shouldn't have been working in that bitter wind.' Susanna handed him his pint pot of warmed ale.

He peered at her from under bushy grey brows. 'Are you becoming a scold too, Susie? As if there is a choice, child. As it is, we'll still be using the piss pots tonight. I must needs shore up the far side.' He collapsed back against the chair, staring glassily into the fire. Star nudged comfortably at his hand but was ignored.

'But surely not just yet, Father. Stay awhile and warm yourself.' Fear stabbed at her. John Tenpenny had been ill for so long and was getting no better. Should he die, they would be distraught, Prudie especially. And then what would become of them? Unprotected women were at the mercy of whatever fate had in store. Suppressing a shiver of apprehension, she stroked his unruly wiry hair.

'Aye. I'll warm myself and then I'll to my work and take a sup at The Cock tonight.'

'You'll not go to the tavern?' Prudie exclaimed in horror.

John turned to glare at her. 'Why shouldn't I? At least a pint of ale will give me some hope of rest tonight and besides, have we not cause for celebration this day?'

Prudie's lips thinned in disapproval. 'You know as well as I that this house has no need to celebrate. Are we still not in mourning?'

'And how will that look, wife? Better to go out and be proud and celebrate with the rest of the town rather than remind them all our Thomas died in vain for the cause we have just lost. Besides, it's been fourteen years long past. Time to make amends with our enemies.'

'I will not be so quick to forget my son. Are you so keen to turn coat, husband?'

John groaned. It developed into a hacking cough so there was some time before he could answer. 'I am not turning my coat tails,' he spluttered indignantly. 'I'm preparing us all to live in a country that now has a king ruling over it. What choice do we have? We still have to live in this town, cheek by jowl with neighbours who will fare remember we were on parliament's side. Even Flete is now raising its glass to the king and with cheerful face. Some folk have too long a memory. What good would it do to bawl out my support for Cromwell? Easy to live by principles but even easier to die by them.' John coughed again and spat phlegm into the fire. Drinking down his ale in one, he heaved his bulk to his feet and returned to the bitter chill of his labours.

Prudie threw herself into his chair and wept into her apron.

Susanna rushed to the woman. Kneeling at her side she crooned, 'Hush now, hush. John is ill-tempered because he's not well. He has not forgot Thomas and his sacrifice. He's being practical, is all. For sure, there are still spies about who would seek their revenge. Better we keep our heads low and our thoughts hidden.'

'And be hypocrites,' Prudie wailed. She raised her tear-stained, exhausted face. 'How could I forget my Thomas? My only son. Did he die in vain?'

'Not in vain, Prudie. He died in defence of the cause we believed in. And we will always remember Thomas. Of course we will.'

The lurcher shoved his nose onto Prudie's lap, distressed by all the noise.

'Look, here comes Star to comfort you. The last pup of Thomas's beloved bitch. He would not forget his master so easily either. But be counselled, Prudie. John is right. He is thinking ahead of how best we can still live in Flete. We will have to bide our tongues and think before we speak.'

The three sat huddled together, listening to the applewood logs hiss on the fire until jolted apart by the door being flung open again. Star growled in his grizzled throat and Susanna put a hand to him. She glanced up, half expecting John's return, only to see a finer dressed figure standing silhouetted against the light.

'Master Lacey!' Prudie cried in alarm. 'Is there a problem with Agnes? Has the babe sickened?'

'No problem I assure you, Goody Tenpenny. I come to pay your fee, that is all. My wife and son thrive, although Agnes is somewhat more tired than her baby. He cries lustfully for her milk.'

'A good sign.' She began to get up.

'Nay. Don't rise, good woman. I understand it was a long night's labour.'

'Aye it was but longer for your wife than I.'

'But a good end, God be praised.'

Prudie nodded. 'A good end. The best. God be praised indeed.'

Robert Lacey didn't move. Instead, he stood gazing about. Susanna took time to study him. She had been good friends with him and Agnes when they'd been too small for their differing social class to matter overmuch, and before hard times had befallen John Tenpenny. Robert had been a good-looking little boy and had grown into a handsome man. And he knew it. The blond curls had darkened but his hair still lay thick under his luxuriously feathered hat. He had swapped childish muddy breeches for a pair in fine worsted, and a Honiton lace collar frothed at the neck of his leather jerkin. He looked just as he should: a wealthy farmer and landowner.

Remembering his manners, he swept off his hat and bent in a bow. 'Mistress Susanna, it's good to see you again.'

'And you, Master Lacey. Congratulations on the birth of your son.' Susanna saw him swell with pride.

'Aye, a new birth for a new time. And what better day to be born than when our king rightfully takes back his throne.'

'Indeed,' Susanna murmured. 'And fitting you have honoured him with naming your son after him.'

Robert's face split into a grin making him resemble the boy she had once played alongside. 'What finer name than our lord monarch's?' Striding over he held out a small leather bag. 'Your fee, Prudie, with our grateful thanks.'

She nodded. 'Let me know should I be able to aid in any other way and my blessings for your wife and child. May they continue to thrive.'

'Amen to that.' Robert reached a hand down to Star but again the dog growled so he withdrew it. 'Thomas's old dog still lives I see.'

'Yes. His dog still thrives even though his master does not.' Prudie's tone was bitter.

Susanna put a tight hand over Prudie's as a warning. What had they just been discussing? The old woman would get them all into trouble if she wasn't more careful. 'Star is the last puppy of Thomas's bitch. You may remember Vixen, Robert.'

'Indeed. I have happy memories of all of us playing as small children. You, Agnes and I. Thomas always with a dog at his heels tolerating us as we chased after it. Vixen was a fine animal.' A shadow fell over his face. 'Simpler times perhaps.' He stared at Susanna, lost in reverie.

Susanna bit her lip to prevent her shouting out, *If only it had been you who had been killed at Stow and not our precious Thomas!* Little chance of Robert Lacey being killed. He had been resourceful in avoiding any warfare. Sucking in a breath she managed her composure and answered, 'Yes. Happy at times and, I agree, simpler too. But isn't that always the way as we shed our childish ways and assume the mantle of adulthood?'

Robert fixed her with a curious look. 'How wise you've grown, Susanna. How wise.' Then he puffed himself up. 'And now I really do have to assume the mantle of adulthood, as father and provider.' He shook his head in amazement, as if the reality was only just sinking in. 'How droll. Me, a husband and a father to a new generation.' He chuckled complacently. 'But what a world little Charles has been born into. What a life he may look forward to. A newly secure and prosperous nation. God save the king!'

The women remained silent but nodded. Susanna, with a sideways glance at Prudie, muttered a cursory, 'God save the king!'

Robert raised his eyebrows, began to say something but changed his mind. 'I must say adieu and return to my new family.' He bowed. 'My thanks again, Prudie.' Replacing his hat with a flourish, he added, 'Good day, ladies.' He turned abruptly on his heel, making his elaborate garter ribbons flutter, and left.

'Watch that man, Susie,' Prudie barked. 'He was fond of you as a child and I see lusty lights in his eyes as he looks upon thee as a woman.'

Susanna watched as a now relaxed Star sloped to the fire and lay down with a groan. 'Aye, I take heed. Fear not though, Prudie, Robert is only just married to Agnes. And now they have been blessed with a child, a son moreover, his eyes will not roam. Fond though he was when we were all children together, we run in very different spheres now. He and Agnes made a good match, a suitable one and some even say 'tis a love match.' She gazed at the blank face of the front door, wondering how many of her own words she believed. There, once, had been the possibility that she would wed Robert Lacey. The baby that had slithered into her hands from Agnes's loins might have been hers. A curl of jealousy gripped her innards, which she stifled. She would not be envious of Agnes being married to Robert. She wasn't sure he had grown into a kind man. And unkind men made unkind husbands. 'Maybe it should be *me* warning *you*,' she added briskly. 'Be careful what you say in front of him. He has high connections, Prudie, how else did he manage avoiding having to take up arms? He could make trouble for you, should he choose. Maybe for us all.'

The women stared at the space once filled by the swaggering man. Echoes of foreboding swirled in the gap he left.

CHAPTER 3

JUNE 2018

Beth collapsed onto the tiny two-seater sofa in her new flat, lifting her feet up onto one of the arms. She gulped her wine with relish, feeling the cool liquid glide down her dry throat. It had been the most exhausting month of her life. She gazed around at the boxes piled high in the sitting room; there was still work to be done. But it would have to wait.

Downstairs, the shop was ready for opening day the following Saturday. Over the last few weeks, the town had become increasingly busy with tourists and Beth was hoping to cash in on the season and make enough to tide her over the first winter. Opening earlier in the year had been the original plan but all the legalities had taken far longer than expected. She took another sip of wine and stretched her toes, luxuriating in her solitude. It was bliss having a workman-free home.

Hearing her phone buzz, she picked it up to see a text from her sister.

> Just got kids to bed. Light nights keep them awake. I have wine. What you up to?

Beth toasted the quietly burbling television and texted back.

> Same. Thanks for all your help, sis. Just as well we're not afraid of hard work.

Told you I was the best scrubber in town. Least I could do.

> Knackered. Heading for shower and early night.

At least the hard work is for you now and not that timber company.

> True.

Beth hugged a cushion, aware the wine had gone to her head.

> Glad I got out of that job.

Putting her glass down, she lolled back, enjoying the scents of her home-made soaps and hand lotions mingling with fresh emulsion as they wafted upstairs. Lavender and rose, bergamot and ginger mingled with the subtle odour of paint.

> Really need to go, Lor. Falling asleep here.

Okay, love. See you at grand opening Saturday.
Night.

> Night.

'Another glass of wine,' Beth sighed contentedly, 'a shower and then bed. It might not be most people's idea of a good night, but it's all I'm up for.' Just before she drifted off to sleep, she promised she'd stop talking to herself.

A thundering knock followed by someone tugging on the old-fashioned jangly doorbell shocked her awake. Cross-eyed with exhaustion she twisted round to peer at her phone. Nine o'clock. It was nine o'clock on a workday. Not late but anyone she knew, family or friends, would have rung ahead. The doorbell rang again, setting her teeth on edge. Getting up stiffly, she made her way down the narrow twisting stairs. Switching on the lights, she saw, to her surprise, standing at the main shop entrance, a couple with a baby.

Crossing the floor, Beth found the keys and unlocked the door. Swinging it open she said, 'Jade, Hugh. What are you doing here?' She didn't quite disguise her dismay.

'Well, that's a nice welcome, I must say.' Jade pushed her way in, wearing the baby in a sling on her front. Hugh followed, looking embarrassed, encumbered by a couple of bags. 'As you didn't come to us, we thought we'd pay you a visit to see what all the fuss is about.' She stopped in the middle of the floor. 'It's not very big, is it?'

'Not sure how much room I need to sell soap and lotions,' Beth answered equably. She was intimately acquainted with Jade's moods. Feeling awkward, as Jade was the first in their circle of friends to have a baby and she didn't know the etiquette, she went to stroke his head. 'Is this Hamish?'

'I didn't give birth to two babies, thank God, of course it's Hamish. And don't touch him!'

Beth backed off in shock. 'Sorry.'

'Jade's a wee bit wary of germs,' Hugh put in, shame-faced, his Scottish heritage sounding in the rolling rs.

'And with good reason. I don't want my little Hamish touched by some random and getting ill.'

'I'm not some random.' Beth bristled. God, what were they doing here?

'Of course, you're not,' Hugh said. 'Forgive us. We're exhausted. It's all been a lot harder than we expected.'

'Harder? Harder for *us*? Harder for me, you mean. You didn't grow a whole human inside your uterus and then push eight pounds of screaming baby out of your fou-fou.'

Beth suppressed her frustration. Jade, when on one of her rants, took no prisoners. 'Would you like to come upstairs?'

'We'd love to,' Hugh said.

Jade looked around, her eyes making tight little movements, as Beth relocked the front door. 'Is it weird living in your shop?'

'I don't. I live upstairs.' Beth led them to the stairs. 'I've only been in a week. The first night was strange, sleeping upstairs knowing it was all empty down here but I'm getting used to it. I've got to know Tony and Fred in the flat next door and there's a couple living opposite so there are people around.'

'Still,' Jade sniffed and hoisted the baby higher on her chest, 'it's not like living on an estate, is it? I'm glad we've got people all around us, families too. They've all been so kind. Bringing us casseroles, offering advice. I like being in a little community.'

'This is a little community. It's just a different one.'

'Don't you miss Exeter?'

'Sometimes. But I'm not far away. I can get my city vibe if I want.' She nodded at Hugh. 'Shall I take one of those bags? Be careful going up the stairs, they're steep.'

Jade stared up. 'I'm not risking taking Hamish up there,' she hissed. 'I might fall and drop him.'

'You'll be fine.' Hugh sighed irritably.

Beth looked from one to the other. Despite her limited experience of babies, she knew the strain it put on a marriage. Even so, these two looked at breaking point. 'Tell you what, I'll go first, you can follow, Jade, and Hugh can come up behind you. If you fall, you'll land on him and he's big and burly enough to cushion the fall.'

'Knew the rugby training would come in handy for something,' Hugh said affably. 'Up you go, Beth, and we'll follow.' He glanced at his wife. 'You'll be fine, and so will Hamish. Or would you like me to carry him?'

'No.' Jade wrapped protective arms around the baby. 'You've got the bags and I can't carry them, they're too heavy.'

'Then do as Beth suggests and follow her up. I'll come up right behind you–'

'What about the bags?' Jade asked sharply.

'I'll leave them here and come back down for them.'

Eventually, Beth got them installed on the sofa, settling herself on the floor. Just to get them this far had been a mammoth task. Was life with a small baby really this fraught? If it was, she'd definitely put off having any. 'Can I get you guys any wine?' She began to get up again.

'Don't be ridiculous, Beth. You know I'm breastfeeding.' As Hugh was about to answer, Jade rounded on him. 'And don't even think of drinking. You're driving home and I will not put my baby in a car with a drunk driver.'

Hugh bit his lip and raised an eyebrow to Beth in apology.

'Tea then, or coffee?' Beth asked, trying to keep the edge from her voice. This was a nightmare. Why had they come if it was all so difficult? 'Water?' she added, hopefully. 'It'll have to be tap, I haven't got around to doing much of a food shop yet.'

Jade summoned a sigh. 'I'll need some water if Hamish wants a feed, otherwise it's a no. Really, Elizabeth, you need to get yourself organised. No food?'

Beth tried not to snap. 'I didn't say that. I said I hadn't got around to doing a big shop and bottled water wasn't at the top of my list of priorities. I've been trying to get the shop ready to open as soon as possible.'

'We noticed,' Jade said, thin-lipped. 'You haven't been to see us.'

'I'm sorry, I really am.' There was an awkward pause. Beth needed a drink to get through this. 'Pass my glass over, will you, Hugh?' As he did so, she smiled over-brightly and thanked him. Grappling for a reason, she added, 'Mum once suggested it was a good idea to leave new parents alone for a while. I didn't want to intrude.'

'That's very thoughtful of you,' Hugh said. He eyed her wine covetously. 'Thank you.'

Jade shifted the baby slightly, pulling the edge of the sling away from his face. 'Oh and your mother's known for her maternal streak, is she?'

'Jade! Honestly, I don't know what's got into you.' Hugh tutted.

'Don't worry, Hugh. I can't argue with that. You've all known me long enough to know once my mother had us, she palmed off our care to anyone willing.' Beth took a large mouthful of wine. Jade was right. Sarah Loveday had had her children in quick succession with two different men, then concentrated on enjoying her life in any way possible. Two little girls got in the way of cheap holidays on the Costa del Sol, the odd job working abroad, and any nightlife Exeter offered. Latterly it had been charity work abroad. Their maternal grandparents had stepped in to look after them. She and Lorna had a close bond, perhaps because of their mother's benign neglect. Her sister was happily married and living in Bristol. Beth had stayed with their grandparents until studying at Exeter university. Both girls had grown up independent, resilient and thankfully free of any neuroticism. They had Judith and Maurice Loveday to thank for that.

'And how is your mother?' Hugh asked gently.

'I've no real idea,' Beth answered blithely. She knew her unorthodox background bemused him. Hugh came from solid middle-class Edinburgh stock and any hint of anything outside the norm bewildered him. She often wondered if this had been behind the transfer of his affections from her to Jade. Observing them now, she wondered how that was going for him. 'Spoke to her last week but that was the first time in ages. I assume she's okay, but I don't know exactly where she is at the moment. Somewhere in Vietnam, I think. Said she was considering training with some relief organisation.'

Jade huffed. 'I can't see Sarah being any use to foreign aid.'

Beth squeezed out a laugh. 'Can't disagree. You never know though, maybe she's put her wild ways behind her.'

'She ought to settle down,' Hugh said. 'Especially at her age. She can't racket around the world forever.'

'It makes her happy.' Beth's voice rose in defence of her mother. When had Hugh got so pompous? She didn't bear Sarah any ill will. She didn't know her well enough for that and she couldn't, in all honesty, complain about her childhood. She'd been fed, kept warm, had a roof over her head – most of the time – and had been loved.

'You never knew who your dad was, did you?' Jade asked pointedly.

Beth shook her head. 'Some bloke Mum met once in a club. Long gone now. All I know is Lorna is my half-sister and we have different dads. She's not concerned about finding out about hers either.'

Hugh snorted in distaste.

'Have you never thought to find out about him?' Jade asked.

Why was Jade harping on about this? They'd known one another since university, she knew all about Beth's childhood. 'Could never be bothered.' Beth shrugged, refusing to rise to the bait, wishing Jade and Hugh would go. 'His absence didn't affect my life, so I've never thought having him in my life would make a difference either.'

Jade jiggled the baby gently as he snickered in his sleep.

Putting her head on one side, she gave a tinkly laugh. 'Oh, Beth, family is so important, I think. I've begun to realise that more and more since having little Hamish.'

Beth bit back a retort. Marriage and parenthood had made Jade and Hugh priggish and complacent. Lorna had a point; it was time to let the friendship drift. They were on very different life paths and had different priorities now. She drained her wine, thinking about how they had all met. They'd teamed up as undergrads during Freshers' Week. She and Hugh had become an item almost immediately and had gone out for most of their three years at Exeter. Then, just after graduation, he'd had a painfully stilted conversation where he explained he couldn't see the relationship going anywhere as he was going to work in the States. After they'd split up, she'd tried to get on with her life, alone. To her surprise Hugh had returned to Exeter, unable to settle abroad, or that's what he'd told her. Only two months after coming back he and Jade had begun dating. There had been enough time – just – to make attending his and Jade's wedding as bridesmaid last year not *too* painful.

Looking at him now, Beth knew she could never be the sort of partner Hugh craved. Jade, on marrying, had immediately given up work, happy to concentrate on being at home. It wasn't something Beth could see herself doing. She found it hard to relinquish her independence; people often commented she appeared to not need anyone. Did she still want Jade and Hugh in her life? Clodagh, another friend from university, and prone to psychological analysis, always claimed Beth clung to friendships beyond their lifespan. 'Your mother intermittently rejected you,' Clodagh pointed out. 'Is it any wonder you hang on to relationships once they're made. The status quo keeps you feeling safe.' It was one theory. She really didn't have anything in common with them any longer. Jade, content with her casserole-donating yummy-mummy neighbours and Hugh, off to work, briefcase in hand, becoming ever more stout and self-satisfied. To Beth, it seemed yawningly conventional. Perhaps she had more of her mother in her than she realised?

Deciding on her answer, she retorted, 'Yeah, well, families come in all sorts of shapes and sizes. Gran and Granddad aren't far away, should I need them, there's still a few of the old uni gang in Exeter and I go out with the folks from my old job every now and again. And who knows, I may even find family here in Flete. Granddad once said he thought he had a cousin who lived here.'

Jade said, pityingly, 'Oh, Bethie.'

Beth had had enough. She stood up. 'I'm going to pour myself another glass of wine. If you're going to sit in my home and criticise my life choices, I think I'll need another. I *was* going to have a bath and an early night.' She glanced at the clock, still leaning against the skirting board, waiting until she had the time to put it on the wall. 'It's gone ten. You've seen the shop, you've seen the flat.' She paused meaningfully. 'Haven't you got to go and do feeding or bathing or whatever tiny babies need?'

Hugh had the grace to look discomfited. 'We couldn't get Hamish off to sleep so I suggested we pop him in the car and maybe the rhythm would send him off.' He glanced tenderly at his son. 'And it worked. Drove along Sidmouth seafront and somehow ended up here.'

Oh, so that's why they were here. Tenpenny House had been a convenient stopping off point.

'And we thought we'd come to see you and your new retail empire,' Jade added sulkily. 'Seeing as you couldn't be bothered to come to see our little Hamish.'

Beth let the sarcasm go. She was getting tired of Jade's snipes. 'I've been busy. And, as I said, I was leaving you to yourselves for a while. The last thing I wanted to do was impose myself on you when you've had this major life event going on. I was leaving the ball in your court.'

Hugh stood up. 'Of course, understood. We'll be on our way now, Beth. Come on, wifey, let's get you up.' He hoisted Jade up by the arm.

Jade fixed Beth with a stare. For a second Beth thought she looked panicked, trapped. Then she returned to form. 'Yes, we'll go. We know when we're not wanted, don't we, little Hamish?' she crooned at the baby.

'Oh, Jade.' Beth sighed, frustrated with the woman's self-pity. 'It's not that you're not wanted. Please come again, just give me a bit of warning next time. Maybe we can meet up for a coffee somewhere?' The words were out. She didn't mean them. Friendships, like habits, were hard to break.

'And that shows, doesn't it, Hamish, how little Beth knows about what it's like to be a new mother. There'll be no spontaneously "meeting up for a coffee" for me any time soon. Bags, Hugh!'

After a repeat, tortuous performance of getting downstairs, Beth saw them out, immediately locking and bolting the door behind them. Leaning against it, she let out an angry hiss of relief that they'd gone. She and Jade had once been such good friends but this brief encounter had been nothing less than torture. Rubbing an exhausted hand over her face, she made her way back upstairs, tripping over the protective cloth the chimney sweep had put down. Her foot rustled against some paper. Picking it up she read Ian's apology:

> *Sorry, will return tomorrow first thing to finish. Ran out of time. Found this. At bottom of chimney on right.*

Going to the inglenook fireplace, which was such a proud and distinct feature of her shop floor, she picked up a small package roughly wrapped in soot-stained newspaper. Opening it, she saw it contained a bottle about the size of her hand. Under the encrusted soot she could see the glass was a dull green. 'This chimney just keeps on giving,' she murmured, peering at it more closely, feeling its age. Clutching it in her hand, and too shattered to ponder on it any longer, she made her weary way up to her bed.

CHAPTER 4

JUNE 1660

It was Susanna's favourite place. She was often drawn here, to this stream bubbling over the shallow beach and curving out of sight, to the raucous quacking of ducks and their comical offspring, to the gulls squawking overhead, to the serenity of the ancient oak whose leaves had provided shelter for many hundreds of years.

As well as the oak standing proudly alone in the middle of the clearing, willows formed a graceful clump, their feathery tendrils tickling the water. A hedge of elm partly separated the pebbly beach from the water meadow beyond. Some said they were witch elm, precious to the old religions, valued in the ancient knowledge. The same people said it was a sacred place. Some still came to hang offerings on the tree branches, as the ancients had. They stole up here after dark, or in the early morning mists. Not wanting to be discovered and be persecuted for clinging on to the old ways. There were scraps of material hanging in the branches even now and someone had placed a small bundle of lady's smock at the foot of its trunk. Timeworn country habits died hard.

Susanna knew the place was considered unchurch-like, ungodly. Along with May pole dances, horse races and gatherings at fairs, the Puritan government had forbidden simple country pleasures. Everything had been sober, pious. Thomas and Prudie had been staunch in their defence of the Commonwealth, stating no one man had the divine right to rule over others and Susanna had been swept along with their fervour but had not much liked the Puritan ethic either. The wars had battered the population; whatever side you supported there had been heavy loss of life. She had heard it said there were too few men in England now, as so many had perished. There was little hope of her finding a husband and she was considered old to be unmarried at five and twenty. The wars and political wrangling had gone on for as long as she could remember and, while she was truly thankful England seemed to have a more settled future in store, the new king was untested. He couldn't be worse than the ones who had ruled before him. None tolerated a woman who wasn't a daughter, a wife, a mother or a whore. There was little margin for any other role. Susanna thanked the Lord every day that she had had the good fortune to be taken in, as a poor parentless babe, by the Tenpenny family. Otherwise, her fate would have been very different. She had been no man's daughter until then. Her lips thinned as she realised that now, unless she could find some man willing to take her on, she would be no man's wife. 'And there are petty pickings,' she announced to the wagtail who dropped at her feet, eyeing her curiously. 'Who'd be a woman, eh? No matter what man is in charge of parliament, my life is governed by the amount of tattle I attract. And, without a man's protection, little bird, it's a dangerous path to navigate.'

Standing, her hand to her eyes to shade them, she thought back to the first time she had come here with Old Mary and

Agnes and Robert. The sharp green smell of the grass and the fluting birdsong revived a distant childhood memory of gathering wildflowers in the meadow probably at this same time of year. She felt, again, the sun fierce on the back of her neck as she'd reached down to pluck flowers, breathing in their sweet scents. The goodwife had taught them the names: wild orchid and cowslip; garlic and anemone in the nearby shady woods. A woman of a low and poor sort with a keen knowledge of the natural world, she had loved the place and tried to share why. All that had changed when she had been accused of witchcraft and hounded out of town. She had been luckier than most, many had suffered far, far worse. Susanna, Agnes and Robert had continued to play, in innocence, by the stream at the place of the old sacred oak long after Mary disappeared. Now Susanna visited alone, childish games long gone, and Robert and Agnes with their own world in which to play.

Despite, or perhaps because of, the slightly dangerous quality to the clearing, Susanna always felt a deep sense of peace here. It was as if the ancients reached forward through time to protect her. She made herself comfortable on a tussock of grass, dropping her feet onto the pebbly beach, and contemplated removing her shoes and stockings. It was a rare hot day and the sun felt like benediction on her back. Taking off her wide straw hat she pushed her coif back a little and lifted her face to the sky, drinking in the heat. At long last summer had arrived and she needed to welcome its warmth into her bones. She stretched and wiggled her shoulders, the heat penetrating her many layers of clothes, feeling decadent and shocking. Under her linen coif sweat prickled on her scalp. Opening her eyes she darted a glance behind her at the meadow, there was no one to be seen on the track, she could hear nothing moving on the nearby drover's lane. It was safe. She slipped off her shoes, her stockings followed. Lifting her skirts above her calves she wiggled her toes, feeling saucy. Then, feeling even more daring, she gathered her skirts about her knees and inched over the pebbles, hopping and squealing a little as the stones bit into her soft feet.

The river made her gasp; it was icy. But it felt freeing and cleansing. Once she was acclimatised, she stood, perfectly still, up to her knees in chilly river water, her clothing bunched up in front and looped in a heavy pile over her arms. It was a magical feeling, a forbidden feeling. If any church member saw her, or had word of this, she would be condemned to Hell. It felt so blissful she didn't care. Susanna giggled, feeling naughty. The ducks, having been scared off, returned and eyed her nosily. One began pecking at the grass bank to her left, her babies bobbing around hopefully and following suit. A stone dislodged creating a great splash. The duck squawked and took off again, flying low over the water and out of sight. The ducklings, paddling frantically, followed, cheeping desperately for their mother. The stone had revealed something sticking out of the bank. Susanna paddled nearer, weeds tugging around her toes which by now were numb with cold. Holding her skirt clear of the water she peered at it curiously. Plucking the object from its hiding hole she held it up to the light and examined it. It was a worn metal knife with an intricately carved bone handle. The metal was unknown to her but was certainly not recently forged. The handle had elaborate circular patterns etched into it, great complicated whirls and curling loops. She sensed it had once been much prized, a precious and useful object. Practical too, with its serrated edge. How long had it lain hidden in the riverbank? Who had it belonged to and to what purpose had it been used?

A horse whinnying in the far distance startled her into

action. It would not do to be caught like this. The shame would follow her through town. Flete folk liked to gossip and if a woman's reputation was at stake, even better. Easing the knife carefully into the pocket hanging from her apron, she waded back to the beach, wetting her skirt hems in her haste. Sinking onto the grassy tussock she tried to rub feeling back into her frozen feet. Panicking, she was trying to drag her stockings over numb, wet flesh when a man on a fine dappled grey cantered along the track through the meadow. The rider reigned the horse in. To her mixed shame and relief – it was still dangerous to a woman's body and reputation to be found wandering alone in the countryside – she saw it was Robert Lacey.

'How now, Mistress Susanna. Have you come to revisit our childish places?' The mare snorted and snatched at the reins, chewing at the bit and foaming at the mouth.

Susanna leapt up, hiding the incriminating evidence of her stockings behind her body. She watched as Robert struggled to gain control of his mount.

When quietened, he slid effortlessly from the saddle and strode towards her. 'Mary fears this place for some reason.' He shrugged. 'I cannot fathom why, she's usually a placid ride.' From his vantage point on the edge of the meadow he smiled down at Susanna. 'We had no fear being here, did we? I always remember such happy and pleasant times, with the three of us playing. I even remember us getting soaked in the river more than once.' His mouth twisted. 'It seems, from looking at your skirts, that you have not outgrown the habit.'

'You named her Mary?'

'Aye. In remembrance of Old Mary. She was always kind to us.'

'She was indeed. The town was not as kind. I wonder what happened to her?'

Robert glanced down, deep in thought. 'I do not know. It was a sad occurrence.' He returned to gazing at her, his chin lifting in defiance. 'But maybe she shouldn't have meddled in ungodly practices. Still, all is in the past now.'

Susanna wondered at the ease with which he dismissed such cruel treatment of an old and vulnerable woman. She remained silent.

'Are you to tarry here a while? Be advised, it's still not safe to be abroad and on your own.' He added self-righteously, 'And think of your reputation, Susanna.'

Had he always been so priggish? As he had inherited his father's estates and land and was a married man with a son he could order her about. Once her childhood equal and friend, now he assumed the mantle of master. Prudie's warning that he could cause them mischief crawled into her mind. For years he had been nothing to them, now the birthing of his son had brought them into each other's lives again. 'I will away this moment.'

'And have you been in the water? Is it not too chill?'

Susanna felt the knife's cold metal, hard and rigid, in her apron pocket. For some reason, she was loath to reveal the real reason why she had been paddling. 'I rescued a duckling.' She stammered out the lie.

'A duckling?' Robert looked amused, his top lip curling under his fashionable moustache.

'Yes, it had become stuck in the reeds there and had been left behind.'

'Your heart is too soft, Susanna. You should have left it for the fox.' He squinted at her. 'Moreover, you lie most unconvincingly,' he said softly. 'You always did.'

'I would rather be thought of as soft-hearted than let a poor creature suffer so,' she replied, feeling her face heat with anger.

'What if your clothes had become drenched and you had

gone under? You were not bathing in your shift as you used to. You are no longer a chit of eight.' His gaze swept from the partlet at her neck to the feet revealed white and naked below her skirts, his meaning clear.

The relief that it had only been Robert Lacey who had found her fled. Susanna was alone and defenceless. Should he choose, he could do whatever he wanted, master over her that he now was. Feeling was returning to her toes and the sharp stones prodding into her feet whipped her into action. 'As you rightly point out, I am no longer eight years old. And I am getting cold. I will be late for my chores, so if you would be so good as to let me put on my shoes in privacy, I will make my way back to town.'

Robert didn't stir. A muscle clenching and unclenching in his jaw was his only movement. He seemed to be weighing up his choices.

Mary the horse rescued her. She threw up her head, nearly yanking the reins from Robert's hand. He pulled violently on the bit, forcing the mare to submit. 'And I must go too. It seems my horse has had enough of this place.' He nodded briefly. 'Good day to you, Susanna. Don't stray so far from town on your own again. Who knows what might happen.'

A warning? Or a threat?

Putting the toe of his boot into the stirrup, he threw himself astride the horse with the easy movement of one who possesses sturdy lithe muscles. Gone were the reedy thin shoulders of childhood, he was in full vigour of manhood, strong and vital. Should he choose to overpower her, she would have no hope of fighting him off.

Survival instinct kicked in and Susanna strived to find her manners to placate him. 'Good day to you.' Although the words were polite, her voice was stiff and unyielding. She would not show him her fear.

He jerked the horse around and cantered off, the hooves making the ground thunder.

Collapsing onto the bank, fear – and something else unidentifiable – rippled through her. It made her tremble so violently it was all she could do to pull on her stockings and shove her feet into her shoes. She needed to be careful around Robert Lacey. Very careful. They all did.

CHAPTER 5

JUNE 2018

Beth dusted the soot off the glass bottle found in the chimney and the curious bone handle knife the magpie had dislodged, put them on the mantlepiece over the 1970s gas fire in her sitting room and promptly forgot all about them. A hot bath to rid her of the strained and odd conversation she'd had with Jade and Hugh, another glass of wine and she'd collapsed into bed and slept the sleep of the exhausted.

Ian returned two days later and finished sweeping the chimney, apologising profusely. 'Someone nicked the catalytic converter off me van. Buggers,' he grumbled. 'Can't leave nothing nowhere.'

Pulling up a stool on the shop floor, he accepted the mug Beth handed him. He was a lugubrious bear of a man in his fifties who liked to chat. Beth, suppressing panic that the shop opening was in two days' time, and she still had tons to do, accepted she needed a break and joined him.

'You got that thing I found then?'

She nodded.

'I've found all sorts sweeping chimneys, like. See, folks

shoved stuff up there to ward off witches,' he explained matter-of-factly over his weak-with-three-sugars coffee.

'Witches?' Beth choked on hers.

'Yeah. Quite common hereabouts. I knows of a farmer not far out of town who still sticks a bull's heart up his chimney, even now.' Ian tapped the side of his nose with a forefinger. 'Country folk don't change their ways as quick as you townies.'

Beth, despite her preoccupation with all she had to do, was grimly fascinated. 'How do you know all this?'

'Oh, folklore and stuff is the wife's hobby. She's big into it.'

'And why did they put things in the chimney?'

'They used to think, way back, that a chimney was a passageway from one world into the next. And witches could travel between the two. So they rammed things up there. Sometimes it'd be a shoe, maybe a flank of bacon stuck with pins.'

'Bacon stuck with *pins*?'

'Oh yes. Stopped her, the witch that is, on her way down, like. Well,' he continued affably, 'no one likes an arse stuck full of pins, do they?'

Beth stared at him, nonplussed. Was he having her on? Gazing at the inglenook, which was now clean and free of soot but remained purposeless, she said, 'I found a handle. I think that came from the chimney too. Once I'd cleaned the soot off it, I could see beautiful patterns carved on it. I think it might be really old. Do you think it was put up there to stop witches?'

'Now, my lovely, you've got me there. I've found bottles like that little glass one, the odd shoe, a mummified cat once, but never the handle off something. Weird.'

She had to ask. 'A mummified cat?'

'Witches had familiars, like. Imps of the devil. They'd arrest the witch and shove her familiar, and it was often a cat, up the chimney. Any other old hags that were tempted to sprint down the chimney would be stopped by the spirit of the cat.'

Beth shook her head. 'It's mad.'

'Seems so to us but back then, probably when this old place got built, people really believed in witches and that she'd do them harm. A few good luck charms shoved up the chimney wouldn't go amiss.'

'She?'

'Well, a witch is a wicked old woman, in't she?' He finished his coffee in one, handed her his mug and began to gather his things. 'Wash that up, love. And I've known a few witches in my time, make no mistake. No offence, like.'

'None taken,' Beth replied, her lips twitching.

'Just glad I met my Sharon. She'll get the invoice to you in the post, she does all my bills and suchlike.'

Obviously, Ian's misogyny didn't extend to not letting his wife handle the paperwork. 'Yes, that's fine.'

'And don't forget, even if you don't have plans to use this old chimney, it's a good idea to have it swept once a year.' He touched his forelock in an old-fashioned gesture. 'This time next year, then?'

'Yes. I suppose so. Ian?'

'Yes, my lovely.'

'Was there a bird's nest up there?'

'No. Why'd you ask?'

'I had a bird fly out. That's when I found the knife handle. Main reason I booked you in to sweep, to be honest. I'm not keen on a repeat.' She shuddered, remembering how the distraught magpie had flown at her.

'You'll get the odd seagull nesting on top. Sometimes the young daft 'uns get themselves stuck.'

'It was a magpie.' She saw him blanch. He made no answer.

Eventually he broke the silence. 'A mock a pie's not lucky.'

He sniffed and wiped his nose with a grimy hand. 'I'm sure it's something and nothing though.' He looked around at the boxes of stock still unpacked, obviously keen to change the subject. 'My Sharon loves a bit of soap.'

'Bring her to the opening on Saturday. She'd be very welcome. Lots of special offers and free Prosecco.'

Ian brightened. 'We'll do that. See you then, Beth.'

'See you.'

When he'd gone, Beth couldn't help but stare at the chimney. It sat there squat and faintly malevolent. Feeling foolish, she went to it and forced herself to bend to squint up. She could see nothing but blackness and a sort of shelf sticking out. A sudden rapping made her heart start violently.

Ducking back out of the chimney, banging her head in the process, she saw a woman standing at the front door peering in, her breath steaming up the glass.

Beth waved her away. 'Not open yet. Come back on Saturday.'

'Can't you let me in now? I don't want much.'

Beth went to the door, irritated. 'No, I'm sorry. We're opening on Saturday.' For good measure she pointed at the sign she'd put up.

The woman muttered, put up two fingers and strode off.

Suppressing a jittery giggle, Beth took the mugs into the kitchen and wondered about modern day good luck charms. If that had been an example of the sort of customers she was going to attract, she'd need all the luck she could get for Saturday.

~

That night, she tossed and turned, sleeping fitfully. The dream, when it came, was urgent, full of hot fear and self-loathing, grief and confusion. Somewhere, smothered, was love, pure and true.

A young woman, dressed in full skirts and a tight bodice stood in front of the inglenook in the shop. She was hiding something. Something important. Her movements were snatched and hurried, panicked. From outside came the snort of a horse, an impatient shout, and the flapping of black and white as a bird soared.

Beth reared up, awake and sweating. Fumbling for her tumbler of water she drank deep. The dream had been vivid and real. She'd felt every confused emotion that had run through the young girl. But it was just a dream. A dream.

Lying back down, she tried to quieten her breathing and get back to sleep, but couldn't switch her brain off. Worries tumbled through her head, mixing surreally with images from the dream. Too hot, she threw the duvet off and was immediately too cold so wrapped it around her again. She became very aware of the empty cobbled street outside, of the echoing space of the shop floor below. Apart from one or two unexplained creaks and groans, which she put down to the old building settling down for the night, she'd not been bothered about being alone here before. The front door of the shop was necessarily secure and alarmed; the side door had a sturdy lock that she bolted at night. Behind the shop was a tiny yard with four solid walls that was only accessible via a gate at the end of the passageway. She was used to living alone, her upbringing had forced her to become tough and self-sufficient but Jade's comments about how weird the set up was, plus the conversation about witches, had created a film of unease. Perhaps, foolishly, she'd never feared physical attack; she'd always been street savvy. But tonight, for the first time, she was in fear of not the living but the unknown, the inexplicable. Turning over, something caught around her throat. She clawed at it. It tightened, choking her. Terrified, unable to breathe, she felt cold sweat drench her body. Then realised it was just the duvet. Scrabbling at it, she flung it away and lay there, panting, trying to make sense of what had happened. She'd never felt terror like it.

'Relax, you silly woman,' she scolded herself. 'It's a panic attack probably. Or stress. Or exhaustion. Or a combination of everything.'

The dark felt oppressive so she scuttled under the bedding again. She was frozen, unable to reach out and switch on the bedside light, fearful of what might be there. In her imagination the blackness crowded round her, the beamed ceiling hung low and heavy shadows reached out. Peeking out she glimpsed a bulky figure looming by the door. Throwing the duvet over her head again, she lay in frozen dread hearing a thump, thump, thump... Was something walking towards her? Or was it blood pulsing around her head? That was the only rational explanation. But she felt anything but rational. In one swift movement she darted her hand out and switched on the light. Immediately, the shadows receded, leaving her sweaty and confused. The ominous figure by the door resolved itself into the dressing gown hanging on its hook. Had she been asleep and dreaming, or had she been awake and paranoid? Was it night terrors? Whatever it was, she hated the trickle of cold fear that slid down the back of neck. Her abject vulnerability. It was as if someone or *something* had been watching her. Pushing herself up against the pillows, she sat until the shaking in her limbs ceased and she was breathing more normally. Searching the room, she couldn't see anything out of the ordinary. The wardrobe door was shut securely just as she'd left it, her bottles and tubs still sat on the dressing table. All seemed serene and boringly normal. Cocking her head to one side she could hear nothing except a keening gull outside. She shivered. It always weirded her out when they called at night. It seemed so unnatural. Her grandmother had called them maws, the old Devon name. Thinking of her solid, reassuring grandmother made her brave, so she padded next door to the kitchen. Tea, hot and strong, was probably the last thing she should drink if she couldn't sleep but it was what she craved. Taking her mug into the sitting room, she flicked on the remote and the television burbled into life. Perching on the edge of the sofa she watched, glassy eyed, until the rushing between her ears calmed and she felt more normal. Eventually *The Weakest Link* repeats lulled her into exhaustion, and she curled up and slept.

～

Considering Beth was running on empty through lack of sleep and energy, the shop launch hadn't gone too badly. She had got through it on adrenaline and caffeine.

Lorna had driven down from Bristol for the day with husband Steve, and both had done sterling work distributing Prosecco, chatting to customers, and giving out goody bags with free samples. Her grandparents had popped in for a while, told her how proud they were of her, given her an enormous hug and then disappeared to treat themselves to a cream tea. The local paper sent a journalist who took loads of photos and Jurassic Coast Radio sent a representative. Beth had done her best to answer their questions, remembered to give out her press releases, handed over the goody bags with samples of her lavender soap and body lotion, and smiled until her face ached. Encouraged by the A-board planted outside on the cobbles and tempted by the free fizz, quite a few people wandered in and the place had had a happy buzzy atmosphere.

Towards the end of the day, when Beth was hoping to steer the last few customers out so she could lock up and collapse, a woman with a glossy black bob streaked with grey, introduced herself. 'I'm Florence Addy.'

As they shook hands Beth found herself coveting Florence's

lime green linen dress, feeling scruffy and work-stained in comparison.

'I help run the Holistic Health and Mindfulness Centre,' Florence continued. 'We're just three doors away, on the corner.'

Beth remembered walking past a building with an opaque window and subtle silver lettering. She'd been so busy, she hadn't taken any notice of it, thinking it was a solicitor's office or something similar.

'Do pop in one day, we'd love to introduce you to what we do.' Florence gazed around her admiringly. 'It's so nice to have the old shop open again. It's been shut up for too long and I always felt it had a wonderful ambience.' She peered into her goody bag and inhaled. 'Lavender! One of my favourite natural scents and this soap smells out of this world.'

'Thank you. And please do come back.'

Florence closed the bag and beamed. She had a gap between her two front teeth. 'I most certainly will! I can see myself becoming a regular. Do you make all your own stock?'

Beth smiled ruefully. 'I make a lot of it, but I'll have to balance running the shop and making the products. I've an outside supplier but I'm hoping to source more locally from someone who uses natural ingredients as I do.'

Florence nodded approvingly. 'I'll have a think. A lot of our clients are artisan makers; they may have something you're interested in.'

'Thank you,' Beth said in surprise. 'Thank you so much!'

'You're welcome. We've a good community here in Clappers Lane. We all try to support one another. Come to one of our small business networking meetings, darling, get to know us all.'

'I will.'

As the woman floated off, Beth put two metaphorical fingers up to Jade and her assertion that there was no community here. She and Hugh hadn't come to the launch, sending a text excusing themselves with some kind of baby drama. Beth understood, she really did, but it hurt all the same. It was another nail in the coffin of their friendship.

'You look pretty pleased with yourself, my lovely, and I don't blame you, it's gone really well.' Lorna pressed a chilled glass into her hand. 'Bet you haven't stopped long enough to have one of these, though.'

'Oh, Lor, thanks.' Beth drank half of the Prosecco down in one. 'And yes, I think it's gone okay.'

Lorna giggled. 'Not sure Steve knew exactly what he was doing but he's done a grand job on that till when necessary.'

Beth shook her head slightly. 'I wasn't banking on making any actual sales today, so I'm really grateful he stepped in. I know it's exam season.'

Lorna blew her husband a kiss. 'Makes a change from him being knee deep in school work.'

'I can't thank you both enough.'

'Nothing from Mum?' Lorna pulled a hopeful face.

'What do you think?' Beth laughed drily. 'With Mum I manage my expectations, the lower they are, the less I'm disappointed. Besides, she's in Vietnam, isn't she?'

Her sister shrugged. 'No idea. Haven't spoken to her since before Christmas. Who was that huge burly bloke with the strong Devon accent?' she asked, changing the subject. 'Said something about sweeping your chimney.'

'That's Ian. He actually *is* my chimney sweep. Said he and his wife might come along. It's nice that he did.'

'More than nice,' Lorna said warmly. 'Mrs Ian bought sixty pounds worth of stock.'

'Did she?' Beth's smile widened. 'Good for her.'

As the last people trickled out, Steve collected the A-board, shut the door and turned back to his wife and sister-in-law. 'A good day. Been a real success, Beth. Well done.' He came over to her and kissed her on the cheek.

'Thanks to both of you. I couldn't have done it without you.'

'What's family for?' Lorna looped an arm through her sister's. She glanced at her husband. 'Now, seeing as Steve's parents are babysitting, we thought we'd take you out for a nice meal. You're too knackered to cook and I know you normally exist on wine and crisps, so we need to get some proper food inside you. Where's good to eat in Flete?'

Beth thought for a minute. 'Fish and chips, kebab, curry? Oh,' she added, brightening, 'there's a new Thai just opened up.'

'Perfect. Get your coat, sis. We're going to hit the town.'

CHAPTER 6

JUNE 1660

Susanna wrapped her shawl around her shoulders and tied it firmly at her middle. Despite it being June there was still a chill wind, and she had to walk to the other side of town near the harbour. Their aged workhorse, Job, had thrown a shoe and they'd scraped enough for a visit to the smithy. In her basket were several soap balls, headily fragrant with lavender. She and Prudie made them to sell at market to eke out a living. If she was short, she hoped the gift for the smith's wife would ease any late settling of the bill.

She led the lame horse as he walked at a snail's pace, holding her skirts above the puddles of mire in Clappers Lane and avoiding the foul-smelling middens. The weather had been odd this year. Her memory couldn't reach far enough back to recall a truly long hot summer; it had been cold and dreary from one April through to the next. This year felt even more out of kilter and unseasonal. There may be a king back on the throne, but the weather had not rejoiced in the fact; the winter had been harsh, the harvests poor and food shortages already making stomachs growl. It should be the best of the year now, with calm seas and blue skies but all was grey and stormy. An ominous greeny-yellow sun slipped from behind a low cloud but gave little light to the scene in front of her. She left the lanes with their overhanging top storeys, to emerge into the wool market. The roughly cobbled square led, along another narrow alley, down to the seafront and along a rutted track to the harbour. It was a good harbour and gave work to many, although a silted up poorer version of before. She remembered Old Mary had once told a tale of Flete being an ancient seaport, a Roman one, but it had fallen into decline after a storm blocked the estuary and thence the route inland. Now it was home to fishermen and those who ferried wool to Flanders. There would be no crossings today, the Flemish cloth merchants would have to do without. Susanna could glimpse an angry sea churning with churlish waves.

She wondered if the bone handled knife she'd found in the river had come from Roman times.

When showing Prudie her find, the old woman had grabbed at it greedily. Peering at it, she decided it might have come from the time of the great empire, many hundreds of years before.

'Or perhaps even before,' Prudie had declared. 'See, these curling, curving patterns are too circular, too natural inspired to be Roman. Tis my understanding theys liked straight lines and squares.' She squinted and looked closer, murmuring, 'There were great tribes that lived here abouts before the Romans. Made beautiful things like this.' She weighted the knife in her hand. 'Made with skill, this one. And I reckons tis a woman's knife. Too small to be a man's, see.' Sucking her teeth, she added, 'This was no weapon. Made for woman's work.'

'What, cutting herbs and cooking?' Susanna had asked.

Prudie shook her head, jowls quivering. 'More likely woman's work *for* women. Cutting the birth string and the suchlike.' She held it up to the firelight where the blade glinted even through its patina of rust. 'A mighty fine discovery, young

Susie, and I've a mind to use it once I've cleaned it up. Reckon it has some old magic about it.'

The words had made Susanna shiver. Nothing good ever came from the word magic.

Now, making her way through the market square, leaving behind the clamour of the oyster sellers and the yelling pie vendors, she navigated narrow Fish Lane. It led to the seafront and was narrow and uneven. Concentrating on her feet and trying not to breathe in the foetid odours, she was almost upon the horse before she spied it. A dappled grey was tied up and attended by a lad from Lucia Pettit's bawdy house. They were almost blocking the alley. As she urged a reluctant Job past the mare's enormous backside and nervously kicking back legs, she recognised her. It was Mary, Robert Lacey's horse. Job stalled in stubborn fright and the boy abandoned Mary, giving the old horse a slap on the rear. It thankfully got him moving again. Susanna kept her head down, hid her face in her shawl and called a quick thank you. She had no desire to meet Robert Lacey again. Whatever had he been up to in the bawdy house? She could but guess. With a fleeting pang of sympathy for his poor wife, still lying in and not yet churched, she hurried on.

At last, she and Job found themselves on the sandy track that ran alongside the sea. Here there were a few hovels, with the smithy in the distance and the harbour beyond. A stiff breeze shifted off the sea, bringing with it the pungent aroma of salt and not quite disguising the stench of poverty and fish guts from the ramshackle dwellings. Old Mary used to gather seaweed and sometimes even eat it, but Susanna was never keen.

'Although, if bellies continue to rumble, the town folk of Flete may yet have to scour the seas for cuttlefish and samphire, eh, Job,' she crooned to the horse. He was making heavy weather of the rubbled path, so she stopped and rubbed his whiskery muzzle. 'Not far now, boy, and then the smithy will make you good.'

The familiar clanging of hammer on anvil and aroma of hot metal reached her as she neared the smithy. Tying Job to the post outside, she went in search of James the smith, only to be greeted by a much younger man. A stranger.

'Greetings, mistress,' he said, pausing in his toil and wiping his sweating forehead with a rag. 'What can I do for you?'

Susanna's mouth fell open. The man was tall and sparely built but with an energy that sparked from him as much as from his blacksmith's furnace. He wore the usual smithy's leather apron, but his shirt yawned open exposing a strong chest covered in a down of dark brown hair. A red kerchief tied around his neck soaked up most of his sweat but it still ran in rivulets down his body. Susanna knew she should avert her eyes from such nakedness but somehow couldn't. A ripple of something undefined and unknown ran through her very core.

She jumped as James strode around from behind the building. 'Cover yersen up, lad. You'll frighten the maid.' He set down the pail of water he carried and addressed her. 'Fear ye not, Mistress Susanna, this is only Barnabas. He is lately come from my sister's house to apprentice for me. He's not yet used to such hard labour,' at this he cuffed the man lightly about the head, 'and gets a sweat on. Fasten your shirt now.'

Barnabas put down his hammer and tugged his shirt together.

'Now, what can we do for you?' James asked. 'Is it old Job? I spied him outside.'

Susanna cleared her throat. She nodded and then finally found her voice. Darting a quick look at Barnabas, who was watching her and grinning, she answered, 'He's cast a shoe.'

James nodded. 'I'll go take a look at the beast. Sit yerself down, maid, tis a long walk for you from Clappers Lane.'

Susanna perched on a roughly hewn stool and surveyed the scene. The smithy had been a feature of her life since childhood. Back then she would accompany John Tenpenny to James's more humble shack in the middle of town. The war had created work for those who wanted it; there had been a need for swords to be forged, armour to be mended, horses to be shod. With the profits James had built a fine new smithy. It boasted robust brick walls and a thatched roof and was on the edge of Flete; a more useful distance from the harbour. A great fire blazed in the purpose-built brick housing, sending flames and smoke up the chimney, tools hung in serried rows on hooks and the great anvil was placed directly in front. Susanna scuffed her feet on the ash-covered floor, woodsmoke making her nostrils prickle. It must be a mighty hot place to labour but she was glad of the shelter from the sea wind.

Barnabas upturned a leather bucket and sat on it. 'You're from Flete then?'

She nodded.

'I'm from Exeter way. I began my apprenticeship there as a boy but my uncle thought I should learn a better trade with him.'

'And I'm sure you will.' She watched as he thrust a hand through his hair, which made it stick up comically at the front. He had a nice face. Not devilishly handsome like Robert Lacey's but wide, with a firm jaw and a strong, high-bridged nose. A healthy flush burnished his cheekbones, speaking of strength and an outdoors life. 'I'm from Exeter too, originally,' she blurted out. 'My parents died in the last plague and John and Prudie Tenpenny took me in.' She sucked in a breath, she hardly ever told anyone about her past; she was sure most Flete folk thought she was Tenpenny kin.

Barnabas nodded. 'I am sorry to hear that. James says they

are good people.' He dipped his hands in the bucket of water James had brought in and rubbed them dry on his thighs.

The action roused something in Susanna. Her throat closed and beads of sweat prickled between her breasts. Her head swooned. She couldn't fathom what was happening.

Rising, Barnabas took a linen wrapped parcel off a shelf and then, balancing on the bucket again, he peeled the cloth away revealing a hunk of bread and cheese. Susanna tried not to watch as he ate. She thought his manners surprisingly refined for a smithy's apprentice. After he had slaked his thirst with cider from a flagon, he wiped his mouth.

Susanna couldn't avert her eyes from his lips. What would it be like to be kissed by such a man? She suddenly felt very hot. Desperate for fresh cool air, she was about to say she needed to attend to Job when James bustled back in, thwarting her escape.

'Yes, maid. It's a shoe, all right. Back hoof. Old Job's picked up a stone and all. 'Twould explain his lameness. I'll see to it now. Get off your backside, Barney. I know you think you've learned everything you need back in the city but you might still learn summat from your old uncle.' He began to gather his tools and placed a ready-made shoe in the fire to heat. 'Will you hold Job's head, Susanna? I know he's a docile enough beast but won't do no harm to keep him calm.'

She nodded and rose to go outside, glad of the chance to flee the noise of emotion Barnabas had stirred. Going to Job, she held him by his bridle and put her face close to his nose, whispering endearments and breathing in his reassuring scent. She was thankful to have an excuse to hide her flaming cheeks.

'He's a fine horse,' Barnaby said, coming to stand next to her, making her jump. He scratched the animal's ears.

'He is. A little old these days. We try to rest him as much as we can but there is always work which needs to be done.'

'You have a farm then?'

Susanna smiled at the thought. Still keeping her face hidden, she replied, 'Less of a farm. We have but a field and some animals. Chickens, a few geese, a cow and a rascally goat. And there are always kittens.'

'On Clappers Lane?'

'Yes, at the very end. There is no dwelling beyond except for the Lacey Manor.'

'So you have had a fair distance to walk this day?'

'I have. And slowly too. Job could not walk fast.'

'Will you be able to ride back? If he cannot bear your weight, I can take you in the cart.'

James yelling at Barnabas to come back to the business end prevented her from answering. Susanna was in a dilemma. It had, indeed, been a long tedious walk and she would not allow Job to suffer her weight upon his aged back, so returning in the smithy's cart would be a blessing of sorts. Besides, she longed to escape to home and unpick the whirling emotions that Barnabas had stirred up. Could she cope sitting next to him for the duration of the journey? Job's nose jolted upwards as James began work so she tried to rid her mind of handsome strangers and concentrated on keeping the horse steady.

When all was finished, she heard Barnabas suggest to his uncle that he drive her back. After a short discussion, to her surprise James agreed. When she paid him and handed over the soaps, he even pressed a morsel of coarse bread and some cheese into her hand, saying, 'You look right famished, child. Eat that on your way. Death is all too keen a hunter for those who are sick.'

Thanking him, Susanna secured Job to the back of the cart and clambered on board to sit alongside Barnabas. She tried not to huddle too close but with the chill wind whipping off the sea, she was grateful for the man's bulk.

'I'll go the long way round,' he said with a smile that made dimples appear. 'Fish Lane is too narrow for the cart and the market square too busy. Is that acceptable to you, Mistress Susanna?'

She nodded, folding her frozen hands into her shawl. Then she changed her mind; she was ravenous, having not eaten since early that morning, so tore into the bread James had given her. The cart swayed and swaggered out of the smithy's yard, throwing her against Barnabas's shoulder and the contact gave her a thrill she had never felt before. Once she'd finished eating, she checked behind to see Job placidly trotting along, all signs of lameness gone.

'He'll be fine now he's rid of that stone,' Barnabas said cheerfully, cramming his hat on as they entered the track that would lead eventually to Butcher's Row and then Cross Street and then home. 'Lots of life left in him.'

'I hope so. We rely on him ever more now that John is always so ill. Prudie and I aren't strong enough to pull logs about or take a load of potatoes and turnips to market.' She felt Barnabas give her a warm glance of concern.

'If you need any help, you know where I am.'

She met his look with a smile. 'Won't you be busy learning your craft? I imagine James to be a hard taskmaster.'

'That he is.' Barnabas grinned, the dimple grooving his cheek. 'But he is a fair man too, and kind. He would not like to see two women in distress and in need.'

'There are many in need in this town,' Susanna replied.

'But they are not you and it is to you that I offer my help.'

Their eyes locked. Susanna felt her cheeks heat and her breath quicken. Was this what the poets of old talked of? Was this love? How could it be when she hardly knew the boy?

'I left a mother, two sisters and a brother in Exeter. I cannot be there to aid them so I offer my services to you,' he said quietly.

'Why would you leave them? Didn't they need you?'

'I needed to learn a trade more. A blacksmith is never short of work and a skilled smith can find work anywhere, even across the seas.'

'Would you go to the new world?' Susanna asked, in awe.

Barnabas let the reins lie on his pony's back. The animal plodded on, knowing its route. 'I might. I've heard fortunes can be made.'

'Should you like to be rich?'

'I should like to be happy and content and provide for my family.' It was a stout reply.

'You would be unable to provide for a family here if you left our shores.' Susanna gently batted away a bee. Old Mary would have said it was bringing her a message from the other world, the one beyond the grave. She wondered who had chosen to visit her.

'I meant my own family. I would like to take a wife and have children. And even though peace is declared, and we have a king on the throne, there is no guarantee we won't have another war here. I seek a peaceful and prosperous life. Maybe that *would* be in the new world.'

It thrilled Susanna to hear Barnabas hankered after a family. He seemed wise for one so young. 'Men make money in wars,' she said tartly.

'Aye. And men die in them too. I was too young to fight last time round and I have no appetite to fight in another. There are many who are celebrating the return of a monarch, maybe they think he will end all future conflict.'

'And you are not so certain?'

'I am not.'

'You could not help your kin if you were so far away.'

''Tis true. Luckily, my elder sister is about to marry well. Her new husband will take on my mother and, aye, my sister too, until she weds.'

'You have a very clear vision.' Susanna meant it. She had given little thought to her own future. Life was busy and hard enough in the present to dwell on what might be. As a woman she knew her choices were limited. Prudie and John would be well advised to marry her and have her off their hands, but they had been good enough not to mention it as yet, even though she was an old maid. She knew, that due to John's continuing sickness, Prudie was finding her work hard and the farm, such as it was, was becoming neglected. If they could not plant the next crops, then they would not be able to harvest them. There was only so much two women could fit into one day, no matter how hard they slaved. A man, in the shape of a young husband for Susanna, would be a welcome pair of hands. But who? She turned to Barnabas. He was becoming ever more attractive, most probably some years younger, but he was no marriage prospect, not when he had his sights set on the new world. A pothole in the track jolted the cart violently and she fell against his strong shoulder.

He put an arm around her waist and held her firm. 'I've got you, Mistress Susanna. I've got you safe.'

CHAPTER 7

JUNE 2018

After the bustle and busyness of the launch, things settled down to a slower pace. Trade was erratic but Beth learned it could be surprisingly good on sunny days when the warm weather drew visitors in. The town, although lacking in the obvious attractions of nearby Lyme and Sidmouth, offered more plentiful and cheaper parking and a constant refrain amongst shoppers was, 'We gave up trying to park in Lyme and we're glad we ended up here'. It boded well.

Beth was less happy with how she was sleeping. Whether it was stress, adrenaline or adjusting to a new regime, sleep evaded her. Having tried her best lavender body lotion, room fragrance and bath salts, alcohol, no alcohol, warm milky drinks, cutting off all screen work hours before bed and numerous other suggestions from Lorna and their grandmother, she admitted defeat and booked an appointment with her GP. They'd wanted her in for a new patient check-up so she thought she could kill two birds with one stone.

That morning she'd come to after another restless night full of weird dreams. This one had been horrible. Vague and muffled with a latent sense of menace breathing somewhere murky below the surface. It had left her sweatily anxious, with a thumping headache and gritty eyes. The sore aching throat she put down to possible hay fever, although she'd never before suffered. She'd eventually fallen asleep for an hour, only to be woken by a persistent buzzing near her ear. It was a bee. She got up, shooed it out and shut the bedroom window before heading for the shower, planning to open the shop for a few hours before closing early for her doctor's appointment. Soaping herself with her own concoction of lavender and tea tree oil body wash, something her grandmother always said about bees came back to her; that they were messengers from the dead.

As she strolled along Clappers Lane, sucking in the briny air, she realised how good it was to get out of Tenpenny House. It had felt brooding and oppressive. During her solitary evenings in the little sitting room above the shop, she'd been easily spooked by the building's creaks, or the soft flit of a bird outside. It was almost as if something was watching…

A gull swooped low and startled her, making her trip on the cobbles. It flew too near her head, cackled and landed not far away, where it pecked aggressively at a discarded sandwich pack. 'Talking about killing birds,' she muttered as her ankle turned over on an uneven bit of pavement. Gulls never seemed this bold in Exeter. Glancing at her watch she began to jog. She was late. Arriving, panting, at the surgery she was told the doctor was running late, so had time to get her breath back and collect her thoughts.

After half an hour or so on an uncomfortable plastic seat, Beth had become hypnotised by the fish swimming languidly in a huge tank in the middle of the waiting room. She was interrupted by a receptionist who emerged to address the waiting room. Icy blonde and skinny, she looked around defensively.

'Dr Carmichael is dealing with an emergency. It's likely to take a while to sort so you can either wait or, if you have to, you can rebook your appointment.'

The old woman sitting next to Beth began to grumble. 'I'm going to register at the other surgery. This place is going to the dogs.' She snarled at the receptionist who glared back.

'You do that, Mrs Davies. You won't be missed.'

Mrs Davies sucked her teeth and said something unflattering under her breath. 'Right cow is that one,' she added as the receptionist returned to behind the desk. 'I'll go with Dr Smith over at the Rope Walk Surgery. Good-looking boy, is Nathan Smith.' She nudged Beth with a sharp elbow. 'He's very popular. Nice young man. He was so good with my Ezekial.'

Beth stared at her startled. What part of the body was an Ezekial? Or was it a disease, tropical maybe? She was just wondering what tropical diseases were rampant in east Devon when her neighbour continued.

'My grandson, that is. No bugger could get to the bottom of it, but Dr Smith wouldn't take no for an answer. Got him referred to a specialist. Right as rain he is now. You waiting or rebooking, my lovely?'

Beth considered her answer. She'd shut up the shop for the day and had only an empty and increasingly eerie flat to return to. 'I might as well wait.' She waved her phone. 'I'll read a book.'

Mrs Davies snorted. 'Do your eyes in reading on that buggerin' thing.' She got up stiffly, holding her back. 'These chairs don't half do my hip in. I'll go an' rebook. Can't be arsed hanging around here all day. I've got *The Chase* to go and watch.'

The old woman headed to the desk. Beth felt a pang of sympathy for the receptionists as the queue of disgruntled patients grew. A man emerged from a door further along the corridor, casually dressed and carrying a briefcase. He looked vaguely familiar. Mrs Davies approached him; obviously moaning. He listened patiently, seemed to sympathise and pointed at the queue. Mrs Davies nodded back to the crowded waiting room and, as he glanced over, he caught Beth's eye.

An instant heat flowered and her pulse hammered. He was attractive. Not overly tall but with that spare build and erect posture that hinted at peak physical fitness. Trying to calm her breathing, she surreptitiously observed him as he took time to calm Mrs Davies. Was this the Dr Smith she mentioned? Beth thought she'd said he worked at another surgery, the one on Rope Walk nearer the seafront. As he consoled the elderly patient, she studied him. Very short light brown hair, greying slightly at the temples, taut suntanned skin across good cheekbones and a strong high-bridged nose. Maybe late thirties. And as sexy as hell. Glancing up, he caught her staring, she blushed and concentrated on her phone. Her heart was racing. Ridiculous!

She found her eyes constantly drawn back to him. When Mrs Davies reached the front of the queue, he patted her on the shoulder and disappeared behind another door. Trying to concentrate on her book, which was failing to grip her, she kept half an eye on the corridor, willing him to emerge and brighten everything up again. Smiling to herself she tried to read, inwardly shaking her head at the almost visceral reaction she'd had. It had been like a bolt of lightning shooting across the clinically sterile waiting room. Weird. She'd never had a reaction like that to anyone before. It was almost as if she knew him already. Frowning, she pictured his face in her head. Maybe he was someone from university or a brief acquaintance from her childhood in Exeter? Someone who had popped into the timber merchants when she worked there? Flicking through her memory she was certain she hadn't met him before, but the feeling of familiarity persisted. Then she gasped. He was the doctor whose picture had been in the local newspaper; the one she'd picked up and read when she'd collected the keys to Tenpenny House. He'd found a book of old recipes or something. She remembered being strangely drawn to the book he'd been holding and hadn't understood why. Certainly a stranger then, and not someone from her past. It made her instant and visceral reaction even more odd.

As the waiting room gradually emptied, she found her thoughts straying to her relationship history. Such as it was. She'd been resolutely single since leaving university, the whole Hugh and Jade business had put her off risking her heart again. Going to their wedding had been the hardest thing she'd ever had to do, despite being genuinely delighted they'd found one another. Since then, her social life had centred on drinks with workmates or university friends who had stuck around the city. Then there had been the courses she'd needed to do to set up the business, not to mention having to sell her house; both had been time-consuming. Life had been full and happy and she wasn't aware of feeling as if she was missing out. Seeing Jade with the baby had been a shock though. Maybe she hadn't been quite as honest to her about the reason why she hadn't visited. True, she'd heard that many first-time parents rejected constant visitors and hadn't wanted to intrude, but was the real reason jealousy? Did she want a bit of all that marriage and baby stuff for herself? Maybe the strange reaction to the sexy doctor was a result of long buried hormones? Or should she just get laid? She hadn't had any of that for a while either. Everything to do with emotions and sex was as rusty and unused as Mrs Davies's hip.

Taking in a deep calming breath and scolding herself, she tutted and focused back on her phone, eschewing the book, and scrolled through Facebook instead. Jade was generous with posting baby pictures. It all looked idyllic but the panicked look she'd glimpsed on the new mother's face had suggested otherwise. Beth made a mental note to phone her friend as soon as possible.

An hour and a half later, she emerged from the surgery into the balmy evening, clutching a prescription for sleeping pills. Blood pressure, weight and general health was deemed fine by Dr Carmichael, who was quite clearly impatient to clear his delayed appointments and get home. Beth had no intention of taking the pills and had felt fobbed off. She was sure the prescription was a ploy to get her out of the consulting room. She hadn't taken to Dr Carmicheal, a stout older man with a flushed drinkers' nose who had barely taken his eyes off his computer screen in order to talk to her. Still, it could be worse, she could have been assigned someone like the sexy doctor with the briefcase as her GP. She grimaced. Getting examined was embarrassing enough, let alone by an attractive doctor who mysteriously inflamed her suppressed and rampant hormones. Head down, studying the prescription, she thought she may as well get it filled. Heading towards the chemists, she bumped into a man emerging from the back door of the surgery.

He smiled apologetically, swapping his briefcase to carry it under the other arm. It was the same man who had been so kind to Mrs Davies. He was even sexier close up.

'I'm so sorry. Wasn't looking where I was going.' He nodded down to the prescription in her hand. 'You were seen eventually then?' He smiled. He had a really nice smile, genuine and interested.

'I was. Thanks.'

He shrugged. 'I'm sorry about the wait. It happens sometimes but when it's an emergency it has to take precedence.'

Beth recalled the older man who had been wheeled out to a waiting ambulance, his face a dirty grey with strain and illness.

Her opinion on Dr Carmichael softened. 'It can't be easy having to deal with that when you come into work expecting nothing more serious than a repeat prescription for blood pressure.'

He thrust a hand into the pocket of his cream chinos and nodded. 'It isn't.'

Beth tried not to notice his wrists with the scattering of light brown hair. *Good grief, girl. When did you find a man's wrists sexy?* She could feel her heart palpitating. Maybe there *was* something wrong with her and she ought to go back in and book another check-up?

'I'm not a doctor at this surgery but I've been in the same position as Dr Carmichael a few times. You're right, we GPs don't often have an emergency that acute but,' at this he raised his eyebrows and grinned, 'we're always prepared for something out of the ordinary. It's what makes the job more interesting.'

'I'm sure.' Their eyes met and held. Beth felt heat flush her cheeks again. So this must be Mrs Davies's Dr Smith. His next words confirmed it.

'I'm Nathan Smith. I'm a doctor over at the Rope Walk Surgery. I've been here for a meeting.' His mouth twitched humorously. 'Also delayed.' He held out a hand and she took it. 'Nice to meet you…?'

His touch was electric. Almost too late Beth realised she was supposed to offer her name. 'Elizabeth Loveday. I'm a new patient. Just been in for my new patient check. As I'm a new patient.' *God, stop gabbling!*

'It's lovely to meet you, Elizabeth.'

Beth couldn't decide if he was naturally charming or too smooth for his own good.

'Have you been in Flete long?'

'Not long. I've moved from Exeter. I've opened the new shop on Clappers Lane.'

His brows rose. 'Ah, the one selling all those delightfully scented soaps? I wandered by on Saturday.'

'You should have popped in. It was the grand opening.'

'You know, I really should have.' He paused and stared at her, seemingly perplexed.

There was a slight stain on the good doctor's cheeks too. His eyes were bright and Beth had the sense that, for this moment in time, she was the only person who mattered to him. She watched, fascinated, as his breathing increased, his chest rising and falling rapidly. What was this thing happening between them?

He cleared his throat. 'I must come and see if I can find something for my sister. She's the most difficult person I know to buy for.'

'Please do. I've a great selection of gifts, all handmade, mostly by me.' Beth swallowed down some unknown emotion.

'Then I will. Welcome to Flete, Elizabeth Loveday.'

'It's Beth. To my friends.'

'Then I hope we'll become friends.'

'Yes.' Had her life depended upon it, Beth couldn't have uttered another word. Breath strangled in her throat. This was the most bizarre reaction she'd had to anyone. It was almost as if she'd known him before and in some deeply profound way. Something inside her recognised him. Shaking her head a little she knew that, until today, he'd been a stranger. What was this? Love at first sight? A *coupe de feudre*? Did she believe in all that? She shook her head again. A breeze shivered through the trees bordering the car park and a blackbird shot across the tarmac cackling a warning. It brought her back to herself. 'I must go,' she said, not moving.

'I must too. I'm late for evening surgery.' He didn't move either, still holding her gaze.

It took one of the nurses to call out a 'Bye, Nathan,' before either stirred. Then Nathan walked with the nurse to her car, and Beth went through the gap in the trees onto the main road and began to walk slowly downhill to her flat. She'd completely forgotten to collect her prescription.

Weird.

CHAPTER 8

JUNE 1660

In the grand bedroom of Lacey Manor, Prudie tucked the covers over baby Charles. She toed the wooden crib and rocked it gently.

'Well, hag,' Agnes hissed, 'what's the matter with him? Why does he ail?'

Prudie shook her head. 'I know not. He is well swaddled and seems content enough, if a little thin. How much of your milk has he had?' Prudie had tried to get little Charles to latch on, but it was to no avail.

Agnes pulled a face and snatched together the lace collar of her nightgown. 'As you have seen I find it a disgusting process. Robert has organised a wet nurse. A girl from town latterly given birth. She is of poor stock but comely and rosy-cheeked. She has come to live with us and will do.'

'You could persevere with feeding him yourself, especially in these first few weeks. It will help him thrive. I believe it is the new fad amongst the fashionable in London.'

'It apparently has *not* helped him thrive,' Agnes snapped. 'He is thin and weak.' She flopped back onto her linen bedding, glaring at the maid hovering anxiously by the door. 'Joan had better feed him gruel as Robert's mother insists.'

'If he will take it, then that would be good but I think him too young for such stuff. Cow's milk watered down may help, but Mistress Agnes, he needs milk, from a wet nurse or better still, from you. Oftentimes a new mother can find nursing a child difficult at first, but I have seen many bonny babes flourish and grow to be healthy children in the town when fed at their own mother's bub.'

'May I remind you,' Agnes spat, 'I am no street urchin from the gutters of Flete. I am a Lacey. And I care little for fashionable talk in London on how to feed my child, I've told you, I cannot do it.' She gulped, on the verge of crying. 'I hate him pulling and tearing at me.' Turning her face to the bed drapes, she hid cheeks flushed with frustration.

Susanna stood near the door feeling helpless. She had at first refused to accompany Prudie to Lacey Manor, not wanting to encounter Robert. Prudie had insisted, saying Susanna needed to learn more of what happened after a child was birthed, wanting to pass on skills and knowledge. She had watched as Prudie tried to get Agnes to feed her son, only for the new mother to squeal and cry that it made her sore. Prudie had fed the infant poppy cordial to make him more amenable but she could sense the old woman's concern. If baby Charles did not feed and thrive, it left him vulnerable to the many sicknesses that continued to plague the town.

As Agnes quietly sobbed and Prudie rocked the crib, Susanna looked about her. Despite knowing the Lacey family since a child, she had never entered the great house. To her eyes, it was a marvellous affair. Richly woven wool rugs warmed the wooden floor quite unlike the rushes and herb-strewn earth at the Tenpenny cottage. Diamond panes of real glass sparkled in the windows and Agnes's bed was draped with fine curtains of blue and cream silk. Susanna had never seen such riches, had not known it possible to live in such a way. She hadn't known the family possessed such wealth and, indeed, it had not always been so. Like so many on the winning side, the Laceys had filled their coffers in the wars. Glancing over at Agnes as the baby began to wail in frustration, she bit her lip. It was a pitiful sound that tugged at her innards. No matter how many fine curtains, or how many silk tapestries, it could not guarantee a healthy child it seemed.

Agnes plucked at her night coif. 'Make it stop.' She squeezed her eyes tightly as if to shut out the infant's cries and thumped the bed with clenched fists. 'Make it stop, I beg you.'

Prudie bent and fed the child drops of cow's milk on the tip of her finger and it soothed him. She stood up, straightening her creaking back with a sigh. 'Cow's milk will do the job if he'll take to it but, if you cannot feed the child yourself, then a wet nurse it will have to be. But make sure she is a clean girl. And keep all windows and drapes closed. The air can carry the pestilence. You say you have a girl already?'

Agnes shook her head mutely.

Joan, the maid, spoke in hushed tones. 'Meg will attend as soon as her beestings has gone and her proper milk has come in but her babe has only just been born.' She came closer and added, 'Rumour is Master Robert is keen for a large family and needs the mistress to be with child again as soon as possible. He will not hear of the mistress feeding the babe herself and you'd be wise not to cross him, Goodwife Tenpenny.'

Prudie nodded. Agnes's fate as a woman was sealed: to bear her husband as many children as possible and in quick succession. She would not even have the safety of her breastfeeding time to keep her from quickening with child again. Prudie sent up a prayer for young Agnes and also for

Meg's poor infant, left to the fate of hand feeding whilst its mother fed the offspring of the wealthy. 'Then let us hope it is soon, the baby needs nourishment.'

'Yes, that's the answer,' Agnes murmured, exhausted. 'And then it will thrive.'

'And try to eat. Something nourishing. Chicken broth or pottage.'

Agnes grimaced; her eyes still tightly shut. 'I cannot face food.'

Prudie sighed. She put a vial of liquid on the oak table. 'Take this in some wine. It will help.' Agnes made no answer but Joan took it.

'I'll make sure the mistress gets some and I'll hasten Meg's attendance. She is the friend of my younger sister.' At Prudie's questioning look, she added, 'Yes, a clean girl from a good family, the Flowers.'

Prudie gave a grim smile. 'I know the Flowers.'

Joan saw them to the door. 'My thanks, Goodwife Tenpenny.' She glanced over her shoulder at her mistress. 'She is not the easiest to care for,' she whispered. 'She says she has no appetite but will eat sweetmeats and cake enough.'

Prudie nodded, taking the small bag of coins that was her payment. 'Better than nothing but press her with meat and warmed wine. She needs goodness and liquids. My good prayers for the babe and mother.' She glanced at Joan's exhausted face. 'And for thee.'

As they left the bed chamber, Susanna asked what she had passed over in the vial.

'Just some yellow wort,' Prudie replied. 'My own recipe. It will help quieten the mother's nerves and maybe even calm her to feed the babe.'

They walked to the top of the back stairs, with heavy

thoughts, their footsteps silenced by the thick runners beneath their feet. They failed to notice Robert Lacey as he stood listening in the shadows.

CHAPTER 9

JUNE 2018

Beth woke from yet another disturbing dream. Someone was nagging at her to do something, to see someone, but it was all too distant and on the edge of her consciousness to register. It was something to do with an ill baby. She could still hear its ragged cries tearing at her insides. Flinging off the duvet which, again, had tightened around her neck making her feel trapped and strangled, she drifted off to sleep only to be woken again, this time convinced someone was in the bedroom. With a stomach hollow with fear and her body running in a chilly sweat, she flicked on the light to see nothing there. Then had dozed uneasily until dawn before falling more heavily to sleep. Having overslept, the third time she woke was from a seriously sexy dream about Nathan Smith.

The temptation to throw the duvet over her head and stay in bed was strong but she had a business to run. And it wouldn't run if she wasn't on the shop floor. Forcing herself out of bed, she showered quickly, keeping the water as cold as she could stand to shock herself awake and then stumbled downstairs to open the shop. While it was still quiet, she switched the kettle on and toasted some bread, keeping half an ear out for customers.

When the bell rang as the main door opened, she'd only nibbled a corner of her first slice. Hastily brushing crumbs from around her mouth she went through to find Nathan Smith standing awkwardly accompanied by Florence from The Mindfulness Centre.

'Look who I've gathered in off the street,' Florence proclaimed. 'I insisted he simply must come in and buy some of your scrummy soap.' She gave him a gentle prod as he grimaced as if to say, *what could I do?* 'Over there you'll find the bergamot and nettle soap I was raving about to you.' Having dispatched Nathan, she came closer to Beth and hissed loudly, 'I'm so glad to have this chance to speak to you. I've just heard the most devastating news.'

'What?' Beth blinked through her confusion and blushes at having the object of her intensely erotic dream in her shop. She became very aware of the scruffy sweater she'd thrown on and attempted to smooth her curls down. She must look a mess. A sleep-deprived, sex-deprived mess.

Florence jiggled her arm. 'Beth, are you listening? They're going to resurface the cobbles in the lane.'

'That's good, isn't it?' Beth forced herself to focus, remembering how she'd tripped on them when rushing to her doctor's appointment.

'It *is* good and we've been nagging at them for donkeys to get it done.'

'But?'

Florence sighed audibly. 'They're going to have to close down the lane in order to do it. I've been on the phone to the council for an hour this morning and, although for most of the work they can keep some kind of access going, for about three weeks, they'll shut the lane completely.'

'For three weeks?' It came out as a squeak.

'And with restricted access for the rest of the time. I mean, it desperately needs doing but what a time of the year to do it! Peak tourist season. And I thought of you, darling, straight away, having only just opened.'

Beth didn't know if it was the news, her bad night, or all the rushing around, but a wave of foggy dizziness descended. She felt herself sway.

'Oh, my lovely, are you all right? Nate, can you grab a chair, I think Beth here needs to sit down. Me and my big mouth. I should have eased you into the appalling news more gently. I really didn't mean to give you a shock.'

Nathan guided her onto the stool he'd grabbed from behind the counter, standing protectively next to her to prevent any fall. He held her lightly around the waist and Beth leaned into him.

'Coffee,' Florence declared. 'Strong and as hot as hell, that's what you need. Stay right there and I'll make some.' When Beth protested, she added, 'Don't worry, I know my way round the kitchen. I've known this building for years and I don't expect it will have changed.'

Beth inched herself away from Nathan. 'How embarrassing.'

'Not at all,' Nathan answered. 'Have you eaten this morning?'

'A bite of toast.'

'Drunk any water?'

'Not really. Half a mug of tea. I slept badly and then overslept and had to rush around to get the shop open.'

'Mmm, that'll do it. Why aren't you sleeping well?' He took her wrist and checked her pulse.

'Bad dreams, a bit of stress over the business, I suppose,' Beth answered, hoping he'd put her racing pulse down to her dizzy spell.

'Your pulse is rapid but that on its own isn't too much of a worry. Is that why you were at the surgery, the not sleeping?' Nathan dropped her wrist and, putting a finger under her chin, gazed into her face.

Beth felt heat colour her cheeks and tried not to notice how vividly grey and alive his eyes were. 'Yes,' she mumbled. 'That and my new patient check. Dr Carmichael gave me some sleeping pills. Zolpidem.'

'And they're not working?'

'I haven't been taking them.' She edged away from his hand.

'And why's that?' Nathan's tone wasn't judgemental, simply curious.

'I don't like to.' Beth shrugged. 'Not sure I really trust sleeping pills. I've heard they make you sleep too heavily and leave you feeling like shit during the day. I can't afford to not be on my game at the moment.'

'Well, it's true some people find that but until you take them you won't find out. And if they do have side effects, the dose can be tweaked, or you can try something else. Maybe a different type of sleeping pill.'

'Sleeping pills?' Florence emerged from the kitchen carrying three steaming mugs. 'Here you are, darling, a smack of best Brazilian. I've put sugar in too. Might buck you up. I don't normally advise the use of caffeine but exceptional circumstances and all that. Come to me, I can fix you up with something gentler and more natural than sleeping pills. What?' She glared at Nathan.

'I didn't say a word,' he said mildly. 'You know I believe in complementary medicine just as much as anything else.'

'And yet you've dished out pills.'

'I'm not Beth's doctor, Flo. I didn't issue the prescription.'

'No, but you would have.'

'You know I can't discuss that.'

'Dr Carmichael then, I assume. If you ask me, he ought to retire. He's too out of touch.'

Nathan remained silent.

'And I know you agree with me on that.'

He looked down at Beth. 'Maybe it would be a good idea if you went to see Flo. If you're unsure about the Zolpidem, then you could try the complementary medicine or homeopathy route. Despite what Florence claims, I'm not averse to patients trying a variety of routes to health but it would be wise to check it out with your own GP too.'

Beth clutched the hot mug to her like a lifeline. 'Perhaps I will.' She glanced from one to the other. 'Sorry to make such a fuss.'

'You haven't!' Florence said. 'Look, there's a business meeting tonight to discuss the way forward and how we can work round the roadworks. Why don't you come if you feel up to it? It's not just the shops that will be impacted, The Mindfulness Centre will be too if people can't park close by. Maybe we can band together to put pressure on the council to get it all done as soon as poss.'

'I have to go, I'm afraid,' Nathan interjected. He reached for Beth's wrist again. 'Will you be all right?' After a short silence, he added, 'It's still fast but that might be the caffeine. I recommend you pop back to Dr Carmichael for another check-up.'

Beth shook her head. 'I'll be fine. Never fainted before or even felt dizzy. I'm sure it was just low sugar or something.'

'Maybe.' He looked thoughtful. 'Best to get it sorted though.' He put his untouched coffee on the counter. 'And I'm really sorry but I do have to go. Flo, can you stay for a while?'

'I really don't need a babysitter.' The words came out sharply. Beth wasn't used to being fussed over. She stood up, relieved to see her legs were steady. 'The coffee and sugar has done the trick. You two go. I'm sure you both have better things to do than look after me.' As they began to protest, she added, 'And I promise, if anything like that happens again, I'll seek medical help.' She shuffled them to the door. 'I promise,' she repeated.

Florence, obviously reluctant to leave, said, 'Meeting at our place seven thirty tonight. Wine to soften proceedings. Please come. You'll get to meet everyone too.'

'I'll be there,' Beth replied, as much to get rid of her as anything. She shut the door on their concerned faces and waited until they'd disappeared from view, then bolted the door shut and flipped the shop sign to closed.

After pulling herself wearily up the stairs, she collapsed on the sofa and pulled a throw over her. In five minutes she was fast asleep.

∽

Waking at one o'clock and ravenous, she made a cheese doorstep sandwich and carried it, along with a mug of tea, to the sofa. Switching on the news, she let the television burble away to itself while she ate. Her mind drifted back to the nightmare she'd had that had so disturbed her. The memory of the baby's cry, ragged and desolate, tore at her heart and, for a second, was so intense, she thought it was in the room with her. Putting down the half-eaten sandwich, she made a sudden decision, picked up her mobile and tapped on Jade's number.

Forty-five minutes later, having eased her work van out of its tight parking space behind the shop, she pulled up outside Jade's house on the estate on the outskirts of Exeter. The road curved round with discreet planting, which would mature in time into a tree-lined avenue. The houses themselves were uniform with subtle architectural differences in an attempt to make it an authentic and organic street scene. It didn't quite work. The houses were built of the same brick, had white uPVC front doors, some with red roof tiles, some with grey. It didn't detract from the fact it was bland new build estate. Still, Beth thought, if it suited Jade and Hugh, then who was she to get snooty. Lots of people would give their eye teeth for a roof over their heads, especially ones desired by most as these were. After navigating around Jade's little Toyota parked on the drive, she rang the doorbell. Hearing an exasperated 'Wait a minute' she did precisely that. A dog walker wandered past and she smiled and greeted her, only to be ignored. So much for Jade's avowal of community.

The door opened but Jade immediately retreated into the house. Beth followed her along the hall. It was her first time in Hugh and Jade's new house and she was curious. Baby Hamish lay in a Moses basket fast asleep in the kitchen diner. The glossy white doors were smeary and the worktops covered in baby bottles, a steriliser unit and unwashed mugs.

'I've just got him off,' Jade hissed. 'We can go into the conservatory.' She picked up a baby monitor, eased herself past a freestanding dryer covered in Babygros and nappies, and collapsed onto a sofa. 'What a morning,' she whispered, the low volume not detracting from the angst. 'He was up four times in the night and wouldn't settle at all today. I'm exhausted. Now he'll sleep all day and be awake all night again. You ringing the doorbell didn't help,' she accused. 'I thought he'd wake up again.'

'Nice to see you too, Jade,' Beth answered, not hiding the sarcasm. 'Is there anything I can do? Shall I make some tea?'

Jade closed her eyes and waved a hand at the coffee table. 'Already made. Don't blame me if it's cold.'

Beth poured them both tea, added milk, and passed a mug to Jade who sat up and clutched it to her like a lifebelt. For a moment they didn't talk and then Jade, having drunk her tea in more or less one gulp, gingerly placed the mug back on the table. With one eye on the baby monitor, she asked, 'So, how's things with you? Still enjoying the single baby-free life?'

'You had a choice to marry Hugh and have a baby,' Beth said, trying not to rise to the bait.

Jade sighed, her bottom lip wobbling. 'I did. And I don't regret it. But it's hard. You can't imagine how hard. It's just an endless grind. Trying to feed him, trying to get him to take a bottle as my milk dried up. The nappy, bathe, feed routine. No matter how soon I've fed and changed him, he messes his nappy and it starts all over again. And my body! I don't think it'll ever recover. My stomach's all squashy and covered in stretch marks, it's still scary to go to the loo, and that's the first mug of tea I've drunk that's even vaguely warm. I don't even get a chance to have a shower and wash my hair.'

Beth didn't know what to say. Caring for a tiny baby was out of her comfort zone. Her memory told her Lorna had coped brilliantly but maybe she'd hidden the truth. 'Does Hugh help?'

Jade sighed again. 'Oh, you know men. He charges in at six expecting a hot meal on the table and the windows cleaned and then gets furious as he thinks I've spent all day doing nothing. If only he knew!'

'Why don't you go and sleep now? I'll keep an ear out for Hamish, do the washing up, give the kitchen a quick clean.'

'There speaks the childless woman,' Jade retorted. 'You don't understand, do you? If I take him up with me, he'll wake up. If I clean the kitchen he'll wake up.'

Jade had missed the point but Beth let it go. 'Put him in another room and let him cry for a bit?'

'And you really can't see why that would be a problem? God help any baby you have. No, I'll make the most of you while you're here and have an adult conversation for once that doesn't revolve around Hugh's desperately boring job or the baby.'

Beth sipped her tea and waited.

'How's the shop going?'

It felt as if, rusty with conversation, Jade had plucked the question out of the air and wasn't really interested but Beth obliged her with an answer. 'The launch day went well and sales have been okay so far. Nothing spectacular but building.' Nothing would persuade her to tell Jade the truth about how erratic trade had been. 'But now the council are planning on closing Clappers Lane to recobble it, so I think I'm going to have to close completely for a few weeks.'

Jade sat up; her interest piqued. 'No! That's appalling timing. I hope you're going to claim compo for the inconvenience and lack of takings.'

'I'll certainly look into it, but I'm not sure there'll be much loss of earnings as I've only just opened up. Not nearly established yet. I'm going to a meeting about it tonight so I'll find out more then. Who knows, it might only be restricted access and I won't have to close at all. Although, I was thinking, if I did have to shut, it might give me time to get a website sorted, make some stock, that sort of thing.'

'Sounds as if you opened before you were properly ready,' Jade reproved.

'Possibly. But if you keep holding off from doing things somehow there's never the perfect moment.'

'That's what Hugh said about having a baby,' Jade said gloomily.

'Would you change your mind if you knew then what you know now?'

Jade glared at her, her blue eyes brilliant with sudden tears. 'It's not that simple.'

'No, I'm sure it's not.' Beth hesitated. 'Are you all right, Jade?'

'Of course I'm not all right! I've just grown a whole human being inside of me and pushed an eight-pound baby out through my fanny. Of course I'm not all right.' She lay back and closed her eyes again, murmuring, 'What a stupid question.'

'But you will be?'

Jade waved the question away with a weak hand. Beth was concerned. She watched her friend as her breathing deepened and she seemed to lapse into sleep. Jade's once beautiful naturally blonde hair lay lank and unkept in greasy strands on either side of her face. Her delicate porcelain complexion that Beth had always admired and envied was blotchy with a ring of spots on one side of her mouth. Apart from the mound of her post-birth stomach, she was skeletally thin. It looked as if Jade was being eaten alive by something vile from the inside. Was this the truth of motherhood or was there something else going on?

She and Jade tacitly understood that, although on the surface they were fine with Hugh moving on from one woman to the other, under the surface lay a new layer of awkwardness. Added to their very different lifestyles it meant they weren't nearly as close as before. But that's what happened, wasn't it? You went through so much change in your twenties, leaving home, university, building a career. It was inevitable that you changed so much that friendships formed in youth drifted to be replaced by others. Beth knew the Jade who she'd encountered over the last year or so wasn't the one she'd been close to at university. Again, she asked herself what she was getting out of this relationship. She thought back to their early university days. Beth, used to being self-reliant, had breezed through the first few months of her degree while Jade, coming from a more sheltered background, had struggled for a while. She'd relied on Beth enormously. Beth hadn't minded. It had been eye-opening learning about Jade's cosseted middle-class upbringing full of ponies and month-long holidays in Cornish cottages. Despite it all, Jade had emerged from her childhood unspoiled and good fun, with the secure self-belief of the wealthy and a mischievous sense of humour. She'd been kind too, and unexpectedly motherly. Beth had always appreciated Jade's motherliness. It didn't make sense that she was struggling so much now. If anyone was destined for marriage and babies, it had been Jade.

As Beth forced herself to sit silently so as not to wake her friend, she wondered if the change had been down to Hugh more than the baby. Was Jade having to live up to some impossible standard of how he thought a wife should behave? Was he oblivious and insensitive? Neglectful? Or worse, was there some kind of domestic violence going on? Surely not. Beth thought back to how Hugh had been when they'd been going out. He was a bit posh, with no understanding of how the less well-off lived, but he'd been kind, sexy in his own way. Still, someone could change in ten years.

Jade woke with a start, wiping a trickle of drool from her mouth. 'Oh my good God, did I fall asleep?' She looked around blearily. 'How long was I out for?'

'Only about fifteen minutes or so.' Beth went to get up. 'I should go. Let you get some proper rest.'

'No, stay a little longer. Hugh won't be back for ages. He's got a late meeting.' Jade yawned. 'I'll just take a peek at Hamish. Check he's okay.'

As she rose Beth caught a whiff of body odour. Her friend really did seem to be neglecting herself.

Jade returned carrying a packet of biscuits. 'Hobnob? I lie to myself and say because they've got oats in them, they're good for me. Suppose I should have served them on a plate with a dainty little doily. Don't ask for more tea, I can't be arsed to make any.' She collapsed onto the sofa again, took a biscuit, bit into it and then threw the remainder onto the coffee table.

'Thanks.' Beth took one. 'And since when have we been doily freaks? Time was, we ate takeaway pizza out of the box and beer from the bottle.'

A tiny smile slid onto Jade's face. 'True,' she admitted. 'Happy days. Simpler times. Remember that grotty house we shared on Union Road? There were actual mushrooms growing in the bathroom. I never dared tell the parents. They would have swooped in on a dawn raid and taken me away from there.'

She began to look the most animated Beth had seen since she'd arrived. 'It was mould and the landlord fixed it but yes, it was pretty grim.'

Jade leaned forward and took another biscuit, crunched into it but then threw it, like the other, onto the table. 'So, any men on the scene? Are you having hot sex with even hotter men? Got to get my sexy times vicariously now because H is going nowhere near my fou-fou for at least the next twenty years. Might take that long before it feels normal.'

Beth smiled, a vision of Nathan rising. She felt her cheeks heat. 'There's no one. Single and fancy free, that's me.'

Jade eyed her speculatively. 'I don't believe you. There is someone. There *is*,' she repeated triumphantly. 'You've gone beetroot. Come on, don't lie to me, I'm your oldest bestie. Spill.'

Beth shook her head. 'It's nothing really. A doctor.'

'A doctor!' Jade exclaimed. 'Uh-oh, now we're talking. Don't ever tell my ma or she'll have me pinching him. She always wanted me to end up with a doctor. Hugh, a mere insurance bod, is somewhat of a disappointment.'

There was an awkward pause as both women realised what she'd said.

'Soz,' Jade said carelessly. 'Didn't think.' She took yet another biscuit and repeated the action of taking one bite then rejecting it.

Beth shrugged but was hurt at Jade's tactlessness. 'Don't worry,' she lied. After another pause, she continued. 'He's someone I've only just bumped into. There was this weird instant connection, though.'

'Oh, I likey! Is he hot?'

'Yeah,' Beth admitted. 'Tallish, lean. Runner's physique. Exudes health.'

'Yabbadabbadoo! What sort of doctor? Medical or academic?'

'GP.'

Jade's face fell.

'What's wrong with him being a GP?'

'I've not found them overly simpatico recently. Trust me, if male doctors had to give birth, they'd be majorly more understanding. I've found the whole medical profession dismissive, to be honest.'

'What have you been having treatment for?'

'Excuse me!' Jade flicked a thumb in the kitchen's direction. 'There speaks the childless woman again. You haven't had your insides ripped apart by childbirth.'

The atmosphere, having been strained throughout, became suddenly icy. A chasm had opened up between them, Beth realised, and she wasn't sure if it could ever be traversed. 'I'd really better go.' As she stood up, Hamish let forth a wail. It sounded uncannily like the baby from her nightmare.

'Yeah, you go,' Jade said in surly tones. 'I'll just go and feed Spawn of Satan and then change him and then wash his clothes and nappies and tidy this lot up.' She pointed to the mess of biscuits she'd made.

'You go see to Hamish, I'll tidy up.'

'No, go,' Jade snapped. 'After all, what else have I got to do? I haven't a shop to run or a hot doctor panting for me.' She heaved herself up and went into the kitchen, calling back, 'See yourself out.'

CHAPTER 10

JULY 1660

The first Susanna heard of the news was from Goodwife Flowers who swooped on her as she walked home from the market. Susanna had sold all her dried herbs and collected a leg of mutton and two fine rabbits. Her basket was heavy. She was slowly walking along Butcher's Row and Mistress Katherine had plenty of time to pounce. She stopped her outside the Fleece Tavern, its door wide open, spilling foetid stinks of ale and sweat. Susanna had reason not to linger, and it wasn't just because of the drunks eyeing her up lasciviously.

'You've heard then?' Katherine pulled at her arm.

Susanna turned to face her. A woman of middle age, she was shrivelled and bent. Katherine by name. Cat by nature. And a cat she was, with sharp tongue and claws. Susanna was always wary of her. On opposing sides during the wars, there lasted an old enmity between the Flowers and the Tenpennys. 'I've heard nothing. What are you on about?'

'The Lacey babe. Died this morn. The barber-surgeon was called but there was nothing he could do. Poor wee child expired this earth just as the cock crowed dawn. And there's my poor girl, Meg, dismissed out of hand. She was the wet nurse, I'll have you know.'

Susanna stood aghast, struck silent to the core. Though she no longer had any great affection for either Robert or his new wife this was wretched news indeed. 'Then I am sad for it,' she managed eventually. 'It is a great sorrow for a mother to lose her child.'

'And for the father too, although there are those who say he would do better to stay more at home and not frequent the taverns and bawdy houses so much.' Katherine pursed her lips. The woman had an insufferably superior air.

'Maybe those who spread scandal should mind their wagging tongues and keep their noses clean,' Susanna said sharply and then regretted her hasty words. Goodwife Flowers was not a woman to cross.

The woman's eyes narrowed nastily. 'Some say his gaze has been turned by an old love. That his heart beats for another, not his poor suffering wife still in her childbed.' She gasped, putting a hand to her mouth, her eyes enormous. 'And now then, didn't Mistress Tenpenny attend the birth and see to the health of the child afterwards?'

Susanna felt a warning prickle. 'What of it? Prudie tends to many births.'

'And yet she's never taken the church's oath to have a licence.'

'You know as well as I she's never seen the need. The women in Flete and hereabouts know Prudie and trust her, even without the church's approval. She has the old knowledge passed down to her by her mother and her mother before. The church has no need to oversee what she does.' Part of Susanna knew she should get away from Katherine and that, by rabbiting on in defence of Prudie, she was digging herself into the midden even further.

Katherine smirked. 'Prudie may come to be grateful for the church's protection should anyone accuse her of not caring properly for the little Lacey boy.' The inference was clear. 'We are not too young to remember witch accusations, Mistress Susanna. Think of Old Mary and what happened to her, aye and her like before.' She stepped back, spat at Susanna's feet and added, 'I make sure I call on Jane Thatcher if in need of a midwife, for she has the church's licence and has taken the oath to serve the town's women.'

'You've said enough, Goodwife Flowers. I'll take my leave of you. Good day.' Susanna turned and half ran to the corner of the wool market. Just before she turned into Market Street, she heard her name being called. Glancing over her shoulder, fearing the woman had had the temerity to follow, she saw it was Barnabas, the smith.

Content that Goodwife Flowers was no longer in sight, she stopped. 'What do you in this part of town?'

Barnabas smiled disarmingly. 'Helping you. Your basket looks too heavy. Let me carry it for you.'

Susanna handed it over. 'In truth, it's making my arm ache. I thank you.'

'Let me walk with you to your home. We'll make better speed with me carrying your burden.' He glanced upwards. 'And the sky looks grey. We'll be in for a shower presently. I can smell rain on the wind.' Barnabas nodded further along the street. Tis in this direction, isn't it? We go by the old stone cross and over Cross Street?'

Susanna nodded. The encounter with Katherine Flowers had left her shaken. She needed to get back to Prudie and warn her what was being said, for if Katherine was scandal-mongering, then the rest of town would be too before long.

Barnabas fell into step alongside her, peering down in

concern. 'Are you quite well, Mistress Susanna? You look mighty flushed if you don't mind me being so bold.'

Susanna shook her head to rid herself of the image of the vindictive Mistress Katherine. 'Oh tis nothing. Town tattle.'

'And yet it has upset you?'

She bit her lip, willing herself not to cry. John Tenpenny had worsened this week; his fever would not break and he coughed vile coloured stuff. Prudie had enough to worry about without adding to her woes. But add to them she must. She needed to know there was gossip about witchery. Why hadn't Agnes called for Prudie instead of inviting some quack barber-surgeon in? What would he know of childbirth and caring for infants? He'd most likely try to bleed the already weak mother and how would that help any?

'Now you look angry,' Barnabas observed.

'I am. I am full of rage.'

'And your pace matches your fury. Slow down, I cannot keep up.'

Susanna relented, stopping on the corner of Clappers Lane. She looked up at him and relaxed a little. Managing a laugh, she said, 'You do me good, Barnabas the smith. You ease my nerves.'

'Then that is all for the good.' He smiled down at her and a warmth filled his face. 'I am mighty fond of you, Mistress Susanna.'

She laughed more freely. 'We have but lately met. How can you become fond of someone of whom you know so little?'

Barnabas's lips curved. 'I know not but it is true. Maybe it is sorcery?' he added coquettishly.

Susanna quailed, she felt her gorge rising and rocked back on her pattens. Putting a hand to her throat, she gazed, wide-eyed at him.

He was quick to recognise her terror. 'I'm sorry. It was a jest. An ill-advised joke to make when we all know women who have hanged. What is it? Tell me.' He put a hand on her arm. 'You have gone very pale.'

Susanna got her breath back. Swallowing bile, she was ready to speak. 'The Lacey child has died,' she gasped, 'up at the manor, and Prudie was the cunning woman who attended. Goodwife Flowers has just accosted me and insinuates there has been talk of,' she hesitated, unwilling to say the word, 'witchery. What am I going to do, Barnabas? How can I protect the Tenpennys?' She stepped nearer and whispered hoarsely, 'Prudie's mouth runs off with her, she's inclined to get indignant and angry. Says things before she speaks.' She put a hand to her mouth to stop the tears. 'Just as I have done with that woman, Flowers. Oh, but she made me so cross I couldn't help myself.' Ice-cold fear solidified in her. 'And that is exactly what she wanted, of course. The sow.'

Barnabas was silent as he digested this rush of information. He studied her and then said kindly, 'I haven't lived here long but even I know how this town likes to talk. Don't fret, Mistress Susanna, it'll all blow out on the next tide. Come, take my arm, we will walk to your cottage, explain to Mistress Tenpenny what is afoot and all will be well.'

Susanna hesitated. She wished her life had no more concerns than that of handsome young men wanting to take her arm. 'If I do, there'll be more tattle in Flete. It's as good as a promise of marriage for some.'

His eyes twinkled. Despite his youth, they had well-worn creases at the edges fanning down his cheeks. A sure sign of a man who laughed long and hard. 'Would that be so tragic? I can think of worse fates.'

'So can I.' Despite her preoccupation and the threat of blethering tongues, Susanna slid her arm through the one he offered.

As they made their way along Clappers Lane, Susanna let a

tight breath release. Life could hold little to fear if she had the protection of such a man. Her snatch at happiness lasted only until they approached Tenpenny Cottage. From within she could hear Star howling. An unearthly and tragic sound containing all the sorrows of the world.

'Something is wrong.' Susanna picked up her skirts and ran. Fear stabbed. 'Something is terribly, terribly wrong.' Flinging open the door, she stopped short. Prudie sat in John's chair by the fire, rocking to and fro, her face shrouded by her apron. At her feet Star sat on his haunches, his long nose pointing at the ceiling, ears flat, howling as if his heart would break. Susanna rushed to the old woman and crouched at her side. Putting a consoling hand on the dog's neck, she said, 'Ssh now, Star. Hush now, dog! What is it, mistress? What ails you, Prudie? Prudie! Speak to me.'

For a long moment, there was no reply and then Prudie stopped rocking. Star ceased his racket and the old woman began to speak, her words dropping heavily into the quiet. 'Oh Susanna, dear daughter, dear adopted child, we have to be brave. We have to be so very brave.' She drew in a harsh stuttering breath. 'For our John is gone. We are left alone. My good John is dead. What are we to do? We are alone. Two women alone and defenceless in the world.' Prudie began to wail again and covered her face, her shoulders wracked by heaving sobs.

CHAPTER 11

JULY 2018

Warm sun and squawking gulls woke Beth at five, along with a dog howling piteously somewhere in the distance. A tremendous sadness hung over her, along with the echo of someone sobbing uncontrollably.

She lay blinking in the pink early morning light, disorientated. Knowing she wouldn't sleep again, she got up and made tea. It would be another long day surviving on too little sleep, but she was almost relieved to be awake. The dream, although shifting and vague, had been full of such sorrow she had no desire to risk returning to it. Why was she overwhelmed with misery? Her whole being felt dragged down. Tears prickled at the back of her throat, but she refused to give in to them. It had been just a dream, that's all. Stirring the teabag vigorously in her mug, she vowed to ring Lorna and their grandparents later, to check all was okay. Resolutely practical, she rarely gave in to superstition, but the pall of sadness lingered and couldn't be ignored. What if it meant something was wrong?

Giving herself a stern talking to, that if any disaster had befallen her family she would have been rung, Beth took her tea back to bed and scrolled through her emails on her phone. Opening one from Jade had all premonitions of doom returning. Thumping her mug down on the bedside table and sliding up in bed to better concentrate, she gasped as she read, barely believing the contents:

> You! You are the one I blame. I married Hugh. He was the one I wanted. He was the one I always wanted. All through university I had to stand on the sidelines and watch as you played with him. You never loved him. Not really. Not like I love him. It was the happiest day of my life when you two split up. You didn't know, did you, that I went over to the States to visit him? That's when we got close. I heard all about how badly you treated him, never wanting to commit, always going your independent way. Miss Aloof, Miss Nothing Can Touch Me, Miss I Don't Need Any Help. I tried to get him to marry me but he kept holding off, saying he wasn't over you, it wouldn't be fair to me. But I got him in the end, didn't I? I'm going to give him the perfect home and marriage. Something you never could. I'll give him baby after baby if that's what he wants. It doesn't matter that it wrecks my body, wrecks my head. I'll be the perfect mother to his perfect babies.

It went on, becoming even more of an incoherent ramble. The gist being Beth had ruined Hugh for Jade. No matter what she did it was never enough, never what *Beth* would do. Jade resented coming second in Hugh's eyes and it was all Beth's fault.

Beth lay back on the pillows horrified and furious. The fucking cow! Who did she think she was? This was way over and above one of her usual rants. Always quick-tempered, Jade often went off on one for about five minutes, about being cut up when driving, or a shop assistant ignoring her, only to laugh it off, sink a wine, grin and carry on a normal conversation. But she'd never, ever put her thoughts down in an email and never as accusatory and as personal as this.

Biting back her anger, Beth searched her memory. Had it really been like that at university? She didn't remember it that way at all. She and Hugh had enjoyed a casual student relationship, but their feelings had been real and they had loved one another. Had she really been remote? Come across as too independent? It was true, due to her upbringing, she relied on herself first and always expected others to let her down but surely there had been a true mutual warmth in her and Hugh's relationship, no matter how young they'd been. And she *had* loved him. Getting over him had been one of the hardest things she'd ever done, especially knowing he'd moved on to her best friend.

She scanned the email again, noting it had been sent at two thirty that morning. Jade had no doubt been up with the baby. Was Hugh up too, or leaving everything to his wife? She knew he'd taken no parental leave and had returned to work straight away. Jade had family but they lived an hour away so she was on her own. Had Beth been Jade she would have felt a little abandoned. Her lips twisted. But maybe, as she was perceived as being so self-reliant, she would have coped better. The flush of anger faded. She thought back to when she'd visited, Jade's spikiness and her strange behaviour with the biscuits. This was more than Jade's usual mulishness; the woman was struggling. But it was still hard to forgive.

She glanced at her phone again. What the hell was she supposed to do with the information? Ring Jade? Demand an apology or at least an explanation? And what was she to blame for, exactly? Jade had got exactly what she wanted, hadn't she? Rage licked at her again. It wasn't yet 6am so too early to ring. She could email back. She could ignore it but was that abandoning Jade? Beth couldn't walk out on a friend who looked like she needed help. Could she ring Hugh, or would that seem like going behind Jade's back? Surely it would feed into her paranoia if she suspected Beth and Hugh were talking about her. Lorna's words came back to her, 'Get rid, they're toxic.'

'Argh! Bloody Jade. What am I going to do about you?' Beth flung the phone onto the bed where it bounced once and then lay faintly accusing. Picking it up again, she scrolled through a few baby forums. They were eye-opening. Scanning threads on 'baby blues' and post-natal depression, none of it seemed to marry up with how Jade was behaving.

'Maybe she *is* a cow,' Beth said to herself. 'A prize bitch. A mean girl. Always has been and I've never noticed.'

Going into the kitchen to make more tea, she slotted bread into the toaster. Was it actually *her* problem to solve? Surely Hugh had noticed how erratically his wife was behaving? Thinking back to when they'd been in the flat all she could remember was how irritable he'd been with Jade and how longingly he'd stared at Beth's wine. Was he really that obtuse? Maybe she should get in touch with him and suggest Jade see someone. But was that fair on Jade, going over her head like that? Maybe there was nothing wrong with Jade other than a deeply bad mood and a huge bout of resentment.

Forcing herself to reread the email, one sentence jumped

out. That Jade had visited Hugh in the States. The information slid greasily into her consciousness. Neither Jade nor Hugh had ever mentioned it. It was yet another betrayal. The image of them having a lovely time in Boston and keeping it a secret hit her hard. She wasn't sure she'd forgive them that. Making her decision, she muttered, 'Not my monkeys, not my circus. If you've got a problem, sort it out between yourselves. If you can write those words, Jade, then you're no friend of mine.'

Taking her plate of toast to the tiny table underneath the window, she stared out upon Clappers Lane. The only life that could be seen was an enormous tabby cat skulking in the shadows of overhanging Tudor gables. Thankfully the howling dog had quietened. She wondered who it belonged to. As far as she knew, no one in the lane owned one. Gulls swooped and cackled overhead and the breeze whipped up white horses on the bit of sea she could glimpse. She sighed. The move hadn't been all she'd hoped for. Footfall in the shop had been impossible to predict. Trade on one day could be brisk, on others non-existent. There was no building of momentum. Beth wasn't sure she'd done the right thing. Maybe sticking to online selling was the way forward. It had been how she'd started but, ironically, trade had been so brisk it had been impossible to do the business justice whilst working at her office job. It had left her precious little time to make soap, customers got irritated at waiting and at not being able to get hold of stuff straight away. Everyone lived in an instant-gratification society, mainlining Amazon Prime these days. Her customers didn't understand the time and effort it took to make a batch of soap. It was why she'd made the compromise to stock from other sources and not make all the stuff herself. She'd thought, having a base where people could come in and buy in person, was the answer. Now it didn't seem the case. The more she thought about it, the more appropriate the idea of closing the shop seemed until she felt properly ready to open up again in a way she wanted to. Flete was getting busy with tourists but they didn't seem the sort to buy handmade soap and hand lotion and, so far, few had ventured off the beachfront long enough to discover Clappers Lane. The resurfacing would put them off even more. Little point in staying open with no customers being able to get in.

The Clappers Lane business owners' meeting had been short and to the point. Latest intel was the work was likely to take four weeks minimum with the lane being partially accessible and completely closed for some hours each day during the height of the repairs. It would be an unholy mess. Beth sucked in a deep breath and made some decisions. She would close the shop, concentrate on building stock, get a proper website sorted and create far more of a social media presence. Relenting, she would also ring Jade as soon as it was a civilised hour to do so. But she wasn't looking forward to it one bit.

Three hours later, Beth slid the newspaper-wrapped parcel containing the bone handle and the glass bottle, still a little sooty with chimney dust, into her bag, clattered down the steep stairs and marched out across the cobbles in Clappers Lane towards the main shopping street. Anger gave her feet wings.

The conversation with Jade had been terse and unhelpful. When Beth asked what it had all been about, Jade had dismissed the email as the ramblings of a nursing mother who was surviving on little sleep. When Beth had explained how disturbed and upset it had made her, Jade had abruptly cut the call. There had been no apology.

'It just isn't on,' Beth mumbled to herself as she strode onto Cross Street, ducking out of the way of a car that hadn't quite successfully navigated the mini roundabout and mounted the pavement. Glaring at the driver, some of her foul mood dissipated. If that's what Jade was going to be like, she'd go low contact; she didn't need the hassle. Lorna would be so smug.

Once on the narrow pedestrianised shopping street, she relaxed a little. It wasn't the most exciting place in the world and certainly didn't live up to its quaint moniker, Narrow Sheep Walk. She halted outside her destination, the tatty door of the town's museum, debating whether to get a coffee first or go straight in.

'Going in?'

It was Nathan. Dressed casually in chinos and a short-sleeved navy-blue linen shirt, he had a hessian shopping bag over his shoulder. He exuded good health and fitness.

'Oh hi, Dr Smith. Seem to bump into you all over the place.'

He grinned attractively. 'Small-town life. And the local GP having quite a considerable amount of leave at the moment. And it's Nathan. Are you feeling better now?'

'I am, thank you.' Beth didn't want to dwell on her health problems so changed the subject. 'You didn't fancy going away anywhere?'

Nathan shook his head. 'Not sure I can be bothered with an airport; the security rules do my head in. Having a few weeks at home.' He pulled a face. 'Forcing myself to catch up with the gardening. I'll do some walking too, get a few runs in. Besides,' he gestured around him, 'why go away when you have the delights of east Devon?'

Beth bit her lip and followed his gaze. She wasn't sure how serious he was being. All she could see was an old-fashioned butcher, a second-hand furniture shop and the usual smattering of charity shops.

'I know what you're thinking. This part's on the run-down side but Flete has real community and, despite it being fairly popular with tourists, we don't get overrun during the summer.'

Beth thought of her takings that week. 'Not so good if you've just opened a business though. I'll need the tourists to keep me going through the winter.'

'True,' he admitted. 'Perhaps once the resurfacing is done, Clappers Lane will be a more attractive prospect. Although I concede there's not much for visitors in this part of town. Having lived in Lyme briefly though, I really appreciate being able to park more easily. And Flete has kept its banks and post office, which is always a bonus.'

'So far.'

'So far,' he agreed.

'And there's the museum.'

'Which is open at the moment, I believe. Are you going in?' He peered at the handwritten sign hanging on the door proclaiming its opening times.

'Yes.' Beth reached into her bag and eased out the parcel. 'I'd forgotten all about these. My chimney sweep found them when he was doing the inglenook in Tenpenny House. It's a bone handle, I think, and a little bottle.' She held the grubby package up to Nathan. 'I wondered if someone at the museum might know more about it. I think the handle might be quite old.'

'Ah yes. Ian. He's quite the character.'

'That's one way of putting it. Unreconstructed male would be another.'

Nathan laughed. He scrubbed a hand over his shorn hair and grimaced. 'He certainly has a unique take on some things.'

'Women especially.'

'And speaking of characters...'

Nathan got no further as the museum door was wrenched open and a tiny elderly woman glared out. 'If you're coming in, come in. Don't stand there yammering on my doorstep all day.'

'Bill. Hi.'

'Oh it's you, Dr Smith.' The old woman's lips pursed. 'Didn't think you lot did house calls no more.'

'Not a house call, Bill,' Nathan said cheerfully. He slid the shopping bag off his shoulder. 'I've something to collect from you, if I may. And this is Beth Loveday. She has a couple of objects she'd like your expert opinion on.'

Bill narrowed her eyes behind owlish spectacles. She flipped a thick white plait over her shoulder. 'Loveday, eh? Come yourselves in then. You've timed it well; I've just put the kettle on. Flip the sign to shut, will you, Beth Loveday, so as we're not disturbed.'

Beth did so and followed Bill and Nathan along a shabby corridor past two rooms full of exhibits and into a tiny back room where a kettle was rattling to a boil. The place reeked of damp and neglect.

'Shift that load of papers off, why don't you, and then you'll have somewhere to sit,' Bill instructed.

Nathan obliged, gesturing to Beth that she take the worn and lumpy armchair. He perched on the arm, a little too close for her blood pressure. He smelled gorgeous, a mixture of soap, sparklingly clean skin and a subtle woody aftershave. She repressed a giggle. After her start to the day, he was just what she needed. He was so wholesome.

They sat in silence while Bill made tea the old-fashioned way, warming the teapot first, adding loose leaf tea and then pouring it into mugs using a strainer. It took time and ceremony.

Nathan gave Beth a sympathetic wink.

Eventually Bill handed over two white mugs. 'Biscuit?' It came out as some sort of threat.

Beth caught sight of the packet of Hobnobs and, remembering the afternoon at Jade's, refused. Nathan, to her surprise, took two. Perhaps he wasn't as much of a health nut as he appeared.

Bill settled onto an uncomfortable looking stool, sipped her tea and peered over the rim of her mug at them. 'Loveday, eh?'

she repeated, her glasses misting up. 'You a relative of old Betty Loveday? She lived down Church Lane. In those Victorian cottages.'

Beth wrinkled her nose. 'I could be. I'd have to ask my grandparents. I'm a bit vague about my family. It's not a very common name though, so yes, maybe.'

Bill snorted. 'You young folk. You never know anything about your family. Never pick at your roots, do you?'

'Well, my dad didn't hang around and my mum disappeared frequently, so my grandparents brought me up. In Exeter. Loveday is my granddad's name. Suppose it's possible this Betty might be a cousin or something.'

'You've got the same given name. Elizabeth,' Bill pointed out shrewdly.

'We have, haven't we? I'll have to ask him. Knowing my mum, she'll have just plucked the name out of thin air.'

Bill snorted again. 'So what have you brought me?'

Beth put down her tea, it was too hot to drink anyway and, once again, brought out the newspaper package. After carefully unwrapping it she held up the handle. 'This. It fell out of the chimney. It's got these beautiful carvings on it.' She handed it over. 'I think it's a handle.'

Bill slammed her mug down on the draining board and took it. Shoving her glasses up onto her forehead, she held it close to her face, squinting at it with one eye closed. 'Fell out of the chimney, eh?'

'Yes, the inglenook at Tenpenny House. I've just moved in. I live in the flat above and I've just opened a shop there. I–'

Bill flapped a wrinkled and age-spotted hand at her. 'Yes, yes, heard all about it. Soap or lotions or some such. The chimney, eh?' she murmured. 'Interesting.'

'A bird got trapped. When it flew out, the handle must have been dislodged.' About to mention witches Beth stayed quiet, taken aback by this spiky old woman. 'It was a magpie, actually.'

Bill's interest quickened. 'A mock a pie, you say? Fascinating birds. Oh yes, I see you shudder. More to them than the old rhyme, you know. Givers as well as thieves. And they mate for life and mourn their dead. Chinese believe they're good luck, did you know that?' She gave a philosophic shrug. 'Mind you, they're associated with witches an' all. Let's have a look at this magpie's gift then.' Bill twisted stiffly and fetched out a magnifying glass from the sink drawer. Holding it to the handle, she pronounced, 'I'd say this was old. Really old. Think it's Roman.'

'Roman?' Beth asked, startled. 'I wasn't expecting it to be so old.'

'There was a big Romano–Briton settlement hereabouts.' Bill nodded curtly in the direction of the museum itself. 'Go have a look. Educate yourself as you young folk like to tell me.' She paused but before Beth could draw breath enough to speak, added, 'And while this might date from Roman times, it's not Roman itself. Not with these concentric circles and interlocking patterns. It's more ancient Briton, Celtic if you will. We had several tribes living in the hillforts round and abouts. It'll be from the Durotriges or Dumnomii tribes.' Bill smacked her lips in appreciation. 'Beautiful thing.' She nodded. 'Durotriges tribe, I reckon. They were known for their craftsmanship.'

Beth had no idea what Bill was on about. She'd research the tribes later – if she could spell them. 'So how old do you think it is and what actually is it?'

Bill focused on her. Her eyes were vivid and youthful, and startlingly intelligent. 'Reckon you're right. Handle off something.' She held it out to them. 'Most probably a knife. See how it's shaped to take a fist. Wider at the end where it must have been fastened to the blade and at the other, so as you could get a good grip.' She placed it into her palm. 'A woman's fist that is. Too dainty for a man.'

'Not a weapon then?' Nathan put in.

'Not a weapon. Too delicate. Too fancy. A tool of some kind.'

'For cooking?' Beth said.

Bill sniffed derisively. 'Doubt it. More likely for something medical. Women of the Durotriges were distinguished healers. Revered. Held positions of great esteem within the tribe. A knife handle as beautifully made as this one wouldn't have been used at the hearth. See, look at the care and skill that's been taken with the carvings. Most likely used to cut up herbs and prepare cures, a sacred knife to add weight to the magic of the healing. Or maybe used in childbirth to cut the umbilical cord. A very special knife would have been used for that. A sanctified one.' She blinked rapidly and let her glasses slip back down onto her nose. 'Just think,' she whispered, 'we might be the first folk to have touched it in over two thousand years. It's got magic, this has. Real magic.'

Beth felt a weirdness wash over her. The air thickened. That the knife handle could be a link to such ancient and potent forces was profound. She wasn't, however, going to let Bill get away with her last comment. 'Except I have it on good authority Tenpenny House was built in the sixteen hundreds or thereabouts. So someone from that era must have put it up the chimney for some bizarre reason.'

'Suppose,' Bill admitted grudgingly, coming back down to earth. 'It's a fine, fine thing. If you feel like donating it to the museum, we'd be glad of it.' She handed it back.

'I had the chimney swept and when Ian did it, he said something about witches...' Beth let the sentence trail, embarrassed. She felt Nathan stir next to her.

Bill sucked her teeth. 'So what do you know about witches?'

'Not a lot. Hardly anything,' Beth amended. 'Just what Ian

told me, that people used to shove things up chimneys to ward them off. I didn't really understand what he was on about. I mean, how can a witch get down a chimney? She'd be too big.'

Bill laughed. 'She would an' all. Chimneys were considered portals. From one world to another. It wasn't the witch's body folk were afeard of, but her spirit.'

'A portal,' Beth said thoughtfully. It made more sense. Slightly. 'So they shoved things up there to keep witches away?'

Bill nodded. 'A child's shoe. A dead cat. Sometimes a spell bottle. Sometimes there'd be protective markings on the hearth. Oftentimes, they'd build the chimney a bit crooked so she'd have more trouble getting through.'

Beth thought of the ledge she'd spied when she'd examined the inglenook. She was finding all this increasingly fascinating. She took the bottle out of the paper. 'Ian found this.' She handed it over and watched as Bill examined it.

'Ah now, this is much more straightforward. What you've got here is a spell bottle.'

Beth and Nathan waited patiently for her to explain further.

Bill tipped the little bottle to one side and peered at it. 'See, inside there's some kind of liquid, just a mite left. Probably wine or maybe sea water. Sometimes they added urine.' She grinned, enjoying Beth's grimace of revulsion. 'They'd add hair or a speck of shell off the beach, a feather or two.'

'But what was it used for?' Beth asked, enthralled.

Bill put it back into her hand. 'Protection.' She shrugged. 'To ward off evil. They'd say a prayer or incant a spell over it, seal it up and put it somewhere safe. Up the chimney or under the floorboards. It's most likely to ward off witches, like Ian the Sweep said.'

Beth stared at the bottle in her hand. A world was opening up to her, one of which she had little knowledge and no understanding. Someone, many hundreds of years ago, had been so desperate to ward off evil that they had collected objects thought special, uttered a fevered and desperate prayer or spell and secreted it away, never to be found until Ian's probing brush knocked it out of its hidey-hole. 'But there's no such thing as witches is there?'

Bill's mouth twisted. 'Think you'd better do a bit of reading, child.'

'Oh.' Beth felt reproved. She placed the bottle on the newspaper on her lap, alongside the knife handle. The only thing she knew about witches was the old Halloween clichés. Old women wearing big black hats and riding on broomsticks. Something else she needed to google. A thought occurred. 'But, Bill, have you ever known a knife or the handle of a knife being put up a chimney to ward off a witch?'

'No. And never heard of summat that old being found up one neither. Must have been precious to its owner with that amount of craftsmanship. Maybe it was hidden for some reason? Maybe it's been revealed for a reason? You got yourself quite a treasure. You got yourself a mystery too.'

Beth picked up the handle and weighted it in her hand. It fitted as if made for her. She agreed with Bill: it was too small for a man; she knew it had belonged to a woman. And, somehow, she was sure it was too beautiful to have been a weapon or something dully domestic. But what else could it have been used for? Was Bill right in thinking it special and sacred? And how had it ended up in her chimney next to the spell bottle? None of this made sense.

'I can give you some websites to look up the stuff you need to know,' Bill said, surprisingly. 'And you can have a look-see in the museum too.'

'Thank you. I'd appreciate that.'

'And you, Dr Smith? You've come to collect your book, I suppose?'

Nathan handed over the hessian shopping bag.

Bill chuckled evilly. 'I had a rare old time looking through this.' She reached out and lifted a leather-bound book off a pile of papers on the floor. 'This is old too.' She scrutinised it for a moment.

Beth only had time to glimpse that it was a thinnish volume with battered covers darkened with age before Bill slid it into the bag and it disappeared. A sudden urge came over her, which shocked her to the core, to snatch it off the old woman and clutch it to her own chest. Where had that come from?

'Any opinions on what it is?' Nathan's voice brought her back to herself.

He was calm but Beth could feel his body vibrate with excitement next to her. She remembered the article in the local rag about him finding an old book. This must be it. She recalled the strange pull it had for her when reading the newspaper article. Forcing her buzzing brain to quieten, she concentrated on what Bill was saying.

'A book of recipes, some fine flower and plant drawings. Remedies, concoctions. No NHS back when it was written. Folk had to heal themselves or ask a cunning woman to help.'

'A cunning woman?' Beth asked.

'A wise woman. A healer.' Bill tapped the bag with an arthritically bent finger. 'Time was women were the ones who had the knowledge and the power to keep folk healthy. They'd be the ones sought out to mend the bones, soothe the fever, aid at the birth bed. Like I said about your knife handle, the ancient tribeswomen were venerated back then. This book's from much, much later. Maybe sixteenth, seventeenth century. Women were healers then too, but 'twas a troubled time for a woman then if you were a gifted healer or cunning woman. You had to tread carefully.' She glared at Nathan. 'Of course, now it's all men doing the healing.'

'Oh come on, Bill. I'm the only male doctor at my surgery. Everyone else employed there is female.'

'That's as may be. But when this was written,' she tapped the bag again, 'the physicians were stealing in, taking over. They'd discredit the women and their age-old knowledge, take over.'

'But why? What was their motive?' Beth was confused.

'Power.' Bill rubbed her finger and thumb together. 'Money.' She leaned forward. 'Men don't like it when women get together, child. Don't like to think about what they're talking on. Take child birthing. For centuries it was women's business. The women of the community, the sisters and mothers and friends would gather together to see the birth through. Used a birthing stool, sat the woman up, let her lean against them as she pushed. Gossips they were called, the women who attended the birth.'

'Gossips?' Beth said, startled. 'But that means–'

Bill nodded. 'It does now, child. Comes from the word *Godsibb*. Women back then needed a network to keep each other safe.' She snorted. 'Things don't change much, they still do! Of course, the men couldn't be doing with women telling each other to keep wary of Old Joe and his wandering hands and the suchlike so they changed the meaning of the word, made it more derogatory, like. And, not only that, but they put the fear of God into women if they were found to be telling tales and spreading nonsense, they'd be stuffed into a scold's bridle with a nail through their tongue.' She stroked the hessian bag. 'But back when this was written, a gossip was a friend. A friend who saw you through the pangs of labour, who kept you safe. It was the only power women had; their community of women.'

She leaned in and snarled and Beth wondered if she were quite sane. 'How many men have you known to be called a gossip?' she asked.

Put on the spot, Beth had to concede to none.

'There you go. The men doctors came along, took over, got

rid of the birthing chairs, put the woman flat on her back and there she was pushing uphill against gravity. And took a handsome fee for the privilege.'

'Why did they do that?' Beth wondered how Jade had given birth. They'd not discussed it. To be honest, Beth hadn't wanted to.

'Easier for the *men* to see what's going on.' Bill sat back in triumph. 'Keep the woman under control and where they want her.'

'That's appalling!'

Bill nodded.

Nathan interjected, obviously unable to keep quiet any further. 'But now we have birthing pools, balls, candles and music, hypno births. Whatever the woman wants plus medical intervention whenever necessary. And we no longer have to choose between the mother or the child. And it was often the mother who was sacrificed. We've moved on, Bill, you've got to admit that. Not everything historical is better.'

Bill huffed, unwilling to concede. 'There's a lot of wisdom in this here book.' She pointed at Beth. 'And it's like your handle, it was precious to her owner. Someone prized it enough to use parchment and leather to keep a record of the remedies. It was special to its owner and it's worth keeping safe.'

'How old do you think it is, Bill?' Nathan asked.

Bill's nose twitched. 'Thinking with your wallet, Dr Smith? This isn't the *Antiques Roadshow*.'

Nathan didn't rise to the barb. 'I'm simply curious.'

'If I were pushed for an exact date, mid-seventeenth century, I reckon. Post Culpepper. Lot of his influence in there.' She handed over the bag reluctantly. 'You take good care of it. There's power in there. Feminine power.'

Nathan took the bag gingerly. 'I will. I promise. And trust me, I'm not about to sell it. We believe it's a family heirloom.'

'Trust you, why? Because you're a doctor?' Bill gave a girlish giggle.

'Seems as good a reason as any.' He smiled.

Bill grumbled something under her breath and then rose stiffly. 'And now, you two young 'uns, I'm going to turf you out. Got to eat me lunch. You've eaten all my biscuits so I'll have to make do with a sandwich from the coffee shop. Scarper.'

CHAPTER 12

JULY 2018

Beth and Nathan were outside, standing on the sun-soaked pavement amongst the tourists wandering beachward.

'As you said, bit of a character.'

Nathan grinned. 'She is. Local legend. But no one knows more local history than she does.' He nodded to the now firmly shut museum door. 'And she runs this place with little help. Coffee? Don't know about you but I couldn't drink much of that tea. Besides, I've a craving for a toasted teacake and I know just the place.' He gathered the hessian bag close to his chest. A passing group of tourists barged into Beth, knocking her into him. He slid an arm around her waist and righted her. 'You okay?'

Beth liked the feel of his strong arm on her body. She felt heat rise where his flesh pressed against her T-shirt and she liked that too. 'I'm fine but wondering where you'll find a place quiet enough at this time of year.'

'Come with me.'

He hitched the bag onto his shoulder and led her across the street and down a narrow alley she'd never noticed in between the chemist and a charity shop. A waft of newly baked bread assailed Beth's nostrils making her tummy grumble.

'Flete's best kept secret, or one of them. The town bakery.' Nathan opened the door of the unassuming-looking shop and its bell jingled merrily. Inside was a counter and one tiny table with two chairs. The view of the old wall opposite wasn't alluring but the scent of fresh bread certainly was.

A skinny man, possibly in his early forties, came out of a back room and smiled in greeting. 'Nate! How are you doing, man? Coffee?'

'Two, please, and two of your teacakes to eat in.'

The man nodded and disappeared again. 'A running mate,' Nathan explained as they sat down.

'A running baker?' Beth queried to the soundtrack of a coffee grinder in a room beyond the bakery. 'Unlikely combo.'

'Travis figures the running helps him eat all the good stuff he bakes and keeps him trim.'

'And is it a philosophy you agree with?'

He grimaced. 'As a GP I'm supposed to say cut down on the sweet stuff. As a realist I say a little of what you fancy does you good and take regular exercise that you enjoy.'

'Wish you were my GP,' Beth replied sourly, thinking back to the unsympathetic and uninterested Dr Carmichael.

Nathan gave her an intense look. 'I don't.'

'Oh! Am I such a bad patient then?'

'Not at all.' He grinned. 'But I couldn't take you out for coffee like this if you were. It's strictly against protocol. And I'd like to ask you out, if I may.'

The wind was punched from Beth's sails. 'Oh,' was all she managed. Before she could get her feelings ordered, Travis brought over a cafetiere of coffee, and teacakes oozing yellow butter piled high on a plate.

'There you go, folks. Enjoy.' He and Nathan chatted about

the next parkrun they were doing and something about a Grizzly run in nearby Seaton that sounded truly terrifying. Beth only half listened. Trying to quieten the emotion Nathan's statement of intent had stirred up, she concentrated on eating. When she'd finished, as the men were still chatting, she googled on her phone the name Bill had mentioned: Culpepper. Born in 1616, he became an apprentice to an apothecary, she read. Wounded fighting for Cromwell, he was most famous for his *Culpepper's Herbal*, published cheaply for the mass market in 1652. Beth wondered what the literacy rate was in the seventeenth century. If Bill was right and Nathan's leather-bound volume showed the influence of Culpepper, it dated it post 1652. And the evidence was clear; it had been created by a person who could read and write. She vowed to research life in the seventeenth century; it was a period of which she knew little. A link took her to Amazon and a modern translation of *Culpepper's Herbal*, so she ordered it.

While Nathan ate, she sipped her second cup of coffee and looked around her. The bakery was tiny, with whitewashed rough walls and a tempting display of bread and cakes on offer. Nothing fancy but delicious-looking sourdough, treacle tarts and the hearty Devon speciality, lardy cakes.

'This is a real find,' she said when he'd finished.

He tapped his nose. 'Only the locals know about it.'

Beth, picturing her own shop and thinking a niche artisan bakery would go down a storm on Clappers Lane, asked, 'Then how does Travis make a living?'

Nathan pushed his plate away. 'I don't think he's that bothered about a huge profit. He lives above the shop, cycles everywhere, opens when he feels like it and bakes what he's interested in making. He's a laid-back kind of guy, if that's not stating the obvious.'

Beth was silent for a moment. Maybe she could learn from

him. But, then again, the laid-back running Travis probably didn't have a mortgage to worry about. Even though small, hers was still a pressing worry. Guilt that she should be in the shop right now snatched at her. 'Interesting philosophy if it works for you.'

'And it's not for everyone. Travis used to be a hedge fund manager. Suffered a breakdown and came to Flete to start again. He's not bothered about expansion or making a lot of money.'

No, he wouldn't be. He's probably already made enough. Beth kept the thought to herself; it seemed too cynical and she didn't want to appear bitter. But it was a business model that wouldn't work for her. She changed the subject. 'So, tell me about the book you collected from Bill.'

Nathan jerked round. His shoulders relaxed as he saw the shopping bag was still hanging on the back of his chair. Turning back to her, he answered, 'It's something Mum found when she was clearing out the attic. As Bill said, it's a book of old recipes and folk remedies. Seeing as I'm a doctor, Mum thought I might like it and, as it looked so old, I thought Bill might be able to tell me more about it. Mum thinks it's something to do with Dad's American family.'

'You're American?'

Nathan shook his head vigorously. 'No. Born and bred in Devon. In Flete, actually. Went away to medical school and then returned after a while.' At Beth's questioning look, he added, 'Parents getting on a bit and wanted to be closer, so jumped at the chance to be a GP in the town. My paternal grandfather, though, was born in Massachusetts. He came over as a GI in 1943, was billeted here in Flete, met my grandmother and they got married just before he embarked for D-Day.'

'Wow,' Beth said, impressed. 'Romantic story. Did they go back to the States?'

'No, he settled here after the war. The book was in a chest of stuff that Gramps had had sent over. Mum had stashed it in the attic from when she'd cleared his house. She thought she'd better look through it before throwing any of it away. It's an amazing thing. Beautiful copperplate writing, delicate drawings of plants and flowers. There's some water damage but quite a lot has survived and it's fairly legible if you persist.'

Beth repeated the information she'd just looked up.

'Ah. That's interesting. I know a little about Culpepper but only had the haziest notion of when he was around.'

'It might narrow down when your book was written.'

'Certainly could. From the little I could decipher – the writing's hard to read – I think Bill's right about it being a book about remedies, so it's much more than a book of nature observations. There are a few recipes for hand salves and foot lotions but one I could just about make out recommended a healing tincture made from oil of yellow wort as it was named. I'm assuming it's hypericum. St John's wort. Has small yellow flowers that are a bit fuzzy-looking. Quite pretty and a common garden shrub.'

'Oh yes. Think my grandparents have some. Bane of my grandfather's life as it gets untidy and he's always having to prune it. What was it used for?'

'In the book it's described as being good for mild depression, or to "soothe and quieten the nerves".' Nathan traced a teacake crumb around his plate thoughtfully. 'In fact, you could say it's still used for that now, as an antidepressant. You can readily buy it in tablet form. It's quite a potent natural remedy, though, and you have to be careful how it mixes with other drugs.' Nathan paused and then added meaningfully, 'In the book it's also called Demon Chaser, which I found intriguing.'

'Demon Chaser,' Beth repeated. 'Are we back to witches?'

'Who knows?' he replied cheerfully.

They lapsed into silence.

Beth could spy a sliver of bright blue sky above the alleyway and hear the screech of a gull as it flew overhead. There was a faint babble of voices as people made their way along nearby Narrow Sheep Walk, heading for the simple pleasures of the beach and an ice cream. In the small seaside town, life was continuing normally. And yet, in this unremarkable bakery she felt something truly profound had just begun. But, for the life of her, couldn't explain what.

'Isn't it odd that we seem to be connected by these things?' she began slowly. 'My spell bottle from around about that time and your book of seventeenth-century folk remedies. Not to mention Tenpenny House itself.'

'It is.' He seemed to be thinking through his words. About to say something, he paused, then said, 'Not sure how your Celtic knife handle fits into all this though.'

'I'm not sure how *any* of it fits together. It's just a feeling I've got that it is.' She stopped, embarrassed. 'I'm not one for flights of fancy normally. I can sort of understand why something would be shoved up a chimney to ward off evil but not why an ancient knife handle would be hidden.'

Nathan shook his head a little, looking strangely relieved. He ran a hand over his chin. 'Maybe it was very precious to the person who hid it in the seventeenth century as well as the tribeswoman? If Bill is right and it's connected to a healing woman, maybe the person who put it in the chimney was one too, and that's why they felt it had a relevance? I know I'm always drawn to the history of medical stuff. A visit to The Old Operating Theatre Museum lives in the memory. In London,' he explained further.' Shuddering, he added, 'Although it was grim. Patients were tough in those days. No anaesthetic.'

'God,' Beth said, appalled. 'Can't imagine going through an operation with no anaesthetic. And what you say makes sense, or as much sense as any of this does. I mean, your seventeenth-century book on healing must have a hell of a story behind it.'

'I'll have to ask my American relatives.' Nathan's brow creased. 'My family originates here in England and emigrated to the US, then Grandpa came back in the war. Members of the Smith family have been criss-crossing the Atlantic for generations. Maybe the book began life here and went to the States with them, back in the day?'

Beth leaned forward, enchanted by the idea. 'Now that is a story! Do you think your family were some of the original pioneers?'

Nathan laughed. 'If that were the case, I think it would be the subject of family legend and I've never heard it said. A lot of American citizens aspire to have gone over on the *Mayflower*.'

'The *Mayflower*?'

'The pilgrim ship that sailed from Plymouth back in the sixteen hundreds.'

'And we're back to the seventeenth century again. We seem to be in its grip.' Beth leaned back, thinking. 'Do you know much about what happened then? I've a knowledge gap.'

Nathan shrugged. 'I'm a medic not a historian but off the top of my head there was the English Civil War, Thomas Cromwell, lots of plague, a mini ice age. Then the Restoration in 1660 when Charles II was put on the throne. Oh, and witches and witch hunts.'

Beth laughed. 'For someone who professes not to be an historian that's pretty good knowledge.'

He smiled. 'I had a grandmother who loved her history. It's to my eternal regret that I disappointed her by becoming a scientist. There are some tales, which she told me at her knee, that stuck.'

'Witches,' Beth said thoughtfully. 'They seem to have us in their grip too.'

'As you say, it is strange that we have this connection.' He paused and then added, 'Would you like to borrow the book to have a look yourself?'

Beth was taken aback. 'You'd let me? Do you trust me that much? We hardly know one another.'

Nathan bit his lower lip thoughtfully. 'That's true. And yet, it's peculiar, but somehow I feel as if I've always known you. I felt it that very first time I saw you in the waiting room at the surgery.' He winced. 'Across a crowded room. Sorry. Too cheesy for words.'

'Very cheesy but you know what? I agree.' Beth was silent for a moment, thinking back to the compulsion she'd had to his picture in the local newspaper, to her visceral physical first reaction to him when they'd met. 'It's weird.'

'It is,' he replied matter-of-factly. 'But there you have it.' He laughed. 'Maybe we knew one another in a previous life?'

Beth didn't answer.

'But yes, I trust you with the book. If you're interested and would like to look through it, I'm more than happy for you to borrow it.'

'Thank you. I'll look after it with my life.'

'No need to go that far. Just treat it with respect.'

'Do I need gloves when I read it?' Beth asked, hazy recollections of history documentaries flitting through her mind.

Nathan sat back. 'I don't know,' he said, nonplussed. 'It's been in an attic gathering dust and damp for decades, I don't think handling it will do any harm. Maybe just make sure your hands are clean and free of any oil or hand cream.'

Beth nodded. 'I will. I promise.'

'Now, back to that date. Dinner, or a film?'

The abrupt change of subject brought her up short and made her blush. After a brief discussion they agreed on a drink then a film at the cinema in nearby Sidmouth. Parting company in the street, Beth watched as Nathan strode away. The heady initial physical attraction hadn't waned, but it had quietened. What was more, it was evolving into something more solid, more grounded. She wasn't sure which she feared the most.

Clutching the hessian shopping bag to her, she turned onto Cross Street to head home. She couldn't wait to leaf through the book to discover what it contained. Maybe there would be recipes for a lotion or some soaps she could make and sell in the shop? Seventeenth-century beauty products selling in a house of the same age might draw customers in. As she reached the untidy cobbles of Clappers Lane, she realised she was no nearer to finding out who had put a Celtic knife handle up the chimney at Tenpenny House and why. Somehow, though, she was certain there was a connection between the book, the bottle and the handle. Just what remained a mystery.

CHAPTER 13

AUGUST 1660

The constables came for Prudie at dawn. Arrested, she was marched, at a pace too fierce for her, to the town lock up.

Susanna had hung on to the old woman's legs but the men were too strong. They shoved her to one side, bellowing they would take her too if she resisted. One kicked her hard in the ribs, his boot stealing the breath from her body. Falling hard against John's chair, she hit her temple and was momentarily out of her wits. Coming to, she heard Star trying to defend her. With all the energy his old body could muster, he ran at the constables barking, baring his teeth and lunging at them, tearing into their clothing. Kicked viciously, he let out a shriek of agony and had crept to hide behind the settle.

Susanna lay gasping, trying to clear her throbbing head. When all was silent and she was certain the constables had gone, she shuffled, on her hands and knees, to where the dog lay panting. She held Star to her until the panting lapsed into whimpering and the aged hound took his last soft breath to lie still. She sobbed into his fur until the body grew cold.

When a footstep dropped on the threshold of the cottage she

started in fear. Had they come back for her? Had they come for her too?

It was Barnabas.

'Where are you? Are you still here, Susanna?' His voice was fraught.

'I am here, Barnabas. Behind the settle.' She thought she'd shouted but the crying had roughened her throat and it came out as little more than a hoarse whisper.

He ran to her, kneeling at her side. 'I've just heard. They took Prudie. On what charge?'

Susanna raised her tear-ravaged face. 'I don't know. It was all such confusion.' She began to sob anew. 'Oh, Barnabas, they injured Star so, his poor old body could not take the pain and he died. I'm so afeared they will do the same to Prudie. Despite her protests, she is not strong, especially not with John gone.' She gathered the old dog in her arms and wept into his neck. 'Oh, Star, why did they do this to such an innocent?'

Barnabas sat back on his heels and let Susanna cry it out. When she had finished, he gently took the dog from her. 'I'll bury Star for you. He should not be left.'

'Bury him,' she began but was too distressed to finish. She wailed into her apron and then took in a deep gulping breath and continued. 'Put him under the old apple tree. He always liked to sit there in the shade.'

He nodded and left.

Susanna wept again into her hands and then scrubbed her face with her apron, wincing at the swelling bruise. She dragged herself to her feet on perilously unsteady legs, biting her lip in determination. Weeping and wailing like this would not help Prudie. She poured a mug of ale, drank it in one, and then refilled it for Barnabas. He would need it after his travails. Poor Star, a dog as faithful as he did not deserve such an end. Tears flowed again; it seemed the weeping wouldn't stop. Stiffening her resolve, she slumped at the table and forced her thoughts into calmness. Somehow, she needed to find out under what charge Prudie had been arrested. It was unlikely the town clerk would lower himself to talk to a woman and certainly not one as humbly born as she, so she would need to ask Barnabas for yet another favour.

In the few short weeks since John's death, she and Prudie had leaned heavily on his aid. They were now defenceless women. Prudie was a poor childless widow with no status in society. Susanna, an unmarried maid with no father to protect her, had even less. Work had dried up. They had attended just one birthing since Charles Lacey's: a fish gutter who lived in one of the hovels on the harbour. Her thirteenth pregnancy, her body was too old and worn out to carry twins. Despite packing the birth wound with linen to raise the womb back into its rightful position, Prudie and Susanna had been unable to stem the torrent of blood that soaked through the straw bedding and pooled on the floor. The mother had perished, and her boys had died only hours after their birth. It had laid Prudie low. Any loss did but this hit her hard. Susanna had watched as Prudie had used the ancient knife to cut the birth string on the first son and then the second. The unwelcome thought that the knife's magic was cursed crowded into her brain.

Increasingly, if they could afford to, women were seeking out the country physician to attend their childbed, the poorer sought Jane Thatcher, the licensed midwife the church had approved. No one came to Prudie. Since Charles Lacey's death, women had lost confidence in the cunning woman's abilities. News in the town had it that Prudie was too old, her skills waning with age. The twin boys' death added to the flame of rumour, but the poor were of little account; they died all the time. It had been the Lacey baby's birth of which they had taken note, all in town had watched with a slavering interest. His death had also been the final death blow to Prudie's midwifery.

Susanna rose wearily, clutching her painful ribs, and poked the fire to make it flame. She stirred the contents of the cauldron; it was only pottage but was warming enough. She would feed Barnabas and decide upon a plan. Cat, the ratter, slunk out of the shadows. He'd had enough sense to flit when the trouble occurred. Susanna bent to caress his silky black head. 'If only Star had had more brains and less honour,' she whispered. 'Prudie is going to be distraught when she finds out her beloved dog is no more.'

Barnabas returned looking grim-faced. 'I buried Star where you suggested but not before your neighbour poked her nose in and asked me what had happened. Apparently, the whole town has been witness to Prudie's humiliation.' Going to the pail in the scullery, he sloshed water over his hands and dried them on his breeches. 'I am afeared for you, Susanna. You've been unprotected without John and now are even more so.' Cat left Susanna and weaved around his ankles. He bent and scratched his ears. 'If only you would offer some assistance, puss.'

'Cat does well enough. He keeps the rats from the wood pile and keeps his mistress warm of an evening. Come, sit and eat.' Susanna gestured to the table and bench. Spooning pottage into bowls she set them down, added a trencher of bread, placed the mug of ale in front of Barnabas and joined him.

Barnabas gazed tenderly at her and then exclaimed, 'You are hurt too!' Surging to his feet, he grasped her wrist to turn her to him. Gently lifting her coif from her forehead, he gasped. 'The bastards hit you?'

She shook her head, wincing in pain. 'I tried to get them off Prudie and they pushed me. I knocked my head into the chair. Tis nothing, just a bruise. I'll make a poultice later. Sit down now and eat.'

He obeyed, reluctant to leave touching her. 'That Hal Thatcher always did have more brawn than brain, but I would not have thought he had it in him to injure women.'

'He's long been known to be a bully,' Susanna replied. 'I've known him since a child. And now he is a constable he has the law behind him for such play.' She added, 'But even so, I would not expect him to treat an old woman so. You know they hobbled her legs and tied her hands behind her back?' She pushed her bowl away, untouched, hands trembling.

Barnabas put his spoon down. He too had lost any appetite. Instead, he drank the ale, gulping it down thirstily. He placed the pint pot back on the table with careful precision and wiped his mouth with the back of his hand. 'What are we to do about Prudie?'

She glanced at him. 'I am grateful you think it's we who ought to do something but it is not your battle, Barnabas.'

This time it was his turn to shake his head. 'It is my battle as much as yours. I've become mighty fond of the old woman. And you know how I feel about you.'

Susanna felt her face heat. 'It is good to know we have you.' Tears thickened in her throat and she could say no more.

They sat in silence, deep in thought and sorrow, then Barnabas picked up his spoon and resumed eating.

When Susanna could speak again, she asked, 'Did my God-fearing neighbour know what Prudie had been arrested for?'

Barnabas tore off a piece of bread and wiped his bowl clean. 'Mistress Anne? She did not. Just had a mighty interest in why the goodwife had been marched off.'

'She has been a good neighbour until recently, but she is beginning to believe the town scandal mongerers. She told me last week everyone believes Prudie took the plague into the Lacey house and that is why the babe died. They think John died of the plague but it was not,' Susanna said fiercely. 'He had an ague, had had it through the winter and it settled on his chest and weakened him. It was not the plague! Prudie would never knowingly take a sickness to a childbed. She has done nothing to deserve any of this.'

'There is no plague in Flete at present. People are tattling because they have nothing better to do. Take no notice, Susanna.'

'But I have to take notice. If there is no plague to blame,' Susanna shuddered, 'then folk's brains will turn to another explanation.' She didn't need to explain. The inference was clear. 'Prudie's life is held in her reputation, just as mine is. We cannot be as free as you men are. Prudie has no husband now, no position. I have even less. We scratched a living before. Now we have little hope. Thank God we still have our cow and chickens and we can eat. We haven't had one person call for a tincture or salve in days. One birth,' Susanna said bitterly. 'One birth and our fortunes are wrecked.'

'You could have protection. If you marry me.'

Susanna put a hand to her mouth, stunned. A proposal was not so totally unexpected, but she had other concerns now. It was one more shock in a day filled with them. Gulping down a tumult of emotion, she reached out and grasped his hand. 'I would not shackle you to such an arrangement. What would the good smith James say? What would your mother and sisters and brother have to say? Besides, Barnabas, I thought you were bound for the Americas and great riches.'

Barnabas slid along the bench to be nearer. 'Then come with me,' he exclaimed, his face alight. 'As my bride. We could have the makings of a good life out there, you and I.'

'Oh, Barney,' Susanna replied, sadness clouding her eyes. She hated to dim his enthusiasm, blight his optimism. 'What a wonderful idea but how can I leave Prudie, especially now? She is not strong enough for such a journey. And she would not leave her home and all she has here.'

He took her hands in his, rubbing his roughened thumbs over her knuckles. Blowing out a frustrated breath, he said, 'Then I will stay and work with you to get Prudie released. But first we have to find out why she is in the lockup in the first place. It will be some trumped up charge, do not fear.'

Relief that she was not in this alone rushed through Susanna. She smiled at Barnabas even though fear insisted on clutching at her heart. Pain shot through her head. She must take some devil's-bit with honey for her wound. Prudie had taught her it lessened the swelling of bruises. She owed the old woman so much. She scanned the room with its shelves of jars and bottles of tinctures and cures, the serried racks of dried herbs and pots of ointments. Prudie's life's work. 'I hope so, Barney. I really hope you're right.'

CHAPTER 14

JULY 2018

Nathan's book was fascinating. It took patience to decipher, but once Beth caught the rhythm of the words and sussed out the 'f' was sometimes an 's' she was enthralled. The drawings and paintings, many faded by time, had their own charm too. Not thick, and more journal than book, it had stained leather covers held together by a tough thong which wound around several times to keep it secure. Opening it the first time, Beth hadn't had a repeat of the strong reactions of before but, somehow, had felt the book was in its right place now. Had returned home.

After copying the recipe for a hand salve with lavender and chamomile, she tried making a small amount and was entranced by its subtle scent and the way it soothed her skin. Having replaced the original tallow fat with olive and almond oils to make it more acceptable to the modern customer, she knew if she could make it in quantity, it would sell.

She'd also taken up Bill's command and delved into some online research on witches. Talk about a research rabbit hole! She'd spent long evenings making her eyes dry and gritty by staring at the screen. She'd also genned up a little on the seventeenth century. It had been an appallingly violent time.

'It was tough reading,' she said now to Nathan. They'd met for a quick drink before going to the cinema. It had turned into dinner and the conversation flowed so much the film had been forgotten.

'In the years 1540 to 1650-ish thousands of people were convicted of being witches,' she declared, spearing a piece of celery off her cheeseboard and crunching it indignantly. 'The Civil War years were the worst.' She shook her head. 'Those Puritans didn't like women they thought were witches one bit. Not sure they liked women full stop. Certainly didn't give them any rights. Did you know over ninety per cent of those killed were women? And they were hanged.' She shuddered, putting a hand to her throat. Not surprisingly, given the sombre nature of her research she'd had another nightmare the night before. It had been a truly horrifying one full of violence and pain, and immersed in hopelessness. She'd woken to find the bedding wrapped tight around her neck again and had yanked it off, gasping for air.

'It was even worse in Scotland. The women were burned, although they strangled them first.' She pulled a face, adding sarcastically, 'So that's something, I mean, putting them out of their misery before burning them. People actually believed you could have a spell cast on you, or be hexed, or that your cattle died as a result of a witch.' Picking up her glass, she was aware she was getting a little drunk. She didn't drink all that much these days and red wine always went to her head quickly; it made her garrulous. 'And don't get me started on that bastard Matthew Hopkins, the so-called Witchfinder General. Talk about a walking, talking perverted misogynist.'

The couple on the next table gave her a startled look and got up to leave.

Beth bit down her next comment. The more she'd read, the angrier she'd become. 'Sorry. Am I getting too loud?'

Nathan shook his head. 'Not at all. I only have a smattering of knowledge about it so I'm interested in what you've found out. Although the story of Salem was well known in my family in the States as we're New England based. Witchcraft again.'

Beth nodded. 'Yes, I read about that too. Over two hundred people accused. I suppose as well as exporting Puritanism on the Mayflower, we sent them a hatred of witches too.'

Nathan drank his wine thoughtfully. 'Mass hysteria is an interesting phenomenon. It's one explanation for what happened in Salem and not as unusual as you might think. There was a case back in 1980 in Nottinghamshire. Over three hundred children fainted at a fair. They called it The Hollinwell Incident. Over two hundred had to be hospitalised.'

'What with?'

'They all reported the same symptoms. Weakness in the limbs, severe headache, dizziness and nausea.'

'And you think that was mass hysteria?'

'It's one explanation. Another is the use of pesticides in the nearby fields. There have been other reported incidents of mass hysteria, often amongst communities of young girls such as in schools.'

'And is that what you think happened in Salem? Mass hysteria?'

'If my memory serves, the supposed witches were accused by young girls and it's often been reported as an example of mass hysteria. Politics and religious fervour played a part too. It certainly took place within a closeted and febrile community with little contact with the outside world.' Nathan crumbed a fragment of bread. 'It's a fascinating subject. I got interested in it as a phenomenon back at med school.'

Beth nodded again and pushed away her plate. The meal had been delicious, the intimate Italian restaurant in Sidmouth perfect for a first date, although she hadn't anticipated the conversation to be so intense.

'Coffee?'

'Yes please. Think I need it to clear my head. Not sure if it's the wine or what we're discussing.'

Nathan caught the attention of their waiter, ordered and then settled back in his seat. 'I've been doing a little digging too. About the connection between healing and women. It's true what Bill claimed in the museum. For centuries women were at the centre of community healing. The Celtic tribes, from where your knife handle may have originated, revered and respected women. They had equal status, were often tribal chiefs, and a cunning woman would be a highly esteemed and prestigious member of the village. There at all the important moments of life. Birth, death, everything in between.'

Beth stared at him, thinking how attractive he looked in his white linen shirt and glowing with good health. 'You sound quite wistful.'

Nathan shrugged. 'Suppose I am. For about a year into my training I thought that's what being a family GP would be about.'

'And?'

He smiled ruefully. 'It can be that still, just not very often. I push a lot of paper as well. Don't get me wrong,' he added, 'it's still rewarding, just not quite in the way my younger, more idealistic self imagined.'

'So, if women were the healers, what happened to change that? Seems to me women became vilified in the seventeenth century for the very skills for which they were once held in esteem.'

'I suppose you could argue it began with the witch trials. I believe lots of those convicted were also the village midwife or healer.'

'From what I've read it was often the way to get your own back at someone you thought had wronged you. A lot of women accused other women. And then mob rule took over.'

'And we're back to mass hysteria again.' Nathan nodded. 'I came across an interesting theory that it's mixed up with industrialisation.'

Beth was taken back. 'Industrialisation?'

'Mm. And land enclosures. Before land was enclosed it was farmed communally and both men and women worked on it equally. Then the land was enclosed, forcing families into urban settlements where men found work in factories and women became increasingly isolated in the house, or took less well-paid work, piece work that could be done at home. The old connection with the land was lost, some of the old remedies forgotten. Physicians came on the scene–'

'Men,' Beth interrupted.

'Yes men,' he conceded. 'Women legally weren't allowed to train to be physicians. There was money to be made being a doctor so they didn't want these women healing others if they could barge in and get paid. The misogyny took a long time to die out, some say it never has. I have an old midwifery training book I picked up in a second-hand bookshop. The hierarchy is laid out very clearly.'

'With doctors at the top.'

He nodded again. 'With doctors at the top. And, of course, back when it was written in the sixties, doctors were male. Even when I was training, I know several of my female colleagues had a really tough time in hospitals. I'd like to think it happens less in general practice.'

Beth contemplated the uninterested and abrupt Dr Carmicheal. She would welcome a female GP. She'd welcome anyone else but him if she was honest; she was still frustrated with how her appointment had gone. 'So they stopped women doing the healing, stopped them training to be a doctor and victimised any that tried. By accusing them of witchcraft and hanging them. It's a fucking disgrace,' she blurted out. She stopped, appalled at herself. 'Sorry. I hardly ever swear.'

Nathan smiled. 'I happen to agree with you. But, as I say, it's only a theory. There are probably far more reasons why the witch trials reached their peak during the sixteenth and seventeenth centuries. They had a whole belief system in the supernatural, which is so alien to us as to be impossible to understand. They really did believe the devil walked amongst them.'

'Have you ever come across anyone evil?' Beth asked curiously.

'I've treated people who were in the middle of a severe mental health crisis.' Nathan pulled a face. 'It's not easy for anyone and especially for the person at the centre of it. Do I believe they were evil, or acting under the influence of the devil?' He shook his head. 'No. Do I believe they were capable of *acts* of evil? Yes. But it's a severe psychosis they're under the influence of, nothing to do with the devil.'

'What gets me,' Beth said heatedly, 'what really gets me is they picked on the vulnerable women in the community when they accused them of witchcraft. Most of those hanged were old, poor, perhaps different in some way, or without the protection of a man. Widows and the like. Women like my grandmother. She's always touting some ancient folk remedy, although in her case, they'd have to fight my grandfather off first.'

'Or made a case against him too?'

Beth sighed. 'Yes.' The restaurant had emptied, they were the last customers. The evening, although in an unexpected way, had flown. She felt as if she'd been talking to Nathan forever. She waited until their coffee was served, along with dainty shortbread biscuits and petit fours, before continuing. Trying to lighten the atmosphere a little, she said, 'I would have been under suspicion straight away.' Tugging on one of her wayward chestnut curls she added, 'Hair definitely has a hint of the ginge, I've got green eyes and am left-handed. Resolutely single without a man in sight and not only that, I make weird concoctions.'

Nathan laughed. 'At least you don't claim any of your potions cure ailments.'

'That's just it, though. I'm right on the cusp of the purely cosmetic and herbal medicine. Some of my stuff is sold to aid sleep, for instance. My lavender body lotion goes down well with those who have trouble sleeping, although it's never worked for me.' She peered into her coffee cup, wondering whether she should risk drinking it.

'That's it then, oh sinister one. Watch what you do or the town gossips will have you up on a charge.'

'Sinister one?'

'Sinister is Latin for left.'

'You're right. I'm doomed.'

'And let's not forget that pre-NHS, when getting a doctor could be a choice between being ill or eating, home-made remedies were all some folk had. Florence would say more should be used.'

Beth smiled; she could picture Florence saying that only too clearly. 'I remember Gran saying brown paper and grease was put on her chest if she had a cold. She's really into her home remedies, is my gran.'

'Not sure how effective that would be.' Nathan's brows rose.

'But I wish people were a little more self-reliant sometimes. I had a woman come in the other day with a broken fingernail.'

'No!' Beth didn't know whether to laugh or be appalled.

'To be fair, it was down to the quick but even so, she only had to put a plaster on it and wait for it to grow back.' He warmed to his theme. 'And if people practised better hygiene and washed their hands more and coughed and sneezed into tissues, it would spread viruses less effectively. And don't get me started on the number of missed appointments. I suppose it gives me a chance to catch up and not run late but I still always seem to.'

'But you'd still rather be a modern GP in the twenty-first century and not a cunning woman healer in the seventeenth?'

'Not much of a quandary.' Nathan drank his coffee and put the empty cup down.

'You said you didn't know much about all this, the witchcraft trials and stuff, but it seems to me you know loads.'

Nathan frowned. 'I do, don't I? Suppose it's becoming a bit of a hobby. Coming from a New England family it's always something you're aware of. And, living here with Bill in the museum spouting forth to anyone who'll listen, my imagination got sparked.' He ate a biscuit whole before continuing. 'Plus, one day when I was wandering around Exeter I came across the plaque dedicated to the last three women in England who were hanged for alleged witchcraft.'

Beth sat up, her interest quickening. 'A plaque? I've lived in Exeter all my life, went to university there. I've never heard of it.'

'It's a little hidden away. On the wall of the old Rougemont Castle at the back of Gandy Street.'

'I know Gandy Street,' Beth said, referring to the narrow lane full of quirky shops and cafés that ran perpendicular to the modern shopping street. 'One of my favourite haunts.'

Nathan smiled. 'I'm fond of it too. Love a coffee there when I've been having a nose round the museum.'

Beth was aghast. She put up a hand to her mouth. 'I've never put a foot inside the Royal Albert. That's shocking, isn't it?'

'It is. We'll have to remedy that as soon as possible. It's a date.'

A frisson sparked in the air.

Beth was vaguely aware the restaurant had turned the music off. They must be desperate to get rid of them, but she didn't want the evening to end. She held Nathan's eyes flirtatiously. 'A date it is then.' Not wanting to appear too eager, she added, 'And, if I go ahead and close the shop, I'll have time on my hands. Will have to find something to do.'

He laughed. 'I'm very fond of the place. It's not enormous but fascinating enough if you like local history. But then I'm a bit of a museum geek. Can't pass one without exploring.'

'So, tell me about these women then. The ones the plaque is dedicated to.' She shook her head. 'I still can't believe I knew nothing about this.'

'It's easily missed. Not very big. Just says, The Devon Witches.'

Beth winced.

'I know. Not very subtle. It commemorates three women from Bideford. Hang on, I took a photo the last time I was there.' He fished out his phone, thumbed through his photos, and passed it over the table.

Beth read, '"The Devon Witches. In memory of Temperance Lloyd, Susannah Edwards and Mary Trembles of Bideford. Died 1682. The last people in England to be executed for witchcraft. Tried here and hanged at Heavitree".' She looked up, startled. 'Heavitree?' It was an area of Exeter she knew well.

'Yup. Where the hospital is now. Apparently Heavitree means heavy or hanging tree.' He laughed without humour. 'I was without my car one day and was scrolling bus timetables online. There's even a bus stop called Gallows Corner there.

Most think the women were buried in the grounds of what is now St Luke's. It's part of the University of Exeter.'

Beth nodded. 'I know it. On the main road into the city opposite Waitrose. And, ironically, houses the Medical School and the Nurses' Academy.' She shuddered and handed the phone back. '1682. It seems a long time ago.'

'It does.'

'And yet women are still subjected to witch hunts. Makes you wonder how far we've progressed.'

'What do you mean?'

'If you dare to voice an unpopular opinion you're soon shot down, especially on the socials. Twitter can be a vile place to be a woman. They're not content with disagreeing with you, it's the violent and sadistic language they come at you with. Threats to your person, rape threats. I've had it happen to me when I dared venture in on a sports discussion.'

'Jeez. I had no idea.' He looked shocked. 'That shows my male privilege, doesn't it? Mind you, the most social media I do is a Facebook page to keep in touch with old uni pals. And that's heavily locked down so patients can't find me.'

'Trust me, it's the best way. If I didn't have to have a media presence for the business, I wouldn't bother either.'

Nathan poured them more coffee. 'You're right though, about 1682. Suppose it is a long time ago. The beginning of the modern age. The so-called Age of Reason. The growth in scientific and philosophic thinking.'

'Seems it arrived in Devon a little late,' Beth said drily.

He grinned. 'Doesn't everything?'

'Seriously though, it also seems late for any women to be accused of witchcraft. Everything I've read points to the worst of the witch hunts being in the sixteenth and early seventeenth centuries. 1682 is knocking on the door of the eighteenth century.'

'It does.' He leaned back. 'I'm afraid I don't know much else about the Bideford Witches but Bill might.' He ate a chocolate and then added, 'How are you getting on with the book of recipes?'

Beth's face brightened. 'Oh, Nathan, it's fabulous. I've already tried the lavender and chamomile hand salve and I'm going to try to make it in bulk quantities. I think it'll sell really well. I'll have to get the ingredients checked for health and safety first, though.'

It was Nathan's turn to look startled. 'You have to do that?'

Beth nodded. 'Oh yes. Wouldn't do to have anything harmful going out. I have to be really careful. I mean, obviously, I can't guarantee someone won't have an allergic reaction but I can do my best. Plus, I have to label everything clearly and comprehensively.'

'If only people actually read labels. I had a patient complain her antibiotics hadn't worked. She not only drank alcohol with them and didn't finish the course but took on them on a full stomach instead of an empty one.' Nathan sighed. 'Sometimes my job is incredibly frustrating. She had two more courses before the problem was resolved. If she'd taken the first lot in the right way, she'd have been sorted three months earlier.'

Beth winced. 'I won't ask what was wrong with her.'

'Just as well,' he added more cheerfully, 'as I can't tell you. Probably shouldn't have said as much as I did. I find you very easy to talk to, Beth.'

Beth wasn't sure how to react. She felt the same. They hardly knew one another but this, whatever *this* was, seemed to be travelling fast in a direction she hadn't navigated before. She contented herself with a smile. Then frowned.

'What's wrong?'

'It's nothing really. Just that you mentioning disgruntled

patients reminded me someone has been putting really stinky reviews on my website.'

Nathan sat up. 'A complaint?'

'That's what's so weird. No complaints just snarky little comments.' She took out her phone, found her website and passed it to him.

'"Do people really buy this crap?"' Nathan read. 'Wow.'

'Read on. It gets worse.'

'"This stuff is such a rip off. Have you seen the prices? Don't buy this crap". Charming.' He handed the phone back. 'Can you block the negative comments?'

'I did. I edited some of the worst out and by the morning there was a flurry of even more vindictive ones claiming I have something to hide. Things like I'm deliberately only putting the five-star reviews up and so on. It's obviously someone who has trouble sleeping as they post in the early hours.'

'Or a bored teenage keyboard warrior.'

'Maybe.'

'Is it worrying you?'

'Only when I remember. Life's quite full-on at the moment so I don't have a lot of time or emotional energy to spare for it, but I can't say it's pleasant.'

'Is it affecting trade?'

Beth shook her head. 'Hard to tell but I'll be moving more and more into online sales while the cobbles on Clappers Lane are being repaired so it might have some impact then.'

'A rival?'

'Who though? No one within a twenty-mile radius is selling anything like my stuff. I'm not in competition with anyone.'

'Do you know anyone techie who could investigate?'

'Yes. My brother-in-law, actually. He could take a look if it gets any worse.' Beth slipped her phone back into her bag. 'Let's not spoil a lovely evening. I'm sure if they get no reaction, they'll go away.' She smiled brightly. 'But thanks for the sympathy.'

Nathan reached over and put his hand over hers. It was warm and reassuring. 'Any time. And if you need more, I'm here.'

They gazed into one another's eyes and a flicker of something important passed between them. Only the long-suffering waiter, asking if they'd finally like the bill, interrupted.

CHAPTER 15

AUGUST 1660

On a day when papery leaves scurried on a dry wind, Prudie was released. It was to their utmost confusion and relief. Barnabas collected her in his cart and drove the exhausted woman back to Tenpenny Cottage. So weak was she from her mistreatment she could barely stumble from it, so he lifted her up in his strong arms and carried her in, ignoring the twitching eyes and loose mouths of those who watched.

Susanna put her in John's old chair, stoked the fire and began bathing the old woman's wounds. She tried to hide her revulsion at the bruised eye, swelling to purple, the deep cut at the edge of Prudie's mouth and the raw marks on her wrists where she had been bound. She tended the injuries as best she could with root of devil's-bit.

All Prudie's power seemed diminished. She was but a withered old woman. She said nothing during these attentions, her eyes cloudy with age and distress, turned away to the fire. Susanna tempted her with pottage and warm wine with treacle but she took hardly anything.

They left her dozing underneath the best wool blanket while

eating their own meal at the table and conducting a conversation in angry hushed tones.

'I need her to take nourishment. She's obviously been starved and had no water,' Susanna hissed in a fierce whisper.

Barnabas tore off bread with strong teeth and chewed thoughtfully. 'Maybe she'll get something down in a few hours. She said not a word all the way back from the gaol. I think her brain's turned. The shock, perhaps, of how she's been treated.'

Susanna leaned nearer, close to tears. 'And she stinks. I hate to say so but I need to get her washed.' It was true, the stench of vomit, urine and fear permeated the cottage.

'Best leave her to sleep for a while.'

'She'd sleep better in her own bed, under a clean sheet and in a fresh shift.'

'Then, once we've eaten, I'll help you do that. You will not manage on your own. I had to fair carry her from the cart.'

Susanna's mouth dropped open in horror. 'You cannot do such an unseemly thing. I cannot allow it. *Prudie* would not allow it.' She glanced at the once proud and indomitable woman. 'What did they do to her?' She knew Barnabas spoke the truth; she would not manage to wash and dress Prudie alone. A tear escaped and rolled down her cheek. 'They arrested a fierce woman who would stand up to anyone who crossed her and we have received back a hollowed shell.'

Barnabas reached for her hand and squeezed it before answering. 'They locked her up and left her. No food, no water, little sleep. These things will undo a person even as strong as Prudie. It's lucky she was let out after only so little as four days otherwise I would have collected a corpse.'

Susanna gasped and covered her face with her apron. She rocked back and forth in her grief.

'Nay, my Susie, don't take on so. We have her back. With food and warmth she'll be the old Prudie and scolding and chasing us all around before you know it. Come, eat. Drink your ale. You have to be strong for the both of you now. If you ail, what will become of Prudie?' He sat patiently drinking, waiting for the storm to pass. When it eventually did, he averted his eyes and ate while Susanna scrubbed at her tear-ravaged face and tidied her hair back under her coif. When she picked up her spoon to eat the now cold pottage, he ventured, 'I still don't know who paid the release money.'

'Someone kind and who wished a poor old woman no further harm, let's hope. Who else could it be? And thanks be to God to whoever it was. For as you say, we have our Prudie back with us alive.' She glanced over to the old woman who seemed more comfortable, her face turned greedily towards the heat of the fire and slightly snoring.

A knock on the door shocked them both but, thankfully, did not wake Prudie. Susanna, wiping her hands on her apron, hurried to the door to find Mercy Prentice standing on the threshold. A trusted friend and an ally from the old days of the war.

'Come in, come in, Mercy. It's been too long.' Susanna ushered her in, aware of two or three women clustered together in the lane and peering with an avid curiosity towards them.

Mercy collapsed onto the bench, her reddened face evidence of her long walk from the eastern fringes of town. 'Tis fair warm out there. I'm not used to the heat, we have little enough of it.' She nodded her acceptance to Barnabas's offer of ale and then glanced over at Prudie, still asleep by the fire. 'It's true then,' she said, once she'd quenched her thirst. 'They let her out.'

Susanna moved the dirty bowls out of the way before sitting down. 'Barnabas collected her this very morning. We have no idea of truly why she was imprisoned or indeed released but we're very glad to have her back with us.'

'Aye.' Mercy blew out a breath and mopped her forehead. 'Then I have news that might be of use to you, Susanna.'

After pouring more ale Barnabas made to go. 'Perhaps I should leave?'

'Stay, Barney.' Susanna put a hand on his arm. 'Whatever Mercy has to say to me, can be said in front of you. You are both trusted friends and allies.'

Mercy looked knowingly from Susanna to Barnabas. 'It's true what they say about you two then? Is a betrothal at hand?'

Barnabas sat down and grinned. 'It will if I have anything to do with it. This good woman is taking some persuading though.'

Susanna smiled, suddenly shy. She and Barnabas and Prudie had been closeted together in their own little world for so long she had forgotten how the outside would see it. She had already compromised herself by accepting so much help from Barnabas. Mercy could be trusted not to blather about finding them in the cottage alone, but others would not be so generous. She had little choice, now, but to accept his hand. And looking at his fine strong features and honest face, she realised she could do a lot worse. Reaching out, she placed her hand over his. 'I'm simply taking my time to think about it.'

Mercy huffed. 'Don't tarry too long. There's many a wench in Flete after this young man. He's a fine prospect.'

They laughed and this time it was Barnabas's turn to blush. The sound roused Prudie who started. She stared round at them, blinking.

'Oh lor, I've gone and woken the poor woman.' Mercy inhaled and wrinkled her nose, her inference clear. 'Is there anything I can do to help, Susanna?'

Susanna gave her a grateful smile. 'Oh, Mercy, you've come at just the right time.'

Between the three of them, they managed to get Prudie up the narrow curving stairs. Susanna and Mercy undressed her while Barnabas heated water. Once the woman was in her bed, clean and comfortable with a wrapped heated brick at her side, the women returned to the downstairs room.

Mercy was sober when she sat back on the bench. Shaking her head she muttered, 'Never did I think I would see such things on an old body.'

Barnabas looked up from where he was stoking the fire. 'What's this now?'

'More injuries, Barney. Bruises all over her ribs, weals on her back.' Susanna's voice grew fiery with anger. 'And more. In places where no old woman, *no woman* should be hurt.' He came to her, put his arm around her and they were silent for a while. Then Susanna shook him off, collapsing onto the bench. 'I cannot believe Hal Thatcher would do such harm. True, he's a bully, but to injure an old woman so!'

Barnabas shook his head. 'I doubt it was Hal. When I collected Prudie there was someone else there. His superior. A Matthias Finch, I believe. He works out of the Exeter Assizes.'

Mercy looked up, shocked. 'Matthias Finch, you say?' She sniffed disdainfully. 'I know of him. A crueller man couldn't be found. Says he does the work of the Lord but his hands and actions say otherwise. He and his team of pricker women convicted that poor woman Abigail Wray some years back. Said she had had carnal knowledge of the devil. If anyone has the devil within, it's Matthias Finch.'

Susanna gasped. 'I remember poor Abigail. She was a friend of Prudie's. Mercy, you said you have information?' she asked harshly. A pall of dread hung low over her. She studied the woman. She always thought Mercy Prentice resembled a cheery little wren, brown-faced and chubby, her good nature shining from her plain face. Now, she looked greyed and thin with shock. If Matthias Finch had been involved in Prudie's arrest, it could mean only one thing. 'Take some more ale,' she said, more gently. 'Or would you like mead? I'll put extra honey in it. It's good for the nerves.'

Needing to be busy, Susanna rose and found out the flagon of mead. Pouring them all good measures, she added some sliced boiled eggs and more bread. 'We need fuel,' she said, to herself more than anyone. The sight of Prudie's naked body had shocked her profoundly. Thin and scrawny with withered flesh that much she knew but the hurt she had received at the hands of those who had mistreated her was beyond all understanding. Shaking her head, she tried to dispel the vision of the many cuts and abrasions inflicted, the angry welts on her back. She gulped back the horror. The dried blood around Prudie's privy parts and on her thighs. What had they done to her and why? Cat jumped up onto her lap and kneaded. She hugged the black creature into her, seeking comfort, feeling the purring reverberate.

Mercy nodded, clutching her pot of mead. 'Although I'm not sure you'll want to hear what I have to say after what we've just witnessed.'

Susanna groaned. 'I need to know. For my own sanity of mind, I need to know who our enemies are and why Prudie has been treated so.'

'Well then, child, I'll tell what I know.' Mercy paused, pressing her lips together. 'It seems Prudie came across Master Robert Lacey and his wife.'

Susanna drew back in shock. And yet, somehow, she'd known the man would be behind their misfortune.

'They were in their fine carriage,' Mercy continued. 'Risen in the world, have the Laceys.'

'Aye. Blood money from the war,' Susanna answered bitterly.

'You know the Laceys?' Barnabas asked.

Susanna nodded sharply. 'He and the Mistress Agnes were once my childhood friends. Our paths crossed again when

Prudie and I attended Charles Lacey's birth. And, remember, that was the babe who died. It seems, lately, Robert Lacey has been wherever I have somehow. In town, at the sacred clearing.'

'The sacred clearing?'

'It's what we called the beach at the bend in the river. We all used to play there as children. It's out beyond the drovers' holloway.'

Barnabas's voice shifted into sharp concern. 'Did he do you harm there, Susie?'

Susanna shook her head quickly. 'He did me no harm but–'

'But?'

'I felt something in him. Some confliction. Maybe evil. Or something.' She huffed in exasperation and scrubbed an exhausted hand over her face. 'I don't know. He's changed since I knew him as a boy.'

'And not for the good,' Mercy added. 'It would seem Prudie got into an argument with the Laceys.'

Susanna stared at her in consternation. 'An argument? About what? I know nothing of this.'

'I know not the details. Talk in the town has it he is after your land. And that is the motive for causing you all mischief.'

'Our land?' Susanna exploded. Cat jumped down in fright and slunk away. 'But we have so little. It cannot be worth anything to him!'

'But it blocks the Laceys' route to the river. And even if you have a small acre, it has good pasture and a river approach for water. It's valuable, Susanna.'

'And here we are scraping and scratching by and sitting on a fortune.' She glanced at Barnabas. 'Maybe Prudie should give up the cottage and we can come with you to the Colonies after all.'

He gave her a tight smile. 'Mercy, you have more to say on this?'

'I have, Barnabas. The land may be the cause of the

argument but others say Mistress Agnes was heard screaming at Prudie about something else.'

'About Charles?' Susanna put in.

Mercy nodded, looking deeply uncomfortable. 'There were... accusations.'

'Accusations? I have heard talk she thinks Prudie took a plague to the birthing room. Mercy, you know this isn't true,' Susanna added urgently. 'Prudie would do harm to no child. There was no plague in this house. John died of ague.'

'It was not accusations about plague carrying, Susanna.' Mercy sucked in a breath. 'It was more serious than that.'

Susanna sat back, her mouth falling open in shock. 'Witchcraft.' Leaden fear and dread dropped into her stomach and the bread and mead threatened to return.

'Yes, witchcraft.'

'This cannot be. Tell me it is not so. We have not had a witchcraft accusation in the town since Old Mary, and before that when Abigail was hanged. I remember going to the hanging as a girl. It must be fifteen years ago.'

Susanna lapsed into silence, remembering how Prudie and John had pushed to the front, holding on to her with a bruising grip. At the time she had thought it was to afford a better view. A great crowd had gathered in the wool market. Street hawkers selling meat pies and oranges, pickpockets darting through, sly looks on their faces as they sped off with their bounty. It had all the atmosphere of the country fairs that used to be held before Cromwell banned them.

The jeers of the townsfolk rang in the air as Goodwife Abigail had been led up to the scaffold, her hands tied behind her back, terror etched on her aged face. As she had been lifted, shivering, up to the rope, she had soiled herself in her fear, the dark stain adding to the blood smeared on her thin shift. The crowd had gone wild, the shaming spectacle adding to their day's entertainment. Prudie had rushed to pull on the old woman's legs to hasten the death and lessen the suffering, then Susanna had realised why they had needed to be at the front. It had been a terrible day. Then she thought of Mary who had been run out of town. Mary who had escaped public humiliation and a death in front of the drooling masses. She wondered what had become of her old friend. Starved and dead in a ditch, no doubt. Maybe a hanging, as long as it was swift, was the better end?

Feeling her heart thump violently, Susanna asked, 'But how can Prudie be accused of witchcraft? Of exactly what crime is she accused?'

Mercy looked at her with shrewd eyes. 'If there's no accusation, one can be made up,' she said bitterly.

'So it was Agnes who brought the charge?'

'Aye. Claimed Prudie had bewitched her babe and that's why it perished. And got her husband to carry out the deed.'

Susanna gasped. 'Robert Lacey ordered Prudie's arrest?' Fear ran like ice through her. She knew this man would be behind all their misfortunes. Had known it since the day he appeared at the threshold offering payment for his child's birth.

'So I've heard. He'll do anything to keep that woman sweet, although the Lord knows why. Needs an heir, I reckon. Doesn't stop him whoring in the bawdy houses.'

'Aye, I've seen his horse outside the one in Fish Lane.' Susanna sucked in a breath. 'Robert got Prudie arrested for witchcraft. It would explain Prudie's beatings.' She put a hand to her throat.

Mercy sniffed in agreement.

'But, Mercy, this puzzles me as it wasn't taken further. I am glad, more than I can say, but why wasn't it?'

Mercy's eyes gleamed. 'And this is where the tale gets even more intriguing, child. If rumour and gossip has it right, Robert got Prudie arrested on behalf of his shrew of a wife but he must have had second thoughts, for he did not appear within the three days with any evidence. Moreover, 'twas *he* who bribed for Prudie's release.'

'Oh,' Susanna cried in shock. 'This makes no sense.'

The woman shook her head. 'That it doesn't. I can only think Master Lacey has no stomach for a witch trial, unlike Matthias Finch. He'll have pricked and examined poor Prudie just for sport and he'll be cursing the Laceys and the town of Flete for he'll not get paid now, without a witch conviction.' Mercy sat back. She emptied her pot of mead, wiped her mouth and continued. 'Robert Lacey is proving a weak man. And what's worse, he's a weak man in search of power. Trying to please his wife so she'll bed him and provide him a son, trying to keep Prudie's enemies appeased but not having the stomach to see through what he's started.'

'And sure, we have enemies enough in this town,' Susanna answered. 'Enemies from the old times. John was a good man but he had a rash tongue and spoke out too loudly and too often. We warned him to quieten but he took little notice especially when he'd taken ale.' She glanced at the heavily beamed ceiling overhead. 'And, much as I love Prudie, she can be the same.'

'I've said it to her myself too many times. We live in troubled times, Susanna. Aye, there's a king fresh on the throne now and those who support him are jubilant. But for how long? Are we to fall into war again? The Lord Protector had support until his death, and despite his milksop son not coming to anything, there may yet be war to make us a Commonwealth again. So, be assured, it is true you have enemies in this town, but you have allies as well.' She looked about her quickly, as if to see who might be listening. 'Ones who will rise to take the cause again. And, more than allies, you have friends. Friends who would be willing to back Prudie against any new allegations. Maybe

Robert Lacey knows this. Maybe that's what is behind her release.'

Susanna contemplated the candle on the table. They had been talking for so long, it had nearly burned down, the tallow leaking into the oak of the table. Her nostrils prickled with its stench; she had never become used to the smell but tallow was all they could afford now. The days of beeswax were long gone. 'Thank you, Mercy. Thank you for all you've done here today. And thank you for bringing us this news.' She clasped the older woman's hand. 'It is good to know we have friends and allies out there.' Sighing, she added, 'We may well need them.'

Mercy got up to go but sat back down again, stiff from sitting for so long. Pushing herself up, making her knuckles white with the effort, she stood. 'I'll be going.'

'I'll happily take you on the cart,' Barnabas offered. 'It's a long walk.'

Mercy shook her head. 'Nay, child. A walk will ease my stiff limbs. Susanna, if I could have some of Prudie's salve, it'll relieve the pain on the morrow.'

Susanna fetched a pot of the herb of Venus and daisy salve and saw the old woman to the door. 'God go with you, Mercy,' she said as she kissed her. 'Be careful. We need your comfort and kindness.'

She watched as Mercy limped down the path to the lane, sending the cluster of tattling women who had gathered there away with a clenched fist. Aware of their keen gaze and mouths twisted with speculation, Susanna closed the door and barred it. Leaning her forehead against its wood, she screwed her eyes shut and wondered what was in store for them all. Cat returned, weaving between her legs under skirts. She picked him up and buried her nose in his thick black fur, taking comfort from his reassuring purr as it vibrated through her. A tightening thickened around her neck and made her swallow. The image of poor old Abigail swinging from the gallows flashed into her head, unwanted and uncalled.

Witchcraft.

The very word sent a slither of cold dread greasily through her. For now, it seemed, Prudie was safe. But if she was under suspicion, then it followed so was the whole household.

CHAPTER 16

JULY 2018

Beth closed the laptop and screwed her eyes shut, trying to unsee the torrent of vile messages she'd just read on her website. There was a mixture of reviews, mostly good. That was okay, she expected feedback. What she hadn't anticipated was the mishmash of gossipy comment, quite a lot of it spiteful and suspiciously in the same style with the same misspellings, added to even the best reviews.

> Smells like poison. Discusting. Yuck, my poor nose!

> This soap looks so discusting, like a lump of burned flesh!

> Gross. Over-priced and over-hyped. Look elsewhere for better stuff.

She suspected most was the hand of some juvenile keyboard warrior and on top of making her review page look untidy and unprofessional, it really hurt. Briefly, she considered closing the site down completely but, with the resurfacing work in full flow outside in the lane and the shop closed, selling online was her only option. She'd tried keeping the shop open but, after the third day of no customers and teeth being loosened by a deafening jackhammer, she'd decided to shut for the duration of the roadworks.

Her mind flipped back to the trolling on her website. She was amazed at how upset she felt. Usually, she was able to shake off negativity, but she'd poured her heart and soul into her business and the criticism, however puerile, felt intensely personal. Maybe she should ring Steve? Her brother-in-law was an IT teacher in a comp. Could she get him to redesign the site and start anew? Glancing at her phone to check the time, she clocked the date. No good bothering Steve in July; he'd be up to his ears in end of term stuff. She'd simply have to ignore the rubbish on her site and hope her customers would too. A prickling hovered in the air and a gull shrieked outside, making her jump. Gazing around at her little sitting room, she couldn't quite rid herself of the sensation that something, or someone, was watching. On top of the trolls, it was all too much.

She'd had another bad night and was muzzy-headed from lack of sleep. Last night's nightmare had been truly horrific. A rope tightened around her neck, strangling the breath from her body, cutting into the tender flesh under her ears. She'd tried to lift her hands to free herself but her arms stayed clenched to her side, paralysed. She'd woken panting and sweating, and stared into the darkness, waiting sleeplessly for dawn.

Rubbing her tired and gritty eyes, she growled bad-temperedly at the empty echoing space and went downstairs.

In the shop's kitchen, which was now clinically clean and her workshop, she made a fresh batch of lemon soap. As ever, the mixing of the lye solution into the distilled water soothed her as she watched it slowly emulsify and thicken. The lemon zest and essential oil she added filled the room with a zingy citrus smell and immediately lifted her spirits. There was something about the scent of lemons that made her feel cleansed and refreshed. Her customers felt the same; it was one of her most popular soaps. She tried to hold on to the positive comments, it was all too easy to dwell on the horrible ones. Turning the soap mixture out into the lined box, she gave it a good tap to rid it of bubbles and put it on a high shelf to 'cure.'

After tidying up she wandered into her little shop, tweaking displays aimlessly. The racket from out in the street seemed even louder in here and it filled her with an itch of restlessness. Grabbing her bag, she made a snap decision, locked up and headed out to the museum.

It was a hot sunny day and, with everyone down on the beach, the museum was deserted.

Bill greeted her with a nod to follow her once more to the back room. Putting the kettle on, she asked, 'So what brings you to my door?' Beth subsided into the armchair, feeling a pile of papers crumple underneath. She made to get up and remove them, but Bill waved her hand dismissively, saying, 'Take no heed, child. The flatter that load of paper is, the better it fits in the bin. It's only a load of bureaucratic nonsense from the council. Squash it flat.' She handed over a steaming mug of builder's tea and perched on a similar pile on the stool opposite. Peering at Beth, she asked, 'Come to ask me about your spell bottle?'

'I haven't, actually. The shop's closed and I got a bit stir-crazy. Wanted some fresh air.'

'And?' Bill didn't miss much.

'And I've been reading up a bit on witches. There's stuff on the internet but it's mostly about Essex and Scotland. I wanted to know more about local stuff. Were there...' Beth hesitated. 'Were there witches here, in Flete?' She wasn't sure why she was so eager to know but Nathan's book, the spell bottle and the Celtic knife handle had awakened a desperate need. The online abuse had unsettled her, added to the nightmares and the sensation of there being someone or something in Tenpenny House watching her. She was in search of answers at least to some of it.

Bill edged a pile of books further onto the draining board and put down her mug. 'What do you know?'

'I know a little about the Bideford Witches and that they were hanged at Heavitree but that's not quite local enough for me.'

Bill's lips thinned and she nodded. 'Three old defenceless women they were. In their last years on this planet, like me. Often the case. If a woman was old or poor or without the protection of family,' here Bill snorted, 'or a man, then she was fair game. It was often gossip that led to their downfall. Someone said a woman had been seen to converse with the devil or to feed her familiars from her devil's teats. In the case of one of the Bideford Witches, they said she'd slept with the devil in the form of a black man.' Bill cackled. 'Bideford was a mighty port at the time, there would have been folk from all parts of the world, of all colours and creeds there. He was likely some poor freed slave but the gossips had him down as the devil incarnate, so there's racism raising its ugly head as usual.' She sniffed and picked up her mug. 'Sometimes it was a way of settling old scores. Of getting back at an old enemy.'

'And what about in Flete?'

Bill settled more comfortably on her pile of paper, crunching it beneath her. 'The Bideford Witches were hanged long after the fervour of the witch hunt craze. Most of it carried on in the fifteen and sixteen centuries. James I was to blame.' She huffed. 'The Scots should have kept him. There was a man who didn't like women, that's for sure. Wrote a book explaining how to deal with witches, didn't he. *Daemonologie*. Even personally oversaw the torture of women suspected to be witches. Nasty bugger. It led to there being whole teams of witchfinders and they were paid well for their toil, you can be sure of that. So of course it was in their interests to find witches. And find them they did.'

'What did they do to them? How did they prove it?'

'You really want to know? Tis not pretty.'

Beth felt the noose tightening around her neck. She swallowed; not sure she did, in fact, want to know the answer. A compulsion warred inside. Needing to know, feeling connected somehow with what these poor women had had to endure, but terrified. She nodded.

'Well, they'd have women in the village or town who were appointed to strip the accused. Local women they'd be, see. They'd search her for the devil's marks. That's where they believed the witch would feed her familiars or imps. And her familiars could be any animal she had around. The dog or the cat they had to keep the rats down.'

'Devil's marks?'

'Warts or hanging skin tags'd count. You're a child but when you get to my age, you get fair few of 'em so it would be easy pickings. They'd examine the accused all over, even the breasts and genitals, that's where they believed the devil's marks were most often found. Torture them with sleep deprivation too. Tie their thumbs to their heels and swim them.'

'Swim them?'

'Throw them naked in the village pond. If the woman drowned, she was innocent. If she rose to the top, she was guilty.'

'How was she expected to swim with her hands tied?' Beth gulped. It was horrific.

'Oh she wasn't,' Bill said matter-of-factly. 'Better spectacle, I reckon, that way, my lovely. Like I said, hard times. Different times. Beyond our understanding.'

Beth shuddered. 'It's all so awful. And it was like that round here?'

'It was as bad as anywhere, maybe worse. Rural folk are slow to shift their superstitions and seafarers are the most superstitious of the lot. They were dread afraid of witches.'

'Were there any witch trials in Flete?'

'One or two that I know of. The most documented is that of old Abigail Wray. Accused of drying the cows.'

Ridiculously Beth had visions of an old woman wiping cattle down with a towel. 'Drying the cows?'

'Making their milk dry up.'

Beth's nose wrinkled. 'But that could happen for a number of reasons.'

'Well, *we* know that but in 1645 they thought different. It was how things were back then. Like they say, the past is a different country. And you have to remember, at that time England was a country riven apart with civil war. Brother pitted against brother, neighbouring family fought against neighbouring family. Folk swapping sides so you never knew who was friend and who was foe. There was chaos, little law and order.' Bill pursed her lips. 'Terrible times. Violent times. Very little worse can befall a country than civil war. And on top of all that it was a time of plague, poor harvest because of the bad weather. Did you know it's been called the Little Ice Age? The Thames froze over in 1607 and they had frost fairs and skating. Must have been a rare old sight but no good weather for years meant no crops. When folk are faced with starvation, hardship, war and a breakdown in civil order they turns on one another. Look for someone to blame.' She sniffed. 'And they believed the devil walked amongst men, superstition was a way of life, see. It was a time when it was thought if a pregnant woman gazed at the moon she was risking insanity in her unborn.'

'Very different times,' Beth agreed but needing Bill to get back to the point. 'What happened to poor Abigail?'

'She was an elderly widow. Lost her sons and husband in the civil wars like so many before her. They reckon two hundred thousand died.'

'Two hundred thousand! That many?'

Bill nodded. 'And mostly men.'

Beth sat back, aghast. 'I had no idea.'

'There would have been lots of women left without the protection of their menfolk, like there always is after a war, and Abigail was one of them. She was a cunning woman, a wise woman, a healer. Used folk remedies to cure, was a gossip who attended births. Remember I told you a gossip used to mean a friend or a helper to a woman in childbirth? They were friends of the woman in labour, would sit behind her, propping her up, comforting her. Giving her mugwort to ease the delivery, or raspberry leaf tea to hasten it. And if the birth had been a hard one, she'd lay a hare skin covered in its blood on her belly to close up the woman's wound.' Bill chuckled at Beth's horrified face. 'I said it was different times, didn't I? Seems barbaric to us but these cunning women had centuries of lore passed down to them by other wise women and that's what they believed would help.' She laughed again. 'Don't think our good Dr Smith would agree though, would he?'

Beth shook her head, her tired mind reeling with the information.

'Well,' Bill continued, 'Abigail, village elder and wise woman, someone who was looked up to, a woman who folk went to in their hour of need, was unlucky enough to be accused by a farmer and taken by the witchfinder. Matthias Finch, he was called. Worked out of the Exeter Assizes.'

'Assizes? Matthias Finch?' A heavy sense of doom landed on

Beth, making her sick with dread. She had come across a man called Matthias Finch before. But where?

'What passed as the law courts at the time.' Bill sucked her teeth angrily. 'Aye, that man was notorious in these parts, right enough.' She paused long enough to swallow tea and then continued. 'He gathered together a team of women to do the strip search and the pricking. See, searching bodies, dealing with plague deaths, murder victims, the infanticidal, was considered women's work. They probably pricked Abigail all over, poor woman, searched her for devil's teats.'

Beth was finding it hard to make sense of this. 'I still don't understand what you mean by pricking.'

'They had a tool. A long sharp needle or bodkin. Stabbed it into the flesh of the accused. If it drew *no* blood and if the poor soul *didn't* cry out in pain, it pointed to her being a witch.' Bill drew in a deep breath. 'Evidence, see.'

'But surely anyone pricked by a needle would bleed?'

'And this is where it all gets knotty. Some women had no chance. If they were needed to be found guilty, if the rich man had an agenda to prove against her, maybe she'd wronged him in some way or argued against him, because of course it don't do for a poor woman to stand up to the wealthy, does it?'

'And that hasn't changed,' Beth said bitterly. The emotion swamping her was anger. She was furious. A red-hot rage filled her. And all over a woman who had lived and died four hundred years before.

'You're right there, child. So, if the witchfinder was after his fee and the accuser was after his revenge they used a pricker with a retractable blade. Plunged it into the woman's thigh or arm and up they held it, blade showing nice and bloodless with the woman not making a murmur because the blade was retracted and it was all an act.' Bill sat back in dark glee.

'Oh my God.'

'Told you it wasn't a pretty tale. The women didn't stand a chance. The pricking didn't stand as evidence alone though. They had to conduct a vigil throughout night and day, not letting her sleep, waiting for her familiars to appear. Or walk her, keep her awake until she was insensible. Sleep deprivation is an age-old form of torture, ask any mother of a newborn. Suppose you could consider Abigail as lucky. By the time of her trial, the ducking stool had fallen out of favour so she went in front of the justices and put on trial. The reason we know so much about her is scraps of the paper documents from her trial exist. They're very fragile but I can let you have a transcript to read. We've got one here in the museum. Poor woman was estimated to be in her seventies and not in good health even before she stood trial. I would imagine,' Bill added drily, 'after all she went through and festering half-starved in a filthy gaol for a few weeks, she'd be in no fit state to defend herself. Having said all that, all the evidence they could gather would count for nowt unless there was an actual confession. The documents show Abigail admitted having lain with the devil and that he had pestered her until she had done his bidding and forced the cows dry.'

'But why would she say that if it clearly wasn't true? Bill, this is shocking!'

'Humiliated, no sleep, beatings, ripped away from all those she loved. She'd probably admit to anything just to get the whole thing over and done with. I doubt by that point she would be in her right mind.'

'And what happened to her?'

'Show hanging. In the market square in town. It was always an event. Folk came from miles around. There'd be a mighty crowd, hawkers, musicians. It would be a day out. There'd be hundreds there.'

Beth's mouth dropped open. 'It was entertainment?' she cried out in incredulity.

Bill gave an evil cackle. 'No internet then. What were folk supposed to do to keep themselves amused?'

'Oh, Bill, that's awful.'

'It is, child. It is.' Bill sobered. 'Reckon the crowds were encouraged as a deterrent. To show everyone this is what will happen to you if you dare break the law. It was an excellent way of keeping women in their place and too frightened to make any trouble, wasn't it? Because, of course, if they did, they risked being hanged for a witch just like the woman they witnessed dangling in front of them.'

Beth picked up her abandoned mug and drank her now stone-cold tea. She needed it, her mouth had gone dry. 'And was it only women this happened to?'

'Mostly but there were some men accused too. At least in England they just hanged you. In Scotland they burned witches.'

'Yes, I read about that.' Beth bit her lip, feeling the shadow of the noose around her neck again. 'I've never heard anything more shocking. And these women were innocents!'

'Of course they were. Maybe guilty of causing a bit of bother by begging, maybe doing something spiteful, or getting drunk and wandering homeless but they certainly weren't having dalliances with the devil. You've seen the plaque put up for the Bideford Witches?'

Beth nodded. 'I've seen a photo of it.'

'A move forward to remembering them and giving them our forgiveness but it don't really go far enough, does it?'

'Nowhere near far enough.'

Bill rose stiffly to her feet. 'Got what you came for?' She shook her head wearily, suddenly looking frail. 'Don't do me any good to dwell on that bit of the past. I'll lock up and make my way home, I think.'

'I'm sorry to have kept you, Bill. And I'm sorry to have distressed you.' Beth reached out and took hold of the old woman's hand. She could have listened for hours more but could see the woman was exhausted.

Bill shook her head again. 'Needs knowing about, child, like a lot of women's history it's not known about enough, but it's not a time in history I like to think about too often.'

'It does.' Beth rinsed the mugs in the sink and followed Bill along the dimly lit corridor to the main door. On an impulse, she kissed the old woman on the cheek. 'Take care.'

'You too,' was the gruff answer and then Beth found herself out in the twenty-first century, the bright hot sunshine and holiday crowds.

CHAPTER 17

JULY 2018

Beth wandered, hardly aware of her surroundings, along Market Street to the old square. Buying a takeaway coffee, she found a bench and sat down.

It can't have changed all that much since the seventeenth century. A half-timbered market hall still stood proud on the cobbles, although the surrounding square was a car park now rather than a wool market. Tourists wandered aimlessly, ice cream in hand, pausing to peer into the shops. Some buildings still wore their medieval cloak if you raised your sight up above the modern steel and glass shopfronts. It was all too easy to picture gallows and a dangling figure. Beth shuddered and closed her eyes. She didn't want that image in her head. Almost unconsciously her hand strayed to her neck, feeling the familiar tightening sensation. And many of these women had been put to death because of what, gossip? A score to settle? Someone had sold a folk remedy or cure that hadn't worked? Deliberately shunning the past and thanking the gods for her twenty-first century life, she searched for her mobile and clicked on her sister's number. After a short call, Lorna promised to ask Steve if he'd look into the negative reviews and vile comments on the shop's website.

'It'll be a while though, sis,' she said. 'I've hardly seen him this week with the hours he's putting in at school. But I know he'll get to it when he's got a minute. You okay?' Without pausing for an answer, Lorna added, 'As soon as the summer hols start we'll pop down and try that Thai again. It was so yummy last time. Gotta go, lovely. PTA meeting looming.'

Beth clicked off the phone, slotted it back into her handbag, closed her eyes and lifted her face to the sun. With her colouring it would give her freckles, but she was greedy for its warmth and life. Someone slid onto the bench beside her and she opened her eyes to see Florence from the Mindfulness Centre. Wearing a vivid purple smock, she had a pet carrier next to her from which a plaintive meowing emanated.

'Are you all right, Beth? You look awfully pale.'

'Hi, Florence.' Beth mustered a smile. 'I'm fine. Just enjoying the sunshine and fresh air.'

Florence huffed. 'Not much else we can do with our businesses closed.'

Beth twisted to face the woman, shielding her eyes from the sun with her hand. Properly concentrating, she asked, 'Has it affected you badly?'

Florence nodded. 'We managed to cadge some space in Kennaway House in Sidmouth but some of our regular clients don't want to travel that far, so most stuff is on hold until the work on the lane's been done. What about you?'

Beth thought for a minute before answering. 'Do you know, I think it's actually been a blessing. I think I opened too soon and before I was properly ready.'

'You looked ready when I popped into your shop at the grand opening.'

'Well, I had the stock and the shop was set up, but I don't

think I was *emotionally* ready. I've been so frantic selling my house, buying the shop, working out my notice at the timber merchants that the change has taken me by surprise.'

'I understand completely, darling. It can happen. You've been through some of the most major life changes all at once. It's bound to take a toll.'

Beth released a breath. 'It's kind of you to see it that way. I was beginning to think I was being a right old wuss about it all. I don't normally let things get to me so much.'

'Not at all. Readiness is everything.' Florence patted her hand. 'It's good that you're giving yourself time. And you've not been well. No more fainting spells? Are you sleeping better now?'

'Haven't fainted again, thank goodness. I really think that was down to low blood sugar levels, it's never happened to me before. But I'm still not sleeping very well. Stress, I expect. The doc gave me some sleeping pills but I refuse to take them.'

Florence cocked her head on one side. 'I promised you something for the poor sleeping, didn't I?' She let out an exasperated sigh. 'What with everything that's been going on, and this little one here, it's quite slipped my mind. Come back to the house and I'll see what I've got to hand.'

'Thank you,' Beth said gratefully. 'I will.' She liked Florence and thought she could be a friend. Peering at the pet carrier, she observed, 'Someone doesn't sound very happy.'

'He's not. I've just taken him to the vet. My older cat scratched him badly. I adopted Frank here as a kitten. All was okay until little Frankie hit adolescence. Now it's like World War Three. And worse, my older cat, Salem, is threatening to leave home. He's been missing these last three nights.' Florence got up and heaved the cat carrier into her arms, its occupant still protesting. 'Come on, I'm positively gagging for a cup of tea. It's not far. Just as well.' She squinted into the carrier. 'Frank, what did they feed you at that vet? I swear you've put on a stone.'

Beth followed Florence along the main street, over Roman Way and to some pretty Victorian cottages in a narrow lane. She held the pet carrier while Florence fished out a key and let them in. A long narrow hall led to a kitchen diner that opened out onto an impressive conservatory.

'Let Frank out, will you,' Florence instructed. 'And I'll put the kettle on. Go and sit in the conservatory. I've kept the blinds down so it shouldn't be too warm in there.'

Beth obeyed, amused at how Frank shot out and disappeared into the hall. She made herself comfortable on a squishy sofa and looked around her. Small stained-glass pictures and dream catchers dangled from the central beam that was wrapped with fairy lights. All along the windowsill, interspersed with pot plants, were large crystals of various colours. It was cluttered and more than a little dusty but strangely soothing. Florence had been right, having the window blinds down had muffled the worst of the heat. An enormous and grumpy-looking tabby cat jumped lightly up onto the outside step, peered in through the door and then sloped off.

Florence entered carrying a tray loaded with mugs and a plate of biscuits. She gazed outside at the departing cat. 'My poor Salem,' she uttered miserably. 'I've had him for twelve years and it breaks my heart to think he feels unwelcome in his own home.' Sliding the tray onto a coffee table covered with magazine and newspapers, she said more brightly, 'Lemon tea and home-made gingerbread. Casey my partner makes it and it's very good.'

Beth reached forward for a mug, breathing in the heady aromas of lemon and ginger. As she did so, the little black cat from the pet carrier reappeared, jumped up onto the sofa next to her, rubbed his face along her arm and settled down.

'Oh, Frank likes you. He normally hides under the stairs for hours after a vet visit.' Florence frowned in disbelief. 'Is he purring?'

Beth nodded, amused. 'Like a steam train.' She looked down at the lithe black body, feeling the vibrations pulse through her. 'It's quite comforting actually. I'd thought about getting a dog but it's just not practical at the moment.'

'Lots of advantages to a cat. Far more independent. I adopted Frank as a kitten from a local rescue.' Florence crunched into a biscuit, adding thoughtfully, 'He was the last to be picked.'

'Why? He's adorable.' Beth tickled Frank's ears and watched, fascinated, as they flicked back and forth. There was a vivid scratch on his pink nose. The result of the spat with Salem, no doubt.

'People think black cats are unlucky, although I've always thought the opposite. It's the same with dogs.' Florence tutted. 'And in an Instagram world they're harder animals to photograph well so people don't want them.'

Beth was shocked. 'People have pets on the basis of how well they photograph?'

Florence laughed without humour. 'They do indeed. The rest of Frank's litter were tabby and white and black and white, and all went before him.' She sighed. 'He's a really lovely affectionate little cat, it's just he and Salem don't get on. I suppose I'll have to contact the rescue centre, see if anyone wants him.'

Frank rolled onto his back, still purring loudly.

'I've never seen him do that with anyone. He's even letting you rub his tummy! He's really taken to you. I've always said cats pick their owners,' she said meaningfully.

Beth looked up quickly. 'Oh no, Florence, I couldn't. I don't know the first thing about cats. I wouldn't have a clue how to look after him.'

Florence shrugged. 'Not a lot to it. Feed twice a day, make sure there's water out, provide a litter tray or let him out. The vet's confident his nose will heal without problem, and I've made sure he's up to date with his inoculations and worming and flea treatments. I use the vet in town and they're very good, so I can recommend them. And I'm only around the corner if you have any questions.' She reached over to give Frank a scratch under the chin. 'Best of all I could come and see him for a cuddle without Salem getting horribly jealous and spiteful.'

Beth hovered on the edge of a decision. Frank was gorgeous. Slinky and long like a miniature black panther and with jewel-bright emerald eyes. She'd never been much of a cat person, always gravitating to dogs. She and Lorna had had a pet-free childhood. She suspected her grandparents had enough to do looking after two lost little granddaughters without adding animals to the household. Her grandmother had always spoken fondly of the collie she'd had as a child and the many cats that shared her childhood home on the Blackdown Hills. Judith Loveday had had a country upbringing and kept Beth amused with stories of keeping a sick lamb alive in the warming oven of the Aga and of hot toddy remedies for a chesty cough. Beth always used to tease her about being part witch. Her mood sobered instantly. In the light of what she'd learned from Bill, joking about witches didn't seem funny anymore. 'Folk might say I'm a witch and Frank is my familiar,' she murmured, not quietly enough.

'They well might.' Florence looked amused. 'With your colouring, darling, you'd give them added fuel for their gossip. Red-haired, green-eyed and left-handed. Oh yes, I'd say they'd definitely mark you out as one.'

'How did you know I'm left-handed?' Beth asked, startled.

'It's the hand you're holding your mug with.' Florence

chuckled. 'And so what if you're a witch or people think you are? Lots of Casey's friends are. She's thinking of joining a coven.'

'There are witches *now*?'

'Of course there are. In fact, I'd say it's a growing ideology. A desire to return to nature's message, a need to feel back in rhythm with the seasons, a turn away from pharmaceutical treatments and a return to herbal and holistic remedies. Did you think they'd been consigned to history?'

'From what Bill at the museum's just told me, yes. I would have said there was wholesale slaughter of them.'

Florence huffed. 'They did their best. It's thought over ninety thousand perished throughout Europe. Hundreds in England and Scotland. Weirdly, in Ireland, and Wales where Casey's from, there were hardly any witches executed. Maybe the Celtic culture is more tolerant and understanding of the less worldly, the more mysterious realms.'

Beth nodded, thinking of a friend she'd had at university. 'My good friend Clodagh, who's from Ireland, believes in the little folk. Fairies.'

'Not much of a leap from fairies to sprites, will-o'-the-wisps to witches. And people back in the sixteenth century completely believed in witches. That wasn't the problem. The issue was society wanted to eradicate them.' Florence's lips twisted as she flicked a crumb of biscuit off her dress. 'And it hasn't stopped even now. Casey's friends have to meet discreetly in case of attack.'

'Attack?' Beth's mouth dropped open. Had Florence used the word "attack"?

'Come on, darling. At a time in history when lesbian groups are under attack for simply meeting together, it's not much of a stretch to think a group of women practising witchcraft would cause a stew. We've even had some members of Flete's Evangelical Church come into the Mindfulness Centre accusing *us* of doing the devil's work. Superstition and fear of what's misunderstood hasn't gone away.'

'What did you say to them?'

'Sat them down with a cup of calming chamomile tea, explained what we did, gave them a booklet outlining our treatments and yoga courses and sent them on their way.'

'I can't believe they did that.'

Florence shrugged. 'It was out of concern, I suppose. Tolerance works both ways. I said we wouldn't bother them if they treated us with the same understanding.'

'Has it worked?'

'Who knows?' Florence's tone was dry. 'I'm sure there were several prayers said for our salvation but at least they haven't been back. It was just as well Casey wasn't there, I don't think she would have been quite so tolerant.' She chuckled. 'And don't forget, in some parts of the Church of England, yoga has only just been accepted.'

Beth was silent for a moment. A whole new world had opened up to her over the last few hours, firstly with Bill in the museum and now with Florence. 'I'm interested in the witch's coven. What do they do?'

'You'd have to ask Casey, darling.' Florence drained her mug. 'I'm sure she'd be happy to explain. As far as I know there's lots of herbal tea and cake, a bit of gossip and the odd spell incantation. I know they take a vow to "do no harm". So much for casting spells on folk. Are you hoping to join?' She nodded to Frank, now asleep and snoring delicately. 'After all, your familiar has chosen you now.'

Beth followed her look. A wave of fondness for the little cat washed over her. 'He has, hasn't he?'

'And I have all his food bowls and toys. You can have those.' Florence bit her lip, her voice quavering. 'I'll miss the little chap, but it would be the perfect solution to the problem. Somehow, I know you'd be his perfect owner, not that anyone really owns a cat as such and I'd also be able to see him occasionally.'

Her tearful expression decided Beth. After all, how much trouble could one small cat be? 'Okay,' she said slowly. 'As long as you don't mind me phoning you up at all hours asking stupid questions. And will Casey be all right with this?'

Florence nodded. 'She will. She's getting as distraught about the situation as I am. You might have the two of us popping over for a Frank cuddle.'

Beth smiled. 'You'd be more than welcome. Both of you.'

'I'll get his stuff together.' Florence rose abruptly, as if now the decision was made, she wanted it done. 'We'll pile it in the car and drive you as near as we can get, given the roadworks.'

'My parking space at the back is still accessible. You can pull up there and we can go in through the kitchen door.'

'Perfect.' Florence stood looking down at the oblivious cat. 'Well, Frankie. Looks as if you've landed on your paws. Come on, little one, let's get you settled into your new home.'

CHAPTER 18

AUGUST 1660

It was a fine balmy day. A snatch of summer before the bitter chill of autumn. It had seemed to be winter for so long, the years monotonously chilly and damp. Golden days like these had been few and far between.

Susanna had forgotten how good it was to have God's sunshine on her face. She stood in the Tenpenny garden, lifting her face to the warmth, straying from her task. It reminded her of the day when Robert Lacey had come upon her at the river beach where she had found the ancient knife. Her mood plummeted. It had been a strange encounter and all ill that had befallen them seemed to have arisen from then. Or had it started when poor Charles Lacey had perished? Picking some rosehips, she scowled. How had that been their fault? They had tended to Agnes as dutifully as to anyone, more so. It was a sad fact that babies died. A sadder fact that women were sometimes unable to provide a son for their husbands. She sent up a fervent prayer for Agnes's womb to be fruitful once again. Maybe then she would cause the Tenpenny household fewer problems. That she would leave them alone and life would resume as normal. Had the two families been on friendly terms still, she and Prudie would have offered a tincture of lady's mantle; it helped quicken conception. But neither dared go near the Lacey Manor now.

Susanna's concentration lapsing, she caught herself on a dog rose prickle. Sucking her finger, she stared unseeing at the plant. She'd been praying a lot recently but no amount of pious utterings on sore knees would make Prudie normal again. Since her vicious encounter with Matthias Finch the old woman was slipping away. Her body was beginning to heal but her mind had been broken beyond repair. Only last night Susanna, on hearing a noise, had woken and gone downstairs to find the front door swinging wide open to the moonlight. A flash of pale had caught her eye and she'd found Prudie, barefoot and in her shift, wandering along the lane, her hands full of blackberries.

'Need to gather them in a full moon,' she'd hissed, wild-eyed. 'That's when theys best.'

Prudie had become possessed of a surprising strength and it had taken Susanna all persuasion to turn the old woman home and into bed. Now, she rubbed her shoulder. A bruise had flowered from where Prudie had lashed out in temper.

Susanna concentrated on the task in hand, picking the rest of the rosehips and some sweet tops of nettles. She would make a soothing tea, and a good nourishing soup from the nettles. Cat slunk to her side and pressed himself against her skirts demanding attention. He had been needy of late and now Star was gone was the sole recipient of their affections. Scratching the top of his head, Susanna murmured endearments before becoming aware of a gaggle of town boys standing at the gate. Putting down her basket, she turned and faced them, unease causing her muscles to tighten. For a long minute they stared at her insolently and in silence, so she asked, 'What brings you here?'

The eldest poked another with his elbow and cackled. 'She asked what we come for.'

The knot of unease hardened into panic. Flicking a glance around, Susanna could see no one else in view. She was defenceless. No dog, no man to protect her. True, they were boys but the biggest was as brawny and strong-looking as a man and probably had the same evil intent within him as some she'd come across.

'I ask again, what brings you here? We have little enough for ourselves and have no food spare.' She gestured to the basket. 'As you can see, I have poor pickings. Just a meal of rosehips and nettles. And that has to feed Mistress Prudie and the smith Barnabas when he arrives.' It was a lie. Barnabas was not expected but she hoped the prospect of a feared and respected man would see them off.

'He ain't coming nowhere near here,' a younger boy called out. 'He's shoeing my mam's horse.' She recognised him and fear made her stomach drop. It was Ned Flowers, one of Mistress Katherine's brood; a family which long had no love for the Tenpennys. 'You're lying,' he sneered.

Susanna sucked in a breath to keep herself calm. 'It doesn't take a whole day to shoe one horse. Barnabas will be here soon.'

The older boy shoved Ned out of the way. 'Aye. He'll come running. Word is you have him enchanted. That you has cast a love spell over him.' He spat over the gate. For all their bravado, the gang had not ventured onto Tenpenny land. His face bore a curious mixture of fear and fascination. 'That's what we're after. A love potion so we can get the girls abed.'

Susanna nearly laughed. For one, the idea that she had bewitched Barnabas and for two, that these boys so recently fed from their mothers' teats were thinking of lying with girls. 'I don't make love potions and if I did, I certainly wouldn't sell any to saucy-tongued lil' tackers, still babes in arms. Get back to your spinning tops and hoops and sticks, boys.'

The anger was sudden and vindictive. 'Don't laugh at us,

whore,' Ned Flowers yelled, his face puce with rage. He shook his fist from his position of safety behind the eldest. 'Get us what we wants. Tell her, Elias!'

Infected by his ire, Elias, the older boy, sneered. 'Yes, whore. Get us what we want.' The others joined in with threats and waving fists.

'Or?' Susanna couldn't help it. A lick of anger coursed through her. How dare these whelps come to her cottage and threaten and curse at her. She took a step nearer, an icy calm descending. Broadening her shoulders and pulling herself to her full height, she stared at them, one brow raised, waiting for them to speak. A bee buzzed by and she brushed it away irritably.

'She *is* a witch. It's all true what they say. Look at her.' Elias pointed a wavering finger. 'She's even now casting a spell over us.'

'Nay, that's her familiar,' Ned yelled. 'She's bewitched the bee to do her bidding. That's what they do. She's a witch, I tell thee.'

This time Susanna did laugh. The idea was absurd – and terrifying. They may be mere boys but many a witch had been convicted on the say so of children. 'I am no witch. If I were I would have turned you all into toads by now.' The words were unwise but panic was making her tongue loose. Cat, sensing trouble, sidled to her and she picked him up, hugging him to her as a shield.

'Witch!' shrilled Ned. 'She's a witch-whore!' The others joined in chanting vile insults.

'Get away from here! You are not welcome.' To her chagrin, Susanna heard her voice become weak with fear. Something hurtled through the air. She looked around thinking it was the bee returning but saw Elias with a handful of stones. He threw another but it fell impotent at her feet. Ned Flowers's aim was surer. A larger stone landed hard on the back of the hand that was clutching Cat. Her yelp of pain excited the boys' anger further.

'Get the witch's beast,' Ned snarled. 'It suckles from her devil's teats.'

Susanna let go of Cat so he could make good his escape but Ned was quicker and a hard shower of stones landed on the cat's rear. He yowled and shot off. Stones rained down on Susanna, one catching her on her forehead. She turned away.

'Hold thy wab, you varmints. Get thee away!' On a banshee shriek Prudie stumbled out from the scullery door, wielding the besom broom. Her skirts were flying and cap askew, wild hair dripping down her back. 'Ned Flowers, Elias Light, get thee gone. With all the power I have I curse you and your kin, you ungodly unchristian folk.' She ran at them, teeth bared, shaking the broom.

Elias took one look and ran, the others followed but Ned remained. He spat at her feet. 'I ain't afeared of you, you old crone.' Shaking his fist at her he added, 'You'll regret those words, see if you don't. We all knows you were on the side of the Protectorate. The wrong side.' He spat again. 'Hag!'

Prudie jabbed the broom at him and, after giving her one more hate-filled look, he ran after the others.

Susanna went to her, put her arms around the old woman's thin shoulders and led her back to the safety of the house. The lump of fear lodged deeper within her. Her throat tightened with the threat of the noose. She prayed they would not all live to regret the old woman's words.

CHAPTER 19

AUGUST 1660

The days crawled by. Unwilling to venture out, Susanna stayed indoors while Prudie dozed fitfully by the fire. Susanna had risked going to market once but the supporters Mercy had claimed to be prolific were nowhere to be seen. She was only too aware of the scandalmongers hugging the corner of Market Street. She had paid for her goods and scurried home, head low, hiding behind her wide-brimmed straw bonnet. Even so, someone had spat at her feet, narrowly missing her skirts. There may well be Commonwealth supporters still in Flete but they were keeping themselves hidden. The powers of the Lacey family and the king had silenced them. She and Prudie had gone to church as usual, to not do so would accelerate even more suspicion, but had spoken to no one and had had backs turned on them. The hissing whispers as they'd walked in and that had fallen to an accusing silence was almost enough to have them turning about and returning home.

Prudie kept to John's old chair, her gnarled and age-stiffened hand rhythmically stroking Cat who now clung to the indoors too. Since the town bully boys had stoned him, he sported an array of scrapes and bruises on his flank and skulked in the house, staying close, any rats forgotten.

Prudie's body was mostly recovered from her time in the gaol but her mind continued to wander. She forgot things and sometimes thought John was still alive. She remembered enough to be wary of any man except Barnabas and shied away, ducking behind Susanna should one come near. In an attempt to stir Prudie back to her old self, Susanna was recording all her recipes and notes in a leather-bound book Barnabas had once given her. Prudie's expertise, as that of her mother and grandmother, was all in her head. Susanna wanted a more permanent legacy. Then, if the worst was to happen, at least there would be some kind of record of her skills. It seemed to her vital and urgent that she do so.

Prudie had good days but more often long hours when her eyes and brain lay vacant. To fill the time, Susanna began to draw finely detailed illustrations to accompany Prudie's descriptions. The old woman came back to life when telling of how wood sage, when dried to a powder, could help with mouth ulcers, of how bay leaves when crushed into oil could cure earache. Thanking the Lord that Prudie had taught her how to read and write, Susanna dutifully noted down that herb of Venus could be used to help the delivery of a baby and to draw out the womb-cake afterwards. Frowning in concentration, she encouraged Prudie to describe adder's-tongue in detail and created intricate drawings of the long broad leaf with its finger-length stalk and serpent's tongue flower. She relished these hours and the bond between them grew ever stronger. Although she had picked up much of the wise woman's lore, she'd had no idea quite how comprehensive it was. It seemed as if Prudie was digging into her damaged mind and reaching deep for the knowledge she had kept there for a lifetime. A long lifetime of skills and expertise and a good life spent healing people, aiding their delivery into the world and easing their passage out of it. It was harsh that it was this very ability that had brought her low and might be her undoing.

'Set it into oil,' Prudie was now murmuring in a voice so quiet Susanna had to strain to hear.

'What is this now, Prudie?'

The old woman flapped a hand in exasperation. 'Lady's bedstraw, child. Are you not listening? Set in oil and place in the sun for twelve of God's days before using.'

Susanna wrote it all down. 'And what is it for?'

'Burns, scalds, remember.' Prudie nodded, staring into the fire as if envisaging herself applying the salve. 'And to ease travellers' feet. Aye. And for scab itch in children too.'

The drowsy late afternoon was interrupted by Barnabas. He entered through the buttery having milked their cow and collected a few eggs from their dwindling flock. Putting it all away, he helped himself to a tankard of ale, pulled up a stool to the fire and his news burst out.

'I have heard tell of a ship, Susie. A ship sailing all the way to the new lands. Tis a Shurt and Strange tobacco vessel. Trade is good from Bideford. The ships take Devon goods to Virginia and bring back tobacco and skins.'

Susanna handed him a plate of cold mutton for his troubles; he was their rock. She had become shy of even venturing into the garden after the stone throwing incident. Abandoning her book, she pulled up another stool and sat between him and Prudie. The old woman had become prone to alarming outbursts and she wanted to calm her should any excitement happen. Wrapping the woman's hands around a cup of vervain tea, she asked Barnabas, 'Bideford? Why would we travel all the way there? It's a good way, Barney.'

Barnabas tore into the meat, obviously hungry. Eating with his mouth full, he answered, 'Because as well as taking Bideford pots to Virginia, they take people. Folk like us who want to start a new life.'

He was aglow and Susanna's heart sank. She wasn't sure if she wanted to leave Flete and go to a foreign and unknown land. Fear clutched at her heart. Susanna glanced at Prudie, who was sipping her tea but dribbling it onto her kerchief, and knew she wouldn't be strong enough for such a voyage. And she knew she could never leave her. But what of the future here? The town would take its lead from the Laceys and Robert Lacey would do as his wife insisted. And Agnes Lacey hated them with a passion, as only a woman who had lost a babe and was seeking a scapegoat could. There had been no news of another pregnancy. If the woman was now barren, things could only worsen for them.

Barnabas slaked his thirst and put his tankard down. 'And what's even more fortuitous, what's the absolute best news, is they'll pay us to go.' At Susanna's blank expression, he continued, nodding. 'I know. Can you believe it is so? They want people like us, young and strong, with skills, to make a new land in the Colonies.' He reached forward and took her hands. 'Oh, Susie, it'll be hard. We'll have to work harder than we've ever done but I know we can make it a success.'

She eased her hands out of his. 'And what if we travel all the way to the north coast and can't get passage to Virginia? What then?'

'Susie, Bideford is a mighty port. There's work aplenty for a smith like me. If there isn't, then I'll repair boats, make barrels. Anything to make enough money to get us out of this godforsaken country.'

Susanna reared back. 'Barnabas, hush your mouth. We're in enough trouble without your blasphemy. What if someone should hear?'

His lower lip jutted out mutinously. 'Can you say there is a

God in Flete? After what He allowed them to do to Prudie, and in His name?' He shook his head violently. 'Tis no God I want to serve under.'

'Walls have ears,' Prudie's voice, shocking in its frailty but no less forceful, hissed out. 'Take a care of what you speak, young Barnabas.'

'Aye, I will, old woman,' he answered, looking chastened. 'But the last ship sails before the winter gales set in and it will take us a goodly while to get over the moor to Bideford, so I need to hasten a decision.'

'Barnabas.' Susanna took his hand back. 'I'm not sure I can make a decision this grave so quickly.' She nodded imperceptibly towards Prudie. 'There are things to consider, animals to sell. What of this house? And what would we do about Cat? We can hardly turn him out to take his chance in the world. He means so much more to us now we no longer have Star.'

This time it was Barnabas who extracted his hand and Susanna sensed his very self withdrawing. 'It is our only chance, Susie. There may not be another ship until next spring and, even then, there may not be one that pays out passage. Can you not see the urgency?'

'Oh aye, I see the urgency. I also see the danger. How are we to traverse the moor? On foot?'

'I'm to buy the cart and horse from my uncle. Lady is no nag like Job, she is strong and will be an asset to sell when we get to Bideford.'

Susanna felt deeply the slight to their faithful old horse. She frowned. Barnabas seemed to have it all worked out in detail. And all without the slightest consultation with her. Resentment licked. Once again she felt her impotence as a female. If only she were a man she could take the reins of her destiny. Chafing at his imperiousness, her tongue became sharp. 'What of this new world? I've heard terrible tales of red-skinned men who wear feathers and little else. How can we live amongst such heathens?' She was gabbling out tattle heard in the town; in truth she had no idea of its veracity.

'Susanna, I never thought I would hear you be so small-brained.' Barnabas gazed at her, stricken, and worse, disappointed. He put his plate down where the pewter clattered against the hardened earth. Susanna winced and feared for its safety. It had been John's and the only pewter they owned. Cat jumped sleekly off Prudie's lap to take advantage of their argument and lick at the mutton grease. 'The native tribes have helped the settlers, traded with them, showed them how to grow crops which yield in their soil.'

'But are they good Christian folk?'

For the first time Barnabas looked uncertain. 'I believe some are. I believe some keep to their own gods. If it means so much, take your God with you and we can build Him a church there.' He inched closer. 'This could be our chance. True, there are fortunes to be made but it isn't the money I'm seeking. It is the freedom to live as I want to live.' He spread a hand around the room, pungently thick with choking smoke from the damp logs Susanna had failed to properly dry. 'Is this living? Cloistered in here day in, day out, too afeared to venture even as far as the garden? There are herbs out there to be picked, apples to be collected. Had I not come today, would your cow have been milked? This is no life.' He sat back, triumphant in his manly confidence that he was right. 'We must go, Susanna. Or there is no life for us.'

'Go if you must, Barnabas. I have yet to decide whether to accompany you.'

He frowned. 'You are concerned about your reputation, perhaps? Of course we would marry before we left. We'd go as man and wife. And if we can't find anyone to marry us here in

Flete, then we'll find someone in Bideford, or failing that I'll get the captain to marry us on board the ship! What say you to that?'

'He speaks the truth, Susie. You must go. It is your only chance of a better life,' Prudie croaked. She turned stiffly, body aged beyond its years by recent experience but, for the first time in weeks, her eyes recovered of some of their old fire.

'And will you come?' Susanna asked with beseeching eyes.

Prudie smiled. 'I cannot. For what use would an old woman be in a new world?'

'It could be your chance for a better life too, Prudie. You have so much healing knowledge. So much power. Much to give to a new community.'

'And that knowledge is yours now, child. I have passed it to you and you have written it into the book. And the book will go with you. Every community needs its healers, women to help other women give birth, ease those into the next life. Important skills to have when you're building a new town. One that may value them more than here and now in Flete.' She sank back against the hard chair, exhausted by the longest speech she had made since returning from the gaolhouse.

'I cannot leave you, Prudie.' Tears coursed down Susanna's face. 'You are everything to me. You took me in when my parents died, gave me a home, tended to me as your own.' She flung her arms around the old woman, weeping into her shoulder. 'I cannot go.'

Barnabas rose impatiently. 'You have made your decision then, Susanna? You are to stay here and be persecuted by the tattlers and gossipmongers in town? You turn your back on opportunity, on a freer life? You reject me? You reject our love and the life we might have had?'

'No,' Susanna wailed. She turned from Prudie, wiping her face on her apron but he had already reached the door. The familiar tightening around her neck made her gasp and scratch at her throat. Her choice was unenviable. Stay in Flete and risk the terrible retribution that came with an accusation of witchcraft, or leave behind the woman who had raised her and who needed her, sacrificing her to an unknown and perilous existence? 'That is not what I mean, Barney. I require time to think it through. Grant me that.'

Barnabas swung open the front door, sticking out his chest and rising to his full height, his masculinity angered by what he perceived as her rejection. 'But that is the very point, Susanna. I do not have the luxury of time and *you* most certainly do not. Good day, Mistress Prudie, goodbye, Mistress Susanna.'

He swept out, slamming the door shut with such violence that the whole cottage shook. Susanna hid her face in her lap and sobbed into her apron. They had lost their friend and protector but most of all, through her indecision and his pride, she had lost the man she loved.

Cat mewed and pushed his head against her face. Gathering him up, Susanna whispered into his black fur, 'Oh, Cat, my pretty. What is to become of us?'

CHAPTER 20

JULY 2018

The decision to adopt Frank, however hastily made, was proving painless. He settled in quickly, established her bed as his favourite place to snooze, was clean with his litter tray habits and was affectionate company. Florence's statement that cats choose their owners seemed to be true.

The only problem came when Beth needed to make a batch of soap. For hygiene purposes she needed to keep the area as spotlessly clean as she could. She didn't want to risk reviews accusing her of making soap with black cat hair in it; she had enough bad reviews as it was. Pre-Frank it hadn't been an issue; she'd scrupulously scrubbed down the kitchen worktops before and after each manufacturing session but Frank was a needy cat and liked to be with her. He hadn't reacted well to the closed kitchen door and his yowling had spoiled the usually meditative quality of the session. She'd tried turning up the radio but Frank had protested even more loudly. As a possible solution, Florence had brought in an old freestanding dog gate she'd found in her shed. Beth wedged it in the doorway between the kitchen and the passageway and to her utter surprise, it worked.

She eyed him now and said, 'Any cat of repute would leap up and over that gate, Frank.' The cat stared back at her from unnervingly intelligent green eyes, found a patch of sunlight on the flagstoned hall and settled down. Now she was within view he seemed to understand what was happening and that she needed to get on with her work.

She tried a batch of soaps scented with sandalwood oil and cinnamon and was pleased with the masculine, slightly Christmassy aroma. She'd just finished clearing up when there was a knock on the side door. Opening it, to her pleasure and surprise, she found Nathan.

He slid his sunglasses onto his head and grinned. 'It's a glorious day. Wondered if you fancied a stroll along the beach and an ice cream?'

'Would love to!' Beth agreed. 'Can't be out too long though,' she added, explaining about having recently adopted Frank. 'It'll be the first time I've left him.'

Shutting the kitchen and shop doors so Frank couldn't make mischief with her stock and contaminate the new batch of soap she'd just made, she was surprised at the relief she felt at escaping Tenpenny House; it had felt oppressive lately. Walking down Clappers Lane with Nathan and skirting around the roadworks, even the ugly orange barriers and lack of workmen couldn't dampen her sense of reprieve.

He was right, it was a beautiful day. 'Thank you,' she said, sheer joy zipping through her. 'This is a great idea. I can't believe I live right near the sea and hardly ever go on the beach!'

Stepping carefully around a pile of cobbles waiting to be re-laid, he answered, 'If I'm really honest, I avoid the beach at this time of year. Gets too busy but I thought, seeing as it's mid-week, we might escape the worst of the crowds and at least we don't need to worry about finding somewhere to park. Besides, I know a place that sells the best ice cream in the world and I want to introduce you to it.'

As they reached the end of Fish Lane and emerged onto the long concrete promenade, Beth gasped. 'It's wall-to-wall sun worshippers! Why was my shop so quiet when there are all these people in town?'

'It often goes that way.' Nathan led her east towards the harbour and away from the worst of the crowds. 'When it's hot and sunny like this, folk swamp the beach. When it's rainy and cold they're more likely to head into town and wander around the shops. Most often, though, they head off to Sidmouth or Lyme Regis where the shops are a little more touristy.'

'Perhaps Flete isn't the right place for me after all, although I could never afford the rates in Lyme or Sidmouth.'

'You might find once the school holidays are over, the tourists will be older with a bit more cash to spend. Trade should pick up then. The visitors who come in the autumn aren't as fixated on the beach; they like a potter around the shops.'

'I hope so. I've invested a lot of time and emotion in my new project.' Beth eyed the grubby-looking pub on their left that was boarded up and closed. 'Do you think the town is on its uppers? Perhaps I *should* open up somewhere else?'

Nathan followed her look. 'Think there are plans for the pub. It's been closed for a while now. Can't understand why when it's right on the seafront. In the right hands it could be a goldmine. Nice place to sit outside too, in the good weather.' He shrugged. 'Flete has its fair share of problems, like every other small town, but there's a bit of investment going on. And Clappers Lane has some great places, doesn't it? Once the resurfacing's finished and you're left in peace, customers will return. Were you making soap when I turned up?'

Beth nodded. 'Just finished a batch. Think it might go down well at Christmas.'

'Smelled fantastic. I'll definitely buy some.'

'I'm afraid you'll have to wait. It has to be left to cure for a minimum of four weeks. Longer if you want it to really harden and therefore last longer when it's used.'

'You really have to think ahead, don't you? I had no idea there was so much involved.'

'One good thing about being closed to footfall. I can increase my stocks for when I reopen and I'm doing a little experimenting with recipes I haven't tried before.'

They reached a wooden hut, painted cream, pink and pale blue, and joined the queue. Once they'd bought a couple of ice creams from a bewildering selection of flavours, they found a miraculously empty bench and sat down. Lapsing into silence, they enjoyed the simple pleasures of chocolate ice cream, hot sun and the sounds of happy children playing on the beach. The sea was glassily calm and a rich blue, shushing and murmuring as it tugged at the pebbles.

Nathan sighed with pleasure and leaned back on the bench, resting his arms on the back. 'Can't beat the place on a day like this. Getting a dose of good old vitamin sea makes all your troubles float away.'

'Vitamin C? I thought it was vitamin D that we got from sunshine?'

'You're right it is, but I was referring to sea as in S.E.A. There's something blissfully soothing about being near the water.'

Beth laughed, the sunshine and outdoors making her feel lighter than she had for days. 'I see what you mean.'

'Florence does an early morning yoga session on the beach in good weather. You should try it. The meditation session at the end is fantastic against the background sounds of the gulls and the sea. Really helps unknot any worries.'

'Maybe I will.' She fished out a tissue and wiped her chocolatey fingers. 'And you were right about the ice cream. That might be my first but it's definitely not going to be my last. What a treat to skive off work and escape to this.' She observed him. With his eyes hidden by Ray-Bans and his skin, tight over a firm jaw and lightly tanned with a spattering of freckles, he looked like a man without a care in the world. 'You don't come across as being troubled. You look supremely relaxed.'

Turning to her, he lifted his sunglasses to the top of his head, his lips curling at the corners. 'The benefit of having a holiday from work. True, there is something I have to make up my mind about but it's nothing unpleasant. I rather thought *you* have problems and an ice cream by the beach in the sun might help.'

'Doctor's orders?'

'Absolutely.'

'Oh, it's nothing really.' She sighed.

'Doesn't sound like nothing, Beth.'

She leaned forward, concentrating on a small child fighting to get his kite aloft. There was little breeze, even down here on the seafront, so she thought it an ultimately optimistic but hopeless venture. Perhaps the same could be said of her shop?

'When I was offered redundancy from my office job.' She flicked a glance sideways to see Nathan listening intently. He must be a good GP, his focus was laser like. 'I used to manage an office in a timber import–export business. It was busy and my colleagues were good fun, but it wasn't something I could see myself doing for the rest of my life. Besides, I worked hard. I worked *really* hard, and I couldn't see the point when it was all for someone else's benefit. I don't mind putting the effort in, but I wanted something more fulfilling, something I could believe in.'

'Hard to believe in teak and pine.' Nathan's tone was dry but neutral.

'Well, I'm sure it's someone's bag but it wasn't mine. It was a job I fell into after university. I hadn't had much stability in my life, you see.' Beth swatted away a pesky wasp, contemplating how much to tell him. 'I never knew my dad, and Mum left my sister and me when we were little so our grandparents looked after us.'

'That's tough.'

She felt his sympathy so continued. 'It was but my grandparents were great. *Are* great.' Beth made a face. 'Had Mum just gone and left us completely, it would have been easier than what she did. She'd return when she got fed up of teaching English in Thailand, or bar work on the Costa del Sol, set up home here, take me and Lorna back and we'd be a sort of family for a bit.'

'And then?' Nathan prompted gently.

'And then, when she was bored of us, depressed by a rainy Devon winter, she'd disappear to another job. Waitressing in Sorrento or serving chips in Mykonos.' Beth gave a hard laugh. 'I can never fault my mother's work ethic, she's always found jobs to do.' She paused, trying not to sound bitter. 'Just never wanted to put the effort into mothering us.'

A silence landed, only broken by the relentless tide and the gulls wheeling overhead.

'That must have been very hard.'

'I suppose, when I got the job at the timber merchants it would have been easier, safer, to stay there. I had my own little house in Exeter, I was well paid and, most importantly, had security. When the redundancy rumours started flying I went into panic mode. Hated the idea of change, was frightened to death of what might happen, of what I might lose. It was my lovely gran who talked some sense into me. She knew I'd always liked making things.' She glanced sideways again. 'I'd always loved painting, the messy craft stuff at school.'

'But you didn't pursue that as a career?'

Beth scowled. 'Too precarious by half. I wanted a job for life and a down payment on a two-bed terrace in Polsloe.'

'Completely understandable. So what did your gran suggest?'

'That I find something I could do to make a living but that I enjoyed more than paper pushing in an office. We investigated some courses. Evening classes and the like.' Beth gave a short laugh as she remembered she and Judith discussing the possibilities: reiki healing, massage, reflexology, paper making, custom-made clothes. 'Nothing was quite right. Eventually found a soap-making course. It was two days of practical sessions and an eight-week long course of all the other stuff you need to know.'

'Like what?'

'Labelling, allergens, marketing and branding, selling platforms and pricing. Your unique selling point. I still haven't pinned my USP down.'

'Wow.'

'Yes, there's a lot to it if you're thinking of going into it professionally as a business. Gran said with my experience in the office, and my creative streak, it might be the solution.'

'But, at this point, you were still working at the timber merchants?'

'Oh yes. Couldn't quite make that leap into the unknown. Far too comfortable being where I knew and where I'd worked for the last ten years.'

'That's understandable.'

'Leaving a secure well-paid job seemed daft. It would be like emigrating to a whole new world or leaving for the moon. But then the decision was forced as, thanks to Brexit, anything import–export suddenly looked uncertain and I was offered redundancy. A nice fat little package of money, plus the proceeds of selling my house brought me to Clappers Lane and Tenpenny House.'

'Brave taking on such an old property. It must be listed?'

'It is but I had no need to change the exterior and my surveyor, to whom I paid a small fortune, assured me it was in as good a nick as any building of that age could be. It was also weirdly well-priced.' Beth went silent, wondering what the real reason was behind what she'd seen as a bargain. Didn't estate agents have to declare ghosts? Shaking the thought out of her head, she carried on talking. 'I reckoned, if it had lasted all that time, it was good for another fifty years or so by which time I'd be retired and out. And besides, somehow, it seemed right. The building seemed to call to me. Daft, I know.' Beth's lips twisted. 'Have to confess I went into it all not really knowing anything about half-timbered buildings. I've since read some horror stories online.'

'That'll teach you to google.' Nathan laughed.

'Yup. So you can see it took a real leap of faith to start the business up, step out of my comfort zone, and that's why I'm so stressed it doesn't seem to be working.'

'Early days though, Beth. And the road closure can't be helping.'

'That's true. I'm wondering if my decision to close down the shop while they resurface is me being a wuss and not facing up to getting the business running properly. Is it actually all about cold feet and lack of confidence?'

'Maybe,' Nathan said honestly. 'Or maybe it's the sensible way to deal with a problem out of your control and give yourself some prep time. And I don't mean for making more stock. More about getting your head in the right place.'

'Florence said something similar.'

'Wise woman is that Flo.'

'Are you good friends?' Beth shoved the chocolate ice cream-stained tissue deeper into her pocket as the wasp had returned and was buzzing annoyingly around. Still, if she was stung, she had her new good friend the GP to take care of it. After looking after herself for so much of her life, it was a strangely comforting thought.

'I suppose we are,' Nathan said thoughtfully. 'We've known each other from childhood. She's local too and we went to the primary school together. She's a little older though.'

A noisy family with three small sand-covered children strolled past. The youngest child, not more than a toddler, was obviously reluctant at having to leave the beach and trailed behind, his bottom lip jutting out in furious fashion and trailing his plastic spade. He scowled at Nathan as he passed.

It made Beth laugh. She turned to Nathan and blurted out, 'How old are you?'

Nathan didn't miss a beat. 'Thirty-eight.'

'Married? Divorced? Children?'

'No children that I know of, to my regret, as I'd like some. One long-term relationship, which began at medical school but fizzled out as we got older. No one since. Never married so not divorced.' His eyes flickered. 'I'm open to another relationship though. I like being with someone. Gets lonely going home to an empty house after a long day. And running only fills up so much time.'

'Where do you live?' Beth was aware it was an inquisition, but she was curious about him.

'In a thirties semi two streets away from where my parents live. I left to go to university, lived in the south-east for a while then came back to my hometown.' He pulled a face. 'Does that make me boring?'

Beth laughed again. 'Not in the slightest. I've only managed to move twenty-five miles away from my roots. Sometimes I feel a touch of my mother's wanderlust and realise there's a big world out there, but I've always been too scared to seek it out. My mum's in Vietnam at the moment,' she added, almost as an afterthought. 'Think she's working for some sort of relief organisation.'

'Wow.' Nathan's brows rose. 'That's impressive. It's perfectly understandable you haven't wanted to go too far from where you felt secure though.'

Somehow his validation made Beth feel better. She'd always felt too safe, too boring for staying so close to her grandparents, but reliving her childhood through the lens of the brief summary she'd recounted to Nathan made her realise *why* she'd stayed near. 'Perhaps I'm not such a failure after all?'

'A failure? Whyever would you think that? You look nothing like a failure from where I'm sitting,' he said robustly. 'You've dealt with one of life's biggies with practicality and logic. Being made redundant is one of the big stresses. You met that challenge and changed your life, worked hard to get your business going. How is that in anyway a failure?'

'Thank you.' Beth blew out a breath. 'That means a hell of a lot. My sister, Lorna, has her children and is an amazing mum. She's found fulfilment that way. I've always measured myself against my mother, though. Always felt I had nothing to stop me from doing as she has: go abroad, work my passage. I've nothing holding me here.' *Or I didn't*, she added silently. Her feelings for this man had begun as a whammy from nowhere and were continuing to spiral out of control.

'But it isn't for everyone, nor should you feel that it should be,' Nathan said gently. 'Come here.' He opened his arms.

Beth slid into them. Being held was exactly what she needed. Nothing could beat the reassurance of someone holding you close and warm. And nothing could top the feeling of strong male arms holding you against a firm chest. Such a simple pleasure but one she'd been denied for too long. She could really fall for this man. He was kind, understanding and the sexual attraction, which had been the initial and unexpected draw, nagged insistently. 'You said you had something you were mulling over?' she said, her voice muffled against his T-shirt.

'Oh, it's nothing really. A job offer. Like you, it would mean moving out of my comfort zone so it's taking some thinking over.'

He obviously didn't want to expand so Beth let it go, content to lie against his ribs, feeling his heart thump steadily. 'You smell lovely,' she said as she breathed him in.

'I could say the same of you.' He kissed the top of her head lightly. 'Soap and something earthy?'

'Sandalwood. One of my favourite oils. One of the bonuses of hanging out with a soap maker is I usually smell good. Beats mahogany sawdust any time.'

She felt his laugh vibrate through his body as she pressed her cheek against the hot cotton of his shirt. He was lean and muscular and wholly exciting. The sexual frustration left her dry-mouthed. She could happily stay like this forever.

CHAPTER 21

JULY 2018

Nathan came back to Tenpenny House. The hot sunshine and the sickly ice cream had them craving tea. Feeling wired, Beth led him up to the flat, trying to remember what state she'd left it in. On the beach, Nathan's sexiness had been a siren call and she could feel her stomach fluttering, not unpleasantly, in anticipation. As they entered the sitting room, she blew out a breath in relief. It was tidy and, better still, Frank hadn't appeared to have done any damage in her absence. After winding around her legs and crying piteously, she fed him his disgustingly stinky food, flicked the kettle on and emerged from the kitchen to find Nathan staring out of the tiny window of the sitting room at Clappers Lane and down to the sea. Jittery, her nerve endings on fire, she admired the length of his lean body. What would it be like to have it wrapped around hers?

Nathan appeared to have his mind on other things. 'It's an extraordinary view,' he said dampeningly. 'Can't have changed since this building was built.'

Beth's libido dulled a little. 'Apart from the roadworks.'

'Apart from them.' He looked around, at the heavily beamed

wall studded with nail marks, at the beam that split the sloped ceiling in two. Shifting his weight, he winced at the creak of the uneven floorboards. 'It's very atmospheric.' Looking at her intently, he asked, 'Do you ever get freaked out being here alone?'

If only you knew. 'Sometimes,' she admitted. This wasn't going quite as she'd hoped. *Kiss me*, she willed him in her head. 'At least now I have Frank to blame for any unexplained noises,' she blurted out. *Go, Beth. Sexy talk!*

'Have there been many?' Nathan's eyes narrowed. 'You said you hadn't been sleeping well.'

Beth put a hand to her throat. She could sense the rough rope from her nightmares eating into her tender skin, scratching it raw. 'I'm sure it's just stress. Florence has given me some tea to drink. That'll probably help. And I'll start looking after myself properly. Eat better, cut down on all the caffeine, alcohol, that sort of thing,' she said, wishing he'd be less the doctor and more the man. She was definitely getting friend vibes. Concerned vibes but nothing more. The disappointment hollowed her out.

'All excellent things to do.' He gave her a mild look. 'Or you could just take the sleeping pills.'

Beth's phone rescued her from having to answer. As a seduction scene, it hadn't gone exactly to plan. Seeing who was ringing, she said, 'Excuse me, I must take this.'

'No problem. Shall I make the tea? That's if you don't mind me poking about in your kitchen.'

'Thanks.' Beth fled into her bedroom, swearing under her breath in frustration. Taking the call from her brother-in-law, she snapped out, 'Steve, hi.'

'Beth, you okay?' he said, sounding taken aback.

Forcing herself into politeness, she answered, 'Sorry. I'm fine. Just a bit of a day.'

'Ah. Haven't long. End of term stuff taking over. Just catching five at lunchtime. Got some news on your review troll.'

A gulp snatched in her throat. Steve never wasted words and, for once, Beth was glad he got straight to the point.

'The vast majority of the really nasty stuff all stems from the same IP address,' he continued.

'The what?'

'It's the address that identifies which computer is sending the message.'

'It's only one person?' Beth felt the room spin. She let out a shuddering breath. 'So can you tell me who's trolling me?'

'That I can't.'

With shaky legs, Beth perched on the edge of the bed, disappointment flooding her. She'd come so close to finding out.

'But I can tell you the rough area where the computer in question is. It's on the outskirts of Exeter. On the east side.'

'You can't be more specific?'

'Really sorry. That's all I'm able to find out. I did dig out some legal advice about online trolling though. I'll ping it through.' In the background someone called his name. 'Got to go. Ring me later if you'd like to talk more.'

Beth said thanks but the line went dead; Steve had already rung off. She tapped the mobile on her palm, thinking hard. She knew quite a few people who lived in the area he'd mentioned. And she couldn't imagine any of them wanting to ruin her business. Her phone vibrated as Steve sent the email through as promised.

Going back into the lounge she saw Nathan had made the tea, found a packet of biscuits and was sitting on the sofa with Frank kneading at his stomach, purring like a tractor. The scene was purely domestic. Any hopes for a sexy afternoon shrivelled. Besides, she had other things on her mind now.

'Always thought of myself as more of a dog person but think I'm converted,' he said as Frank headbutted his hand.

'Looks like he's taken to you too.' Beth collapsed onto the sofa and poured the tea. Nathan had made it the old-fashioned way in her one and only teapot. She handed over a mug and drank half of hers in one go, clattered it back on the coffee table and lay back with a sigh.

'Bad news?'

'Good news. Sort of.'

'That's clear as mud then.'

Beth gave a short laugh. 'Sorry. Didn't mean to be enigmatic. That was my brother-in-law. He promised to look into the background of all that horrible trolling.'

'I remember you mentioning it.' Nathan sipped his tea thoughtfully. 'Still coming in then?'

'Oh yes. If anything, it's got even more vitriolic.'

He shook his head. 'It's crazy. Why would anyone do such a thing?'

Beth blew out a breath. 'Beats me. Steve couldn't identify exactly who's been doing it, but he tracked it down to one computer in Exeter. Looks like it's one person who's on a mission to destroy my business.'

Nathan put his mug down and returned to stroking an ecstatic Frank. 'Tough thing to deal with.' He frowned. 'Why, though? Why would anyone want to do this? Has your brother-in-law got any ideas on how to combat it?'

'He sent me this through.' Beth scrolled down the email Steve had sent. '"Keep track of any online mentions using an automated search engine tool",' she read out. 'That's an idea. I don't currently use one.' She sat up. '"Respond to any complaints calmly and provide evidence to back up your counter argument". That's interesting. I've been studiously ignoring all the comments as I thought it would just fan the flame. You know, give the reviewer the attention they crave.'

'I've no idea about any of this I'm afraid, but it sounds a good strategy,' Nathan said ruefully. 'At the surgery we have set procedures we have to go through, but it's all dealt with by the office staff. It all sounds time-consuming though, Beth.'

'You're not wrong there, but I suppose I have to look on it as an investment of my time to create a good online image.' Beth's brows rose as she read on. 'It says further down to "seek legal advice, which might provide damages, injunctions or formal apologies".' She pulled a face. 'Sounds serious.'

'And expensive.'

'Isn't getting anyone legal involved always expensive?' She concentrated on the email again. 'Oh, here's some stuff I can do preventatively. "Create positive content".' Pulling a face, she added, 'Thought I was doing that. "Share any content that highlights my strengths". Suppose I could add in a few pages on the site quoting some positive reviews. As well as the vile stuff, some customers have been really appreciative. They've even sent photos showing my soaps in action. Those would look good up on the site.'

'Feel better?'

Beth looked at him questioningly.

'You were very pale when you came in.'

'Well,' Beth shook her phone gently, 'this gives me something practical to work on, which appeals. But I still don't know who it is who wants to destroy everything I'm trying to achieve. It's a really horrible thought that someone out there is sitting in front of their computer right now planning the next message. It's so random but incredibly hurtful.'

'Chances are that it *is* someone completely random and not an orchestrated campaign.'

Beth put her phone down with a sigh and reached for her

mug. Nursing it, she said, 'Has the same effect though, doesn't it? Eats away at my self-belief and dents confidence in the business. It doesn't help that I'm nowhere near established yet.'

'Show me your website,' Nathan said decisively. 'Let's have another look at these comments.'

She picked up her phone again and passed it to him, watching as he read down the list of vitriol.

He bit his lip, then said, 'A lot of these are complaints you can respond to, aren't they? Like the ones about a possible allergic reaction. And the one about the soap not lathering up well. I assume that's because of how it's made?' He glanced up at her.

'Yup. All my ingredients are natural. I don't add any detergents, so my soaps won't froth like commercially made ones.'

'That would be a good thing to put. It's a positive too, isn't it, that your stuff is unique and not mass produced, and completely natural.' He shrugged. 'I mean, I know diddly-squat about all this, so it's an objective opinion but–'

'But helpful. Thank you. Although you need to read on for the worst stuff.'

He read down the reviews and flinched. 'Jeez, I think "Miss Most Dissatisfied" needs to see her GP if her "undercarriage" is as uncomfortable as she's claiming.'

She stifled a laugh. 'Carry on reading.'

He did so, exclaiming, 'Beth, you can't leave these comments up!'

'I know, they're vile, aren't they?' She shuddered.

'They are. They really are. And it's encouraging others to join in. Look, the most recent review has twenty-odd responses.' He handed the phone back. 'They're about other products not purchased from you but it's all adding fuel to the fire.'

Beth read the latest missive and blanched. '"Gross. Blocked

drain. Discusting. Don't buy from this rip-off site. Made me smell sweaty and made skin break out. Over-priced rubbish. Cannot espresss my dissdain". It's the same person. I recognise the appalling spelling.' She sighed. 'I thought, if I ignored it all, whoever is doing it would get bored at not getting a reaction and go away.'

'Have you a way of previewing comments before they go up?' Nathan looked concerned.

'No, but Steve said as soon as term finished, he'd build a new site for me where I can have better control like that. I set this one up in a hurry and it's pretty basic. Until then, I think you're right, I'm going to have to delete everything. That doesn't take long but monitoring the site will.'

'I think, as you said, it might be time worth investing. Take these stupid comments down. They're not informative or in any way helpful, are they?'

'You're right. It's time I pulled my big girl pants on and dealt with it. I've been letting it slide for too long.' Her phone pinged another email through. Not really concentrating, she opened it and clicked through to the link. Rearing back, she threw the phone down. It thumped onto the rug. Pressing a hand to her mouth, vomit rose in her throat.

'What is it? Beth, what's the matter?' Picking up the phone, Nathan glanced at it. His face paled. 'Jesus. What is this?'

'I don't know but it's not me.' She pointed a quavering finger at the phone. 'Please, please believe me, that is not me on that porn site.'

CHAPTER 22

JULY 2018

Beth covered her face with her hands and rocked to and fro. She couldn't rid her mind of what she'd just seen. The tangled limbs, the nakedness. The link had taken her through to some kind of porn site. And while the body doing unspeakably hardcore things wasn't her, the face of the woman undoubtedly was. The revulsion rippled through her, turning her insides liquid. Leaping up and sending Frank scattering, she ran to the bathroom and was sick. Sitting huddled in front of the toilet, questions scrambled her brain. With shaking hands, she stood and splashed cold water on to her face. In the bathroom mirror, her face was haggard. Who was doing this? Why? How? 'Who hates me this much?' she muttered to her ashen reflection.

She stumbled into the sitting room and collapsed onto the sofa, trembling. 'I can't get warm,' she stammered through chattering teeth. Vaguely, she was aware of Nathan leaving.

He returned with the duvet from her bed. He lifted her legs and put them on the arm of the sofa. Settling the cushions behind her back, he tucking the duvet round her. 'You've had a shock.'

He disappeared again and this time returned with a scalding

hot mug of tea. Wrapping her hands around it, he said, 'Drink it. It's disgustingly sweet but it'll do the trick.' He sat on the floor, caressed Frank and lapsed into silence.

Beth lay, sipping the tea – Nathan was right, it was disgusting. Gradually the shaking subsided and she could feel warmth flowing through her veins. Her mind, though, wouldn't stop racing. Unpleasant online reviews were one thing and something she could control but having this splashed all over the net was... she couldn't pin down *what* it was. Her sense of worth fragmented, shattered. The thought that people were leering over the image was revolting. And everyone knew once something was up on the net, it stayed there.

Trembling again, she jolted up, spilling tea. 'Oh God, what if people I know see it? They'll think it's me. You don't think it's me, do you? It's not, I promise you.' For some reason it was important to hammer home the fact. Weirdly, she wondered if, at some point in her youth, when drunk, she had taken part in something like that. Had allowed photos of herself to be taken. Wracked with uncertainty, she thought back to her university days. While they'd all liked a drink or two, she couldn't think of one occasion when she'd been so drunk she hadn't known what was happening. Their little group of three, Jade, Hugh and herself, had always looked out for one another. It had been a promise they'd made when palling up in freshers' week. With student union alcohol being all too temptingly cheap and the horrors of spiked drinks, the risk was ever present. Banding together, they'd looked after each other. They'd been such good friends. But the self-doubt lingered even though she was certain she'd never done anything like in the picture, let alone been photographed. A sob threatened but Beth refused to give in to self-pity. It wouldn't get her anywhere. 'You don't think that was me, do you?' she repeated.

Nathan looked up in concern. 'Of course I don't. It's clear what's happened.'

'Then tell me because I sure as hell don't know.'

'I think someone has stolen your photos off somewhere. You've a Facebook account?'

Beth nodded, the tears threatening again. 'One page for the business and a personal one. But I hardly ever use that. It's just to keep in contact with old friends from uni and Mum sometimes. She occasionally puts up a pic from the most recent exotic place she's in. Do you think they've got the photos from Facebook?'

Nathan scrubbed a frustrated hand over his hair. 'It's a possibility.'

'Bastards!'

'I mean, I'm no tech expert but I'm assuming it's an easy enough thing to Photoshop the face of one person onto the body of another. The bigger mystery is who's done this and why. Have you got any enemies? Any aggrieved exes?'

She shook her head. 'The only serious relationship I had ended when we split up after graduating. He went to work in the States and when he came back, he married my best friend. They've...' She drew in a tremulous sigh. '...they've just had a baby. Hugh,' she hesitated, feeling her face heat, 'took a few pictures of me in the nude and wouldn't delete them but I'm certain he wouldn't do something like this. He's too straight, too boring.' As she said it, she realised how true it was. Hugh was a nice bloke but ever so slightly dull. He wouldn't even know the phrase deepfake porn. 'I can't think of anyone else who would want to do this.'

'And your privacy is locked down, on Facebook, I mean?'

'Yep. Only friends. And my friends list is private. Honestly, Nathan, I'm hardly on it. Don't have time. Would rather read a book.'

'Me too.' He sighed. 'But it figures that it's likely a friend of yours as they'd have access to your pictures. Scary stuff.'

Beth thought again of all those men salivating over the image. She swallowed. 'It's terrifying.' It came out as a tiny whisper, and she hated it. Hated what this was doing to her.

He reached out a hand and held hers. 'I'm loath to suggest this but you've got to have a look at the photograph they've used.'

'Why?' Beth stared at him, wide-eyed, not believing he could say such a thing.

'To see if you recognise the one they've stolen. I wouldn't advise reading any of the comments loaded below,' he added gently.

'Why?' she repeated, stupidly.

'They're vile, Beth, trust me you don't want to look. I can make a note of the website but I need you to examine the picture. And then we can file it away somewhere but keep it as evidence.'

She shook her head violently. 'I just want it gone.'

'Not sure that's wise.'

'Why?' It seemed the only word she could muster.

He grimaced. 'Because I think it's time you got the police involved. You probably don't want to right now but when you've had time to think it through, I really think you need to report it. Are you up to that?'

She nodded. Taking her phone, she forced herself to stare at the image, concentrating as best she could on her face. She was almost certain it wasn't one Hugh had taken; the angle and lighting was all wrong. Then flicking over to Facebook, she scrolled through the pictures on there. 'There's nothing that matches,' she wailed in frustration. 'There are hardly any pictures of me on there. I'm not keen on selfies.'

'Then we definitely need to contact the police. I think you'll be able to do it online. Up to it? The sooner you do it, the faster they can track down these sites and get those images removed.'

'Can they do that?' Beth brightened.

Nathan huffed out a short breath. 'If I'm really honest, I don't know but I think we need to press hard for it. Want me to hang around while you do it?'

Beth gave a quick grateful nod. 'Yes please.' She'd never been in a position where she'd wanted someone else around. For most of her life she'd relied on herself to get by. But now it felt good to have the strong and reliable Nathan to support her.

∼

After a frustrating hour, she'd finally been able to put in a report online, been given a case number and the promise that Devon and Cornwall Police would follow up. Beth felt slightly calmer, less frayed around the edges. Her brain was working better. She supposed the initial shock had worn off. She knew, though, this was false optimism, doubting anyone could retract the image and she'd have to live with it. There was some comfort in that, in terms of porn, it wasn't too extreme, but it was bad enough.

Slumping back on the sofa next to Nathan and Frank, she sighed. 'I should have stamped down on all this online grot weeks ago. Think my brain's been fried by everything else that's been going on.'

'Like what?' Nathan ignored Frank's batting paw and twisted to face her.

'Nightmares. Uber stressed. Not sleeping. A weird...' she hesitated.

'Go on.'

'You'll laugh at me. It's so absurd.'

Nathan took her hand. 'I promise not to laugh at you. Trust me, I'm a doctor.'

That made her smile. 'I suppose you've heard most things before.'

'I probably have. It's what makes the job so fascinating. And frustrating.'

Beth looked up quickly. 'Why frustrating?'

'Sometimes there isn't an easy explanation or remedy.'

She bit her lip, ridiculously on the verge of tears again. Taking in a deep, shuddering breath, she chided herself to get a grip. 'I think that's the case with me.'

'So tell me what's been going on. What's *really* been going on. I've a hunch it's more than not sleeping.'

She fixed him with a stare. 'Promise you won't laugh?'

He lifted his hand from where it was caressing Frank and crossed his fingers. 'Scout's honour.'

'Were you ever a scout?'

'Nope.'

This almost made her laugh. She gave a resigned shrug. 'Okay then. Here goes.' Shaking her head a little, she added, 'Even as I'm saying this, I can't quite believe I'm telling another human being.' His grip on her hand tightened. 'It's quite possibly fantastical nonsense but here goes. So, I've been dreaming a lot. I think it all started when the spell bottle and the knife handle were found in the chimney. I wanted to know more about them so got googling about witches.'

'I remember you saying you'd been doing some research.'

'I also went back to see Bill and she told me about...' her voice faltered, 'about a witch trial *here* in Flete. About what they did to this poor old woman who was probably just a wise woman.' She met his eyes. 'A healer like you. I've got a bit obsessed with the torture they inflicted on these women, I suppose. It's made the nightmares more vivid, more real.' Her hand strayed to her throat. 'Sometimes I can even sense a rope, a noose around my throat. Tightening, strangling.' She risked another glance at Nathan but he was simply listening; intent but impassive. 'It gets worse. I think I see things. Nothing concrete: a shadow here, a tiny movement right at the corner of my eye. A sense that someone's standing behind me. Watching me.' She sucked in a deep breath and screwed up her face. 'I feel I'm being haunted. And I feel it's all connected to this house, to the things found in the chimney and...' she hesitated again, 'your book.'

'The book of recipes?'

Beth nodded. 'We both know it's more than that, though, don't we? It's a record of folk remedies, of cures, all mixed in with the more ordinary, more banal soap and hand cream recipes. It's as if someone was putting down a whole life of knowledge and wisdom. Some parts are almost impossible to decipher, as if the words had been scribbled down as quickly as possible so as not to lose the information. And I really think it's connected to this town.' She gazed around, almost fearfully. 'And probably even this house.'

Nathan chewed his lip as he pondered her statement. Eventually, he blew out a breath and answered. 'Jeez, Beth, that's a lot to process. As far as the book's concerned, I'm not sure how that can be. As far as I know my grandpa brought it over from the States with him when he settled here.'

'Well,' Beth said defensively, 'that's just a hunch.' There was a silence. Finally she broke it. 'And, about this other thing, me thinking I'm being haunted, what's the verdict, doc? Am I mad?' She let loose a nervous giggle. What must he be thinking? But then nothing ordinary had ever coloured this relationship, if that's what it was becoming. From the first fierce recognition of their attraction to this frenzy of witches and spell bottles, seventeenth century history and his ancestor's book. At least his hand still held hers; she couldn't have scared him too much.

'We don't use the term mad anymore but, for what it's worth, I don't think you are.'

'What should I do then? The lack of sleep is the worst. It's driving me crazy. I can't think straight, can't make simple decisions, my head's all over the place.'

Nathan let go of her hand and slid himself more upright on the sofa. An offended Frank jumped soundlessly from his lap and slunk off. 'Let's begin with the practical,' he began decisively. 'How long since your last eye check?'

Beth was startled. 'My eyes are fine. Twenty-twenty vision.'

'Have you been to an optician recently?'

'I can't remember.'

'That answers that question. Get yourself booked in for an eye test. I can recommend the one in town, they're very thorough. Is what Flo gave you working for your sleeplessness?'

Beth shook her head. 'Hasn't touched it. Neither has giving up wine and caffeine.' Looking guiltily at her mug of tea, she added, 'Well, I've almost given up caffeine.'

'It's in chocolate and hot cocoa too. And probably chocolate ice cream.'

'Well, that's just unfair!'

'I know, I know.' He grinned charmingly. 'All the nice things but that's the way it is, I'm afraid. I'm also afraid that sleep hygiene is a bit hit and miss and experimental to see what works for you. Getting the light levels right in your bedroom, the optimum temperature – the cooler the better – not drinking liquids too late so your bladder's not waking you up. That sort of thing. I can dig out a leaflet or some online advice if you like. Lavender helps some people but for others it acts as a stimulant. As I said, it's very hit and miss. Physical exercise can help. Getting active and out in the fresh air.'

'I should have stuck with my first instinct and got a dog. Not a pesky attention-seeking cat,' Beth said mournfully as Frank returned, nudging at her knee. 'And I suppose the next thing you'll say is take the sleeping pills.'

'I'd certainly advise those but as a last resort. What have you been prescribed? Zolpidem, wasn't it?'

Beth nodded. 'And I really don't want to take it.'

Nathan smiled ruefully. 'There comes a point where you have to weigh up which is worse, the insomnia or the side effects of a drug. And not everyone suffers from side effects. You may find it solves your problem without issue. And it's a short-term medication so you wouldn't have to take it for long.'

'What about my other problems, though? The seeing things, the feeling of persecution and paranoia?'

'Well,' Nathan said carefully, 'they could be a direct result of the lack of sleep. There's a reason why sleep deprivation is used as a torture method. It's pretty hardcore.'

'Or?'

'Or you could look into going down the analysis route, counselling, techniques for combating stress. Maybe a referral to a consultant psychologist.' He paused, seeming to think through his words. 'Or even get the clergy involved. A priest could do a blessing. Might be worth a try. There's no easy answer, I'm afraid. It's a case of eliminating possible causes.'

Mention of a psychologist had terror running through Beth. She lapsed into silence. In the distance the church bell rang out the hour. Seven o'clock. She and Nathan had been closeted up together in the flat for hours. 'Sounds like a long road,' she said eventually.

'I'm afraid it is. Beth, I'm sorry not to be able to give you a straightforward answer. I should really be cutting this conversation short and tell you to see your GP.'

'I would but I didn't find Dr Carmichael very... erm... understanding.'

'Try Dr Ekene. She's younger, new to the practice. Just

because you're registered with Carmichael doesn't mean you have to see him.'

'Thanks, I will. It might just be worth trying another GP,' Beth acceded. She couldn't go on like this for much longer. Despite Nathan's assurance that the words "going mad" weren't used anymore, she feared that was what was happening. 'Thanks for listening, Nathan,' she said awkwardly. 'It seems that's all you've done today. I've really unburdened onto you, rabbited on and on.'

He took her hand again. 'Hey, after what happened with that email, I was happy to help, not that I could all that much.'

'And you still haven't said what you're trying to make your mind up about.' It was good to get the conversation back on a normal footing.

Nathan shifted uneasily. 'It's a job. A sort of research post.'

Beth was surprised. 'Oh, that's good.'

'It could be. Earlier this year I would have said it was exactly what I wanted.' He shot her a burning look. 'Now I'm not so sure.' He let go of her hand.

'Why?' Beth found herself holding her breath again.

He gave her a troubled glance. 'It's in the States.'

CHAPTER 23

AUGUST 1660

'What do you do here, sir?'

Robert Lacey stood over Prudie's chair, watching her saw at rags with the old knife Susanna had found in the river. She put her basket down and hurried over, fear pooling in her stomach. Nothing good could come of having Robert Lacey in their house.

He bowed. 'Ah, Mistress Susanna. I come merely as a courtesy, to see how you fare.'

Blocking his view of Prudie, she cursed the old woman's busy fingers. She had lately become obsessed with using the ancient tool to whittle tiny human forms from scraps of firewood and she clothed them with rags. Susanna knew others would see the dolls, innocent in their manufacture, to have all the appearance of witches' poppets.

'And not to do your wife's bidding again? What was she doing out and about and not yet even churched? Making trouble for poor old women? You would do better to keep control of her, Master Lacey.' Fear made Susanna's mouth run wild. She put a hand behind her back and found the old woman's shoulder. She squeezed it comfortingly. It had been the Laceys' doing that had ruined the good woman's mind and put pay to their livelihood, but it would do no good to risk one of the old woman's rants.

'And you would do better to hush your mouth when speaking to your betters.' Eyes narrowed, his breathing quickened. In anger? In lust? Coming closer, he added, 'But you were never frightened of me, were you, Susie?' He ran a finger down her cheek.

She could smell the clean linen of his shirt, the leather of a saddle, the stench of horse, the faint whiff of mud on his boots. All the scents that made the man. She did her best not to flinch. Perhaps she should seek out Barnabas and beg him to take her to Virginia. She needed to escape this man. He had a strange effect on her. Her chin rose. 'I have no fear of you, Robert Lacey. I never did as a child and I certainly don't as a woman.'

Sweat glistened on his brow. 'Then perhaps you ought to. You had better mind what you say to me, Susanna. For I have the power to shut you in the lock-up too.' Although his words were threatening, his tone was mild. He hooked a thumb under her chin, forcing her to look him in the eye. 'You have much to be grateful to me, Susie,' he crooned. 'For it was I who paid off the gaoler and persuaded my good wife not to take her accusations to the courthouse. Otherwise, your Prudie would be dangling from a rope by now. Do I not get a show of gratitude?'

'I have nothing for which to be thankful to you or your family.' Susanna met his gaze boldly, refusing to back down although her insides had gone to liquid. 'Your wife is the cause of all our undoing. Prudie went to her childbed in good faith and administered to her as well as anyone, indeed far better.' His thumbnail was scratching at her throat but she stayed resolute. What had she to lose? If he decided to kill her now, then so be it. 'Babies die, tis God's will. Thank the Lord your wife is yet healthy and able to bear more children. Tis God's will wives die in childbed too. You need to show thanks to the Lord that He spared your wife. You will go on to have an heir yet, Robert Lacey.'

Menace, and something else Susanna couldn't identify, hung hot and heavy in the air. She tried to quell her panicked breathing. What had he in mind? To despoil her? To kill her? To accuse her of witchcraft too and let the justices rid him of his problem? For a long moment they stayed in position, the only sounds Prudie's stentorian breathing as she sat oblivious and the crackle of the flames in the inglenook. Susanna watched as emotions chased over his features: pride, fury, desire. Then desolation.

His eyes flickered and to her utmost astonishment, welled with tears. Releasing her and turning away, he collapsed on the bench. Throwing his hat upon the table, he called out gruffly, 'Ale, fetch me ale.' He covered his face with his hands, his shoulders heaving in unmanly fashion.

Alarmed, Susanna filled a pint pot of ale and slid it along the table to him. She observed from a safe distance while he struggled to get his blubbing under control. She had never seen a man cry before. Not even John when news of Thomas's death came to their door. Perching on the very edge of the bench opposite, she waited.

'I only wanted a son, Susanna. A son to be heir to all I have made. To see us into this glorious new age with our new monarch. I even named him Charles in the king's honour. I had thought to see him thrive and grow. Play in the meadows, make sport with a spaniel. Learn how to hunt and shoot and ride. And all that has been taken from me.' He groaned piteously. 'Agnes refused to feed him herself, you know. I told her, tried to convince her it was the fashion in London now, to nurse your own child and many highborn women were doing it, even the ones at court. She tried and failed. Said it made her bubs sore and ail. Said feeding her own child was abhorrent. Persuaded me if she did not feed him herself it would hasten the quickening of our other children in her womb.' He slammed a fist onto the table. 'She failed at making our son flourish and thrive. Then he took agin the wet nurse's breast and he withered as I watched, unable to do anything. Now Agnes is a shrew and will not let me upon her. I need to beget another child in her, I need children to continue my name.' He drank a great draught of ale and wiped his mouth roughly.

Susanna sat silent. She could not guess his mood, could not frame the right words. The wrong ones might provoke an attack upon her, but to be too sympathetic an ear would surely act as an invitation. She wanted nothing to do with Robert Lacey but he was in her house and he was her problem to deal with. She was a woman alone now. Prudie too old and weak to help and Barnabas absent.

If only the Laceys had reached out to Prudie, the thought came unbidden. She could have helped, fed the child nourishment, given a tincture of motherwort, even found a new wet nurse. But they hadn't. Agnes had chosen, instead, to fire her anger and heartache into accusations of the most grievous kind. 'You are heartsick, Robert,' she began quietly, 'and Agnes is grieving her first-born babe. It has made her mad. But time will heal your hurt. Eventually you will have more sons, other children. They will not replace little Charles but will help you grow a family, a happy family. And yes, continue your name.'

He raised his head and stared at her, his face ravaged by tears and grief. 'I thought I loved Agnes. I thought it to be a love match as well as a suitable one. Her face is pretty and her ways were pleasing but as soon as the ring was put on her finger she turned. She welcomed me into her bed but grudgingly, even on our wedding night. Indeed, I have had more pleasure in Mrs Pettit's house.'

Susanna winced, feeling a reluctant pang of pity for Agnes.

Many a husband brought disease to their marriage bed from the bawdy house. Many a highborn woman had sought Prudie's hop flower to expel the poison of the French disease. And many of them had taken her lady's mantle water to aid conception. She and Prudie had oft seen a pattern. First a desperate plea to rid them of their husband's pox followed by an equally desperate desire to bear him a child. Had they more faithful husbands who kept their wick dry and untainted, then maybe encouragement to conceive would not be necessary. The pox was well known to make a manhood diseased and droop. She turned her attention back to Robert. He was speaking again. A great ramble of self-pity.

'I should have wed you, Susanna. You would have been lusty in my bed and bore me healthy sons.'

She suppressed a laugh bordering on hysteria. She eyed him, a little of her fear draining away. He had aged since their encounter by the river. Worry and grief had etched lines into his handsome face and there was even a touch of grey in his beard. He'd been her childhood friend; she'd once thought him her enemy. Perchance he still was. She didn't know what to think – or how to interpret his moods. 'That would never have been accepted in the eyes of society,' she began cautiously. 'You are so much higher born than I.'

'And what? I could not have risen you up to meet me?' He drank some ale and slammed the pot back onto the table. 'The tattlers would have forgot soon enough, Susie.'

Aye, she thought. They would not have dared to speak in front of a Lacey but to his lowborn wife they would not have been so kind. She considered what it might be like to be married to such a man. To live in a grand house such as Lacey Manor, to dine on pheasant and freshwater fish, to wear silk next to her skin. She wondered if he was a kind lover. The image of his poor horse as he had snatched at her reins and dug his heels into her flank that day at the riverbank decided her. 'You have a wife,' she said, keeping her voice level. 'There is no other in the eyes of God and the church.'

'Yes,' he groaned. 'I have a wife. And such a wife. Screaming like a banshee at old women in the street. Her feral moods have but increased since the death of Charles. I do not understand her anymore.' He glowered at Susanna, his nostrils flaring. 'As her husband it is my right to take her to bed even if she struggles and swoons and weeps upon my shoulder, but I cannot do it. To see her wail so shrivels my desire.'

Susanna felt her face heat. She had no wish to think of Agnes used in such a way, even if it was a husband's due. 'Visits to Lucia Pettit's bawdy house will not help you get a son, Robert,' she said tartly. 'At least, not one to which you can own.'

He smoothed his beard and moustaches down. 'It will not but it helps *my* madness. It helps me forget.' He sounded almost sulky.

'I am sorry for you.' Susanna couldn't believe the words left her mouth. But she was. She was sorry for Robert Lacey. For all his wealth and power, he was lost.

After draining his pint pot, he answered gruffly, 'You must be careful, Susie.' Again he glared. In an abrupt change of mood, he added, 'I cannot promise to control what my wife says or who she accuses and you have enough enemies in Flete to take delight in your downfall.'

Was this a warning, or a veiled threat? 'That's as maybe but we have allies too. Besides, has not your adored king signed an oath to forgive all those who trespassed against him in the war?' Sarcasm dripped from her tongue.

'He has. He has vowed to make people forgive and forget. He is all for tolerance, I wish you could see that.'

'Aye, tolerance is easy when you have won. And easier still if you wear the best fur and gold and sit upon a throne being fed sweetmeats. What loss has he known, when the Tenpennys lost the good, bright boy that was Thomas?' She clamped a hand over her mouth. Her words were leading her into dangerous territory.

'No one was sorrier than I to hear of Thomas's death.' He leaned forward. 'But twas Thomas's decision to go and fight. He died for the cause he believed in, as many men did, on *both* sides.'

'And yet you did not venture onto a battlefield. You profess to admire men who fought for Cromwell but could not bring yourself to fight for your beloved crown!'

Robert thumped the table again. 'I had responsibilities here!' His cheeks flushed. Anger? Shame?

'But you would want Prudie to give up the cause her son died for? She lost her son just as you and Agnes have lost a son, but at least yours was but a babe and had not grown to be a much-loved man.' Exhaustion made her tongue sharp.

Pain heated his eyes. 'In Charles, I lost a son. In Thomas, I lost a friend. And yes Charles was only beginning his life but he was loved too.'

His tone was so tragic, it leached the anger from her. 'I am sorry.' Susanna hung her head. She had gone too far. 'Of course you loved Charles.'

He looked away before getting himself under control. 'Can you not see? Is it beyond your wits to realise that I am trying to help you and Prudie?' Nostrils flared; he drew in a breath. 'There are factions,' he began, slowly and deliberately, 'your so-called allies, in this town that would use Prudie as an excuse to rise up in rebellion. John and Thomas were held in high esteem–'

'I know that,' she interrupted.

'But don't you see, Susie, we're fighting a new battle but a far more subtle one. It is not fought on the battlefield, but in men's hearts and minds. We...' he paused and corrected himself, '...*I* must needs persuade Flete that the new king is good and true, and they must forget their old ways and embrace the new.'

Susanna darted a look at Prudie. She supposed his words made sense. In truth she was tired of politics. It made little difference to her who ruled. Her life was one of petty drudgery whether a common man or God's appointed king sat in power. Prudie, however, even though now feeble brained, would never give up the Lord Protector.

Robert followed her look and harrumphed. 'And that is the crux of my problem with you and with Prudie. You must see I cannot tolerate any anti-king thinking, and that would surely rise if they saw you being persecuted. I have to rout out the parliamentary men and their spies. They are too many and cause too much trouble. We cannot risk them rising to power again. We must defeat them entirely.'

A quiver ran through Susanna.

Robert leaned back, calmer now. 'It would do you service to swear allegiance to King Charles. I cannot and will not see parliamentary uprisings in Flete.'

For the first time Susanna met his gaze directly. 'Is that the reason why you paid for Prudie's freedom? To quell a Protectorate riot?'

He huffed. 'She was lucky I got to the gaoler in time and that he's an easily bribed man. As it was, I was too late to stop that butcher witchfinder Matthias Finch. But I warn you, my influence is spent beyond the town court. If it gets as far as the Exeter Assizes, I can do nothing. I have little power in the city. I warn you again, Susanna, and in the strongest terms, if Agnes decides to take her accusations to be heard again, Prudie is as good as hanged.' He nodded to the poor creature dozing by the fire, oblivious to the high emotion in the room. Robert's lips thinned. 'I saw the poppets she was making. And the knife with its devil's marks on the handle.'

'Then you had better curb your wife's tongue and get her with child as soon as possible,' Susanna bit out, the dread fear returning and making her words sharp. 'Maybe it will turn her thoughts back to more wholesome notions rather than tormenting our family.'

A smile played about Robert's mouth. 'Always so fierce, so defiant. I am right. You would be an ardent companion in bed.'

'But not yours.'

He sighed and looked down. 'Not mine.'

Susanna wondered if he had the fight within him to attack her, but defeat had taken hold and his shoulders drooped. Mercy Prentice was right; he was a weak man. And worse, he was a weak man in a position of power over a town that was still in turmoil. She didn't envy him one bit. He rose, straightened to his full height and replaced his hat with its extravagant curling feather. He was assuming the mantle of a Lacey in front of her eyes and the strange little interlude seemed to be over.

She stood too, refusing to be in the weaker position of sitting below him. He came to her and held her shoulders. Was she about to suffer for witnessing his brief show of feebleness? Her brain ticked over in a frenzy. What to do, what strategy could she employ should he decide to take her? How near was Prudie's knife? Could she edge towards the fireplace and snatch it? He was so close she could feel the heat from his body as his fingers dug into the wool of her waistcoat.

Breathing roughly, he stared down at her. 'I hear you are to Virginia.'

Her mouth fell open in shock. It was the last thing she expected him to say. How did he know? She had no breath to put him right as his next words astounded her even more.

'Then you will be in need of funds,' he continued briskly. 'So I will take Job off your hands.'

Susanna began to shake. 'You cannot take our horse!'

'He is a nag. Not much left in him to be of any employ. And you'll need the money more.'

She couldn't follow his logic. Why, when he considered Job of no use, did he want to buy him? 'But how am I to take goods to market?'

'You are to be affianced to the smith.' He nodded curtly, avoiding an answer. He pressed nearer and she braced herself for the onslaught, but he only dropped a kiss on top of her cap. 'You will be in need of money for the Americas. Take my advice, Susanna, go, take your escape route. I cannot promise to be able to protect you further here.'

And, with that, he swept out.

CHAPTER 24

AUGUST 1660

Susanna trudged along Clappers Lane. Although not hot, the day was clammy and humid and sweat beaded underneath her coif. Irritability added to her unease. Where had the old woman gone?

She'd awoken to an empty, still house, even the fire had burned low. With no time to stoke it, she'd rushed out to find Prudie. Disaster was coming; she sensed it.

Searching along the lane, holding her nose against the stench of the tannery and the alehouses and nearly being knocked senseless by a rooting sow got loose, she came to the crossroads and the ancient cross that stood there. Her heart thumped in her throat. Further on was Market Street and the square, surely a woman as frail as Prudie could not have got so far? As she neared the stone, yelling and jeering filled the sky. As she turned into Cross Street, she saw a crowd gathered outside the Flowers' cottage. Susanna picked up her skirts and ran, splashing through a great pile of steaming dung. She saw, to her horror, young Ned Flowers and his mother Katherine baying over Prudie who crouched low.

'You took plague into that house.' A gobbet of spit

accompanied Katherine Flowers's venom. It sailed through the air, thankfully landing short. She scoured her mouth and rubbed her hand on her apron. 'And if the plague didn't kill that babe, your hexing did!'

'You've made my cows dry, you whore!'

'Devil's harlot.'

'I seen a mock a pie fly into Tenpenny Cottage. I seen it with my own eyes. Tis the devil in bird form summoned by the witch!' Anne, their neighbour, cried.

'Witch!'

'My grass has died,' Samuel Thatcher, Hal's father, yelled. 'It's been cursed. What has I to feed my animals come winter?'

'She put a curse upon Elias Light,' Ned shouted. 'I saw him weaken and he is still abed.'

'Aye,' screamed his mother. 'The boy's full of sores and fever. She did that. I heard theys had a blackamoor visit an all. That's the devil come a calling. Reckon he sucked her bubbies!'

A rock flew and Prudie staggered. Falling back against the cob wall, she hit her head.

'Let me through,' Susanna cried, fear making her voice shrill. 'Let me pass. In the Lord's name, let me get to her. Have you no shame, Anne? Prudie is your neighbour, she has been a good and true friend. What nonsense about a magpie do you talk?' She shoved at Samuel Thatcher. 'Let me get through, I tell you.'

'I saw the devil's imp fly in the window,' Anne, puce-faced and furious spat out. The mob behind jeered their agreement. 'That was the devil himself in magpie form!'

'And to add to this lie are you to say Cat is also a devil's imp?' Susanna gasped as Samuel took hold of her. Gripping her in his strong farmer's hands, he pinned her arms to her side and grabbed her breasts painfully. 'Hal's apple didn't fall far from the tree, did it, Samuel Thatcher?' she yelled, kicking him in the shins and feeling him wince as she made contact.

'Did ye hear that?' Katherine Flowers cried. 'She's admitted Cat is the devil's imp! Keep hold of her, Samuel. We'll hang them both.'

Samuel lisped into her ear from his mappy mouth, his breath foul and reeking of The Cock's sour cider. 'Aye, for where a witch lives, there lives another, Mistress Susanna. We've been watching you. Reckon Prudie did for her husband, aye and her son before him. My son arrested Prudie on suspicion of using witchery against the Lacey babe and she should have hung for it then. Trust me, won't be long before she dangles from a tree. Along with you, you little beauty, but not afore I've made good use of you.'

Susanna struggled desperately but his grip, fuelled by alcohol and vengeance, tightened. 'You always were a king's man, weren't you, Samuel,' she spat. 'And now you're arse-licking the Laceys.' From the corner of her eye, Susanna could see Prudie slumped against the wall, being kicked in the ribs by Ned Flowers. She aimed another kick at Samuel Thatcher's legs but her foot caught in her skirts and she missed.

'Aye. And I'd like to show you what a king's man does to a bitch who was against him.' His vile mouth closed in on her neck and he shoved a filthy hand down the front of her bodice.

'Let the wench go!' From nowhere a deep and authoritarian voice sounded.

'Ned, lay off and come here. He has a sword!' Susanna heard Katherine cry. 'And there's two more of them acoming.' Her voice held the sharp note of panic.

All at once the sword's point was at Samuel's chin, forcing his head high and exposing his throat. 'I said, sir, to let the Mistress Susanna go.'

Susanna flailed as Samuel let go. She fell to her knees in the street's mire, gasping for breath. She still felt Samuel's greasy nails digging into her breasts, pulling at her nipple, and didn't think she'd ever feel clean again. Into her ringing and befuddled ears she heard distant hooves galloping closer.

'Be off with you, man, before you feel the kiss of my broadsword,' her rescuer menaced.

Susanna lifted her head in time to see Samuel Thatcher run. In his wake, the crowd dispersed. A woman bent over Prudie, tending her. Thank the good Lord it was Mercy. The man who had saved her held out a hand. As she rose to her feet she had wits enough to see he wore a simple leather jerkin, a metal chest plate, and a wide sash around his waist. His head bore a broad-brimmed black hat. It was the old uniform. The uniform of the old war. Above his kerchief-covered mouth were wise and concerned eyes.

Two soldiers flanked him, bearing pikestaffs, and a third sat astride a fine bay horse, leading another horse, a grey.

The rider slid from his mount and led the grey over. 'Colonel, your horse.'

Susanna took her chance and ran to Prudie's side. 'Does she live?' she demanded. 'Mercy, is she dead?'

'No, she lives,' Mercy replied, tears streaming down her rounded cheeks. 'The old body has taken yet another beating, but she lives still.'

'Lift her up onto the horse,' the colonel ordered. 'We must get them home. Hurry! The constable's men may be near.'

The foot soldiers lifted Mercy astride the bay and then slung Prudie, non too gently, behind the pommel.

The colonel mounted his own horse, put a hand down to Susanna and pulled her up to sit behind him. They cantered down Clappers Lane, hooves ringing resoundingly out on the cobbles, with the foot soldiers running behind.

Susanna held on to the colonel for dear life, bumping and

sliding on the horse's glossy saddle. Once at the cottage, the soldiers carried Prudie in, gave harsh instructions to lock and bolt the door and jam furniture against it, and then melted away as quickly as they had appeared.

Mercy and Susanna carried Prudie to John's chair and then half lifted, half slid the heavy oak settle against the front door.

'It's all we can do.' Susanna wiped her hands down her apron and collapsed onto a stool, weak now the fight was over. Brushing away her dishevelled hair in a weary gesture, her fingers encountered her linen partlet, worn around her neck, and now ripped beyond repair. A result of Samuel Thatcher's rough dealings. A great shudder tore through her at what might have been. At what might come. Through clenched teeth she whispered, 'If the mob want to gain entry, they will. Fetch water from the scullery and we can bathe Prudie's wounds. I have some devil's-bit spare for her bruises.'

'Again.' Mercy shook her head sorrowfully.

'Again.' Susanna raised hopeless eyes to the woman. 'Why did Prudie go out? Why did she court trouble? We have enough at our door.' Letting go a breath, she added, 'Did you see what she did?'

Mercy shook her head. 'Only a little. I came upon it too late. She was shaking something at the Flowers family. Taunting them. Spitting out some words I could not hear.'

Susanna rose and went to Prudie. Eyes wild, she was muttering, her lips working. 'Hush, my dear. Hush. You're safe now,' Susanna lied. 'We'll have wine and the last morsel of the salted gammon presently. Maybe I'll make apple fritters. They're your favourite.' She bent closer to examine the swelling bruise on Prudie's cheek and saw she had something clutched in her hand, her knuckles white and clenched around it.

A rag doll.

Veering back in horror, she knew what had been shaken at

Katherine Flowers. Knew why the woman had been so furious and vindictive to Prudie. With difficulty, and ignoring the old woman's pitiful shrieks, she prised it out of her hold and threw it on the fire. It burned slowly, the fire was too low on wood. Slowly the little white face blackened and the flames caught the edge of her skirt, curling and singeing the scrap of material. A rancid smell arose from the greasy uncleaned wool used to stuff the body. It sickened Susanna and she clasped a hand over her mouth.

'Would I for Barnabas and the Americas, for there's no escape for us here now. We are doomed,' she whispered, tears prickling, her throat hollow with fear, the familiar tightening clutching at her neck. 'We are for the gallows.'

CHAPTER 25

JULY 2018

'So, Nathan is going to America,' Beth repeated to a staring Frank as she washed up the tea things with unnecessary force.

He'd left after a brief and stilted conversation. She hadn't taken in much detail.

'Mum and Dad are going over to visit family,' he'd said, 'and I've got the opportunity to do some research and work there. I could tag it onto a holiday.'

He'd gone on to explain it was funded by a medical exchange charity. Beth hadn't been able to focus properly, it had been a jumble of blurred words after the phrase "Leaving for the States". But "temporary" and "three years" jumped out.

She tipped the mugs upside down to drain, hardly believing the hollow disappointment that washed through her. She'd known him a matter of weeks and yet, from the first, had felt a vital connection. She recollected when she'd first seen him, across the waiting room at the doctor's surgery when he'd been talking so kindly to the old woman, what was her name? Mrs Davies, that was it. She remembered the feeling of her insides liquifying with longing for him. The attraction had slammed into her, leaving her breathless. It had made no sense then. Made none now. Never before had she reacted to another person in such a way. The sense of visceral recognition had been acute. Intense. Maybe, she forced a laugh trying for humour and startling Frank, she should have jumped his bones and got him out of her system. Somehow, though, she knew the more she had of Nathan Smith, the more she'd need.

It all seemed so long ago now. That first meeting. An eternity. With a jolt she realised it was only last month. It was ridiculous, she felt she'd had him in her life always. Everything else had dropped away; she'd occupied a claustrophobic, obsessive little world dominated by witches, spell bottles and – him.

Going to the tiny table in the sitting room, she slumped at it, watching as a gull caught a thermal and lifted away, the sun catching its white underbelly and its legs neatly pinned beneath. For a second the movement was repeated in several of the small panes of the old window at once creating a kaleidoscope of images. 'It's stupid,' she said to an oblivious cat. 'I have no hold over him, nor do I want it. Oh but, Frank, I hoped that this weird friendship, connection, *thing*, between us might develop into a relationship. But am I ready for one?' The cat answered by lifting his back leg and scratching his ear vigorously. Even if a relationship proper didn't happen and she could ignore the hard impatient tug of sexual desire that was ever present when she was near Nathan, she'd hoped for a friendship. She liked being around him. And she sensed it was mutual.

When Nathan had finished speaking, he'd watched her closely, waiting for a response. 'It sounds a really good opportunity,' she'd said limply. And, not long afterwards, he'd gone.

Beth put her head in her hands, thinking of her mother's wanderlust and feeling bereft all over again. The sense of abandonment was intense. Her mother had left her to travel the world. Hugh had left her for Jade. Now Nathan was repeating the pattern. What was it about her?

Her elbow nudged the recipe book. He'd forgotten to take it home. Sliding it closer, she picked it up and carefully turned the pages. They were familiar to her now, as were many of the concoctions. She admired the beautifully detailed plant drawings and the densely written words, the lettering with its loops and swirls. She laid it back on the table, smoothing her hand over the stained leather front cover. Then she picked it up again and weighed it in her hands. For the first time it struck her how heavy it was. It wasn't a chunky book, barely the thickness of her thumb, so maybe the weight came from the leather binding. She placed it on the table, front cover down, and lazily leafed through from the back; an old habit of reading books from childhood. Lorna had hated her doing it, questioning why she spoiled the book by risking knowing its ending. Beth had laughed at her sister, explaining she was impatient to know what happened and when she did, she could relax and enjoy reading how the plot panned out. She smiled at the memory, at their squabbles. Different with nonfiction, of course. They were made to dip into from wherever. Examining the back cover and its dark stain that travelled from corner to corner, she wondered what story it could tell.

'Where have you been, little book?' she murmured. 'What adventures have you had?' Lifting it up and flicking through from the back again, she stiffened. There was something here. Something different. Frowning, she looked closer. Yes, she was right, the last page was much thicker. A few pages of parchment seemed stuck together. Holding it so it was the right way round, she turned the pages slowly, comparing the weight and thickness of each page. When she came to the last, she examined it. Yes, definitely thicker. It bore the recipe for the lavender and chamomile hand salve she'd tried out. Weird. It was a repeat. And the only recipe to be repeated. The one she'd followed was near the front. Excitement mounting, she peered more closely. Running her fingertip over the surface of the page, she was almost certain she could feel a rectangular ridged shape in the centre. Subtle but unmistakable.

'It's almost as if there's something else in there,' she whispered in excitement to an uninterested Frank. 'Another page. Hidden.' Eyes wide, she turned to stare at the cat. 'What could it be? Another recipe? A spell?'

Two things were certain. The book belonged to Nathan and without his permission, she couldn't investigate further.

Frustrated, she put it down. She couldn't possibly mess with it. After all, weren't there recommendations about how you handled old books? She'd been careful with it whilst it was in her care but, even so, a book expert would probably throw their hands up in horror at how it had been treated. History documentaries featuring white gloves and weird links of heavy beads to hold books open at the required page came back to her. Sliding it to one side, she stared at it in horror. Had she damaged it by simply looking through? How would she explain that to Nathan? She let out a growl of exasperation.

Their easy camaraderie would be in jeopardy now he'd revealed his plans for the States. She had no choice but to back away. She couldn't risk her feelings when he was about to move halfway around the world. It had taken too long to heal after Hugh's behaviour and, even now, the hurt lingered. She let out a snort. Another man who had disappeared off to the US. A wave of loneliness engulfed her. She wondered how Hugh and Jade were getting on. Guilt snatched at her. She'd resolutely gone non-contact ever since the awful email and ensuing telephone call. She hadn't forgiven Jade her vitriol or her complacent excuses. Perhaps she should get in touch? Perhaps *they* should get in touch with her? They were supposed to be her oldest friends! Picking up her mobile, she tapped in a quick, noncommittal message asking how things were, then left texts with a couple of university friends in Exeter, suggesting drinks or a meet up for coffee. It would be good to get out of this seventeenth-century witchy, Nathan-dominated bubble.

Gazing round at her little sitting room, resolutely ignoring the quicksilver shadow that flitted at the corner of her eye, she glimpsed her laptop. There was one thing she could do to keep herself occupied and it would be useful too. Lifting the computer onto the table where it nudged up against the old book, she allowed herself a smile. Two types of technology four hundred years apart; they couldn't be more different. Opening up her laptop, she clicked on her website and began deleting all the poisonous comments. It felt good.

CHAPTER 26

JULY 2018

Four days later, Beth phoned Nathan and suggested she return the book. Had it been an awkward, stilted conversation, or had it been her imagination? He'd given her his address and she walked round to his house, clutching the book incongruously housed in a Tesco bag for life.

Standing outside the nondescript thirties semi, with its pebble-dashed exterior, she thought it looked cosy, a world away from Tenpenny House, and an unlikely home for one of Flete's most eligible bachelors. The front garden had been paved to provide a parking space. Nathan appeared to drive a new-plate black Golf. She was finding out more about him with this brief visit than ever before. There had been little ordinary about their previous meetings. Even the flirtiest conversation had taken place against the febrile background of history and witchcraft, not to mention the confessional about her childhood. She hadn't asked much about him at all. Trouble was, he was all too easy to talk to and an unusually good listener. It was peculiarly exciting seeing how he lived but she stamped down on it. After all, there was little point finding out about him if he wasn't going to be in her life. Her fiercely guarded and delicate heart needed protecting. The connection with Nathan had been instant and intense and, weirdly, she sensed her fate may have been entwined with him. But it was over. She'd drop the book back to him, explain what she'd found and go. It was all too depressing.

'Beth! Hi.'

Nathan appeared at a side gate. He was wearing linen shorts and a loose T-shirt. Her insides pooled with lust.

'Have you been standing there long. I'm so sorry, I was in the back garden.'

'No.' The reply was oppressive.

'Okay. I'm really sorry.' Stepping back, he added, 'Look, come in. Have a cold drink. It's warm today.'

'I've just come to bring your book back.'

He stared at her intently. 'I know but you can stay for something to drink, surely?'

Beth bit her lip. She needed to hand over the book and be gone but if she stayed maybe she could persuade him to look at the back pages. She might even discover the book's secret; it was too tempting. Besides, it was warm, and she'd got hot walking. 'Okay. Just for a while then, I'm very busy.'

His mouth quirked in humour as he led her along a narrow passageway at the side of the house. 'I'm sure you are. Come into the garden, it's shady here.' He showed her to a wrought iron table and chairs on uneven patio slabs and disappeared back through the French doors that must lead to the kitchen. Beth could hear him opening cupboards and clinking glasses. She was itching to go in and have a nose around but stayed resolutely where she was. The less she knew of Nathan Smith the easier it would be to forget him. She concentrated, instead, on the garden. It was small and rectangular with a lawn that sloped slightly upwards. One or two pots of geraniums were dotted about but, other than those, it gave off a faint whiff of neglect.

'I don't have much time to spend out here, Leah's always nagging me about it,' he said, returning and putting down a tray with large tumblers and a jug full of juice, rattling with ice.

'Leah?'

'My sister. Older. Bossy.' Sitting opposite her he poured. 'Home-made lemonade.' Noting her surprised look, he laughed. 'Not mine, I hasten to add. My mum's. It's her latest obsession. That and making disgustingly healthy smoothies.' He handed her a glass. 'This is good, though. Just the right amount of tartness and sugar.'

She sipped. He was right. In ordinary circumstances she might have asked about his mum, who sounded lovely, and why she was into making smoothies, or even about his sister and why she was so bossy, but she thought in the circumstances, it was better to stay mute.

'Are you all right, Beth?'

'I'm fine.' This was awkward. Horribly so. She ought to make conversation about something. Anything. 'I deleted all those horrible reviews and comments, by the way.'

'The ones off your website?'

She nodded.

'Good for you. I bet that was a great feeling.'

'It was. Cathartic.' She slid a sideways glance at him. 'If something's not working, it's good to cut it out of your life.'

'Absolutely,' he said cheerfully. 'Any come back? Any repeat reviews?'

Beth shook her head. 'I was a bit worried about that but nothing so far and it's been four days. Let's hope they've got bored with me and moved on.'

'And anything from the police in response to your report?'

'Nothing.' One reason she'd got so warm walking over was her choice of clothes. Normally, when this hot, she'd pull on a pair of cut-offs and a vest T-shirt. Now she wanted to hide her body. Her jeans and grey sweatshirt were anonymous and sexless. Changing the subject, she added, 'I enjoyed looking through the book, Nathan. It's fascinating.'

'Have you finished with it? I'm more than happy for you to keep hold of it a while longer if you want.'

'No.' She put her glass down and pushed herself back up the chair. 'Actually, I think there might be something hidden in it.' It was no good, she couldn't keep this chilliness going any longer. Clasping her arms around her in excitement, she blurted out, 'Oh, Nathan, I think your book has a secret!'

'A secret? What kind of secret?' He too put his glass down. Curiosity flushed his cheeks.

Beth rubbed her hands on her jeans. 'I was having a last look through and I began from the back.' She lifted the plastic bag and slid the book out onto the table.

'Weird way of reading a book.'

'That's what my sister always says. She can be a bit bossy too.' Beth grinned, seeing Nathan relax as she responded more like her normal self.

'And?'

'And I could feel a rectangular ridge on one of the back pages. Also, I'm pretty sure the last three or four pages are glued together.'

Nathan sat forward, excitement radiating off him. 'Well, what was it? What did you find?'

'I couldn't *do* anything to it. It's your book. I didn't want to be accused of, oh I don't know, historical vandalism or something.'

'Point taken. Let's take it inside and have a look, shall we?'

Beth nodded. Picking the book up and cradling it in her arms, she rose and went into the house. She hesitated until her eyes adjusted to the lack of bright sunshine and then followed him through a black and white, shiny modern kitchen, across a square hall with a parquet floor and into a dining room. It was dominated by a circular table, old-fashioned and of a deeply polished mahogany.

'My grandparents' dining-room table. Seems fitting we examine the book on it. Hold on for a moment, I'll find a cloth to put it on so it doesn't slip all over the place.'

'We might need a sharp knife too.'

He glanced at her, brows raised. 'Okay.'

'And could I wash my hands? They're all sticky from the lemonade.' She paused, embarrassed. 'I should really have considered this before, but I don't think we should touch it with greasy or sticky hands.'

He nodded. 'I'll go find a knife and wash my hands in the kitchen sink. There's a downstairs loo just over the hall.'

Crossing back over the hall, she sidestepped several pairs of running shoes and found the cloakroom. The sanitary ware was Germoline pink, and quite possibly original from the nineteen thirties. It made her giggle; she must be on the verge of hysteria. Washing her hands with Neal's Yard Geranium and Orange, she caught her reflection in the mirror. Flushed face, green eyes vivid and alive. What were they about to find out?

When she returned, Nathan was waiting for her, with what looked suspiciously like a scalpel in his hand. He waggled it. 'Left over from my days as a medical student. Scarily sharp. Show me where you think something's hidden.'

Her heart thumping, Beth turned the pages until she came to the last few. 'See how much thicker the pages are here.' She lifted them between finger and thumb. 'The parchment is so much more dense. I mean, it could be dodgy manufacture. I googled how it's made and it's treated and stretched very thin animal hide. The other pages could almost pass as paper but I remember Bill explaining it was parchment. Remember she said it was expensive and must have been a very precious object to its owner?'

Nathan nodded. 'To its original owner, maybe.' He laughed ruefully. 'I remember Dad saying my grandpa didn't value history overly much. I suppose he'd lived through too much of it.' Seeing Beth's confusion, he added, 'He went through the Sicilian campaign and then D-Day. Think he only wanted to look to the future, not dwell on the past.'

'Understandable.' She looked down at the book lying mysteriously on the table. 'He valued it enough to bring it over with him when he finally settled in Devon though.'

'Actually, I think it got shipped over from the States with a whole pile of his stuff in trunks.'

Beth didn't want to think about the States at the moment. 'But back to the book.'

'Of course.'

She showed him the ridge on the last page. When he peered closer, saying he couldn't see anything, she took his hand and directed his finger along the raised part of the parchment. Quelling the sexual attraction that was always present whenever he was near, she said, 'It's so subtle, so carefully hidden, you can hardly tell it's there. See how it's disguised by the pattern inked around the margins.'

'I really wouldn't have noticed if you hadn't pointed it out,' Nathan replied, breathing quickly. 'However did you spot it?'

Beth shrugged. 'I don't know, really. I was having an idle moment glancing through it and the first thing I noticed was it's a repeat recipe of one earlier. Why would there be two recipes the same? Bill said parchment was expensive, so why waste material repeating the same information? Then I looked closer and ran my finger over the page.' She stopped. 'I don't think I should have done that. It probably goes against all good practice. I noticed that this page is thicker and slightly raised in the middle, so I wondered if there's something underneath.'

'There's only one way to find out.' Nathan raised the scalpel.

Beth stayed his hand with a shaking one of her own. 'Do you think we ought to do this? Is it the right thing to do? Shouldn't we take it to a museum or something?'

Nathan considered her, still holding the scalpel aloft. 'It's my book. It belongs to me. Bill's seen it. She didn't say it was especially valuable to history, didn't have any great monetary value. Or I seem to remember she said that.'

'She said it was prized by its owner.'

'Then we'll treat it with respect but now you've suggested it might be hiding something, I won't be able to rest until we find out. Agreed?'

Beth nodded eagerly. 'Agreed.'

'But maybe video it on your phone or something? Then, if we commit the historical crime of the century, we've evidence we did it with care.' He noted her shocked expression. 'I'm joking. But it might be an idea to film it anyway. Will your phone do that?'

'Yes.' Beth reached into her back pocket and drew out her mobile. Setting it to record and hoping she could keep her shaking hands steady, she said, 'All set.'

Nathan flicked on a table light, and then, frowning in concentration, the tip of his tongue held between his lips, began to tentatively cut at the left-hand edge of the raised shape. 'You're right,' he said, emotion making his voice gruff. 'There is something here.' Slicing carefully along the length of the left side, he put the scalpel down and teased out a wodge of parchment. He let out an enormous breath. 'There. Not too much damage done.' He looked up at her, eyes blazing with excitement. 'Now we just need to find out what this is.'

CHAPTER 27

OCTOBER 1660, AT SEA

We have been at sea these past three weeks. There are no chattering, gleaming magpies, only shrieking seabirds with avaricious eyes and fearsome beaks. At first many folk were very sick, including Barnabas. For the first two weeks he sat on deck, his arms hugging the mizzen mast, moaning most piteously. I tried him with adder's-tongue but it made little effect. Perchance Prudie's remedy was for land born sickness only.

Prudie. Each time I think of her my heart dies some more.

I have had little enough time to come to terms with what I did. Barnabas assures me I had no choice and didn't Prudie herself give me her blessing? But still my heart grieves over her loss and over my treachery. How am I ever to live with myself? With what I have done? My perfidy is as a dagger to my insides.

We have another three weeks at sea. Much time for me to write down the sorry affair and to beg my Maker for His forgiveness. I have to confess, though, increasingly I doubt my God exists. Barnabas still proclaims his own disbelief in such a cruel God and I constantly hush him, for there are many pious families aboard. They all hope for a new life in a new land and a freedom to worship as they believe they should. Barnabas hopes to make his fortune. And I? I am running from the terrible thing I did.

But I must start at the beginning.

After Prudie's tormenting and teasing of the Flowers family, however justified, Mercy and I barricaded ourselves into the house. I knew it was but a matter of time before the constables came. As indeed they did. Hal Thatcher, accompanied by his loathsome father, made the front door look puny as they rammed it open, despite the settle shoved against it. I cried out to Mercy to flee as they had no quarrel with her but association with us might bleed into guilt, and she fled out through the scullery carrying dear precious Cat. I did not want him kicked to death as had happened to my Star. I know she will give our darling Cat the best of homes. Indeed, it was reported later that she collected the goat, our cow, the chickens and the geese. We would not have use for any animal where Prudie and I were going.

The men were rough. Even now I have bruises and swellings as evidence. They were too afeared of Prudie to do too much harm, or maybe it was because her old flesh made their desire shrivel. For myself, I feared the worst. To my surprise, Robert Lacey came with Hal and Samuel Thatcher and they did as he ordered. Apart from their heavy hands and Samuel Thatcher's sneaky fingers groping between my legs I was untouched. As Robert had explained to me, there was little he could do to help now it had come to this, but he did what he could, and I entered the gaol with my maidenly virtue intact.

After our three days in the town lock-up, Mistress Agnes brought evidence to the town hall and it was heard before the clerk. Others joined in. Elias Light's mother accused us of bewitching her son and making him ill, Farmer Bastin told of how his cattle were milk dry. And, of course, our old enemy

Katherine Flowers accused Prudie of using a poppet to bewitch her family. Anne, our once dear neighbour and friend, repeated her nonsense about seeing the devil in the form of a magpie fly in at our window. But it was Agnes Lacey's accusation that Prudie had made her babe so sick that he ailed and died that sent us to the Exeter Assizes.

'Witchcraft,' she said. 'It was witchcraft that killed my beloved baby Charles. And it was witchcraft that has made me barren ever since, so that no babe will quicken in my womb.'

They tied us and put us in an open cart, and for two days and two nights we travelled to Exeter Castle. I feared for Prudie. Her mind broken by all that had befallen her and her body not yet healed from the kicking inflicted by that bastard child Ned Flowers. May he rot in Hell. It rained on us and we had no shelter. I huddled against Prudie to keep her warm but our hands and feet were like ice, which the day's sun did little to warm. In the night I lay, jolting and sleepless, in the wet and mess of my own soiling, hearing the mule snort and watching the stars in the black sky above. I confess I prayed for death. At least for Prudie. Death would be welcomed as an escape from what was to come. I remembered poor dear Abigail and her sufferings. I remembered Prudie's marks and scars from her pricking and the blood that ran down her thighs from her privy parts. I did not want this for myself, but mostly I did not want a frail old woman like Prudie to endure it again. They had tested and pricked her, searched for devil's teats and found none. The witchfinder Matthias Finch would not let her escape his grip a second time.

Mostly I stared at the sky and saw the gallows patterned in the stars. I recollected Abigail's hanging in Flete's wool market fifteen years before and remembered watching as Prudie had rushed to yank on the woman's legs to give her a swift end. That was going to happen to us; they would put a noose around our necks and have us dancing and kicking until we died. I prayed some kind soul would pull on our legs to end our suffering quickly as Prudie had for Abigail.

I had never returned to Exeter, the city of my birth. Since being taken in by John and Prudie, I had never left Flete. There had been no need.

It was early morning when we breached the city boundary, and it was just waking up. I'd hoped no one would be abroad to witness our shame. In this, we were unlucky; it seemed the good folk of Exeter rose early. As we entered the teeming streets, with their close-quartered houses and lanes running with mire, people began jeering. Somehow the locals knew what we were and why we had come. One man, teeth bared and brandishing his fist, ran at the cart, shaking it and making it judder violently. It frightened the mule and made our driver cuss and lash out with his whip. Prudie came to, looked about her with bleary eyes, so I comforted her as best I could. We were spat at and had clods of horse shit thrown at us. The cart rumbled over the cobbles, swaying so roughly I feared it would tip us out and the city rabble would tear us to pieces. As we neared the castle gates and the cart slowed to pull uphill, the streets narrowed and became ever busier. I had never seen such crowds. All about reeked with midden filth. The fresh sea air of Flete seemed very far away. A dog yowled as someone kicked it out of the way, beggars held out piteous hands, molls lifted skirts suggestively and a pie seller drifted past holding his wares high on a board, the scent of meat and pastry making my mouth salivate and my stomach heave with hunger.

Rougemont, the red stone castle. Our destination. We slowed along a narrow lane to enter the gate. It rose, sombre and oppressing and malevolent. As I looked up to the city crest on the wall and the cold blue sky above, I thought it would be the last daylight I should ever see. Even with my faith in the Almighty ebbing away, I still prayed.

Just as we were to leave the clamorous streets and enter the castle, a wild-eyed woman loomed over the cart. As best I could, with my tied hands, I tugged Prudie to me and shrank back. Was another gobbet of spittle or lump of shit about to hit us? But the woman smiled toothlessly and faded away. Out of the sky a black and white bird swooped, its long tail fanning out into a glistening diamond. A mock a pie. A magpie. Our friend. Flying down it dropped a half-eaten meat pie into my hand. Tears coursed down my cheeks at this sudden and unexpected kindness but the bird was gone before I had brains to thank her.

I tore a piece off for Prudie and stuffed it into her mouth but she was too far gone to recognise it as food. Cramming some into my own mouth I moaned through the chewing of it. It was mutton, gristly and fatty, but to my empty stomach, nectar. The cartsman turned, looked down upon us and with a howl of exhausted fury, snatched the rest for himself.

I lay back, sucking my fingers for the last morsel of greasy meat and watched as all darkened overhead and we entered Hell itself.

CHAPTER 28

JULY 2018

'Fuck.' Beth fell back onto a dining room chair. 'What was *that* all about?'

Nathan had struggled at first to read the document out loud. The spidery handwriting, with its long lower loops and ds with a high backwards upper loop, was in places neat, but in others it ran about the page. Frustrated, he'd dashed upstairs and returned with a magnifying glass. Using it, he'd tried again to decipher the words, bending over the paper, holding the glass close.

He collapsed onto a chair at the opposite end of the dining-room table and stared at Beth. 'And there's another two pages, but my head's spinning. I need a break.'

Leaving the parchment where it was, for some weird reason it seemed the right thing to do to cover it with the tablecloth, they went back outside. It was still hot and sunny, a normal day at the seaside: gulls called overhead, sparrows cheeped and hopped about in the garden, and someone nearby had begun to mow a lawn. It was in stark contrast to what they had just read.

Sitting back at the white wrought-iron table, they stared at the jug of lemonade. A wasp crawled up the inside of it, buzzing down to swim in the liquid and then escape and crawl up again.

Nathan jumped up and in a swift movement, threw the jug's contents onto the lawn. 'Don't know about you but I could do with a proper drink. You walked here, didn't you?'

Beth nodded, watching as the wasp flew off, high on sugar. Something was nudging at the back of her brain.

He returned with the tray this time laden with white wine, glasses, a bowl of olives and a bag of Kettle chips. After pouring them both a generous glassful, he sat down. 'As you so rightly say, what was all that about?' Tearing open the bag of crisps, he tossed it onto the table. 'Help yourself. I'm too wired to make anything more substantial, but I'll order pizza later if you like.'

Beth took a deep swallow of wine and a handful of crisps. Crunching them without really noticing, she found her voice. 'It was amazing. So, this... woman, we think?'

Nathan nodded. 'I'd guess so. The threat of sexual violence is clear and she mentions her maidenly virtue.'

'Of course. So this woman is on board a ship.' She shook her head in frustration. 'I have so many questions. When?'

'I'm assuming about the time the book was written and didn't Bill say that was seventeenth century?'

'So sixteen something. And she mentions some pious people on board.' Beth remembered the conversation they'd had about Nathan's American ancestors. 'Your Pilgrim Fathers?'

'Who knows? Possibly. I'm pretty sure emigration amongst some religious groups was high about then. In fact, throughout history, emigration to the States was seen as a last chance necessity. During the Potato Famine, the Highland Clearances in Scotland and so on.'

Beth leaned forward. 'You think they were sailing to America?'

'Educated guess. The writer says she has many weeks of

voyage in front of her. She also mentions Exeter Gaol so it figures she left from the south west. I've no idea how long it would take to sail from Devon to the east coast in the sixteen hundreds but it must be a good couple of months.'

'Or maybe it's a transportation ship to Australia? I've only the haziest idea when those happened.'

'Me too. Who knows, maybe when we've read some more it'll make the destination clearer, might even give us a name. Wouldn't it be great to find out who's written it? Maybe it's the same person who wrote the actual book, or used it to heal?'

'A name!' Beth shot up in her seat, spilling wine. 'I know some of those names!' That was it, she'd heard some of those names before but where from? Reaching forward she glugged the rest of her glass before turning to him, eyes alight. 'I don't know how but I've heard those names before. Someone has mentioned an Abigail and Matthias Finch to me.' Wracking her brains, she thought hard. 'But who? Was it on the net, something I've read?'

Nathan waved his hand hopelessly. 'You've been doing a lot of reading around, researching. It could have been from anywhere.'

'Bill. It was when I talked to Bill. She mentioned an Abigail.' Beth snapped her fingers together, finally remembering. 'That's it! Bill told me a woman called Abigail had been hanged for witchcraft in Flete market square.'

'In the actual square?' he asked, alarmed. 'Where we park now?'

Beth nodded. 'It's all coming back to me. It drew quite a crowd. It was back in the mid-seventeenth century, I think. During the civil war. It was seen as both warning – a deterrent against crime and certainly against witchcraft – and entertainment. People would flock into the town from the countryside to see the spectacle.'

'God, that's vile.'

'Sounds as if Prudie went to it and hastened poor Abigail's end by pulling on her legs.'

Nathan gave a grim nod. 'It can take a while for someone hanging to die unless the neck is broken instantly. It would give the poor woman a quicker and less painful death.'

Beth shuddered. The sense of something rough tightening around her neck was very real. She tugged at her sweatshirt collar and forced herself to reply. 'Wonder if that put her under suspicion as a friend of the accused? And I know the name Matthias Finch too. He was a witchfinder. Bill's got documents in the museum all about it. He was paid to find witches.'

Nathan's brow rose. 'Bet he found lots guilty then.'

'Oh yes,' Beth warmed to her theme, remembering more about the disturbing conversation she'd had with Bill. Anger blossomed hotly again. 'They had all sorts of tricks to make them appear guilty. And they didn't need all that much evidence. Just hearsay, gossip, finding devil's marks, accusations they had familiars, which were only their animals, you know, the cat that did the ratting, the goat that provided milk. Bill reckoned it was used as a way of getting back at your neighbour who'd wronged you.'

Nathan leaned forward. 'And our mysterious author says that, doesn't she? It was all about this Prudie making people ill.' He sat back again, looking thoughtful. 'The seventeenth-century version of a medical negligence claim.'

'If you like. And it must have been weird after the civil war. Lots of old scores to settle, I would imagine.'

'When did it end?'

'They. There was more than one civil war but I suppose you could claim it all ended when Charles II was put back on the throne in 1660.'

'You've done your homework.'

Beth shrugged. 'I've become fascinated by the whole period in history. Hold on, I'll google the first transportation to Oz.'

Nathan sipped his wine and waited patiently.

'I know you have to take what you research on the net with a pinch of salt,' Beth said, after scrolling through her phone, 'but it says here, the first transportation ships were sent to New South Wales in 1788.'

'Too late for us then. My money's on the US.'

'Mine too. Our writer could have sailed from Exeter Quay, I suppose, or could even have gone from Bideford.'

'Bideford?' Nathan said, surprised.

Beth nodded. 'I remember reading about the Bideford Witches after you mentioned them. Hard to believe now but Bideford was this enormous port in the seventeenth century, mostly dealing in the tobacco trade to and from Virginia. You could buy a passage on a tobacco ship sailing to the Colonies and sometimes even get a paid passage. They were desperate for young people with skills to settle the new land. Wonder what Barnabas did when he wasn't being seasick? Obviously not a fisherman.'

Beth thought back to her conversation with Bill, more detail returning. 'Abigail Wray *that* was her name, was hanged in 1645 and our writer says that was fifteen years before, so that makes the year she's writing in 1660. Bang on the beginning of the Restoration. If you were living with a neighbour who's a royalist and you were a Cromwell supporter, I bet an accusation of witchcraft was one way of getting revenge. I mean, people fought one another, fought in *battle* against their neighbour.' She bit her lip. 'It's impossible to imagine, isn't it? Or, more prosaically, if a neighbour had said something spiteful about you, or maybe stolen something, it was a way to get back at them. We've all read about modern neighbourhood spats that began over a disputed boundary, or a tree shedding leaves, and escalating into an expensive court case. People get really worked up about things like that.'

'At least there's recourse to a legal system now. No need for a witch hunt.'

'There are enough witch hunts online,' Beth said quietly.

'Your horrible review comments?'

'Not to mention my starring role in some deepfake porno.' Beth pulled the sleeves of her sweatshirt protectively over her hands. 'But at least I only have the loss of my reputation at risk, not my life. And at least I don't get put in front of a magistrate on a jumped-up charge based on superstition and hearsay. Oh! I've just remembered something else, those accused of witchcraft often confessed. And a confession was the evidence used to hang them. They were tortured, so I assume by that point they were out of their mind.'

'It sounds as if this Prudie was already. The writer's trying to protect her. I wonder if both women had been accused of witchcraft or just Prudie? I imagine she must have been one of Bill's wise or cunning women.' He poured them both more wine. 'And we still don't know how or why the book and this confessional document ended up in the States.'

'But we know it began its life here in Devon. And in Flete itself. It's so exciting. Do you think this was one of your ancestors? They took it onboard as they emigrated and, weirdly, it's returned to its original home via your grandfather. I always knew there was something special about it.' She waved a crisp at him triumphantly.

Nathan laughed. 'You did. That's quite a thought that Prudie and this other woman might be related to me. Imagine, me being related to a witch!' He frowned. 'Both women are going into Exeter Gaol, so it looks likely that both have been accused of witchcraft. But it also looks as if one of them got out. How? We've only got half the story here, Beth. We need to read on.'

'If your eyesight is up to it, I'd love to.'

'Before we go back indoors, could we talk about the decision I've got to make about this job?' He paused. 'I felt we left it… undiscussed.'

'You have to make your own decisions, Nathan,' Beth replied crisply. 'It's up to you what you do with your life. As I said, it sounds like an amazing opportunity.' She finished her glass of wine in one. 'And now, I don't know about you, but I'm dying to find out what the next pages have in store. Let's go and find out, shall we?'

In her head she could clearly see the magpie flying at her from the chimney, soot encrusted and malevolent. Had it been the same one that had flown in at Tenpenny House all those years before? One for sorrow. An omen.

CHAPTER 29

OCTOBER 1660, AT SEA

I will not talk of the gaol. Suffice it to say we received little kindness there. Once shoved in, we were left to our own devices, so I found a corner away from the other prisoners and sat with Prudie. She dozed and fretted but was out of her mind enough to be spared the worst of the sights and stench I had to endure. When my eyes adjusted to the gloom, I wished they hadn't. In my mind I still see what no woman should have endured. The walls streamed with filth and rats running over our feet, but this was as nothing to the piteous humans held within. I huddled with Prudie, became a beggar like the others, snatching bread and water out of the hands of those too weak to fight back, or those dying or dead already. I prayed that we would be called up to the courthouse soon.

In this, it seems there was great haste. The Assizes had been delayed from the summer due to fear of plague and were meeting late. Those who wished to find us guilty wanted to do so in a hurry so they could scurry back to London.

I lost all track of the days; there was little light, just a brazier that the guard huddled near, and much oppressive darkness. All was unending hell. But, after a time, a guard came with a lantern. The light exploded into my eyes and it hurt to look upon it.

'You!' He pointed at me. 'You are to see a visitor.' He unlocked my leg irons, making much of running his hands up my calves. Seizing my arm, he hauled me up.

'I am not going anywhere. I cannot leave Prudie.' I tried to struggle against his hold but he was too strong and I too weak.

Laughing, he spoke, 'You think you have a choice? If the Keeper thinks you should talk to your visitor that's what you do, witch!' He held on to my upper arm with a grip so fierce I knew it would add bruises to the ones already present. In this way, we shambled along interminable subterranean passageways until he threw me into a room brightly lit with candles belching out stinking tallow.

A man sat at the table there. He was sombre and upright, in a black cloak and hat. 'Sit down, Susanna. Take some wine. And there is meat and bread here too.'

Not Barnabas who I had half-hoped it would be but, of all men, Robert Lacey!

I fell on the food, cramming it into my mouth with both hands. Taking great gulps of wine, I drank it so greedily, it ran down my chin unheeded. When I had my fill, I sat back, rubbed a hand over my face and sighed. The feeling of a full belly was good.

'Have you eaten enough? Drunk sufficient wine?'

His mild questions made me sit up straighter. I became aware of how I must look. Capless, hair trailing onto my shoulders, my skirts ripped and soiled, my partlet long gone, leaving my bosom exposed. I must have looked and stank exactly as what I was, a bird of the gaol, captive and miserable. I nodded, unable to speak. What was he doing here?

'I am glad. I'm sorry to see you here, in this state. But I recall I warned you.' He sighed heavily. 'I warned you there was little I could do should my wife take her accusations to the town clerk. And now you are here, in Exeter Gaol and my influence is all but negligible.'

I stared at him. My old childhood acquaintance, the man whose loyalty had stayed with the crown and whose closest friend had fought and died on the other side. His hair, showing under his hat, was now streaked with premature grey, as was his beard and he looked gaunt. The weight of ruling over our little town of Flete was obviously hanging heavy. Or was it the tribulations of his unhappy and childless marriage? Poor Robert, married to a woman who had promised him so much but had grown sour too soon. I wondered if Agnes was happy in Lacey Manor with her silks and laces.

Finally, I found my voice. 'Is that your purpose here? To gloat and preen over my downfall?'

Robert towered to his feet. Slamming the table with his fist so fiercely that the jug of wine jumped, he roared, 'Damn you, woman. You will forever vex me.'

I shrank back against his sudden and noisome anger. Was he here to threaten me? Or, and at this thought the bread and meat threatened to return, had he come to have what he had always wanted? I hardly thought I was still desirable to him in my gaol-soiled rags. He could have prettier and cleaner company in Lucia Pettit's bawdy house back in Flete. And, whatever depths I had sunk to, I was not prepared to stoop so low. He would have to take me by force or not at all.

He sank back on the chair, poured a glass of wine and drank it down in one. His hand was shaking. 'Do you think it gives me pleasure to see my dear friend in such a place?' He gestured to my sad rags. 'In such apparel? So starved she shoves food down her throat with no recourse to the manners she once had. Half-undressed and filthy. Smelling of the gutter and,' he picked up a nosegay from the table and pressed it to his face, 'worse.'

I crossed my arms over my naked shoulders. Without my partlet and in only my shift and bodice, I felt vulnerable. 'So you have come to insult me?'

He stared at me, sadly, I thought. 'We could have made a fine pair, you and I. A happier marriage Flete would not have witnessed. You would have had everything I could afford to give you.' He bit his lip. 'And you would have born me many fine sons. Aye, and maybe a dainty daughter or two. But instead you are intent on throwing away your life with a half-mad hag who cares so little for her own life that she taunts the best-known tattler in town with threats to bewitch her.'

'Prudie can't bewitch anyone. She's a good, pure woman. She's the woman townsfolk have gone to for healing these past thirty years,' I protested.

Robert set his elbows on the table and looked me directly in the eyes. 'And I know this. I also know she bore no ill will to my son but tried to help him and his mother. Flete, however, believes otherwise. Even you must admit that since John died, Prudie's mind has weakened. She has attacked those in town who are most likely to stir others up against her and, which in turn, has brought out factions who would defend her and the memory of John and Thomas Tenpenny and the beliefs they held dear. And those factions, Cromwell's spies, you know I must destroy.'

'The war is not yet over then,' I bit out. 'Even though you never took to battle, you now seek to cut down the old parliamentary enemy.'

His shoulders slumped wearily. 'For there to be peace in our part of Devon, I have no choice. I cannot allow the king's enemies to prosper and rise up against the monarchy again. It led to chaos before; it would lead to chaos again. And bloodshed. Is that what you want? Do you not want a peaceful, prosperous England?'

I glared at him through narrowed eyes. 'You think two defenceless women have such power as to stir up Commonwealth battles?'

'But you were not defenceless, were you, Susie? Cromwell's men came to your rescue. You cannot deny this. They see you and Prudie, as John and Thomas's kin, as tinder to the fire of their rallying cry.'

'Then let us die and with us so will their cause.' I slumped back against the chair, arms still crossed over my chest, staring sullenly at the foetid floor.

He leaned back, studying the table as he rolled a crumb of bread between his finger and thumb. The concentration was deceptively casual. 'I can do nothing to save Prudie from the gallows, for she will truly swing and that I cannot prevent.' A throaty sigh escaped him and he looked almost overcome with some sad emotion. Flicking a glance to me, he added, 'But for you I may be able to suggest something to help. It may save your skin.'

Frowning, I asked, 'But what can you do? I had thought your influence ended at Flete? You have no jurisdiction here in the city. You are as powerless as I.' I wanted to wound him with my words, hurt him as I had been hurt. Although part of me, I admit, wanted to turn back time and, had he ever offered, accept his hand in marriage. How different my life would have then been.

The corner of his mouth twitched but he did not rise to meet my anger. 'This is partly true and I had thought I would have no power over the court's proceedings but a Lacey cousin will sit on the bench. If I am correct in my thinking, you may be able to do something to save yourself.' He fixed me with his gaze. 'But what I am about to say will require great courage and daring. Aye, and a gamble too.' He leaned forward again, almost beseechingly.

'But it is your only chance, Susanna. If you don't take it, then you will surely die.'

'What? But what can I do? Surely there is nothing. I am for the gallows too. In truth, it would be a kind of escape from all of this.' I shivered and gazed around at the windowless stone walls. Who knew where I was. Somewhere in the cavernous depths of the castle. Matthias Finch demanded his pound of flesh for his fat fee and, having let Prudie slip through his fingers once before, would not let it happen again. What could Robert have that would possibly save me from the ordeal I was about to face?

His answer chilled me to the core. And my agreement to his request would surely send my soul rotting to hell.

CHAPTER 30

JULY 2018

'So we know her name!' Beth exclaimed. She and Nathan were back in the dining room, poring over the document. 'Susanna. Tenpenny, if she's related to Prudie. Oh my God!' She stared at Nathan, breathing heavily in her excitement, her words tumbling out any old way. 'Do you think she's connected to Tenpenny House? She must be! It's too much of a coincidence for her not to be. It's hardly a common surname.'

'It isn't. Although we've come across a Susanna before.'

'When?' Beth demanded, eagerness making her harsh.

'Wasn't one of the Bideford Witches called Susanna?'

'Let's have another look at the photo of that plaque. The one on the castle wall.'

Nathan scrolled through his phone and passed it over.

'She *was* called Susannah,' Beth said. 'Susannah Edwards. With an h on the end. And hanged in 1682. Too late for our Susanna? And besides, I've read about the Bideford Witches. They were old women. Everything points to our Susanna being young. Funny, isn't it, you don't think of Susanna as being a particularly seventeenth-century name. Seems too modern.'

Nathan gave her a fond smile. 'You're very invested in our Susanna.'

'I am. I feel a connection to her. I always did to the book but now I feel it to her too. Don't ask me why,' she added impatiently. 'Maybe it's the Tenpenny thing.'

'As far as I know there are no Tenpennys in Flete now, although there is still a Flowers family and a large Thatcher clan. And, of course, there's the Lacey Manor Nursing Home. I'm assuming that must have been Robert Lacey's manor.' He added, with a worried glance, 'Mum's maiden name is Lacey.'

'What?' Beth sank back against the hard and extremely uncomfortable dining chair. 'Oh Nathan, this is getting weird. You're a Lacey?'

'Descended from, I'm assuming. Mum's family have always been in Flete.' He grinned, slightly embarrassed. 'Nothing exotic or unusual about the name Smith. That side of the family could be from anywhere, although Grandpa Smith's family hale from Worcester, Massachusetts.' He shrugged. 'No idea what happened to the Lacey money though. Think Mum's from the poorer branch of the family.'

'When did the manor house change into a nursing home?'

Nathan frowned. 'Years ago. Way back. Just after the Second World War, I think. Mum never really talks about her Lacey heritage. She's not big into history, unlike her mother, my grandmother.'

'Yes, you've mentioned her before. Would she know anything more about Lacey Manor?'

He shook his head. 'We lost her two years ago.'

'But you could be related to this Robert Lacey? The one who visited our Susanna in gaol.'

'I could well be.' Nathan eased a kink out of his shoulders. 'Bill might know more.' He shook his head wonderingly. 'I've never questioned my heritage before.' He gave a short laugh.

'Funny. Never pursued the link between Mum and the manor. It's just always been there and none of us have ever been bothered about it.'

'He's an odd character, this Robert Lacey. Obviously an influential man in Flete at the time.'

'And a royalist. That'll please Mum, she's mad on anything to do with the royal family. Huge Prince Charles fan.'

Beth's brow furrowed. 'But it sounds as if Susanna and Prudie were on the other side. So, why is Robert trying to help her?'

'I don't know, Beth.' Nathan scrubbed a frustrated hand over his hair. 'Susanna mentioned something about them once being friends. Maybe that's it? And it sounds as if he's in a difficult position. His wife has accused Prudie and Susanna of witchcraft, this has stirred up some old allegiances, which are using the women as an excuse to cause trouble in the town. He has to be seen to get justice done and quell any parliamentary rebellion, but the woman he loves is accused and facing the gallows. Yes, a strange man but complex and compassionate too.'

'So you think he loved Susanna?'

'Maybe. In some way. Or it was lust, or he was on a power trip? But if that was the case, he could have raped her. He's powerful, she's a prisoner and extremely vulnerable.'

Beth shivered, glad she only had twenty-first century problems to deal with. 'Jeez. It's bad enough being a woman now, but back then you were nothing in society if you were poor or unmarried. Worthless.'

'And I'm guessing our Susanna was both. Plus she was in gaol, there was a clear power imbalance and he still respected her. Sort of.'

'Even though she was on the losing side.' Beth snorted. 'And if he loved her, why didn't he stop her going to gaol in the first place?'

'I don't think he could,' Nathan said thoughtfully. 'If he's lord of the manor he's in a position of power in Flete, and as I said, he has to make sure justice is seen to be done. He said to her he can't allow parliamentary forces to rise again. He was in an impossible position.'

'Not as impossible as poor Susanna and Prudie, chained up and thrown into a dungeon,' Beth replied hotly.

'True.' Screwing his eyes shut and shaking his head, he said, 'There's something about all of this I'm not liking.'

'Just the one thing,' she began to joke, then saw his face. 'What?'

'The Tenpenny connection, me possibly being a descendent of Robert Lacey. The way the book has returned to its home.'

'What are you saying, Nathan?'

He didn't answer but rose abruptly and went outside. Beth joined him at the little garden table. He looked white and pinched and poured himself a glass of wine, which he drank down in one.

'It all feels as if it was meant to happen,' he began slowly. He laughed shortly and bit his lip. 'I can't believe I'm saying this, but think back to when we met.' He gazed at her, his eyes burning into hers. 'You felt that instant attraction, didn't you?'

'Love at first sight?' Beth scoffed. His decision to leave for the States still rankled.

He smiled. 'Maybe. But I was thinking it was more that we'd met before.'

'But we haven't. Trust me, I'd remember.'

'Beth, I don't mean in *this* life.'

Her jaw dropped. 'Are you really saying what I think you are? Are you talking about *reincarnation*? Come off it, Nathan, you're a scientist.'

'Then how would you explain everything that's happened? The book returning to where it was written, me being a Lacey, you owning Tenpenny House.' He spread his hands. 'This connection we have, this feeling we have between us that began as soon, no *before* I got to know you.'

'You're scaring me.'

'I'm sorry, I don't mean to. It's just I'm floundering for another explanation. There are too many parallels. Prudie being a healer, me being a doctor, you making your lotions and potions.'

'Oh come on, I'm hardly in the same league as a cunning woman.' Her neck felt stiff and tense. Maybe she was coming down with a headache.

'No, but you sort of inhabit the same world.'

Beth fell silent. She was thinking. 'It *is* weird,' she began slowly. 'I have been reading up on courses in herbal medicine.' As the words left her mouth, Beth realised how much sense training to be a medical herbalist made. The last few weeks had crystallised something in her. She loved making her soaps and body lotions but inspired by the book, she wanted to ramp up her knowledge, her skills, to another level.

There was another long pause, a silence, only punctuated by sparrows cheeping in the trees. 'But until you just pointed that out, I would have said I hadn't any idea to study anything of the sort.' She could feel her heart pounding. This felt very important somehow. 'I'm not sure I buy your reincarnation theory, but I'll agree the past and the present are colliding in a very peculiar way. I mean, you may have made the book and Tenpenny connection yourself–'

'It took you to discover Susanna's hidden document and you were the one to research witchcraft,' he interrupted.

'But I'm a Loveday not a Tenpenny. Like you I've never researched my family tree so I suppose there could be a Tenpenny in my heritage somewhere, but I'm pretty sure if there was it would be the talk of the family. My gran, like yours, is really into all that. If she thought there was a witch in the family, trust me we'd know about it. All she ever mentioned was Flete being the Loveday family hub and that there has always been Lovedays here until the last one died childless. She was Betty Loveday, a distant, very distant, cousin of my grandfather's.' She stopped, her mouth hanging open. 'Unless–'

'What?'

'Didn't Susanna say the Tenpennys took her in? So she may have been adopted. Maybe she's not a Tenpenny at all but a Loveday! It's all supposition and guess work though.'

'It adds flame to my reincarnation theory.'

Beth's shoulders slumped; she was finding it hard to concentrate. 'It's all too fantastical to be true. I mean, things like this just don't happen, do they?' A huge bee droned past, low and sluggish and she gently batted it away.

Nathan watched as it flew up into the afternoon sky. He shrugged. 'Basic tenet of some major religions. Buddhists and Hindus believe the essence of a living being transmigrates into another after death. I find it quite comforting.'

'Reincarnation – but the soul doesn't have a *choice*, does it? You can't decide, oh I'm dying, I know I'll come back in the body of Nathan Smith Devon GP four hundred years after I die.'

He smiled slightly. 'No, that's true.' He blew out a breath. 'Maybe, then, Robert Lacey and Susanna Tenpenny had unfinished business that they wanted us to finish?'

'But what?'

'I don't know, Beth. It's just a theory.'

'It's a bonkers theory.'

'I agree. And this all makes about as much sense to me as it does to you.'

Beth surged to her feet so violently her chair toppled over and crashed onto the patio slabs. 'Sorry.' She turned around to pick it up, flustered. 'This is all too much. I need to go.' But she sat back down, legs weak, too confused to move.

'Don't go, not just yet. I'll order pizza, we can finish the wine and read the last bits of the document. I'm even getting quite used to the s being written as f now. I promise there'll be no more talk of reincarnation.'

'I mean, things like this just don't happen, do they?' She rubbed her temple. She had a humdinger of a headache. The air felt heavy and languorous. Maybe they were in for a storm.

'Not to me.' He took her hands. Gazing earnestly into her eyes, he added, 'Look, Beth, I can't claim to know what's going on here. For all I know, it could simply be a load of coincidences, but it doesn't *feel* like that, does it? It feels important. Very important. And *you* feel important. To me.'

Beth's breath hitched. She stared back. She could love this man. His obvious physical attributes aside, she could really love the man that lay below all the running-honed muscles. But he was going away. She slid her hands out of his hold. 'Do you think you're Robert Lacey then?' she asked pettishly. 'Unlike you, I'm not sure I like the sound of him and I don't think Susanna was all that keen either. I think he sounds distinctly dodgy. Evil even.' Her head began to swim. Too much wine on a hot day. Words were streaming from her mouth that weren't totally her own. She needed to fight this attraction to Nathan. There was no future there. 'Are you evil, Nathan?'

His lips compressed at her icy tone. He gave a short laugh. 'I'm not evil. I'm not one hundred per cent good either. I'm just a man, Beth. Trying to do his best with what the world has given him. Do *you* think you're Susanna? About to be hanged for witchcraft?'

Beth's throat closed, the familiar and threatening scratchy rope tightening around it. She tried to swallow and couldn't. Shaking her head, she whispered, 'No, of course I don't.'

Tugging again at the neck of her sweatshirt, she added, 'It's just too much to take in. It's mad, Nathan. It's–'

He picked up on her hesitation. 'But you agree it feels important.'

She couldn't deny it. There *was* something going on and it *did* feel significant but whether or not it was reincarnation, even the word made her giggle in a panicked way, was yet to be proved. 'I'll admit it all feels meaningful and I'll admit to a series of startling coincidences, but reincarnation? That's a leap too far for me. Maybe we'd better read the rest of Susanna's stuff. Maybe that will give me more of an idea of what's going on.'

Nathan gave her a keen look. 'You okay? You've gone very pale.'

'I've got a headache. Sitting in the sun drinking wine will do that.'

He rose, disappeared into the kitchen then brought out a glass of cold water and some paracetamol. 'Take these. It's hot out here, you're probably dehydrated. We need to get some proper food. I'll ring for a takeaway.'

Swallowing the tablets with difficulty down a raw throat, Beth wondered if she was sickening with something. The water was nectar and soothed and cooled. 'Thank you. I'll be fine. I'd rather finish reading the document and save eating for afterwards.'

'Then, if you're sure, we'll read first.'

Beth nodded, eased the kinks out of her neck and accepted his suggestion. 'I'm sure.'

CHAPTER 31

1660

For my sins and to my eternal shame, I took Robert Lacey's advice. I agreed to what he suggested, may God forgive me.

I could not fathom why he should be doing such things as feeding me and bribing the justices to take my evidence. Robert was a hard man to puzzle. A once proud father, a devout Christian and loyal to his merry monarch. Weak in power and a whorer. From what little I had heard of our sovereign ruler, he had this in common with the new king.

From our meeting I smuggled a hunk of venison pie and some bread, and fed Prudie. Sitting with my back to the other poor souls to hide my bounty, I broke it into tiny fragments and tried to tempt her to eat. It was like feeding a babe but once Prudie had tasted the first mouthful, she was eager for more. I'd stolen an apple too, and bit into it with a moan of ecstasy. The fresh juice ran down my chin, freshened my mouth, the texture of the crisp flesh reminding me so much of our old apple tree at the cottage, with poor Star buried beneath, that I almost sobbed. But I had not the time for sobbing and wailing. I had to talk to Prudie about what Robert had suggested. It was an idea so horrific the apple stuck in my throat. I bit off a sliver and pressed it upon Prudie. It seemed to revive her a little and once my eyes adjusted to the gloom again, I could discern a gleam of understanding in hers. I wasn't sure which was worse. Prudie having her senses whole again and understanding the terrible truth of what I had to tell her, but then going to her trial and death sensible of what she faced, or suffering stultified wits. There was comfort of a sorts in oblivion. While she chewed and sucked the pieces of apple I gave her, I ate the rest. Aye, core and pips too.

When we'd finished the sorry meal and sucked our fingers free of any stickiness and crumbs, I held her face in my hands, forcing her attention on me. 'I need to speak with you, Prudie,' I hissed. My voice quavered. 'I need to tell you something.'

Her understanding quickened. I could see some of the old Prudie returning. I released her but she grabbed hold of my arm, her fingers gnarled and bony, biting into my flesh. 'Who called you?' she demanded. 'You were gone. You had gone when I woke.'

'Twas Robert Lacey.'

'That name got through.' Her eyes widened in shock. 'And what has he to do with us? Come to tighten the noose?'

I shook my head. 'I don't think any of this is his doing.'

'Tis his wife's doing. He should have better control over her mouth.'

'Like John did with yours? You were always your own woman, Prudie. And you taught me to be the same.' I spread my hands. 'And look at the trouble it has brought us to.' She flinched and as soon as the words were free of my mouth I regretted them. 'I'm sorry, I did not mean to be so cruel.'

Her lips twisted, creating grooves in her age-thinned begrimed skin. Drawing in a deep breath, she muttered, 'Nay, child. Had my dear John lived he would not have seen us here.'

With a gleam of the old Prudie, she added, 'That's if he hadn't shot his mouth off in The Cock after too much ale.'

I bent nearer. 'It was his old soldiers who came to our rescue,' I whispered urgently. 'Not that it did us much good. We still ended up in here. I never caught the name of the good colonel who helped us and saved us from the mob.' I shivered, remembering my lucky escape from the hands of Samuel Thatcher.

'Aye, theys were good men and it gave us time.'

She was right. It had given us time, not a great deal but I had endeavoured to hide or destroy anything I thought they could hold against us. The poppets had all gone on the fire and I had emptied as many jars and pots as I could into the privy.

Prudie started. 'The book! What did you do with the book? And my knife,' she began to whimper. Her wits were returning with all haste. 'My precious knife. Twas a special one, it had magic in it, Susie. That knife was of the old magic.'

I looked about me, panicked. These were not words I wanted others to hear. 'Shush now, my dear Prudie. All is well. I hid the book beneath my rags in the pail in the scullery.' I thought the men rampaging through our belongings might quail at turning over my stinking and bloodied monthly cloths. 'I'm grieved to say I cannot recall seeing the knife,' I lied. In my haste to cover our traces, I had dropped the old knife and it had broken. I'd kicked it under the settle. An omen, I had thought, and it had made my insides curl with fear. Prudie began to wail and rock to and fro in distress. I didn't want attention brought to us so, clasping her to me, I crooned, 'Hush now, Prudie. What is lost, is lost.'

'It was our power, Susie. All our women's power. A knife of centuries of wisdom. It was truly special,' she keened. It was a heartbreakingly hopeless sound. But I could not agree with her. My opinion was it had brought nothing but trouble upon us. In the unlikely event I should ever be fortunate enough to get back to Tenpenny Cottage, I would curb its magic with some of my own.

We lay huddled together for some time. A rat, scenting our food, skittered past, its nose pressed to the grime in the hope of a pastry crumb. I had no fear of it, it was a prisoner of circumstance just as we were, but it reminded me of Cat and I wondered how he was faring. In a dim corner a woman yelled and cursed, disturbed by Prudie's distressed howling no doubt, then fell into wracking coughs. Gaol fever wandered freely in here. Many a woman fell silent and lay still, to be dragged out unceremoniously when night fell.

Eventually, Prudie lay quiet and exhausted. 'We'll have no need of earthly belongings where we'll be going,' she murmured, reaching out to hold my hand. 'Or should I say, where *I'll* be going.' Her bright eyes, as beady and knowing as the rat's, peered at me. 'For I wager your Robert has a scheme for you. A strange and complex man he may be, but he loves the bones of you, Susanna.'

She knew. How, I could not fathom. Mayhap there was more of the witch in Prudie than I thought. I nodded, sobs heaving at my throat. 'He has a plan which might save me. Oh but Prudie, how can I do such a thing?'

She drew me nearer. 'Susie,' she hissed urgently, 'my fate is what it is. I have had a long life. It's been mostly a good one, one of service to my town. A son safely delivered and a good husband.' The words came out all in a rush, as if she knew she had little energy to expend. 'I've lost all now, excepting you, dear girl. It's my time to go, to meet my Thomas and my John. I have no fear of what's to come but have a great dread of what might befall you. Do what you have to. Save yourself, child.' She fell back against the filthy wall. 'You have my blessing.' Her eyes closed, hands clutching at the rags covering her chest. Her mouth moved. She was uttering something. A prayer? An incantation? I could not hear. Fevered whispers surrounded me. Word had reached us that the delayed Assize judges had arrived from London. We were to be delivered to trial on the morrow.

～

The cart taking us the short distance to court was similar to the one we had travelled to Exeter in, open to the skies and to the hate of the mob. News had spread that the Assize was sitting and there was to be a witch trial, and crowds had gathered for the spectacle. At one point, on the steep hill rising to the gates of the great courthouse, the poor mule staggered and fell to its knees. Prudie and I jolted from one side to the other and clutched each other in panic. I took in a blur of angry and curious faces, heard the baying, the calls to 'Hang the witch. See how the hag bewitches the road!' and squeezed shut my eyes, holding my hands to my face to stop being hit by the rotten cabbages and clots of mire.

We were led, with those around us jostling and jeering, prodding and poking, to a wooden structure, enclosed on three sides but with nowhere to sit. My legs, weak from being shackled, shook and trembled and I clutched the front of it, looking out to a bench raised high above us on a dais. All was dark wood, white walls and noise from the public gallery. The crowds quietened when the justices entered, bewigged and pompous, to sit. All men. Of course we were to be judged and sentenced by men, by those from outside of Devon, with no understanding of our situation. Their faces were devoid of any emotion, and I looked around frantically for Robert Lacey and his promise of a lenient cousin. I could see only baying men, teeth bared like predatory animals. I could feel nothing but the memory of their lascivious hands groping. We were but chattels, less than human, a problem to be snapped out with the rope at the gallows. The justices sat with great ceremony and arrangement of their fine robes, and the noise rose again, full of excitement and fervour for a hanging.

A clerk, sitting below the bench, rose and hushed the crowds. When all was as silent as tolerated, he barked out, 'Prudence Tenpenny of Flete, hold up thy hand.'

Prudie did so. I was proud to see it firm and not trembling. She seemed to have gained granite strength from somewhere, her legs holding steady, unlike my own.

The clerk continued. 'Thou art here indicted by the name of Prudence Tenpenny, late of Flete, widow, for that thou didst bewitch the babe Charles Lacey unto death and that thou didst by witchcraft consume the body of Elias Light.' He paused, letting the baying crowd subside. 'How sayest thou, Prudence Tenpenny, art thou guilty of this felony as it is laid in the indictment whereof thou standest indicted, or not guilty?'

The rabble hushed. Those at the front of the gallery leaned forward, eager to hear a witch's voice.

Prudie took in a breath. Her chin rose. 'I tended to the babe as best I could and to the best of my skills. The babe sickened and died but it was naught to do with my care.' Her answer was met with uproar and derision. She rose to her full height, straightening her back, glaring at the justices. 'As for the child, Elias, I had nothing to do with his illness. Had Mistress Light come to me, I should have happily given tincture and herbs to aid him.'

More jeers and scoffing. 'Hang the witch, for the crone is guilty!' one yelled out.

As the witness statements were read out, all those taken down at the town hall at Flete, I feared my legs would betray me. I was heartsick and sore. Would I have the courage to do as

Robert Lacey had suggested and Prudie had asked? Had I the bravery, or cowardice to put myself forward?

I knew not whether the authors of the witness statements had travelled to Exeter to hear them and see the result of all their efforts. I could see no one from the town, no friend or foe, in the room. At each statement, at each mention of devil or witchcraft, or sucking teats those in the public gallery yapped out their pleasure at such ideas. We were mere entertainment, and they wanted their fill. I felt crowded out, my ears hurt with the pain of the noise and fear clutched at my very innards, but Prudie stood erect and proud, ignoring all. Eventually the petty tattle, the lies and embellishments ended.

'We have heard the witness statements,' the clerk intoned. 'I ask you again, Prudence Tenpenny, how do you plead?'

Prudie simply repeated what she had said before. It enraged the entire court.

One of the fine men on the bench spoke. 'Very well, Mistress Tenpenny,' he said, barely containing his irritation. 'I shall call witness Matthias Finch.'

The public gallery erupted at the mention of his name. The witchfinder was notorious.

He took to the witness stand. I was half-fainting by this point but was vaguely aware of him being questioned, of his avowal that he had found no marks on Prudie's body, no teats from which the devil could suck. I dared hope Prudie would be found innocent but then he sneered, and said, 'I am happy to examine the hag once more. I can do it here; I have my tools. For it maybe I find something missed before.' He turned to the gallery in triumph. He was playing them as fine as any actor. 'And then, gentlemen, we shall have our evidence.'

This pleased the rabble greatly, for they anticipated great sport, and much cheering resounded. One of the justices whispered to the first one who had spoken. He was familiar in some strange way. Was it, could this man be Robert Lacey's cousin? My heart leaped at the idea. Searching the gallery, I looked for Robert's face and, right at the back, perceived his tall figure, dressed in black, wearing his fine broad-brimmed hat with its extravagant feather. The feather bobbed as he nodded, willing me on.

'Hold your tongue, Master Finch,' the justice said. Those in the gallery wailed their disappointment. 'And silence those of you in the gallery elsewise I shall clear it.' Apart from some grumblings, they quietened. To miss out on the spectacle was too much to bear contemplating. It was the most entertainment they'd had all year. 'We have one other witness here who is to speak and it is someone who knows the accused most dearly,' the justice continued. 'Mistress Loveday, speak, child. What have you to say?'

This was the moment. This was when I needed to spout forth what Robert had coached me into saying.

'Come along now, speak up. You have lodged with Mistress Tenpenny for some years, is that correct?'

I managed a nod.

'And so you have witnessed her at work?'

I nodded again.

'And?' He was losing patience with me. 'Speak, child, or I will have no alternative but to send you both to the rope. Or should I have you examined by Master Finch too?'

The thought of young flesh being exposed and prodded before their eyes was too much for the gallery. They exploded.

The justice held up his hand for silence.

This was it. I had no choice. In speaking I would save myself but send Prudie to the gallows. I felt her hand inch towards mine and she clenched her fist around my trembling fingers. She was telling me to proceed. 'I– I was taken in by Prudie and

John Tenpenny when I was but a child of five. I have lived with Prudie these past twenty years.'

The justice raised his bushy grey brows in enquiry. 'So you have seen her consort with the devil, allow the devil to suckle at her teats, perhaps change into another creature or fly about the place?' He leaned in for the kill. 'Have you seen witness of Mistress Tenpenny conjuring up spells to bring harm to others?'

Prudie's hand squeezed mine.

'I have seen her heal and help people.'

The rabble in the gallery hissed their frustration. One yelled, 'Prick the slut, let us see the witchly flesh, let us see her devil's teats!' Amongst much lascivious cackling, I was aware of a scuffle and the thwack of fist upon flesh before someone was thrown out.

The justice narrowed his eyes at the gallery before turning to me and exhaling loudly. 'I should like this session to convene before luncheon and I warn you, Mistress Loveday. I ask you again, have you seen her conjure up spirits, have you seen her transform into a cat or a hare or some other such creature, have you seen her fly? Has she conjured up the devil's work to bring harm unto others? Did she bring harm unto the Lacey babe?' He sniffed and leaned forward. 'Or are you as guilty as she? Are you a witch too, Mistress Loveday? Say your piece and we may look kindly upon you, child, for you are as yet young and untried in the world.'

'I am happy to prick her, justice,' Matthias Finch piped up, his face alive and leering. 'I shall examine her in all her orifices for any mark of the devil.'

'Say what you must, Susie,' Prudie commanded, yanking on my hand. 'I will not see you suffer at the hands of that man. Say it.'

I lifted my chin. I could not do it. Scanning the gallery, I caught sight of Robert, his face white and taut, his eyes narrowed, urging me on. Should I believe him and trust I might receive leniency in return for my betrayal of the woman I loved? To my left Matthias Finch's face glistened wetly, I could smell his foul breath. I recalled what marks he had laid upon poor Prudie's body, how he had tortured her. I remembered her thighs running with blood. His upper lip curled, baring long yellow teeth, and he licked his lips in anticipation of running his hands over my body, of thrusting his fingers into my privy parts. If I said my piece, it may help spare Prudie from a repeat.

And, God forgive me, I could not endure the same torture.

The words ripped from my mouth before I had scarcely known I had said them. It was as if someone else was saying them, that something else had control of me. 'I saw Prudie Tenpenny fly. I saw her with the devil. I saw her conjure spells to bring harm to Elias Light.' Against the baying and roaring crowds, I yelled, 'For she is a witch. Prudence Tenpenny is a witch!'

The courtroom erupted, a cacophony of abuse and jeering that jabbed at my ears and thundered into my head. The clerk called for order to no avail, several were rough-housed from the public gallery, I clung on to the wooden rail in front of me, my hands white-knuckled, my whole being spasming in guilt of what I had just done.

Prudie. A still point in a reeling, lurching scene from Hell. I watched, astonished, as she raised her hands, spreading her fingers as if conducting the air. Small, frail, dressed in filthy rags, a poor old woman of no consequence from a small fishing town, she now held the power. All noise was sucked away. The courtroom gradually fell quiet, a few subdued whispers and then all was silent. Was she about to make her confession? I fervently prayed so. For if she admitted to the crimes of which she had been accused, Matthias Finch would have no more dominion in this room. She would go to be hanged but would suffer no more indignity at his hands.

'Mistress Tenpenny,' the clerk asked, his voice wavering, in no way as bullish as before. Prudie had cast her spell. 'Do you now wish to speak?'

Prudie's chin raised. She fixed her glare upon the justices on the bench above her. I saw one adjust his robes nervously. She had them within her thrall.

'I stand before you as a widow and bereaved mother,' she began. 'My life has been one of service to my family and to the mothers and sick of Flete. I asked little from life: food enough on my table, peace to live my life as I wished.'

The lead justice leaned forward, irritated. 'We ask again, Mistress Tenpenny. Art thou guilty of this felony?'

Prudie met his gaze with a withering one of her own and he fell back with a gasp. 'The world has condemned me as a witch,' she snarled, 'then so be it, I meet my fate as one.'

To my surprise, apart from a sort of fluttering sighing, there was no reaction. It was as if the room was terrified into silence.

'Take her away,' the justice said wearily.

Prudie began to shriek. Mad shrill words that made little sense. 'Heed this warning, men. From this day forward, treat your sisters, the mothers of your children, the women from whose loins you sprang with better care. For there will come a day when women and the power they hold will defy you. Once again they will rise. You may beat us, strip us, use us ill but we are of the world, of the earth and sky. Of Mother Nature herself. Treat us with disdain at your peril.'

'Take her down,' the justice yelled, losing his composure. 'We will hear no more of this nonsense.'

As she was dragged to her death, I could still hear Prudie screeching in the distance. Where had she found this strength? 'Let it be known, men of Exeter Assizes,' she screamed, 'my story and those women who have suffered before me, will be known! I will tell it. It will out...'

I heard no more. All was red and blackness. My grip loosened on the rail and I slid into oblivion.

∽

2018

'Oh dear lord.' Beth sat back, trying to absorb the dreadful details Nathan had just read out. 'So Susanna betrayed Prudie as a witch to save herself. She betrayed the woman who had brought her up, who was her mother in all senses of the word.'

They were back in the cool of the dining room. Nathan had laid down Susanna's papers and was turning a glass of water around in his hands, staring at it intently. Looking up, he said, 'Seems that way.' His voice was raw. 'And who can blame her. What a truly barbaric time. No defence lawyer, no counsel. Just you against the judge and the superstitious nonsense dreamed up by your accusing neighbours.'

'I don't *blame* her,' Beth said hotly. 'I don't blame her one bit. From what you've just read out, Prudie gave Susanna her blessing. Wanted to save her from what that bastard Finch wanted to do. And it sounds as if Susanna was trying to save Prudie from another examination. God, I can feel the sexual violence jumping out at me. The vile, perverted misogynistic monster. What chance did Prudie have?'

'None. Especially as Susanna condemned her. And then Prudie, herself, confessed. And what a speech.'

'She was determined to have her story told. And it has been. The knife! Susanna mentions a precious knife. Could that be the one found in my chimney? Prudie thought it contained magic but Susanna broke it. Why did she leave it there and not take it with her?' Beth's words were tumbling out any old way. Her thoughts following, jumbled and incoherent.

'I've no idea but it's hinted that the knife is very ancient. Far older than four hundred years.

'And our book must be Susanna's. Those must be her remedies, or the ones Prudie passed on to her. It's all so unbelievable. To have this connection with things that happened four hundred years ago!'

'And yes, this must be Susanna's book, everything is pointing that way.' Nathan gazed at her. 'But you're missing the important point. The betrayal is truly shocking but you're missing something.'

'What?'

'Susanna's surname. Beth, she *is* a Loveday. Like you.'

'Oh, Nathan.' Beth felt vomit surge in her gullet and her headache thicken. She clasped a hand to her throat in shock. 'A Loveday? So my ancestor?' She stared at him unable to speak, then, after a long silence whispered, 'I don't like this. I don't like how this is all crowding around us. What the fuck does it all mean? Why do they want us to know their story?'

'Beats me.' He swallowed his water in one. 'I'm not sure I can bear to read the rest.' He glanced at the parchment lying accusingly on the glossy table. 'But I'm not sure I can bear not to know. There's one more short extract. Shall we?'

'I don't think we have a choice. I think they're compelling us to get to the end.'

He nodded and, lifting the parchment, began to read once more.

∽

1660

I shall not dwell on the hanging. I was told Prudie was taken to Heavitree and put to her death. She made a good end, they said. I hoped it was true. Even though I was not witness, the images have haunted my days and nights ever since. I roll and rock and shriek and call out in my sleep, my husband says. I prayed there was a kind soul who hastened Prudie's ending as she aided Abigail all those years ago.

The next hours were a blur. Prudie was ripped from me and I collapsed. At some point I was taken to a room, I think in an inn, and stripped of what was left of my clothing. I feared I was in for an interrogation by Matthias Finch after all and that I had not escaped the court's justice, but an old woman attended me. She forced me to stand on shivering limbs and briskly washed me down. Dressing my hair under a fresh coif, she clothed me in a clean shift and skirts and force fed me gruel, humble stuff but nourishing. Throughout all this I remained numb and compliant. The shock of what had happened, of what I had done rendered me mute. I did not come to properly until bundled into Robert's carriage. We were on our way back to Flete, it seemed. But I was not to stay there. After he had revived me further with brandy and fed me morsels of bread and cheese, Robert began to talk.

'Hear this, Susanna. I must say this quickly or I fear I may lack the courage to say anything at all. I have paid passage for you and the smith, Barnabas, to Virginia. You will go to Flete, collect what belongings you require and take a cart and horse to Bideford. There, you will marry the smith and sail to the Colonies.' He inhaled, making his nostrils flare. 'It is impossible for you to stay in Flete, as you must realise. Not only would your life be in peril but I cannot risk you becoming the nub for parliamentary spies. I will not risk the peace of my town.' He leaned back against the carriage seat and a breath shuddered out of him. 'I have given the town the justice they bayed for,

Prudie is hanged and now we must move on. Create a new world. A peaceful one where our old enmities are gone. We have our king upon our throne and the wars are at an end, praise be.'

I stared at him, mouth agape, exhaustion making my reason weak. Fire from the brandy got through. 'Justice is done? An old woman, an *innocent* old woman, is hanged by the neck?'

He shifted uncomfortably. 'It was a sacrifice that had to be made,' he muttered stiffly through thinned lips.

'She was my mother!' I shouted. 'She nurtured me, helped me learn reading and writing. Taught me the ways of the world, passed on her skills and learning. She was my mother.' The last was uttered in a helpless whimper. I was too choked by tears to continue.

Robert bowed his head. 'I am sorry. Sorrier than I can say.'

I couldn't see his face, hidden as it was by the brim of his hat. 'Are you?' I demanded. 'Are you really sorry?'

He twisted towards me and to my surprise took my hand which, despite the old woman's scrubbing, was still black from gaol grime. The stains would take a long time to fade.

'Prudie was an old woman, Susie. An ill old woman, not long for this world. What choice had I? To let her continue to cause mischief or appease her old enemies and end the matter for good? If acquitted, how could she return to Flete? The old arguments would begin again, the unrest stirred once more. Where else would she go? Driven out like our old friend Mary, to die in a ditch? How could she travel to Virginia with you? She wouldn't last the voyage.'

Prudie had said much the same. But the words, the logic, didn't help. Tears coursed down my cheeks. 'It was I who sent her to the gallows. It was I who hung that rope around her neck. I killed her, as much as any justice and hangman.'

To my shock, he gathered my hands to his mouth, kissing them fervently. 'And I could not let that happen to you. I couldn't bear to see you hang too, my dearest, my own.' His tears began to fall and they joined mine. 'For everything I did, I did it for you, my beloved. For I love you. Have always loved you. I made a rash and stupid marriage and not once have I stopped regretting it. Prudie gave up her life, you will sacrifice your life in Flete, and I have to live with the knowledge that you will marry another man. But at least you will have a life.'

'You love me?' My mouth fell open.

He raised a tear-stricken face to mine and nodded. 'Of course. Always.'

This was too much. Robert had saved me from hanging with a bold plan that had succeeded – but at a terrible cost. He had swept in, bribed Barnabas to take me on and which was to exile me from my homeland. A hysterical laugh forced its way out. Barnabas was the only winner here; he had achieved his aim and at little endeavour from himself. I had lost Prudie, would have to live with the guilt of what I had done for the rest of my life. And I was to be banished far from my home. Married to a man who would no doubt be kind but who I wasn't sure I truly loved, not beyond the physical yearnings of a callow young girl. I would start a new life in strange and frightening lands. With him. Beholden to him, as wife to a husband should be. Where was my autonomy? Not for the first time I cursed my sex and poor position in life. 'Would I were a man, you would not order me about so!'

It brought a wry smile to his lips. 'If you were a man, I should not love you so.'

I stared at him, thinking on his words. For a moment I considered rejecting his machinations. Could I return to Flete and live there? How would I make a living, alone and friendless? The Flowers family would not let me be, neither would I escape Samuel Thatcher's attentions. Women like me, without a man, were fair sport. I recalled his lust-reddened face with a shudder.

I was defenceless, with no power, no prospects and only my wit to commend me. Far more happily situated women had entered Lucia Pettit's bawdy house as a last picking in life and I would not stoop to that. Robert was offering me a new home, a husband's protection and a new beginning in a land where I could be anything I invented. It was dizzying and terrifying in equal measure. I knew I had no choice but to accede, but it didn't make me resent it any less. And he had done all this because he loved me. I wasn't sure how much of his passion I believed. He had to solve the Prudie problem and had done so. Surely I was just another hindrance?

He took my hands again and stared burningly into my eyes, seeming to read my thoughts. 'Tis true. I love you, Susanna, God forgive me,' he said gruffly. 'And for this I let you go. If I loved you less, I would make you stay.'

I softened. Maybe his emotions were truer than I gave credit.

The carriage jolted us together. He threw off his hat and kissed me, soft and tender. It took me by surprise. I had expected him to violate me. Many men would have done so. To my astonishment, I felt myself melting into his embrace. It was as if meant to happen. As if everything in my life had led to this moment. My senses quickened into life as never before. The kiss held the promise of beginning and the pain of end. And then, all too soon, although perhaps soon enough, the carriage lurched and we were apart again.

'Damn these cursed roads.' He bit off another oath and turned to the window.

I reached for his hand, desperate for his touch, and he twisted back to me in surprise. His sensitive embrace had unmanned me. I began to see him in a different light; not so much my enemy, but indeed my saviour. He had risked much in order to help me. I may not agree with how, but I could see no other solution for my future. Perhaps, I marvelled, he did love me a little. Heaving breath into my lungs, I said my piece. 'I accept your plan, Robert. I will go to the Colonies with Barnabas.' It would seem Robert Lacey loved me more than a little. I gasped out, 'Maybe, in another life I could have loved you, had things been different.'

'Had things been different. Had we inhabited different lives.' He stroked a wondering finger down my cheek, staring deep into my eyes. 'I shall never forget you, Susanna Loveday. Til the end of my days on this earth. I shall not forget you, no, nor in this life and the next.' He gave me a little shake. 'I will seek you down the centuries, through time itself, to love you again but as you *truly* deserve.' He kissed me again, this time his lips were full of yearning, full of unfulfilled passion. It left me dazed and breathless. 'To the next time we meet,' he said violently. 'And to the next time we love. One more kiss to seal my promise for it's one I will honour, as God is my witness.' Holding me to him, he once more kissed me. Then he leaned back against the seat, a trembling hand to his eyes, hiding the emotion.

And as such we sat, all the long way to Flete, intimate in the closeted space of the carriage, lost in misery and thoughts of what might have been, and so very far apart.

∽

2018

The rope tightened, scratched at Beth's tender skin, snatching life's air from her body, making her eyes bulge. She felt the room spinning, fading from view. The last thing she was aware of was Nathan's anxious face hovering above, his worried voice asking her if she was all right.

CHAPTER 32

JULY 2018

'Thank goodness you're looking better.'

Beth lay back on the sun lounger in the shade of Nathan's garden. Evening was deepening, with the trees dappling long shadows. Somewhere a blackbird sang a rich and lilting tune. All felt cool and soothing.

She glanced over at him and sipped the water he'd given her. Her throat felt less scratchy, the swollen soreness had disappeared and her head had cleared. Maybe, with all the hot weather a thunderstorm was building and the pressure had affected her? It was the more logical explanation. She refused to dwell on the other. Suppressing a shudder, she said, 'Feeling much better.' She eyed up the pizza that had just been delivered. 'Gearing myself up for a slice of pepperoni.'

'Do you good to eat. Wine, hot sun and a shock is a potent combination.' Nathan got up, put a slice of pizza on a plate, added a paper serviette and gave it to her. 'I don't normally press food on people, but I really think you should eat. You had me worried back there but your BPs okay now and your colour's returned.'

Beth picked off a slice of juicy red pepper and nibbled in

silence. She didn't want to examine the cause of her fainting, didn't want to remember the dreadful feel of the tightening noose. Closing her mind against the image of poor Prudie dangling, kicking from the gallows, she concentrated fiercely on the lush greenness of Nathan's garden, on the scent of dampening grass, on the reassuringly ordinary sound of the blackbird. Once she'd begun eating, she found she was ravenous so gobbled down two slices of pizza in one go. Feeling replete and far more like her normal self, she eyed the man sitting at her side. He was deep in contemplation, sipping a glass of wine. The low sun accentuated the fine planes of his face, slanting and exaggerating his cheekbones. In profile his nose was prominent and strong and she noticed, for the first time, how smooth and clear his skin was. Was he really the reincarnation of Robert Lacey? Was she Susanna Loveday? Had she and Nathan been put here to find love again and to do it better this time? How could that be? It was all too fantastical. Weird as hell but alluring.

She touched her still tender neck. The fainting fit and the only too real sensation of the rope around her neck had been all Prudie. She had been the one to lose her life to the noose. Beth closed her eyes in a vain attempt to empty her mind of the sickening falling sensation and the kicking out into the void as the noose strangled. It had been terrifying and she'd been glad to sink into oblivion to escape. Maybe Prudie was trying to tell her story too? That poor innocent old woman. All she'd done was use her knowledge to heal and had been driven mad by the taunts of those with a vendetta. No wonder she'd lashed out. Beth thought how brave Prudie had been. And Robert Lacey. What a man. They'd all got him wrong, even Susanna. Flawed he may be, but he'd loved her so much he'd paid for her new life and provided her with another man in order to save her.

Nathan was silent, his brows knitted together, deep in

thought. In other circumstances she could really fall for him, Beth thought. The instant recognition and physical lust when they'd first met had deepened into a respect and liking for the man. He was good to be around. Something within her unwillingly acknowledged the relief of not being alone, of not having only herself to rely upon. They still hadn't discussed him going away. Too much seventeenth century and not enough twenty-first. She wondered what the job was, he could be gone for months or years. And now, more than ever, Beth felt rooted in Flete. She wanted to make a life here. The idea came to her so suddenly she nearly spilled her glass of water. She would continue with Prudie and Susanna's healing! Train in herbal medicine. She'd research courses as soon as she got home. The excitement began to form into a solid plan. Maybe she could rent a treatment room in the Mindfulness Centre? It would be the perfect place. Susanna had been trapped in a time where women had little power, had had no choice but to tag along with Barnabas and make her life fit round his. But she had all the privileges the twenty-first century bestowed on her. Unsure just how it would fit in with running her shop, Beth was filled with a strength and purpose she hadn't felt for a long time, maybe had never felt. Learning Prudie and Susanna's story had brought together all the strands in her life: her grandmother's weird and wonderful folk remedies, her shadowy and mysterious Loveday ancestors. Prudie had ended her life in the worst possible way, having given it up to the healing of others. Susanna's was blighted by a betrayal so deep she would surely have carried the scars for the length of hers. Beth owed it to both women to continue their legacy.

How had Susanna and Barnabas managed? Had Susanna built a life in Virginia and been able to carry on healing? Surely hers would be skills much needed in a newly formed community. If the theory was correct and Nathan was descended from Susanna and Barnabas they must have had children. Beth hoped she'd been happy, or as happy as she could, but it must have been a brutal life.

Nathan put his glass down with a clink as his phone trilled. 'Excuse me, will you be okay if I take this?'

Beth nodded as he went into the house to take the call. She'd made up her mind. As soon as she felt able, she'd ring around and enquire about courses in herbal medicine. She'd employ an assistant in the shop to ease some of the pressure. Build a proper business, to hell with the troll reviews. If she built up enough loyal repeat custom surely the negative comments would lessen or at least have less of an impact and be seen for what they were; openly and emptily malicious? She wanted to do this! She wanted to honour Susanna's memory and commemorate Prudie by becoming one of them – a healer. Finishing her glass of water, she was relieved to find her throat no longer ached and her head had cleared. In fact, she felt healthier and more energetic than she had for weeks.

Her thoughts were interrupted by Nathan's return. He looked shocked. Sitting down, he began speaking without preamble. 'That was my cousin in the States. She's just uncovered some family history. It was bugging me why, if the theory that Barnabas Smith is my ancestor is correct, he settled in Virginia in the south when all my family comes from New England in the north. There's been a story kicking round the family for generations. About a sea captain sailing between the Caribbean islands and the southern ports and Boston.' He glanced up, looking uncomfortable. 'Slaves and sugar one way, tea and whale oil the other.'

Beth remained silent, wondering what was coming next.

'Cousin Lilian has just found out that an ancestor on the Smith side was indeed a sea captain trading between the north and south. Born in Virginia, he sailed to Boston and married a local girl there.' He blew out a breath. 'His father was Barnabas Smythe who was a blacksmith by trade, married to a woman called Susanna. It's all there in the town records. The Jamestown history centre has a website record of who settled the town in Virginia. Their names and occupation. Everything. Lilian checked it out online.'

Beth leaned forward, hardly daring to breathe. 'And?'

'Barnabas the smith and Susanna his wife had nine children. All raised to adulthood, which must have been unheard of back then. John was the youngest, who went on to become the sea captain, married Anne and began the northern branch of the Smiths. At some point we must have lost the y and the e.'

He gazed at Beth with glistening eyes. She was moved by his emotion. 'Good old Susanna,' she said, pleased for a woman she'd never met and yet knew so well. 'Nine healthy children. She must have used Prudie's recipe book expertly. So you're a direct descendent of Barnabas and Susanna?'

'Just as you may be.' He clasped her hand. 'So, is this thing reincarnation or tribal memory? Something else?'

'I don't know,' she replied, thinking back to the weird strangling sensation that had caused her to faint. 'I really don't know, Nathan. Nor do I know if this is all over or what we do to bring closure.'

He shook his head a little. 'Can we, do you think, sort it out together?'

There was so much more to discuss, to sort through but Beth was numb. Drained, she couldn't find the right words to answer, so just nodded quickly in response. 'I need to go,' she gasped, suddenly, desperately needing escape. Without waiting for his answer, she rushed out.

CHAPTER 33

AUGUST 2018, TWO WEEKS LATER

After leaving Nathan's house so abruptly, Beth had walked home. The gathering gloom and cool of the summer evening did much to cleanse her brain and soothe her mind. She needed distance, craved space to sort everything out. She just hoped he'd still be around to talk when she was ready. She'd collapsed into a lonely bed, then slept like the dead.

And now it was nearly two weeks later. And so much had happened.

Her first instinct, the morning after leaving Nathan's, was to delete her Facebook pages, wanting to rid her life of any social media completely. To make a fresh start. However, her mother was ignoring all calls and texts, so it was worth trying Messenger. For once, she didn't blame Sarah for going off grid. After her own online abuse, she could see the appeal. Having asked Lorna if she had any information and drawn a blank, and knowing her grandparents knew nothing, her mother was her last and most obvious source.

Hey, Mum, she typed, before she had time to chicken out. *Wanted to ask you something. Do you know the name of my dad?*

Then all she'd had to do was wait. There was always the

chance her mother wouldn't know, of course. From what Beth had been told of Sarah's early life, it had been a non-stop wild partying time. A smile curled at her lips. The same couldn't be said of her daughters. Lorna had married her first boyfriend and concentrated on making a home; it didn't take too much psychoanalysis to work out she was ferociously replicating what had been missing from her own childhood. As for herself, Beth had kept her distance from anyone too demanding on her emotions, unwilling to risk attaching herself to someone who, like her mother, might disappear. That was apart from Hugh. It was why the transference of his affections to Jade had hurt so much. They were among a group of only a few people Beth had allowed herself to get close to. That didn't stand up to too much analysis either.

Nearly two weeks into her self-imposed retreat, she hauled herself out of bed, made tea and stared out of the sitting-room window at the sunshine and the sliver of sapphire sea in the distance. It had been a tumultuous time.

Sitting down on the sofa, she cuddled Frank, gaining comfort from sinking her fingers into his thick black fur. She tried hard not to keep checking her phone. Nothing. No message from her mother. No call from Nathan. Florence had been coming over later to see Frank but had cried off, so the day stretched ahead, empty. She'd become a good friend. Had recommended a Betonica medical herbalism course in Uffculme, not too far away, had encouraged her to talk. Had warned her not to remain so closed off from people, to accept help when it was offered. To open up her heart.

Beth's phone vibrated and she jumped on it. She was disappointed to see it was only Bill from the museum.

'Beth,' she began without preamble. 'I've been digging into the Lovedays.'

'Hi, Bill. What have you found out?' Beth had popped into

the museum and updated her with the new information she and Nathan had found out. There had been something niggling. If Susanna had originally been a Loveday from Exeter, why was Flete associated with the surname?

'Old Betty died childless,' Bill continued.

'Yes, I knew that.'

'Hold your breath to cool your porridge, child. She came from a big family of Lovedays in Exeter. Turns out some of 'em came to Flete in the mid-nineteenth century to work in the cement factory.'

'Cement factory?' Beth said, startled. It wasn't quite the romantic tale she'd envisioned.

Bill laughed. ''Twas on the front, the cliff end. It's the Masonic Hall now but least said of that lot the better,' she huffed. 'Do a bit of hunting around and you'll find a few more Loveday folk round here. So, you can consider yourself descended from proper born and bred Devon Lovedays.'

'Thank you, Bill.'

'Told you, you young things should take more notice of your roots. The past makes sense of where we are now. Always has. Always will.'

Beth thought of Robert Lacey and Susanna Loveday. Of Prudie Tenpenny and Barnabas the smith. 'You don't know how true that is.'

Bill cackled. 'Oh, don't I? See that you and your doctor come by the museum and bring Susanna's secret document. I'd like to give it the once over with my old eyes.'

'Will do.'

Bill clicked off before Beth could say anything more. She stared at the phone in her hand. The gaping hole, now Susanna and Prudie's story had been told, was making itself felt; she needed something to keep her busy. Her finger hovered over her contacts list. There was someone else she had to ring. The information that had come in from Steve and then the police had been conclusive; the person behind the trolling and online harassment had revealed themselves. Her stomach rolled as she hesitated over the ring button. This was someone she knew. Someone who had once been very dear to her. The police had made it clear she could take it further should she wish but Beth had asked them if she could think about it. More than revenge, or justice even, she wanted an explanation.

Her university friend, Clodagh, had been right after all. It took so much effort to allow people into her life, she hung on to them beyond the friendship's lifespan and despite what they did to her. And now it was finally time to break the habit.

The previous week, having to grit her teeth and force herself back onto Facebook, she'd spent a tedious couple of hours scrolling through the photographs on her feed and those on her friends. One had jogged a memory. It was a snap of herself, Jade and Hugh standing in a pub beer garden taken the previous summer. The photo on her feed was a good one of them all, taken by Alec, another university friend, but it triggered a memory. When Hugh and Alec had gone to buy another round, Jade had taken a close-up selfie of just the two of them, joking that now she was an old married woman, there wouldn't be many more evenings out like this. Beth had turned to her friend, thrown her head back and laughed just as Jade had taken it. Beth hadn't liked the photo, her face was flushed by too much sun and wine and her hair had gone frizzy, so she'd deleted it soon after Jade had sent it. Jade said she'd deleted it too. Beth had checked and double checked, it was nowhere on her Facebook or Twitter accounts. Nor was it on Jade's. But the angle of her arched throat and the low ray of sun glinting on her long silver earring was identical to the one used for the online porn.

After talking it through with a muzzy-headed, end-of-term exhausted but sympathetic Steve, and then the police, everyone had come to the same conclusion; it was circumstantial evidence that pointed to Jade being behind the online abuse campaign. Something deep inside Beth had known it all along. She'd denied it, refusing to believe her oldest friend, her *best* friend, could do something this vile. Comically misspelled fake reviews on her website were one thing but to deepfake hardcore porn was beyond despicable.

Beth had taken to her bed and had lain unsleeping and unblinking, holding Frank and remaining motionless for days. Eventually a rage of tears had her balled into the foetal position until Florence had rescued her, fed her chamomile tea and wholegrain toast and forced her into the shower.

Weirdly, Beth thought now as she stared at her phone, she could have coped better had it been Hugh. For a woman to do this to another woman was a particularly wicked kind of betrayal. Susanna had betrayed Prudie but Beth could see the reasoning behind it. It had been a life-or-death decision. And, according to Susanna, it had been with Prudie's blessing. Why would Jade want to do something this utterly cruel?

Fury blazed through her, making her jab on Jade's number. For once she didn't check to see if it was a possible nap or feed time, she didn't care if their routine was interrupted.

'Hello, Beth.'

It was Hugh. For a second, Beth was so taken aback she didn't know how to reply. Why was Hugh answering Jade's phone? Glancing at the clock, she also wondered why he was at home at two o'clock in the afternoon on a work day. 'Hugh. Hi. I wanted to speak to Jade.'

'Oh, Beth,' Hugh's voice broke.

'What's happened?' The anger drained away. Something was wrong. Very wrong.

'It's Jade. She's–' Hugh muffled a sob.

Beth waited impatiently for him to control himself.

Apprehension made her stomach hollow. Whatever Jade had done, their history went back a long way. She thought back to how trapped Jade had looked briefly when they'd visited the shop that time and her suspicions had been raised about what kind of husband Hugh was. Surely he hadn't–

'She's had some kind of–' Another long stuttering pause.

Beth could hear him breathing hard. She forced herself to think rationally. Of course Hugh wouldn't do any harm to his wife, not purposefully. He might buy into thinking he'd bagged a nineteen fifties housewife maybe. Beth remembered Jade saying he was often late home from work, expecting a meal on the table. A bit of pompous neglect possibly, but she must remember not every man was vile and perverted like those she'd come across in the seventeenth century–

'Breakdown.'

Oh God. This was way out of his sphere of understanding. He came from the stiff upper lip, pull up your trousers and get on with it school. 'A breakdown?' A sharp pang of concern stabbed. Hugh wouldn't cope well with this. 'Have you got anyone with you?'

'Yes. My parents flew down yesterday. Mum's looking after me.'

The concern was swiftly replaced with irritation. 'And who's looking after Jade?'

'She's been admitted into a...' Beth heard him drag in a painful breath, '...a unit over in Dorset. It was the closest bed they could find.'

'Jeez. And what about the baby?'

'Hamish is with her.'

'That's good. Isn't it?' Hugh wasn't the only one floundering here. This was beyond Beth's experience too.

'I don't know. I suppose. I wouldn't have the first idea of how to look after him.'

The irritation returned with a vengeance. 'He's your son too, Hugh.'

'I know, I know. It's just Jade didn't let me anywhere near him. Didn't really let anyone near him. I thought she was doing so well, being such an excellent mother. Lame excuse. I didn't see what was going on in front of my eyes.'

'And what happens now?'

'I'm not sure. They said it's post-natal psychosis. Hormones messed up or something. Jade will be treated and come home at some point. I'm going over to see her tomorrow so I'll know more then.'

Beth swallowed painfully. 'Give her my...' she trailed off. 'I hope she's better soon.'

'That's good of you, Beth, under the circumstances. I know what she did, you see.'

Beth couldn't speak for a moment. 'You *know*?'

'The last few days, it's been difficult. Jade was raving about something to do with photos and online porn and then she mentioned you. To be honest, by that point she was hallucinating too so I didn't know what was real and what was, well, I didn't have a clue what was going on. I'd never seen her like that.'

'Oh God. It must have been horrible for you both.'

'It's been...' his voice trailed off into a hoarse whisper. 'After she was admitted I got into her phone and it was all there. Everything that she's done.' He began to sob and Beth heard his mother, in her delicate Edinburgh accent, consoling him in the background. 'No, Mother, I have to say this. Beth, if you want to press charges I'd completely understand. The evidence trail is all here. Screenshots of the nasty comments on your shop's website and,' he gave a wailing cry, 'the Photoshopped images.'

Beth stayed silent. At the other end of the line she could hear ice clinking into glasses and liquid being poured. The

MacDonald clan were having a stiff drink; she could almost smell the single malt. She didn't blame them. Justice was within her grasp. What Jade had done was contemptible, wicked even. But had it been the actions of a rational person? Nathan's words that he'd met people who had done evil but had never met anyone *actually* evil came back to her. What good would it do Jade, or herself for that matter, to drag it through the legal system? How would little Hamish react if, when older, he found out? 'I don't know what to do, Hugh. That… stuff stays on the net no matter how hard you try to delete it all.' She blew out a frustrated, angry breath. 'But what would I achieve taking it to a prosecution? Oh God, Hugh, it's all such a mess.'

'I know, Bethie.'

She heard him gulp again. He must be tanking the whisky. 'Why do you think she did it?'

'I've no idea.' He blew his nose and went quiet, then continued. 'She often complained she felt she'd lost her sense of self, moaned how bored she was. Was definitely sleep deprived and they use sleep deprivation as a torture method, did you know?'

'I did, as a matter of fact.'

'And she was always saying how jealous she was of you.'

'*She* was jealous of *me*?' Beth gave a hard short laugh. 'She was the one who ended up with you as a husband and father of her baby. What did I have for her to be jealous of?'

'Your own business. Independence. She always admired how you didn't seem to need anyone. That you forged your own path.'

'I didn't have much choice, did I?' Beth answered with asperity.

'No. No you didn't. I'm sorry about all that, you know. I feel I messed you around. Jade, well, Jade just swooped me up and before I knew it, we were making wedding plans.'

'You knew exactly what you were doing, Hugh, don't kid yourself. Besides, I was never your idea of a perfect wife, was I?'

'You're the one who got away, Bethie,' he whined. 'I realise that now.'

Beth couldn't believe she'd heard him correctly. Anger sparked again. 'You made it perfectly clear you wanted nothing to do with me as a girlfriend!'

He didn't answer.

'Look, I hope Jade recovers, I genuinely do. I won't press charges, I promise. But this is the end of our friendship.'

Hugh began to bluster. 'Well, I can quite see you wouldn't want to see Jade again.'

Revulsion bubbled up. 'I mean the friendship between the three of us. I don't want to see either of you. Ever again.'

'Oh, Beth, you can't mean that!'

'What do you think, Hugh?' Beth replied softly. 'Send Jade my sincere wishes for a full recovery,' she added and clicked the phone off.

She sat back, shoulders unknotting. Exhaling, she lifted her mug and drank cold tea wishing it was something stronger. She'd hung on to Jade and Hugh for too long. They were remnants of another life, university life, and it was all a long time ago now. Jade was wrong, she *did* need people but not people as toxic as that.

Glancing at her phone again, she saw a message had finally come through from her mother. The information, weirdly, came as no surprise. It was as if she had always known. It made many of the experiences she'd been having that summer make a sort of sense. It was the final, irrevocable link.

And there was only one person she wanted to share the news with.

CHAPTER 34

AUGUST 2018

Nathan opened his front door at her first knock. His face split into a warm and, she thought, relieved smile. 'Beth, how wonderful to see you.'

She stepped into the hallway that was filled with scent of Geranium and Orange from the cloakroom and noted the line of battered running shoes. It all felt very familiar and yet strange.

Despite Nathan asking to work together through this weird thing that had happened to them, Beth hadn't wanted to contact him. She'd needed to process Jade's betrayal. Lick her wounds. Begin to rebuild her self-confidence. She planned to open the shop soon and it almost seemed like an act of defiance; she was desperate to get her business going again. Florence had been amazing, fussing over her, feeding her nourishing vegetarian casseroles and soups, and soothing tisanes while they'd researched the course on medical herbalism she yearned to do. Beth had been startled to discover how rigorous it was but she was still determined to train. Florence had even offered a treatment room in the Mindfulness Centre when she was qualified. Everything was coming together as if meant to be.

However, until today, she hadn't been ready to see Nathan.

He was an added complication she didn't want to deal with. Another layer of tugging emotion on top of all that had happened. Maybe it had been the good food, Florence's tender care or simply the sense that something had come to its conclusion, but Beth felt lighter and untroubled. Happier than she'd felt for years.

'I've been meaning to come over.'

'And I'm very glad you have. Luckily, you've caught me in.'

'Saturday seemed a good day to catch you. Are you back at work now?'

Nathan nodded. 'I was lucky to get as much leave in one go as it was. Back in the surgery now so my colleagues with children can take some leave in the school holidays.'

Of course. The season had shifted into full summer holiday mode. The town and beach were packed, cafés and pubs full of people bent on enjoyment, despite the worst the British weather threw at them.

'Come on in. I'm supposed to be mowing the lawn, but I've given up and I'm having a beer.'

'A beer would be great.' She followed him through to the garden, thinking he looked tired. Worry lines creased at his eyes and he looked too lean.

Settled at the little white wrought-iron table she refused a glass and drank Peroni from the bottle. The garden was lapsing into a cool shade. A lawn mower sat abandoned, its tank of cuttings radiating the powerful scent of damp grass, which made her nostrils tickle. 'You look exhausted.'

He nodded and rubbed a hand over his face. 'Always a shock to be back at work after such a long break and it's been manic. Lots of tourists in town so lots of cases of terminal sunburn and forgotten prescriptions. On top of everything else.' He gazed at her penetratingly. 'More importantly, how are you? Have to say you're looking incredibly well. You've had me worried. Have you been for a check-up?'

'No need. I feel better. Sleeping brilliantly, no more headaches or other weird symptoms. I feel lighter.'

'You look it. Good. I'm pleased and surprised. It hasn't been the most relaxing few weeks.'

She smiled. 'That it hasn't.'

He stared into his bottle, lips pursed. 'I've had decisions to think over too.'

Ah. So he was going to the States.

In an abrupt change of tone he added, 'What's new with you?'

Beth sucked in a deep breath. 'I found out who was behind the deepfake porn.'

Nathan leaned forward. 'That's fantastic news.' He took note of her expression. 'Isn't it?'

She gave him a brief explanation. 'Last I heard she was in hospital receiving treatment.' A wave of sadness overcame her. For Jade. For their friendship.

Nathan took a gulp of beer, obviously shocked. 'That's a tough thing for you to work through, Beth. For Jade too. I've only ever dealt with one case of post-partum psychosis. It can be devastating at the time but, with the right drugs, recovery can be good. And you say the baby's with her?'

Beth nodded.

'That will help. She should receive counselling and help with learning how to bond with the baby.'

'I feel guilty.' Beth turned the beer bottle around in her fingers.

'Whyever so?'

'I knew something wasn't right. From the very start when Jade and Hugh came to the shop with the baby, I could tell how hard-wired they both were. But Jade's always had these highs and lows, wild moods, rants about random stuff. I just put it down to Jade being Jade but an uber version. And when I went to see her, there was something definitely off. She was exhausted and quite clearly hadn't had a shower for some time, bit my head off at whatever I said, fell asleep in front of me.'

'Having a newborn is hard work and a hell of a shock to the system, even if you think you're well prepared.' His lips twitched wryly. 'Or so my sister tells me.'

'It was more than that though. When I visited, she was behaving really peculiarly. Picked up a biscuit, took one bite and put it down. Then took another and repeated the action. Then left them crumbled all over the coffee table. That wasn't like her, and it was weird. Obsessive.' Beth examined her bottle and gently teased a corner of the damp label off. 'And she was so bitter, angry even. At the time I blamed lack of sleep.'

'And it could easily have been that. Not getting enough sleep is torture.'

'I should have done more. Asked Hugh what was going on, had a proper conversation with Jade but she more or less threw me out. Then she sent me this vile email and that was hard to forgive, especially when she dismissed it as being something she'd done when up with the baby in the night and there was nothing to it. Nothing to it for *her* but the words hurt *me*.' Beth swallowed some beer. 'But we'd been drifting away from one another for a while, ever since she and Hugh got together really.' She glanced at Nathan who she saw was listening intently as was his usual way. 'I think we all pretended to be ever so civilised, but the friendship was beginning to crack. I'd had enough and went low contact but I could have helped.'

Nathan was silent for a moment then added, 'I doubt, even if you had mentioned something to either of them, that they would have taken any notice. In my experience, with post-birth depression and trauma it's only when things reach crisis point that people acknowledge they need help. She'll get better. It might take some time, but she'll recover. Maybe then you could even think about resurrecting your friendship. If you want to?'

'Possibly.' After thinking it over endlessly she'd conceded that, at some point in the very distant future, she may pick up the pieces of the friendship. Jade hadn't been in her right mind when doing such horrible things. 'It was a foul thing to do to another human being.' She shivered, the vile image crowding her vision. 'And I'll never be able to get it completely taken down. It'll be swimming around in the swamp that is social media forever.' She hesitated.

'But?'

'But even if there's the vague chance of getting back in touch with Jade, I've no desire to ever set eyes on Hugh again. That I've decided.'

'Because?'

Beth sensed his quickening interest. She repeated what Hugh had said on the phone.

'The bastard!' Nathan exploded, slamming his beer bottle down. 'His wife has just given birth and is seriously ill and he hits on you?'

'Yeah.' Beth let a giggle escape. 'It would be funny if it wasn't so appalling.'

Nathan met her eyes and snorted. 'Glad you can see the funny side.'

'I can't see me rebuilding a friendship with Jade when I think her husband is a twonk.'

'No,' he agreed.

They sat in silence. Beth jumped as a flock of swifts screamed overhead. Two magpies stood on the lawn eyeing them curiously. One stalked, comically stiff-legged, and then took off, the other following, soaring into the sky. Black and white, their long blue-green tails trailing iridescence in the sunshine. Two for joy, her gran always said. And Bill claimed they mated for life. Was it a sign? A blessing?

Beth glugged back more beer and set the bottle on the table with a decisive clunk. 'In other news, though, I've found out I'm a Tenpenny.'

'You're a Tenpenny?' Nathan's eyes sparkled. 'That's amazing. How come?'

'My dad. He never stayed around so I never knew him and his name isn't on my birth certificate.'

'So how did you find out?'

'The simple way. I asked Mum. I tracked her down in Vietnam. She eventually messaged me back. His name was Lance Tenpenny. Looks like I'm part Loveday, part Tenpenny. Which is pretty weird.'

'It's all completely bizarre but I suppose finding out you're a Tenpenny is no weirder than the rest of the stuff we've found out. How do you feel about it?'

Beth shrugged. 'I've never felt my life lacked anything with him not being a part of it. Doubt if he even knows I exist.'

'Do you think you'll try to trace him?'

'Don't know,' Beth said slowly. 'Not right now but maybe, at some point in the future. It's not a common name so I should think it'll be easy enough. It's more exciting thinking I could be connected to Prudie.' Her hand strayed to her throat. 'The creepy dreams, the vile choking sensations, the overwhelming feeling of being watched. I couldn't understand how they were connected to Susanna when she wasn't the one who was hanged. But it makes more sense now.' She gave a short laugh. 'Or as much sense as any of this does. It was Prudie as well as

Susanna who was desperate to tell us their story. Prudie especially.' She flicked Nathan a half-embarrassed glance.

He saluted her with his beer and drank. 'Amen to that. So a Tenpenny has returned to Tenpenny House.'

'Yes. Peculiar, isn't it? Almost as if it was meant to be.'

'And do you think you'll stay there now?'

Beth nodded. 'Yes. I feel as if it's where I want to be. And it's got a different atmosphere now, much lighter, more welcoming. It was getting to the point I didn't want to be there on my own but now I feel it's really my home. Trade might pick up too. At least customers can actually get to me without clambering around orange safety barriers.'

Nathan's lips twitched. 'I saw the road works had finished.'

She looked at him questioningly. 'If you were in Clappers Lane, why didn't you come to see me?'

He put down his bottle and ran a finger across it, wiping condensation away. 'I sensed you needed some space after all that's happened. It's been pretty crazy, hasn't it? Lot to get your head round.' He paused. 'Besides, I wasn't sure I would be welcome.'

It was on the tip of Beth's tongue to say he'd always be welcome but it was crushed out of her with a sudden shyness. Instead, she blurted out, 'I've been talking things over with Florence. Decided I'm going to enrol on a herbalism course. An introductory one to begin with, see how I get on.' She hesitated. 'I want to be a medical herbalist. Carry on what Prudie and Susanna did. Sort of.' A frown creased her brow. 'A tribute to them, I suppose. And to the women who went before them. The ones who used the ancient knife with the carved bone handle. All those women who were revered and valued.'

'Sounds amazing, Beth.' Nathan gazed at her proudly. 'How will it fit in with running the shop?'

She wrinkled her nose. 'I've no idea,' she said with a laugh, 'but somehow I'll make it work. I'm even considering rebranding the shop and reclaiming the name witch. How does "The Witch's Magpie" sound?'

'Perfect.' He leaned back on his chair and beamed. 'All sounds positive. *You* sound positive. As if everything's slotting into place.'

'It is. Talking things over with Florence has made things make sense. She speaks very highly of you, by the way.'

Nathan's lips twisted. 'Apart from when dissing my vocation, Flo and I are good friends, always have been. I just wish I could get her to see complementary medicine and my kind could work together more but that there are some illnesses only orthodox medicine can treat. I'm not the enemy, Beth.'

'She doesn't think that. *I* don't think that.'

He met her look. 'Don't you?'

'No.'

'Even though I've Lacey blood running through my veins?'

'I think,' Beth began and then halted. 'I think Susanna and Robert had a complex relationship. I also think Robert loved Susanna very much. He must have done. He saved her from the gallows and sent her to a new life in Virginia where it sounds as if she was happy enough with her smith.'

'I think she probably was.' Nathan smiled a little and reached for his phone. He scrolled through it. 'My cousin found another list on the Jamestown website.' He handed it over. 'It's the names of all the Smythe children. Susanna must have been a skilled medic to raise them all to adulthood.'

'She must have been indeed. I hope I'm half as skilful.' She shook her head wonderingly as she read the list. 'How amazing to know their names, to see them written down. Oh!' A lump of emotion lodged in her throat. 'Susanna, Barnabas, Abigail, Mercy, Robert, James, Thomas, Prudence and John. They named their children after all the important people in their lives.' She passed the phone back with a trembling hand. 'That's wonderful and so touching.'

'It is.' He smiled with warmth. 'She must have loved Robert a little to name a son after him.'

'She must have done.' A pause fell into the space between them. 'I never, ever thought you were the enemy, Nathan. In fact, quite the contrary.'

He gave her a hard stare. 'Answer this, Beth, and think before you give me your reply as a lot depends upon it. How do you feel about me? About us?'

'Can't you guess?'

He shook his head, exasperated. 'No, or why would I ask? I find you hard to read, to unpick what you're thinking. I felt, I think *we* felt the bond between us. I know I was instantly attracted to you. It hit me like a sledgehammer and then I thought something was building, in between all this weirdness we've had thrown at us, but then I felt you withdraw. I tried to give you space, I really did. But if you hadn't have come over tonight, I would have been hammering on your door.'

'Would you?' Beth's breath hitched with need.

'You've been driving me wild ever since we first met. You must know that.'

'I l-like you, Nathan.'

He bit his lip, his shoulders dipping. 'Like?'

'Maybe, in other circumstances, I could have loved you.' Why was she lying to him like this? She burned for him, body and soul.

'In other circumstances? I don't know what you mean.'

'You're going away. I don't know for how long or whether it's permanent. I wouldn't blame you. You've got family in the States and the chance to live there for a while. It's a great opportunity.' He began to speak but she put up her hand. 'Let me finish. Maybe there could have been something really good happening between us, but I can't risk getting involved. It happened before, with Hugh. We were so close. I suppose I let myself think we'd always be together but he wanted, or thought he wanted, something else, to *live* somewhere else and he broke up with me. Ironically, he only lasted a few months over there but as soon as he returned, he got together with Jade.' She bit down on sudden tears. 'It took me years to get over it. When you've grown up with a part-time mum you guard your heart well, Nathan. It messes you up. Rejection is something you live with because if,' she sucked in a ragged breath, 'your mum can't stick around to love you, it doesn't make you feel very loveable. If your own mother doesn't love you, why should you be worthy of anyone else's love? And you only give your love reluctantly and to someone you're certain will return it. Not to someone about to embark on a whole new life in a country on the other side of the world.' She shook her head wildly. 'I couldn't risk that heartbreak again. Can't you see?'

'I do.' Nathan exhaled heavily. 'And that's what this is all about?'

'Yes. Mixed up with all the Robert Lacey, Susanna Loveday stuff. That and thinking I was possessed by something trying to strangle me. Not to mention my new business being trolled and being a victim of deepfake porn.' Beth attempted a laugh but it came out shaky and half-hearted.

'It's been quite the summer.'

'It certainly has.' She couldn't see why Nathan wanted to have this conversation when he was going away. 'It's not exactly been the best of times to think about beginning a new relationship.'

'But you'd consider a relationship? With me?' He leaned forward with a jerk.

Beth opened her mouth to speak and then shut it again, afraid of what she might say.

'Why the hesitation?'

Beth blew out a hoarse breath. 'Oh yes!' She thought she'd said the words out loud but maybe she hadn't as Nathan reached out and took her hand.

'Okay. I'm just going to launch into this and say it. I'm risking making an utter fool of myself but what the hell. Nothing ventured, nothing gained. Firstly, all this stuff that's been happening to us: Robert Lacey and Susanna, Prudie and her amazing story. I know we said we ought to work through it but I've been thinking.'

He paused and Beth stiffened. What was he about to say?

'I think… I think I don't agree with that,' he continued. 'What about we just accept it all? Maybe we are Robert and Susanna born again.' He shrugged. 'Maybe we're not. We could delve into their history even more and, maybe, the time will be right to do so at some point.'

Beth nodded. 'I'd like to find out more about the Flete Lovedays, especially my namesake, Betty.'

'And I can see why,' he said eagerly. 'I feel the same about the Lacey family. But I also think that's for another time. I think, right now, we need to concentrate on the here and now. Us. However it's come about, the important thing is, through them, we've found each other.'

She stared at him, her heart doing all sorts of somersaults.

Nathan sucked in a breath, his nostrils flaring. 'You must have felt this thing between us,' he began slowly. 'I mean, it's absurd but, for me, it started when I saw you in the waiting room. I was trying to help Mrs Davies and she was chattering on, bless her, as she does, and all I could think about was this woman who was staring at me with these blazing green eyes. Beth, I haven't stopped wanting you since. Ever since then, I've found every which way to run into you, spend time with you.' He smiled ruefully. 'You must have noticed. This town isn't that small that you bump into the same people time and time again. And, when all the Prudie and Susanna madness happened, I was desperate to help. Yes, I was intrigued for myself, of course, and wanted to discover the truth about my ancestor's book but mostly I could see the impact it was having on *you*, how it was destroying you little by little. And that, in turn, was destroying me. I love you, Beth. From the moment I saw you I loved you. I knew, just as Robert did, that I'd do anything for you, to love you until your dying day. And beyond.'

'But you're going away,' Beth said, tears thickening.

He shook his head and sighed. 'I hadn't got to the point of making an irrevocable decision. Was still thinking about it. Until now.' He met her eyes, tears of his own glittering. 'I'll turn them down. I won't go anywhere.'

'Why?'

'Because of you, Beth. It's always been you.'

She inched towards him, her chin lifting invitingly, lips parted. 'Oh, Nathan.'

He kissed her. It was a good kiss and exploded with all the emotion that had been simmering. His lips tasted of beer and hot sun. And love.

After several delirious minutes, he moved her away from him. Holding her shoulders, he gazed into her eyes and said, very sternly, 'I'm not Hugh. I'm not your mother. I'm intent on staying around for as long as you'll have me. Your heart is safe with me. I promise that, Beth. We'll face problems, all couples do. We'll work through them. Problems aren't the end of a relationship but the beginning. And the beginning of something even better. I won't run off at the first sign of trouble. I want you for good, for all time. All I ask is you think about whether you can love me back, if only a little.'

'Love you a little?' Beth gasped in happiness, hardly believing this was finally happening. She threw her arms around his neck, which was deliciously hot from the sun. 'Oh, Nathan. I love you more than just a little. I've always loved you. Even before we met.'

And, kissing him back with all the fierceness she possessed, proved it.

EPILOGUE

FLETE, OCTOBER 2019

'I'm still feeling guilty about making you give up that amazing opportunity in the States.' Beth slipped her hand into Nathan's and felt its reassuring grip. She'd discovered he had talented hands. Cool, clever and ones that could create ecstasy. They were standing in Narrow Sheep Walk waiting for the unveiling of the plaque.

'I wouldn't have missed all this for the world.' Nathan bent nearer. 'I have everything I've ever wanted right here.' He held her close and kissed her, whispering, 'And let's go to the US for our honeymoon.'

Beth's heart stopped. 'Is that a proposal, Dr Smith?'

'It might be, Ms Loveday.'

'Then I might just accept.' She kept the tone light, but he knew her true meaning in her kiss. Their bodies knew each other well now.

The past year had been crazy. The shop was going from strength to strength; Beth had employed a manager and assistant and begun her medical herbalism course. Even though she was only studying the introductory module, it had proved far more gruelling and science based than she'd anticipated but she was relishing using her brain again.

Last week Casey had led a cleansing ritual where Beth, Florence and Bill from the museum had blessed the witch's bottle and the Celtic knife handle and returned them to their hiding place in the inglenook chimney. Tenpenny House, lighter since Beth and Nathan had uncovered Prudie and Susanna's story, now felt immensely calm and serene. Beth was no longer afraid of being there. She'd never discover exactly why the spell bottle and the handle had been hidden, but it felt right to have them back in the place they belonged.

And Beth and Nathan had worked together on this passion project, the end product of which was now in front of them. The town council had been reluctant at first, suggesting it was a time in history they wanted to gloss over, but Beth had rallied support from the Clappers Lane Small Business Association and, most importantly, Bill with her contacts at South Western University in nearby Exeter. Together they'd all forced it through.

The plaque had been erected on the museum wall next to its front door and was being unveiled by the mayor. Months of hard work had gone into this. A small crowd had gathered, Bill did a speech, a moving one about injustice and wrongful persecution of innocent women. It was followed by one from the mayor, resplendent in ceremonial garb, her chain of office glinting in the low autumn sun. And then the plaque was revealed.

Beth gasped as she read the words. Nathan's arm came round her shoulders, warm and strong, and she felt his kiss, tender on her hair.

In memory of Abigail Wray, Prudence Tenpenny and all other innocent women of Flete unjustly accused of the crime of witchcraft. In hope of an end of persecution and intolerance. May their souls find peace.

ALSO BY GEORGIA HILL

New Beginnings at Christmas Tree Cottage

New Beginnings at Lullbury Bay

∼

<u>Coming October 2025</u>

New Beginnings at the Little Christmas Inn

A gorgeously festive, feel-good story full of quirky characters, cosy pub nights and Christmas magic.

ACKNOWLEDGEMENTS

Just like Beth, the more I researched how women were treated during the sixteenth and seventeenth centuries, the angrier I became. Then, when I discovered the story of the Bideford Witches, inspiration struck. The research was fascinating but often harrowing. There is a lot of information about the Bideford Witches and it's a fascinating story. John Callow's *The Last Witches of England* is a detailed account, and Frank J Gent's YouTube videos are well worth a watch. If you get the chance, see Scratchworks Theatre Company's *Hags* which is a funny, thought-provoking and moving version of the women's story. For women's health I am indebted to the excellent and very readable *Maids, Wives, Widows* by Sara Read. There is no Flete in east Devon but if you know the area you may guess which little seaside town I based it on! I'm also guilty of moving the date of the Exeter Assizes. I had so much help with this book. Thank you to Greg Poulos for providing all things American, Eleanor Small for info on horse and cart journeys, and thanks to Wendy Jones for information on a GP's life. Huge thanks must also go to the lovely Kate Ryder for equestrian details, to Julia Roebuck for supplying techie detail and to Jane Bheemah who told me Heavitree means Hanging Tree and which got the writing juices well and truly going. I also owe an enormous debt of gratitude to medical herbal practitioner Su Bristow who gave me so much information on complementary medicine. All mistakes are mine alone. A big thank you to lovely Team Bloodhound who are fabulous to work with. And finally, thank you dear readers. Come find me for a chat on social media. Despite Beth's experiences I'm still on Facebook and X!

www.facebook.com/georgiahillauthor

@georgiawrites

A NOTE FROM THE PUBLISHER

Thank you for reading this book. If you enjoyed it please do consider leaving a review on Amazon to help others find it too.

We hate typos. All of our books have been rigorously edited and proofread, but sometimes mistakes do slip through. If you have spotted a typo, please do let us know and we can get it amended within hours.

info@bloodhoundbooks.com